From the poverty of postwar England and Ireland to the glitz and glamour of Hollywood's golden age, a beautiful, sweeping family drama that illustrates that the bonds between a mother and daughter can never be broken

*A*n *unwanted child*: San Francisco, 1958. On a dark December night, a baby girl is left at the Sisters of Charity Orphanage on Telegraph Hill.

A mysterious suicide: One year later, movie star Frances Fitzgerald takes her own life. Her husband, wealthy business-man Maximilian Stanhope, is rumored to know more about her death than he's letting on, but nothing is ever proved.

A terrible secret: What is the connection between these two events? That's what Frances's daughter, Cara, wants to find out. Abandoned by her mother when she was just seven years old, her childhood is filled with hardship and loss. As a young woman she finds professional success as a journalist, but on a personal level she still struggles to trust those around her. Soon Cara becomes convinced that uncovering the secret be-hind her mother's death is the only way to lay her demons to rest, but learning the truth may end up tearing her apart.

ALSO BY TARA HYLAND

Daughters of Fortune

SINS OF
THE MOTHER

A NOVEL

Tara Hyland

ATRIA PAPERBACK

New York London Toronto Sydney

ATRIA PAPERBACK
A Division of Simon & Schuster, Inc.
1230 Avenue of the Americas
New York, NY 10020

Originally published in Great Britain in 2011 by Simon & Schuster UK Ltd.

Published by arrangement with Simon & Schuster UK Ltd.

First Atria Paperback edition August 2011

ATRIA PAPERBACK and colophon are trademarks of Simon & Schuster, Inc.

For information about special discounts for bulk purchases, please contact Simon & Schuster Special Sales at 1-866-506-1949 or business@simonandschuster.com.

The Simon & Schuster Speakers Bureau can bring authors to your live event. For more information or to book an event, contact the Simon & Schuster Speakers Bureau at 1-866-248-3049 or visit our website at www.simonspeakers.com.

Designed by Jill Putorti

Manufactured in the United States of America

10 9 8 7 6 5 4 3 2 1

Library of Congress Cataloging-in-Publication Data

Hyland, Tara.
Sins of the mother : a novel / Tara Hyland.—1st Atria Books trade paperback ed.
    p. cm.
1. Poor families—Ireland—Fiction. 2. Mothers and daughters—Fiction. 3. Teenage pregnancy—Fiction. 4. Irish—California—Fiction. 5. Family secrets—Fiction. 6. Cork (Ireland : County)—Fiction. 7. Hollywood (Los Angeles, Calif.)—Fiction. I. Title.
PR6108.Y53F35 2011
823'.92—dc22

                                        2011003158

ISBN: 978-1-4391-6512-6
ISBN: 978-1-4391-6514-0 (ebook)

To my parents
Pamela and John Hyland

SINS OF
THE MOTHER

Prologue

Sister Marie scurried along the dark corridor as fast as her pudgy little legs would carry her. Even though she would never admit it to the other nuns, alone in the cloisters at night she often got scared. This evening was worse than usual. A storm had knocked the electricity out again, and the flame from her candle cast eerie silhouettes on the stone walls, as though shadow demons lined the path on either side, lying in wait for her to pass.

"The Lord is my shepherd, I shall not want," she murmured under her breath, trying to draw courage from the words. "He makes me lie down in green pastures."

As she continued to recite the psalm, Sister Marie shivered, this time from cold rather than fear. Even the heavy wool habit couldn't keep her warm at this time of year. Just before Thanksgiving last week, the weather had finally turned. The cold, bright sun set earlier these days, and then the infamous San Francisco fog rose up from the sea, covering the thick legs of the Golden Gate Bridge before rolling in toward the shore, the white mist creeping across the city and snaking its way up here to the Sisters of Charity Orphanage on Telegraph Hill. Sometimes, lying awake in her eight-by-ten-foot cell, Sister Marie imagined the fog oozing in through the keyholes and under the doors, like something from one of those monster movies her younger brother liked to watch.

Stop that, she scolded herself. It was this overactive imagination that had led the canoness at her last convent to suggest that she might not be suited to life as a nun. But even though she had struggled through her postulancy—the six-month period to determine whether she should take the veil—Sister Marie hadn't wanted to give up. It had finally been agreed that she should be allowed to continue with her novitiate—the training to take vows—but on the condition that she go outside of the closed order. Moving to the orphanage had seemed like the best option. She adored children and had always known that motherhood would be the hardest aspect of secular life to renounce. Now she wouldn't have to.

The orphanage had been founded by the Sisters of Charity back in the nineteenth century, funded with donations from the city's upper-class Catholics. At present there were ninety-seven children in the institute's care—and tonight there was about to be one more. A call had come through late that evening, just as the nuns were about to retire, asking if they had room for another child. It was a baby, apparently only a few days old. Apart from that, no details had been imparted about the new arrival: not its sex, nor the reason for it being abandoned here. It was most curious.

Sister Marie had been assigned to stay up with Mother Superior while she waited for the child. But as the hours dragged on, she'd begun to grow bored. Tired of her fidgeting, the reverend mother had eventually sent her to fix them both a late-night supper. It had been bad enough getting down to the kitchen in this creepy building. Now, on the return journey, the nun's progress was slower, as she was carrying a tray laden with mugs of cocoa and a plate of thickly sliced bread, spread with butter and jam. It would have been slower still if a gust of wind hadn't blown through the corridor at that moment, extinguishing her candle and plunging the cloisters into blackness. With a little squeal of fright, Sister Marie let go of the tray. The crash of metal and china on the floor echoed around the vast walls, sending her scuttling the last hundred yards to Mother Superior's office.

She burst through the door without knocking. "Reverend Mother," she panted, hardly able to get the words out, "you'll never guess what happened . . ." Without pausing for breath, she launched into an explanation of her adventure. It was only as she started to calm down that she took in the scene properly: Mother Superior was on her knees, clutching a string of rosary beads, and had been in the midst of praying. "Oh, my goodness!" A hand fluttered to her chest. "I interrupted you! I'm sorry, really I am. About supper, too."

"Enough of your apologies, my child." Mother Superior's voice was low and calm. "I have no need for refreshment. Just, in future, perhaps, you could make your entrance a little less dramatic. My old heart can't take the excitement."

There was the barest hint of amusement in the rheumy eyes—the novice was renowned throughout the order for her histrionics. Using the desk, the old nun hauled herself up, her joints creaking as she stood. She winced.

"Are you all right, Mother?" Sister Marie rushed over to take her elbow.

"'Tis nothing." She waved the younger woman away. "The cold brings out my arthritis." She lowered herself slowly and painfully into the wooden chair and then nodded at the seat opposite. "Sit yourself, child. We still have a long wait ahead of us, I fear."

With that, Mother Superior bowed her head and fell into a contemplative silence. Sister Marie opened her mouth to speak and then closed it again, knowing she ought to resist the urge to talk. That was something else she found hard to deal with—speaking only when she had something worthwhile to say. As she was a natural chatterer, these periods of quiet went against her nature. It was so much easier for the reverend mother, she thought enviously. There was a stillness about her, a sense of serenity that the novice was certain she would never possess, no matter how many years she was here.

In the dim candlelight, Sister Marie studied the older woman's face, soft and lined, as fragile as crepe paper. She was well over seventy now and still going strong. She spoke little about herself, although there were rumors of a decade spent in the missions in Africa, her time cut short after contracting a disease that had weakened her heart. But despite her physical fragility, there was still an unmistakable inner strength about her.

Sister Marie sensed that, like the abbess at her last convent, Mother Superior had doubts about her suitability to take the veil. Secretly she did, too. Life as a nun was even harder than she had imagined. The tiny cell, starkly furnished with only a wooden bed, writing desk, and dresser; rising every morning at 5:30 to go to chapel for an hour of prayer. But although the superior was free to dismiss a novice at any time, Sister Marie guessed that the decision of whether to continue would ultimately be left to herself. The reverend mother was one of those rare people who did not sit in judgment and truly believed the words "Let him who is without sin cast the first stone."

The two women continued to sit in silence, with the younger nun trying hard not to fidget, alternately wishing for the visitors to hurry up and arrive so that she could go to bed and feeling guilty for the thought crossing her mind. Eventually, she must have nodded off in the chair, but the sound of a car drawing up on the street outside jerked her awake.

Sister Marie jumped to her feet. "That must be them." She couldn't keep the relief out of her voice.

A moment later the bell rang, confirming that she was right. Only then did Mother Superior stand, too.

Outside, whoever had rung the doorbell had retreated to the warmth of the car. It was a fancy car, too, Sister Marie noted. Black and sleek, a Lincoln Capri, and this year's model, 1958. That the car was expensive surprised her. Usually when a newborn came to the orphanage, the mother was an unmarried girl who'd gotten herself in trouble and the baby would simply be left on the doorstep. But this was clearly a very different situation. Sister Marie wondered if Mother Superior knew any of the details; unfortunately, even if she did, she was unlikely to divulge them to her gossipy underling.

Sister Marie looked on with undisguised curiosity as the driver stepped out of the car. He was a tall, distinguished man in his late forties, with dark hair, dark eyes, and a navy cashmere coat that must have cost more than it did to feed the entire orphanage for a year. The collar was pulled up, as though he wished to disguise his identity—or maybe she was just being fanciful again. He walked around to the back of the car and opened the rear door, reaching in as though to retrieve a bag. From her position on the stone steps, Sister Marie couldn't see inside, but she thought she heard a woman weeping softly. Perhaps she was mistaken and it was just the newborn, though, because a moment later the man emerged carrying a small bundle of blankets, which promptly started to howl.

Without making any attempt to soothe the crying child, he crossed the drive to where the reverend mother stood. His face was blank, and he didn't say a word, leaving Sister Marie to assume that all relevant information had been imparted over the telephone earlier. Mother Superior took the child from the man's arms. The baby was obscured by the blanket it had been wrapped in, so the older nun pushed the material back. As she caught her first view of the child's face, she frowned, as though something wasn't quite right, and then a moment later her expression softened.

"God love you," Mother Superior murmured tenderly. Her composure recovered, she looked up at the man and said, "You can be sure that the child will be raised as a good Christian."

The man nodded once to acknowledge her words, then headed back to the car.

Sister Marie followed the elderly nun inside. Goose bumps covered her arms, and the hairs on the back of her neck were standing on end. She still hadn't laid eyes on the baby, but she sensed that something was amiss with the child. Whatever was wrong, it had been enough to unsettle the normally unflappable Mother Superior. And that knowledge disturbed her more than anything else.

PART 1

1946–54

Small Beginnings

Mighty things from small beginnings grow.
—JOHN DRYDEN, BRITISH POET, 1631–1700

1

"Stop! Not here—someone might see!"

Franny broke from the man's embrace, struggling to sit up in the long grass. Her breaths were coming short and fast, although it wasn't all due to the fear of being caught. Wanting was written across the girl's flushed cheeks. But she was determined not to give in to her desire. Before marriage, it was a mortal sin, and while she liked to think she was too sophisticated to believe the Church's teachings, it was hard to ignore seventeen years of sermons.

Still lying on his back, Sean reached up with one large, callused hand and brushed a lock of auburn hair from her face. The rich red color reminded him of the glossy coat of the sika deer that roamed the Irish countryside, he was always telling her. He had a way with words, did Sean.

"Ah, come on now, my pretty little colleen. There's nothing wrong with what we're doing."

That was easy for him to say. If her parents found out about them, there would be hell to pay. Canoodling with a boy from the neighboring farms would have been bad enough, but Sean was a laborer, a hired hand toiling on her father's land. To the snobbish minds of those reared in small-town Ireland, that would be the worst crime of all.

Sensing her fears, Sean gave her the hangdog look she had grown to know so well over the past few weeks. "All I'm wanting is a bit of a kiss and a cuddle. You wouldn't deny a hardworking man like me a little peck on the lips now, would you?"

Franny felt her resolve weakening—as it always did when it came to Sean Gallagher. With his impish grin, black hair, and blue eyes, he

reminded her of Clark Gable in *Gone with the Wind*. Like Rhett Butler, Sean was a free spirit, unconcerned by social conventions. He had
grown up in Limerick but hadn't been back for years. Instead he liked
to travel, going wherever there was work. When England had needed
extra laborers to work in the munitions factories during the war, he
had been one of those to go over. Her parents looked down on his
wandering spirit, but to Franny, desperate to escape her hometown and
see the world, there was nothing more attractive. Until four weeks ago,
she hadn't thought that someone so exciting would ever come to sleepy
Glen Vale.

He'd arrived from Cork at the beginning of June, to help with the
fruit-picking. The first time Franny had seen him, Sean had been standing on a stepladder, thinning out the apple trees, his bare back glisten-
ing in the late-afternoon sun. While her sister had stood by giggling,
Franny had bravely gone over to speak to him. Of course Maggie—the
nasty little snitch—had told their mammy all about it later, and she'd
gotten the strap. But it had been worth it to get Sean's attention.

"Just stay five more minutes," he pleaded, reaching up to lace his
fingers through hers. As he tugged her toward him, she caught his
scent. He smelled of his day working in the fields: a strong, manly odor.
"Look, there's no one close."

Franny glanced around. He was right, of course. The meadow was
fallow and far from the farmhouse. No one ever came out here. But
still . . .

"No," she insisted, getting to her feet. "It's late and Mam will be wanting help with the tea. If I don't get back soon, she'll tan my backside."

"I wouldn't mind doing that meself," Sean said, reaching up to playfully slap her on the bottom.

"Ouch!" Pretending to be offended by the overfamiliar gesture,
Franny drew herself up. "You, sir, are no gentleman." It was a line from
Gone with the Wind, said in a perfect imitation of Vivien Leigh's southern drawl. Franny had a talent for impersonations and within a few
minutes of meeting someone could mimic his accent and mannerisms
perfectly.

It took Sean a moment to get the reference. "And you, miss, are no
lady," he returned in a somewhat stilted impression of Clark Gable.

They grinned at each other for a moment, enjoying the shared joke.
Sean took her hand. "Meet me later, will you?"

Franny hesitated. It was never easy for her to get away.

"Oh, come on, sweetheart," her beau chided. "Otherwise I might have to take a trip into Cork and find meself a new woman."

He said it in jest, but to Franny the words were like a threat. It was her greatest fear: that Sean would lose interest in her if she didn't do what he wanted. He'd probably met all manner of sophisticated women in England; how was she, a little farm girl, to compete?

But drawing on all her acting skills, she managed to hide her anxiety. Keeping him guessing was the best way to keep him interested, she'd decided long ago. "Maybe I'll meet with you," she said, with a touch of haughtiness. "And then again, maybe I won't." Without another word, she picked up her skirts and started to run back toward the farmhouse, her golden-red hair flowing out like flames behind her.

As she ran through the cornfields, the long sheaves scratching at her bare legs, Franny knew she would be in trouble again. Not that *that* was anything new. She was always being told off, usually for skiving from her chores to go to the cinema in the neighboring town.

"What are you doing, wasting your time at the pictures?" her father would grumble.

But Franny couldn't get enough of the Hollywood films, which allowed her to escape from her dull life for a couple of hours. She went to the movies whenever she could, and she dreamed of one day being a star like Rita Hayworth, Betty Grable, and Jane Russell—of living in glamorous Los Angeles rather than boring Glen Vale.

Franny hated the rural area where she'd grown up. Located about forty miles outside of Cork, the village and surrounding countryside housed no more than three hundred souls. It was an impoverished, gray place, where the men either worked or drank their lives away and the women were given to religion and childbearing—and raised their daughters to expect nothing more from life.

But Franny did want more. She had been born to stand out. At seventeen, she looked exactly as Irish girls were meant to, in a world where Maureen O'Hara set the standard. Along with her vibrant auburn hair, she had large, mischievous green eyes, skin like freshly churned butter cream, and a small, upturned nose sprinkled with pretty freckles. Her soft, voluptuous body would have given Lana Turner a run for her money, and her flame-red hair was matched by a passionate nature, her personality as vibrant as her looks. It was as though she had been recorded in Technicolor, while the rest of the county languished in black and white. Her big plan was to escape Glen Vale as soon as possible. And today, she was one step closer to getting what she wanted.

Slipping a hand into her pocket, she was relieved to find that the letter was still there. It had arrived that morning, informing her that she had been accepted to train as a nurse in London. She was thrilled. Not because she particularly wanted to be a nurse but because it was her chance to leave Ireland. Once in England, she would find some way to do what she really wanted—become a movie star.

But first there was one large hurdle to cross: getting her father's blessing. She knew he wouldn't want her to go. He couldn't see beyond Glen Vale, had never been farther than Cork, in fact. He wasn't an adventurer like Sean, who was already talking of going back to London. "The city's in ruins after all the bombing. They'll be needing builders, mark my words," he'd told her. Franny often daydreamed about the two of them living in England together.

As she neared home, Franny felt her spirits deflate a little. The farmhouse and surrounding outbuildings were low, uninspired brick structures, built for function rather than aesthetics. Outside, she used the water pump to cool the heat from her face. It wouldn't do for anyone to suspect where she'd been. The kitchen windows were steamed up, meaning she was late for dinner. Cursing, she quickly dried her hands on her apron and hurried inside.

Flinging the kitchen door open, Franny was greeted by the wet, salty smell of boiled bacon and cabbage. She pulled a face. It was always this or stew—why couldn't they eat something different for a change?

Her mother was bent over the stove, using a fork to test whether the potatoes were cooked. Seeing Franny, she automatically tsked with disapproval. "Where've you been, child?" Theresa Healey was typical of Glen Vale women. Once she had been a beauty like Franny, but years of childbearing and poverty had worn her down. Franny's greatest fear was ending up like her mother.

"With Sean Gallagher, no doubt." This was from Franny's elder sister, Maggie. It was said nastily rather than as a joke. Maggie liked to cause trouble, especially for Franny. At twenty, she was a plain, dour girl who envied her younger sister's pretty face and buoyant nature.

Their mother looked over sharply. "I hope there's no truth in that, my girl."

Franny said nothing, just contented herself with a scowl at her sister, who poked her tongue out in reply. Unlike Franny, Maggie had no interest in anything other than getting married. Skeletally thin, she had a mean mouth and cold eyes, and the permanent look of someone who felt she'd been handed a raw deal in life. "It's not fair," she would moan. "If I had only half Franny's looks I'd be wedded by now." But privately Franny thought the lack of suitors had less to do with her sister's appearance and more to do with her constant bellyaching.

Theresa sighed wearily—something she did a lot—and said, "Supper's about ready, so best get setting that table, girls."

"Yes, Mam," Franny and Maggie chorused.

They studiously ignored each other as they began laying cutlery and plates. The crockery was mismatched, and apart from the basics, it was a bare table: flowers and napkins were a luxury the household couldn't afford. At six on the dot, Theresa started to serve up. The men didn't need to be called in from the field—the daily routine never altered.

Franny sat on one side of the table, and Maggie took a seat opposite—the better to glare at me, Franny thought—with their mother between them at one end. Sean came in next, greeting the women warmly. Franny had warned him early on not to sit next to her, afraid that they might give themselves away, so he seated himself beside Maggie, winking at Franny as he did so. Franny's father, Michael, arrived last. As he took his place at the head of the table, a hush fell over the room. They all bowed their heads for grace.

"For what we are about to receive," Theresa said, as she did every night, "may the Lord make us truly thankful."

With that, they all opened their eyes and began to eat. Theresa had already doled out the meat, making sure the men had the lion's share, and now they passed dishes of boiled potatoes and cabbage around the table. This was all done with the minimum of words. There was never much chatter at mealtimes. Michael Healey was a silent man, and, as the head of the house, his preference filtered down to the others.

"So how's the work going?" Theresa asked.

Michael shrugged and made a noncommittal noise. It was up to Sean to say, "We should be finished soon."

"And have you made any decision about what you'll be doing after that?"

Everyone tensed as Michael asked the question that came up at least once a week. It was no secret that once the fruit was collected he wanted to keep Sean on to help with the harvest. The farm was getting too much for him lately, and, as he was fond of complaining, it wasn't as if he had any sons to help him out. Of the six children Theresa had borne, there had been only one boy, Patrick. A strong, strapping lad, he should have taken over the farm one day. But, like Franny, he had been eager to see the world. While her father, a Unionist man who hated the English, had agreed with Prime Minister Eamon de Valera's policy of keeping Ireland out of the war, Patrick had seen it as his chance for adventure. On the day of his eighteenth birthday, he'd gone to England to volunteer. Less than a year later, he had died on the beaches of Normandy. Now Michael's only reference to his son was to complain that the English had robbed him of his help on the farm.

Other than Patrick, Maggie, and Franny, there had been three stillbirths, and after the last, the doctor had warned Theresa against trying for more children. That meant Michael had no natural heir to the farm. It was because of this he wanted Sean to stay on to help bring in the wheat, but the young man had always been typically noncommittal. As before, the farmhand said now, "I've no idea what I'll be doing, sir. I'll see when the time comes."

The older man shook his head in disapproval. "It's a strange way you live, going from place to place, with no security or roots."

"Da!" Franny chided, hating the way her father took every opportunity to put the boot in with Sean.

"Well, it's true. He lives like a tinker."

There was an awkward silence, but Sean didn't seem upset. "It suits me that way. And it'd be a strange world if we were all the same, wouldn't it?"

Franny beamed at him. He was well able for her father, and that was something she admired.

Now Sean patted his belly and burped loudly. "As usual, that was delicious, ladies. I've never eaten so well as I have since coming here. You'll be hard pressed to get rid of me."

He winked at Mrs. Healey, who scowled back. She knew Sean Gallagher's type. A lovable rogue: charming and entertaining, but not someone you'd want near your daughters. Seeing the enraptured look on Franny's face, she felt a twinge of unease. She'd have to keep a close eye on that one. Her youngest child was a romantic and far too pretty for her own good.

"There's no need to thank Franny for the meal," Maggie piped up. "She didn't help a bit."

Their father seized on the information. "Is this true, Franny? You've been shirking your duties again?"

Franny glared at her elder sister, longing to wipe the smug smile from her face.

"Yes, Da," she said, trying to look contrite.

"And where were you this time?"

Studiously avoiding looking at Sean, she said, "Out walking. I didn't realize how late it had got."

Her father snorted. "You've got to learn some responsibility, my girl."

"Yes, Da."

But he ignored her and continued talking. "In fact, I think it's about time you started helping out a bit more around here. Your mother's slowing down. From tomorrow, you'll take over looking after the small livestock. That should keep you out of mischief."

Franny was horrified. She couldn't think of anything worse than being around those filthy, smelly pigs or the goat that always seemed to find a way to chew her hair.

"But what's the point? I'll be off to England in a few weeks." It was more of a question than a statement. No one rushed to agree with her. "Da?" she prompted.

"What?"

Franny felt a flicker of fear, knowing how easily he could get into a temper. But she couldn't back down now. "I said, I'll be in London soon. We talked about this, me going to train as a nurse. Well, the letter came today. I've been accepted," she told him proudly.

She took out the crumpled envelope to show him. She'd read it so many times that it was already well worn. He ignored her outstretched hand and continued eating.

"Michael," Theresa chided gently. "The child's trying to show you something." Franny flashed her mother a grateful look. She was more sympathetic than her husband to her daughter's wandering spirit. She knew there was no point trying to clip their youngest's wings.

With a grunt, Michael threw down his fork and snatched the letter from Franny. He quickly scanned the contents and then tossed it onto the table. "What would you be wanting to go over there for?"

"Because there's nothing for me here!"

"Now's not a good time. Maybe next year."

Franny had heard this before. It would be the same every year, until she was too old or too worn down to have her dreams anymore. She looked desperately at her mother for help, but Theresa dropped her eyes to the table. Michael wasn't a violent man, not like some, but he still wasn't above the odd whack when the mood took him. Franny was on her own.

"But, Da—"

He banged his fist on the hard wooden table, cutting her off. "Will you ever shut it, girl!" His eyes flashed dark and angry, and instinctively she recoiled. "I'll hear no more on the subject."

He grabbed a hunk of bread and mopped up the meat and gravy on his plate, shoving the makeshift sandwich into his mouth, brown juice spilling out and down the sides of his face. Franny looked at him in disgust. Her gaze moved to Sean, and she saw sympathy in his eyes. At least he understood how she felt, that she couldn't stand to be trapped in this place, never having the chance to live.

Sean got up then. "I'd best see to the livestock before dark." He carried his plate to the sink and washed it. As he let himself out, he gave a backward glance at Franny. She saw the invitation in his eyes as he left.

Up until then, she still hadn't decided whether to see Sean that night. But in that moment, Franny made up her mind. She *would* go to him, after all. She would prove to him, and to herself, that she was meant for more than this dump. And to hell with the consequences. Who knew? Maybe then he would take her with him when he left Glen Vale.

2

"Her eyes, they shone like diamonds," Franny sang out, swaying jauntily as she did so. "I thought her the queen of the land . . ."

It was Saturday night, and the Healeys were hosting a *ceili* in their cramped parlor. About twenty people were there, from nursing babies to elderly grandparents, and they had spent the evening storytelling and singing, everyone taking a turn. These weekly gatherings of friends and neighbors had been a part of Franny's life ever since she could remember. As a child, she had been raised on the folk songs, and as soon as she'd been old enough, she'd started singing them herself. She loved having the opportunity to perform.

As everyone in the room joined in with the chorus, Franny couldn't help wishing that Sean was here to watch her sing. But he hated the *ceili*s, calling them old-fashioned, and preferred to go out drinking poteen with the other young farmhands. So instead, they'd secretly arranged to meet later, and Franny couldn't wait.

It was another hour before the evening finally came to an end. By then Franny was itching for everyone to leave so she could sneak out to see her lover. As she stood waiting impatiently with her mother and older sister, Conrad Walsh approached. A bashful young man, good-looking in a conventional way, he wore a brown suit that was shabby but neat: a little like him.

"You played well tonight," her mother told him. He'd accompanied the singers with his accordion. She nudged Maggie. "Weren't we saying that earlier, love?"

Maggie could only nod at Conrad—she was always struck dumb around him.

"Well, thank you, Mrs. Healey, and you too, Margaret." He looked past her to where Franny hung back. "But I think the real star tonight was Franny." He smiled shyly at her. "I haven't seen you around much lately, how've you been?"

"I'm grand, as always, Con," she returned jauntily. Unlike Maggie, she found it easy to talk to boys, especially Conrad Walsh. Having grown up on the neighboring farm, he was almost like a brother to her. A quiet, studious young man, he had more finesse than the rest of the lads in the area. The priest had wanted him to go on to the university, and he'd talked at one point about becoming a doctor. But after his father had died of a heart attack the previous year he'd been forced to take over the farm. Now he was supporting his mother and five siblings, and from all accounts doing a fine job of it. "He'll be the making of that place," her father was fond of saying.

Still looking at Franny, Conrad said, "Are you going to the dance on Friday?"

"What else would I be doing?" she teased.

He was referring to the annual summer social, held in the local town hall. Franny was hoping Sean would take her.

"Well, er . . ." Conrad hesitated, clearly wanting to ask her to go with him. But as he looked between Maggie and Theresa, he chickened out. "Save a dance for me, will you?"

Ignoring the furious look on her sister's face, Franny smiled up at him. "It'll be my pleasure."

Conrad blushed deep red. Then, after mumbling good-bye, he hurried back to his elderly mother.

Later, after everyone had left, Michael said to his wife, "I saw you talking to Conrad Walsh."

"He's a good lad," Theresa acknowledged.

"Aye," her husband agreed. "No doubt he'll be coming to ask me the question about Maggie soon."

Consolidation of smallholdings like the Healeys' and the Walshes' was becoming more widespread. It was common knowledge that Michael Healey favored a tie-up between the two farms, through the marriage of his eldest daughter to Conrad.

"Humph," Maggie snorted. "Conrad's never going to notice me with *her*"—she glared at Franny—"flaunting herself in front of him."

"Oh, give over." Franny had heard the same accusation many times before. Her easy way with men was seen by the small minds of Glen Vale as evidence that she was forward. But though she liked flirting with boys, Sean was the only one who meant anything to her. Conventional Conrad couldn't measure up to the dangerously handsome laborer. "If you want Conrad to notice you, it might help if you opened your mouth when he speaks to you."

Unable to think up a smart retort, Maggie turned to their father. "Mark my words, Da. There'll be no marriage between me and Conrad while *she's* around."

If she'd been hoping to gain some sympathy, she'd picked the wrong person to appeal to. Michael simply shrugged. "Well, if he's not keen on you, Maggie, then our Franny will do just as well."

"Michael!" his wife scolded.

But it was too late. Maggie let out a cry of distress and raced up the stairs to her room.

"What?" Michael looked around in bewilderment. To him, this was business; female sensitivities had no place here. "What did I say?"

Franny ran after her sister. She found her in the tiny bedroom that the two girls shared, lying facedown on the bed, crying. Franny went to sit beside her, putting a comforting hand on the other girl's shoulder.

"Ah, come on with you," she said, trying to jolly her elder sister along. "It's not like I want Conrad. He's all yours, sis, I promise."

The words were meant to be comforting, but Maggie rounded on her, red eyes flashing. "Oh well, thank you kindly." She pretended to touch her forelock. "How very generous of you to let me have your castoffs!"

Franny was immediately contrite. "Oh Maggie, you know I didn't mean it like that."

But her sister didn't want to hear it. "Get away from me, you little hussy," she hissed. "Go to that gypsy you're so willing to open your legs for." Seeing the shocked expression on Franny's face, she smiled nastily. "You think I don't hear you sneaking out at night to see that Sean? I know *exactly* what you're up to with him, and I'd have told Mam by now if I wasn't sure you were going to get into trouble all on your own. So go to him and leave me alone, *dear* sister. I want nothing to do with the likes of you."

Maggie turned away then, burying her head into the pillow. Franny sat there for a moment, speechless. The venom in her sister's voice had shaken her. It frightened her more than discovering that Maggie knew about Sean. She wanted to make things right with her elder sister but didn't know how, so instead she got up and left the room. She would let Maggie calm down and try to reason with her later.

It was hard for Franny to forget her sister's vicious words. Even much later, when she was lying in Sean's arms, she couldn't stop thinking about them.

"She must really hate me," Franny mused.

Sean, busy grazing her neck with his lips, raised his head briefly. "Ah, forget about her. She's just a dried-up old cow."

"Sean!" It was one thing for Franny to criticize her sister, but she didn't like to hear it from others, even her lover. However much Maggie irritated her, they were still blood and he was the outsider.

Sean was immediately contrite. "Look, I'm sorry. It's just we have so little time together, and I don't want to waste it talking about your feckin' sister."

It was a good point. There were precious few opportunities for her to sneak out to meet him. Why bother taking the risk if they weren't going to enjoy themselves?

"As always, you're right," she conceded. Then, to show she was sorry, she tilted her head back and kissed him. After a moment, Sean groaned deep in the back of his throat and pulled her on top of him.

It was a month since that first night she'd come to him, and by now they had the routine down pat. The first time hadn't exactly been pleasant for Franny. It had been more awkward and embarrassing, really, and she remembered quite a bit of pain. She had bled on and off for a few days afterward, and at first she'd wondered if something was very badly wrong; she'd even sworn to herself that if it cleared up she'd never do the same thing again. But once everything was back to normal, it was easier to forget her fears than refuse Sean.

Sometimes Franny wished they could go somewhere other than the small, hard bed in his one-room cottage. It wasn't exactly the most romantic setting. He'd promised that once he had some money together he would take her to a hotel in Cork. They'd spent hours planning the occasion; concocting the lie she would tell her parents so she could stay away overnight. But, like a lot of Sean's promises, the longed-for treat had yet to materialize.

Now he turned Franny onto her back, kneeling between her legs. It was only then that she realized he had forgotten something.

"Wait!" she said. "What about the—?"

He looked confused for a moment, and she hoped he wouldn't make her say it out loud. She didn't particularly like the French letters that he'd gotten off a soldier while he was in England—"the army gave them out to all the men"—but if they stopped her getting pregnant, she was happy to use them.

"I've run out again," he said, sitting back on his haunches. She averted her eyes, wishing he'd cover himself up. However intimate they had been together, she couldn't get used to his unashamed nakedness.

"Could we not do . . . the other stuff, then?" she asked, as delicately as possibly. This had happened once before, a few weeks earlier. They'd gotten around the problem then by Sean showing her other ways to pleasure him. Unfortunately, this time he didn't seem interested.

"It's not the same," he said, moving back across the bed toward her. "I want to be inside you."

An image of her worn-down mother popped unbidden into Franny's mind, and she shrank away from him.

"But I don't want a baby!" She made no effort to keep the alarm out of her voice. She wasn't sure what worried her more—eternal damnation or getting pregnant. Before, her monthlies had always been something to dread. But now seeing the reassuring stain on her knickers was a cause for celebration.

Sean burst out laughing, and she felt more of a fool than before. "Is that what's worrying you? Well, you've got nothing to fear on that count." Then, to her embarrassment, he began to explain how she would be safe if he didn't spill his seed inside her.

"But why haven't we done it that way before?" She wasn't willing to give in quite yet.

"I didn't think you'd believe me."

Franny bit her lip and said nothing.

"Don't you trust me?" It was the hurt look on his face that did it for her.

"Of course I do." It was always so hard to win an argument with Sean, even when Franny thought she was in the right. Somehow she always ended up giving in to him. "I just don't want anything to go wrong, that's all."

He grinned down at her. "Don't worry, I'll be careful. I swear."

Afterward, Franny lay in Sean's arms. Usually the cuddling was her favorite part, but today she couldn't relax. Birth control was illegal in Ireland, so it wasn't easy to get hold of the French letters. Luckily Sean knew somebody who worked down at Cork docks, and he smuggled them in from England. The black-market price was exorbitant but worth it for the peace of mind.

"Are you going to see that friend of yours soon?" Franny asked now.

Before he fell off to sleep, Sean promised drowsily that the next time he went into town he would sort something out.

But a week later, he came back from Cork empty-handed. Apparently his contact hadn't been around, but he swore that he would go back the following week to see him.

Unfortunately, when the next weekend arrived, the docker still wasn't anywhere to be found. Franny worried about continuing to lie together without taking any precautions. But she had no one to discuss her fears with, no one to ask whether it was normal or not—apart from Sean. And he kept assuring her that it was perfectly safe and that he was being careful. And after she'd given in that first time, it was hard to justify why they should stop.

3

"Are you planning on stirring that anytime today, missy? Or are you hoping that if you stare at it long enough it will make itself?"

The sharp tone in her mother's voice jolted Franny out of her daydream. The women were in the kitchen, baking a barmbrack for Halloween that evening. Looking down at the mixing bowl in her hands, she saw that the yeast mixture was no closer to being folded into the flour than when she had started twenty minutes ago. The girl sighed then, and it was as though she had all the troubles of the world on her shoulders.

"Sorry, Mam. I'm not feeling too good."

Theresa peered at her daughter. Franny was a good little actress and certainly not above feigning sickness to get out of work. But the girl's pale face and listless demeanor told her that this time she wasn't faking.

"If you're not well, then why don't you go upstairs and lie down?"

Franny considered this for a moment, and then said, "Thanks, Mam, but I think I'll get some air instead. That'll help clear my head."

Theresa gave a brief nod. "Go on with you now. Maggie can do your chores instead."

"That's not fair!" Maggie burst out. "Why does *she* get out of working?"

"Because she's sick," their mother said firmly. "She'd do the same for you if you were poorly."

Maggie snorted her disbelief. "The only bug she's got is laziness," she muttered. Franny had already taken off her apron and was on her way out of the door, but hearing her sister's words she turned back.

"Will you ever give over, Maggie?" Her green eyes flashed with anger. "No wonder no man wants you. Your moaning is enough to make anyone with sense run a mile!" With that she flounced out of the kitchen, banging the door behind her.

Maggie stared after her, open-mouthed.

"What's up with her?" Theresa was genuinely confused by her younger daughter's behavior. Franny was the good-natured one in the family. She usually brushed off Maggie's little jibes with a laugh. It was unlike her to be cruel.

Maggie, recovering quickly, said, "Mooning over her man, no doubt."

"What man?" Theresa looked over at her sharply. "That Sean, you mean?"

Her elder daughter hesitated for a moment, as though she was about to say something, and then seemed to change her mind. "Oh, I don't know. I'm just guessing. Forget I said anything."

Theresa didn't press her daughter further, but as she began to knead the dough, her thoughts were on Franny. She had a bad feeling she knew exactly what was up with her youngest. And if she was right, it would mean trouble for them all.

"Bless me, Father, for I have sinned. It's been a week since my last confession."

Franny felt the same prickle of nerves that she experienced every time she knelt in the confessional box. It didn't matter that the priest was behind a curtain and couldn't see her face, he knew precisely who she was from the moment she opened her mouth. She wasn't even sure why she'd come here today. But after escaping the farmhouse she hadn't known where else to go, and the tranquillity of the old stone church at least provided a quiet place to think. It had just been a coincidence that the priest was holding confession that afternoon, and she certainly had her share of sins to confess. But now she was here, her courage had deserted her.

"Go on, child," the priest prompted.

The girl opened her mouth to speak but couldn't form the words. After all, what was it she meant to say—that she had fornicated, not once but several times, over the past few months and that her actions had resulted in what she had feared most: a baby, a bastard child, conceived out of wedlock and likely to be born that way unless she did something quickly?

Franny's suspicions about her condition had been there for a while now. She'd kept her worries to herself for as long as possible, praying for a miracle, but when nothing happened she had finally plucked up the courage to tell Sean the previous day.

"Are you sure?" he had asked immediately.

It was a question she had put to herself a million times. Sometimes at night, lying on her back in bed, she would place a hand on her flat stomach and feel sure that no child could be growing inside. But however hard she tried to convince herself, she knew it wasn't true. It had been four months since she'd started sleeping with Sean and two months now since she had bled.

"Yes, I'm sure," she said quietly.

It was admitting it out loud that set the tears off. Up until then, she hadn't cried—she'd been in too much shock. But now she let her fears out. Needing the money, Sean had given in to her father and stayed on to help bring in the harvest, but with the winter closing in, he would have to move off soon in search of other work. She needed to sort this out with him before that happened.

Sean put his arms around her. "Hush, don't cry, my pretty colleen. There's nothing broke that can't be fixed."

Franny let him hold her as she wept. He continued to whisper reassurances, until her sobbing finally slowed. "Oh, Sean," she sighed despairingly, resting her head on his shoulder. "What are we going to do?"

There was a moment of silence, and then Sean said, "I have an idea."

Franny tipped her head up to look at him. "Tell me."

"There's a woman I know of, back where I lived in London," he began carefully. "She's a midwife, as good as any doctor. She helped a couple of girls I knew when they were in a similar situation."

It took Franny a moment to understand what he was saying. She pulled back from his arms. "What do you mean?" she said warily. "You're not suggesting getting rid of it?"

He spread his hands in surrender. It was a gesture she was used to seeing. Initially she had liked Sean's carefree approach to everything, but lately she had also begun to realize the other side to this: he wasn't keen on responsibility.

"But I thought we'd get wed." The words were out of her mouth before she could stop herself. She watched his face blanch.

"Married?" He choked over the word. He stood up abruptly, and she fell back on the bed. "Ah, now, let's not get ahead of ourselves." He said it with an air of forced jollity, even attempting the cheeky grin that she'd come to know so well, trying to charm her. "You know I'm not the marrying kind."

"Well, maybe you should have thought about that before you invited me into your bed," Franny said crossly.

They stared at each other for a long moment. Franny held Sean's gaze, determined to shame him. Her heart was beating so fast that she feared it would explode. Was he going to let her down? But then something in his expression changed; his face grew serious.

"You're right, my darlin'," he said gravely. "'Tis time I started taking my responsibilities seriously." He went over and took her hand. "We'll find a way through this—together. I promise."

Hearing that, she'd felt relief flood through her: he was going to stand by her after all. And, she reasoned to herself, was it any wonder he'd reacted badly to begin with? Finding out that he was going to be a father was bound to be a shock to him. It had hit her hard enough.

After their conversation, Franny had found it impossible to sleep, as she thought about everything that had been said. It wasn't an ideal situation, but they could still make this work. They would have to get married straightaway, and of course they would need to stay here on the farm for a little while, at least until the baby was born. But after that they could go somewhere else, just the three of them. To England or America, and start a new life. It didn't have to be the end. Not as long as they had each other.

Franny had been so eager that morning to tell Sean about her plans that she had gotten up while it was still dark and hurried over to his little cottage. When he didn't answer the door, she tried the handle. Inside, it took her a moment to register the scene: the stripped mattress, the empty wardrobe. Sean wasn't there. Nor were any of his things. He had left her.

She was so shocked that at first she didn't notice that there was an envelope on the bed with her name on it. Seeing it, she felt hope rise within her. Perhaps he'd left instructions for her to meet him later, she thought wildly as she tore it open; maybe he wanted them to elope and he had gone to sort out the arrangements. But inside, all she found was a note with the address of the English abortionist he'd spoken about, along with two pounds—the equivalent of two weeks' wages. Was that all she was worth?

For one moment she thought quite seriously about not taking the money. But then good sense overrode her pride. Maybe if she could have thrown the money into his face it would have been worth it, but Sean wasn't around to witness her grand gesture, so she might as well keep it. After all, whatever happened now, she had a feeling she would need every penny in the future. So she tucked the letter into the front pocket of her skirt and left the cottage for the last time, her troubles weighing heavily on her.

Franny couldn't bring herself to tell Father Brian the full extent of her sins. So after she'd made her penance for what she *had* confessed—ten Hail Marys, four Our Fathers, and an Act of Contrition—she headed back to the house. It was Friday, which meant fish for supper. As soon as she entered the hallway, the smell of boiled haddock struck her. It was bad enough at the best of times, but in her present condition she felt even worse than usual. That meant it was easy enough to plead illness still, so she didn't have to eat any food or make conversation. She just sat quietly, eating a piece of dry bread and sipping weak tea as the rest of the family discussed their day.

Sean's absence hadn't registered on them yet. It was his day off, and often he took himself into Cork. When he hadn't turned up for dinner that night, they had simply assumed he was still there. Franny made no effort to correct them. If they started asking questions about why he'd disappeared so abruptly, she'd probably break down and tell them, and she couldn't face that yet. As it grew dark, Maggie announced that she was going off to bed. Franny would have loved to lie down quietly, too, and have some time to reflect on the day's events, but, unable to face her sister's taunts, she opted to stay up instead.

Franny and her parents spent the next hour together in the small parlor, listening to the wireless. By the time the program ended, the fire was almost out, too, the soft red embers flickering and dying in the hearth.

Michael got to his feet. "I'm off up." He didn't pause to give his wife a kiss good night, simply headed out the door.

Hearing his retreating footsteps on the stairs, Franny stretched. "I think I'll be heading up myself, Mam."

Theresa didn't look up from her knitting as she said, "Not so fast, my girl. Now we're alone, I think it's about time we had a little chat about what's been going on between you and Sean Gallagher."

Franny froze, her mind racing. Had Maggie told on her? It seemed unlikely. Which meant her mother was just guessing and she could still brazen this out.

Trying to keep her voice steady, Franny asked, "Whatever do you mean?"

At that Theresa's lips tightened. She put the ball of wool and knitting needles down and leaned forward in her armchair, her eyes flashing with anger.

"Oh, don't play me for a fool, my girl," she hissed. Her voice was low—anything above a whisper could be heard by the whole house—but she still managed to convey her fury. "I've known for weeks what's been going on, but I turned a blind eye to it—more fool me." She shook her head, as though unable to comprehend her own stupidity. "I thought you were just fooling around out there with that . . . that *tinker*. But seeing you sick today . . ."

Theresa closed her eyes for a moment, as though hoping this would all go away. But when she looked up at Franny again, her expression was hard. "Well?" she demanded. "He's got you in the family way, hasn't he?"

Franny hesitated for a moment and then slowly began to nod.

"And he's done a bunk, has he?"

Again Franny nodded.

Now that the full extent of the situation was known, Theresa looked at her beautiful, willful child, who had always been so troublesome, and wanted to cry.

Seeing the disappointment on her mother's face, Franny's composure deserted her. "I'm sorry, Mam—really sorry. But I love him, and I thought he loved me, too. I know it was wrong to go to bed with him, but he said we'd be married."

Theresa snorted dismissively. She couldn't stand to hear her daughter trying to justify herself. "Do you not have a brain in your head? He'd tell you anything to get you in the sack with him."

"It wasn't like that!" Franny insisted, desperate to make her mother understand. "We made plans together. He was going to help me get out of Glen Vale. Maybe he'll still come back for me—"

"Don't tell me you actually thought he'd stick around?" Theresa said in disgust. "Men like that are after one thing. And once they've got it, they're off. You can't rely on them."

"And who wants a reliable man?" Franny demanded. Suddenly everything she felt was pouring out. "Was it so wrong of me to want some passion in my life? Because that's what Sean gave me. I don't want to live out my days in Glen Vale, never seeing anything of the world. I don't want to slave away on a farm for years, with some brute of a husband expecting me to stay in the kitchen or the bedroom. I want more than what you've got."

Hearing her life being criticized, something in Theresa snapped. Without warning, she struck her daughter hard across the face. "How dare you, you stupid little slut!"

There was a stunned silence. It was the first time Franny could ever remember her mother striking her. She'd had her fair share of beatings over the years, but they'd always been from her father. Finally the enormity of the situation struck home. All Franny's bravado deserted her. Suddenly she was a child again, needing comfort from the woman she usually scorned. Burying her head in her mother's lap, she started to cry. "I'm sorry," she sobbed. "I wish I hadn't done it. Oh God, how I wish I hadn't."

Hearing her daughter in pain, something broke in Theresa, too. She hadn't meant to react like that—it was just that she was upset and disappointed, too. But now she couldn't scold Franny any longer.

"Hush. Don't cry," she soothed, stroking the girl's hair. "It doesn't have to be the end of the world. We'll sort something out, *a leanbh.*"

Hearing her mother calling her "my child," Franny immediately felt better. It meant she had been forgiven. Franny raised her head. "Really?" she said hopefully.

"That's right." Theresa smiled reassuringly, pleased to have brought some comfort. "I'll tell your father what's happened. Then first thing in the morning he'll go down to Father Brian. The priest will speak to Conrad Walsh and his mother."

For a moment, Franny was confused. What did Conrad and Mrs. Walsh have to do with anything?

"Conrad's a good boy," her mother went on. "He'll do right by you."

Suddenly grasping what Theresa meant, Franny felt another wave of sickness wash over her—and this time it had nothing to do with being pregnant. Marrying Conrad might seem like a solution to her parents, but to her it was a life sentence. She would turn into her mother—condemned to childbearing and rearing. She would rather live with the shame and stigma than face that.

She wanted to tell her mother how she felt, but Theresa would never understand.

"Now go on up to bed with you," the older woman said, overly bright. "We'll have this all sorted by tomorrow night, you see if we don't."

In a daze, Franny mounted the stairs to her room. Luckily Maggie was already asleep, snoring loudly, dead to the world. Lying on her bed, Franny made herself face facts. She couldn't marry Conrad, of that she was certain. He was a nice enough lad, and his prospects were better than her parents' had been—there was talk of him getting electricity and running water out to his farmhouse—but those additional comforts wouldn't compensate her for a life without passion or excitement. She didn't want to eke out an existence in Glen Vale. There was far too much still to experience. But how could she tell that to her parents? How could she tell them that she rejected their choices, everything that they toiled for every day? And what alternative did she have?

Instinctively, her hand slipped into her front pocket. She took out the note with the address that Sean had scribbled down.

England. She could go to England.

No, the sensible side of her said; there was no way she could go. It would be better to stay here, where she had family to support her. She didn't dare go out into the world, not in her condition, not on her own . . .

But Franny had never been one to listen to her sensible side, and desperation made her even more ready to act. She had the money that Sean had left her, and she had an address—a place to go. Maybe if she headed there, she might be able to find him and convince him to do right by her.

Swinging her legs over the side of the bed, Franny got up. Tiptoeing across the floor, she eased open the chest of drawers. Hastily, she threw a few items into a bag. She needed to go now, before her courage deserted her.

4

"Are youse gonna do something about that racket," Kevin Casey demanded, "or should I sort it meself?"

Annie Connolly looked up at the ruddy-faced giant standing in her kitchen and sighed. She could have done without this grief. The kids were finally asleep, and she'd been sitting at the kitchen table having a well-deserved cuppa and a rare moment of peace. Now that was blown out of the water.

She didn't need to ask what Kevin's beef was—she could hear it for herself. The girl was crying again. Given that she had the attic room, you'd think she'd be out of hearing, but the noise filtered down through the thin floors, uneven walls, and badly fitted doors. The crying itself didn't bother Annie—she'd seen so many tears over the past few years that she'd become immune—but the other lodgers were beginning to complain. Kevin wasn't the first. She didn't blame the big man for being annoyed. He worked long, hard days on the docks to send money back to his family in Ireland. The last thing he needed was some wailing girl disturbing his precious kip.

Annie got to her feet. "Go on back to bed with you, Casey. I'll sort this." Much as she'd like to leave it to him, it was her duty as landlady to make sure everything ran smoothly. It was one of the many crosses she had to bear these days.

Before the war, Annie had been doing all right. She'd come over on the boat in the early 1930s, and met her husband, Devlin, in one of the Irish clubs. Like Kevin, he'd been a docker, and after getting promoted to overseer, his increased wages had allowed them to buy a place of their own in Whitechapel. A redbrick Georgian house on Cannon Street Road, it was in the heart of the Irish quarter, built up by the influx of immigrants in the mid–nineteenth century who'd come seeking work on the nearby docks. The Connollys had made a good life for themselves there. Annie had given birth to two girls, Bronagh in 1937 followed by Maureen the year after, and the little family had been living happily and prosperously in the East End.

But then the war had hit.

Devlin hadn't been the brave sort. As soon as conscription had been introduced, he'd headed back to Ireland to hide out with relatives for the duration of the war. The irony was, a week before D-Day, he'd gotten into a bar brawl in Dublin and ended up with a broken bottle through his jugular. He'd bled out right there on the dirty pub floor, leaving Annie alone at thirty-five years old, with three small children—the third, a boy named Daniel, conceived during a weeklong trip over to see Devlin in 1943—and without even the war widow's pension to keep her going.

Luckily, she'd had the house. It wasn't much—at four stories high, it was tall and narrow, with two rooms on each floor and an outdoor lav—but it was her only asset. Mercifully, the building was on one of the few streets that had remained untouched by the nightly bombings, and so Annie had moved herself and the kids into the basement and started renting out the rest of the bedrooms. Kevin Casey was typical of the type who lodged there. A casual laborer, he followed the work, moving from place to place. He'd been here for a couple of months now, bedding down on a mattress in a room with two other men in a similar situation.

For people like Annie, postwar London was a grim, gray place. Once the initial D-Day celebrations were over, it had become apparent that other than an end to the bombing, nothing much else had changed. Rationing remained in place; rebuilding was slow. The likes of Annie still had nothing. She tried to treat her boarders fairly. A lot of her compatriots who had gone up in the world exploited their position, offering disgusting rooms to those who had no choice but to put up with it. Annie wasn't like that. But even though she strived to be fair-minded, she was no soft touch, as her newest tenant was just about to find out.

Along with making noise, the girl up in the attic had committed what was to Annie an unforgivable crime: she was behind in the rent.

Annie had been planning to have a word with her the following day, in case the girl was planning a moonlight flit, but the crying incident had brought the confrontation forward. As she mounted the stairs, Annie prepared herself for a blowup. It wasn't as if she was running a charity. She had her own mouths to feed. And that was something she'd need to remember now when dealing with this one.

Thump-thump-thump. Franny slunk down further on the bed, as though that would protect her from the person outside.

"Come on, now. Open up. I know you're in there." Franny recognized the voice—a woman's, with a strong Galway accent. It was the landlady whom she'd met when she first arrived here a month ago. A tall, large-boned woman in her midthirties, she'd looked as though she was a force to be reckoned with. When she was booking in, Franny had heard her telling off one of the navvies for the state he'd left the outside privy in and had decided then that she never wanted to get on the wrong side of Annie Connolly. But now she was.

It was only four weeks since she'd left home, but to Franny, alone and lonely, it felt like forever. It had been easy enough to get a boat over. There had been plenty of women traveling on their own, most of them heading to Kilburn or Cricklewood, places in north London that were bursting with factories and employment opportunities for newly arriving immigrants. Franny had envied them, wishing she were young and carefree, coming to England to start a new life. But pregnant and ruined, she had other concerns.

After arriving in London, everything had gotten harder. Armed with Sean's hastily scribbled directions, Franny had headed over to the East End. She'd gotten off the tube at Whitechapel with the intention of finding somewhere to stay for the night before starting to search for him the next day. But once outside, she'd quickly become lost in the overcrowded, filthy warren of streets that ran from the station down to the Commercial Road. It had been an eye-opener. They might not have had much money back home, but this was a different kind of poverty: an ingrained acceptance of being bottom of the heap. A country girl, used to wide-open spaces and green fields, she'd found the noise and dirt disorientating.

Finding somewhere to stay hadn't been easy. NO BLACKS, IRISH, OR DOGS: it was an all-too-familiar sign in the windows of boarding houses. In the end, a tall, thin man with a dark beard and funny cap had taken pity on her. She was in the Jewish area, he'd explained before kindly pointing her down toward the Thames and Annie Connolly's place, saying "She's an Irish, too; she'll find a place for you if you've got the money." After that, it hadn't taken long to find the lodging house. It hadn't seemed like much, but Franny had felt relieved to be able to afford a room of her own; she'd heard plenty of stories of overcrowding on the way over.

But once she'd seen the little attic, she'd realized that she wasn't as fortunate as she'd imagined. It was at best eight by eight feet, and the ceiling sloped so steeply that the only place where Franny could fully stand up was in the middle of the room. Sometimes she preferred to wander the freezing streets than face coming back to such a depressing place—especially as it wasn't exactly warm inside. It was almost December now and so cold that she would wake in the mornings to find icicles hanging down inside the window as well as outside. Franny couldn't remember the last time she'd been warm. She had on all her clothes now, but still she was freezing.

And what was worse, it had all been for nothing. She hadn't been able to find Sean—she'd asked around, but no one had heard of him, and no one was interested in helping; they were all too busy with their own problems. So now she was stuck. Her money was running low, and she had nowhere to go, no one to turn to. She couldn't go back home, not in her present condition . . .

Thump-thump-thump. The knocking came again, interrupting her thoughts, the thin door rattling under the strength of the landlady's fist.

"Just so's you know," the voice broke through the door, "I ain't leaving until you get out here."

Something in the woman's tone warned Franny not to test the threat. Reluctantly, she got up and went to let the landlady in.

When the girl opened the door, Annie was shocked by her appearance. The last time she'd seen Frances Healey was a month earlier, when she'd first arrived. Tenants came and went so frequently that the landlady hardly noticed them anymore, but the pretty little Irish girl had stood out, with her rich auburn hair and large green eyes. Annie knew the girl had been avoiding her since then; in her two years of letting out rooms she'd seen every trick in the book. She'd let it go, thinking the younger woman might sort herself out, but seeing her now, Annie realized that whatever was going on with this girl couldn't be good. Her lovely face looked strained, and she seemed to have lost weight. She could do with a good meal inside her.

Not that it was Annie's problem. If this Frances Healey didn't have the rent, the landlady had no intention of letting her stay another night.

"You're a week behind." Annie didn't mince her words. "I imagine, since you've been avoiding me, that you don't have the cash?"

As Annie spoke, the girl moved forward a little into the dim landing light. Her eyes were red and tearful, reminding the landlady of why she'd come up here in the first place.

"You're right, I don't have the money," the girl answered in her soft Cork brogue. "But give me another week, and I'll get it to you."

"Sorry," Annie said curtly. "I told you at the beginning—you don't pay up, you're out. You've got half an hour." Annie made to turn away, but the girl put her small hand on the woman's arm, stopping her.

"But I don't have anywhere else to go."

"Well, that ain't my problem." The older woman made her voice deliberately harsh. She'd heard too many hard-luck stories in her time. If she'd listened to them all, she wouldn't have this house still. "If it weren't for you messing me round, I could've let that room to someone else this past week. I've got bills to pay and all, missy. My kids have got to eat, too, you know."

At that, the girl looked devastated. "I'm sorry. I didn't think. Look, I've got a pound here." She rifled through her coat pockets and held out her hand to show the note, as though to prove she was telling the truth. "But I need it," she said quickly, closing her fist and sticking it back inside her pocket, as though she was afraid that Annie was going to whip it clean away from her.

The young woman's remorse seemed so genuine that Annie felt her heart soften a little. She was used to people trying it on, but this girl seemed different. Despite her better judgment, the older woman suddenly wanted to know more about this Miss Healey and why she was here.

"So what do you need the money for?" the landlady asked.

Franny's face closed up. "I—I just need it, that's all," she said evasively.

It was the girl's guarded expression that finally told Annie exactly why she was there. Suddenly it all made sense—the crying; the desperation to stay. There was a woman two streets away, Mrs. Riley, who served as an unofficial midwife in the area, and she was known to provide other services, too. Annie hated the old bag.

"So you're up the duff then?" Annie was matter-of-fact. "And you're here to get it seen to?"

The girl looked horrified. "No, that's not it," she protested weakly, but Annie was already shaking her head.

"Look, it doesn't take a genius to figure it out. And trust me, I won't go blabbing to the police." There was a pause, and then, before the Galway woman could stop herself, she asked, "When're you getting it done?"

For a moment Annie thought the girl was going to deny it again, but then her shoulders sagged and her eyes filled with shame and misery. "Tomorrow morning," she whispered.

Annie sighed heavily. It wasn't that she was opposed to what the girl was planning to do. For someone young and alone like her, it might well be the best decision. But it was the thought of this pretty little thing being at the mercy of that old butcher, Mrs. Riley, that bothered her. A couple of months earlier, Annie's neighbor and friend Evelyn Dunne had fallen pregnant. Struggling to feed six children already, she hadn't been able to face having a seventh. She'd kept the news from her husband and secretly saved up the money to go to Mrs. Riley. "With any luck she'll mess me up enough so that this don't happen again," she'd joked to Annie beforehand.

But it hadn't seemed so funny afterward when, white-faced, Evelyn had described how she'd lain for an hour on the filthy kitchen table while old Mother Riley had poked at her first with a knitting needle and then used a crochet hook to scrape the fetus away. Seeing her friend doubled over in pain, Annie had urged her to go to the Royal London Hospital, just a five-minute walk up the road, but Evelyn had insisted she was fine. Later that day, the woman's twelve-year-old daughter had found her dead in bed, the mattress soaked through with blood. The trail had led the coppers back to old Mother Riley, but no one was speaking up, so she hadn't been charged. It wasn't the first time she'd gotten away with something like that.

"Look." This time when Annie spoke her tone was softer. "Maybe I was a bit hasty before. Why don't we head downstairs for a brew, see if we can't sort something out, eh?"

The girl's gratitude was so palpable that it was almost enough to convince Annie that she'd made the right decision.

Over a pot of tea in the cramped kitchen, Franny told the woman everything that had happened to her over the past few months. It was a relief to have someone to talk to. She'd always complained about the constraints of the farm, being beholden to her parents. But alone in London, she'd had to grow up fast, and it wasn't easy or pleasant. She hadn't realized how lonely she was until now. For the first time in a while, she felt as if someone cared. And it was nice to be out of that cold, damp room. The kitchen might be old and worn, but it was spotlessly clean, and the landlady wasn't as fierce as she'd first seemed.

Annie listened patiently to the girl's story, sympathetic if a little scornful. The girl was breathtakingly naïve. Imagine! Expecting to come to London and find this Sean Gallagher! And even if she had found him, she was as likely to get him down the aisle as Annie was to meet the king.

"So how far along are you?" she asked now.

The girl dropped her eyes, clearly embarrassed to be talking about something so personal. "Three months," she mumbled. "Maybe four."

"Well, it's probably too late to get rid of it anyway," Annie said.

The girl looked devastated. "Then what am I going to do?"

There was real fear in her voice. Annie realized that the younger woman was looking to her not only for an answer but a solution. And although it went against every instinct of self-preservation, she was inclined to break her cardinal rule and take pity on the girl. An idea had been forming in her head as Franny told her story, and now she decided to share it.

"Look, maybe I can help you out. You could stay here until you get yourself sorted. Not for free, of course," she added quickly, not wanting the girl to get the wrong idea. "This ain't no charity—you'll have to pay your way like everyone else. But I'd give you a good rate. I need a bit of help around here, and in exchange you could keep that room you're in. And I know of a few cleaning jobs that could bring in some extra cash. That'll allow you a bit of breathing space. You can have the baby and then decide what you want to do from there."

Franny looked at the landlady in astonishment. This was the last thing she'd been expecting when the formidable woman came hammering on her door earlier. "You'd do that for me?" She sounded almost confused, as though she couldn't believe her luck. "But why?"

Annie shrugged, as though it were no big deal. "You seem like a nice girl, and that bloke of yours sounds like a right so-and-so." She snorted her disapproval, showing exactly what she thought of the man in question. "You ain't the first to get caught, and you won't be the last. We've all been there, love, and I reckon we women have got to stick together, right?"

At that Franny threw her arms around the woman's neck. "Thank you, thank you!"

Embarrassed by the display, Annie pushed the girl gently away. "Hey, there's no need for that," she said gruffly. "You might not be thanking me after you've spent a day on your hands and knees scrubbing some snotty cow's floor!"

But despite the harshness of her words, Annie Connolly was secretly feeling happy about the arrangement. It would be nice, she decided, to have another woman around the place.

5

Mrs. Simpson ran her index finger along the mantelpiece, checking for dust. Franny stood nervously by. This was always the worst part. She could just about handle cleaning the house, but she hated the way the old bag then went around painstakingly checking everything she'd done. Having worked there for the best part of two years, she was hardly likely to start cutting corners now.

"And did you polish the good silver?" The upper-class accent was affected, the snotty disdain was not. Maybe it would have been easier for Franny to swallow if she'd been cleaning at one of those big white townhouses in Mayfair or Belgravia, but they all had their own live-in staff. So she was stuck with snobs like Mrs. Simpson, middle-class women who lived in newly built semis in Islington and Hampstead and were married to men with white-collar jobs—the kind who only recently could afford their own help and liked to look down on their cleaner as a way of asserting their social status.

Franny struggled to hide her impatience. She was itching to get out of there. "Yes, ma'am. And dusted the crystal," she added, preempting the next question. She hated the cut-glass animals that the lady collected and couldn't understand why she took such pride in the ugly ornaments. It had been made clear to Franny that if she dropped one, it would be deducted from her wages. "Is that everything?"

Unable to think of anything else to pick on, the older woman went to her large leather handbag. She made a big show of keeping it on her whenever Franny was in the house—as though she expected the younger woman to steal from her. Counting out the money from her purse, Mrs. Simpson handed it over reluctantly, clearly resentful of having to pay her cleaner.

"Thank you very much." Franny pocketed the cash quickly. She didn't bother to count it: there was never a tip, never a little extra, even at Christmas. But she made sure to sound grateful every time, aware of how much she needed to keep the woman sweet. Mrs. Simpson was always making little digs about how expensive Franny was, threatening to find someone else. So far Franny had stood firm, mainly because Annie had told her to. "You're charging less than you should be already," she'd insisted. "She's just trying it on." Franny knew this was true, but she was also aware of how precarious her position was. As a cash-in-hand employee, she had no rights, and she wasn't sure how easy it would be to find new work.

Mrs. Simpson saw her to the door—again, Franny suspected, to check she wasn't taking anything with her, rather than out of any sense of good manners. It was only half past four, but outside it was already winter dark. The air was so cold that Franny could see her breath forming clouds of condensation. Buttoning her coat with icy fingers, she jammed her hands into the pockets and hurried to the tube station to begin the forty-minute journey back to Whitechapel. It would have been easier to go straight to the club where she worked in the evenings, but that would have meant not seeing Cara, and she hated when that happened. Franny had promised her daughter that she would be back to put her to bed, and she was determined not to let her child down.

Motherhood had brought out the best in Franny. Cara, her daughter, made all the hardships worthwhile. And over the past two and a half years, there had been many hardships. The East End slums could get you down. Overcrowded tenements, unemployment, the constant poverty . . .

The birth itself hadn't been easy. Cara had been a big baby, and although Franny had full hips, her pelvis was small. Annie, experienced in these matters, had acted as midwife, mostly because they couldn't afford a real one. To Franny's shame, she hadn't been very brave. Afterward, Annie had joked that they'd been able to hear her screams five streets away, but at the time it hadn't been funny. Thirty hours of labor in that airless room—because the attic might be cold in the winter, but that couldn't even begin to compare to the stuffy heat of the summer, when not even the faintest breeze seemed to filter through the tiny window.

Worst of all, she'd gotten an infection afterward. She'd been sick and feverish for days, until Annie had finally been forced to get the doctor round. He'd given her some antibiotics, which had cleared up the blood poisoning, but he'd also said that she might struggle to conceive again. Frankly, after everything she'd been through, Franny wasn't sure she cared. She loved her daughter more than anything, but she wasn't sure there was enough money in the world to make her go through *that* again.

On the way back from the tube station, Franny bumped into a neighbor and got caught up talking, so it was nearly six by the time she reached the lodging house. Cara must have been listening out for her, because as Franny stepped into the hall, her daughter came waddling out to greet her. At twenty-one months old, she had the soft roundness of a toddler and was all rosy cheeks and big green eyes. It was those eyes that were her only gift from her mother. Even at this age, Franny could see more of Sean in her, and the crop of dark hair on her head was all her father.

"Mama home! Mama home!" Cara tugged at her mother's skirt as she spoke in her pidgin English. Turning her attention to her daughter, Franny felt the tiredness melt away. It was times like this when she remembered why the constant struggle was worthwhile.

"Come here, sweetheart." She scooped the child up for a cuddle. "Oh, you're getting heavy, aren't you?" she teased, pretending to buckle under her daughter's weight. "What have you been putting in here?" As she began to tickle Cara's tummy, the child laughed delightedly, and Franny felt the instinctive pull of love for her daughter that still took her by surprise.

At first, when she'd started living with Annie, she'd thought about having her child adopted. It would have been the easiest solution, to give her baby to a well-to-do family, where she'd be guaranteed a good upbringing while also allowing Franny to get on with her life, her mistake left firmly in the past. But as the months had gone by and she'd started to get bigger and become attached to the child growing within her, she'd realized it wouldn't be that easy. It helped that there were a lot of women in the area bringing up children on their own, their men either lost in battle or demobbed and departed back to where they'd come from. Franny was just one more, her situation hardly worth dwelling on.

"All right, Auntie Fran?"

Annie's eldest, twelve-year-old Bronagh, came out into the hall. Along with her ten-year-old sister, Maureen, they took turns watching Cara when they weren't at school. The two girls doted on Franny's child and were like little mothers to her. Franny knew how fortunate she was to have found Annie. Her lodging house might not be much, but she was ruthless about keeping it clean; a lot of the other tenements were overrun with rats and mice. But best of all, the Connollys were like one big extended family to her and Cara. Annie's children, even five-year-old Danny, treated Cara like one of their own. Cara had already formed an attachment to him. Now that she could walk, she toddled around after him, trying to call his name like he'd taught her: "Da-nee, Da-nee."

"How was she for you today?" Franny asked Bronagh. Like her mother, she was a strapping girl, big for her age, but she had a sweet, gentle nature and loved children, often talking of becoming a nurse or a teacher one day. "Not too much trouble, I hope."

"No trouble at all." The girl nodded toward the common kitchen that the Connollys shared with all their lodgers. "Mum's in there, we've just finished our tea."

Cara tugged at her mother's sleeve. "Dindins?" She turned hopeful eyes up at her mother.

Franny smiled down at her. "That's right, pet." Annie had offered time and again to let Cara have her dinner with them, but it was one of the few rituals Franny was reluctant to relinquish. She was out working so much that it felt important to maintain some role in her child's life, so she always made time to feed Cara and put her to bed, even on the nights she had to work at the club.

Shifting Cara onto her hip, Franny carried her through to the kitchen. Annie was in there, picking nits out of Danny's hair. Like Cara's, his hair was as black as the soot from the chimney, and they might have passed for brother and sister if it hadn't been for his swarthy complexion. At five, he was a good-looking boy, tall and strong for his age and already a handful. If there was mischief afoot in the street, he was usually at the center of it. The previous week, he'd brought home three tins of corned beef he'd stolen from Mr. Burke, the grocer. When Annie had found out what her son had done, she'd marched him back to the shop, made him return the tins, and then let Mr. Burke take him out the back for a thrashing before giving him a good whack herself. He hadn't been able to sit down for a day but had taken both punishments with a stoicism that had astounded the two women.

"There's not much to eat," Annie greeted her friend.

Franny grinned. "There never is."

With his mother temporarily distracted, Danny took the opportunity to squirm from her lap and, whooping loudly, ran from the room and out of the front door.

Cara stretched out her hands to follow. "Da-nee! Play with Da-nee!"

But Franny held her fast. "No playing at the moment. It's dinnertime now."

Annie shook her head in despair at her troublesome son. "He's got the Devil an' all in him, that boy," she remarked darkly, not for the first time. "Like his father."

But she didn't bother to chase him, knowing he could already well look after himself. Instead, she started to do the washing up, as Franny began to prepare dinner for herself and Cara.

A quick hunt through the cupboards and larder revealed that Annie was right: there wasn't much food left. It might be three years since the war ended, but rationing was still in place. It was the end of the week, so all the eggs and cheese had gone, which meant it was bread and dripping again. Franny cut three slices of bread, spread them with the beef dripping, and then sprinkled salt on. She gave one piece to her daughter and kept the other two for herself, but seeing how quickly Cara devoured her share, Franny gave her another half from her plate.

Annie saw what she was doing and remarked disapprovingly, "It's you who should be eating that, Fran. You're dead on your feet, girl, and you've got a long night ahead."

But Franny, busy watching her daughter stuffing the bread into her mouth, only laughed. "Give over with your fussing. I'll get something at the club later."

After Cara was fed, Franny took her upstairs to their little attic room and put her to bed. As always, her daughter insisted on having a story read to her. Conscious that she had little time left before she needed to leave, Franny reluctantly agreed. But luckily the child was tired from her day of playing, and her eyes began to close after a few pages.

With her daughter asleep, Franny went back down to fetch her bag from the kitchen. Annie was still there, in the middle of washing up. "She's all settled?"

It was more of a statement than a question, but Franny nodded anyway. "You'll check in on her, won't you?"

"You know I will."

With that Franny set off for her second job.

Forty minutes later, she arrived at Piccadilly Circus. Just walking out of the tube station, she felt her spirits lift. It might only be a few miles from Whitechapel, but the West End felt like a different world. It was all bright lights and modern motorcars, the wide, clean streets filled with well-dressed couples on their way to restaurants or theaters—or to supper clubs like the Victory Club, where Franny worked.

She'd taken the job at the club a few months earlier. It wasn't just for the money, although the extra cash did come in handy—it was more because it gave her something to aim for. She was sick and tired of sticking her hands down other people's lavatories. After nine hours on her knees cleaning up strangers' filth, her arms and back were sore and her morale at rock bottom. Sometimes she would look at her poor hands—the skin red and cracked from hours spent in cold water, the cuts stinging from the ammonia and vinegar used to clean the bathroom—and wonder where everything had gone wrong.

So she'd gotten herself hired as a coat-check girl at a swanky West End supper club, hoping that it might provide an opportunity for her to get into performing. Because she still hadn't forgotten her dream of becoming a famous movie star one day. And if she was going to get discovered anywhere, it would be at the Victory Club. Renowned throughout London for being a sophisticated, glamorous venue, major stars often headlined on the weekends. There was also a house band— playing bluesy jazz—along with a host of young, up-and-coming acts.

The entrance to the club was right opposite the tube station, down a set of red-carpeted stairs. Like the other staff members, Franny wasn't allowed in that way, so she slipped in the side door and hurried to the dressing room to change into her uniform. The other girls complained about having to wear the costume, but Franny loved it. She could never afford to buy anything new, and though the outfit might not be special, it was at least a change from her usual plain navy dress and cardigan.

Each night she would pretend to herself that she was getting dressed up like one of the performers.

The changing room was one long, busy room, with a row of dressing tables on either wall. Men and women changed in the same place. For the stars who played at the club, there were two plush rooms next door, but the majority of the employees had to content themselves with more basic facilities. Franny pulled on opaque tights and a leotard, which were both black, and then added the trimmings of the outfit—the tailcoat, arm cuffs, and little hat, all in red. She finished fastening the frog closures of the matching choker, then headed outside so she was at the cloakroom when the club opened at seven. Hazel, a sour-faced bottle blonde who worked the same shifts as she, was already there.

"We're in for it tonight," the other girl said gloomily as soon as she saw Franny. "The place is booked solid."

"Course it is! Vera Lynn's top of the bill."

Franny couldn't keep the excitement from her voice, but Hazel just grunted in reply. She probably would have said more, but right then two large groups arrived at once, and the girls had no more time to talk as they rushed to check the guests' coats.

Hazel was always moaning about the Victory Club—the hours, the work, the pay—and said that she couldn't wait to leave. But Franny couldn't see what she was complaining about: she loved everything about the club. Here, there was no evidence of postwar hardship: rationing didn't apply in restaurants, so the menu featured such luxuries as beef and duck, pheasant and venison. Wine, brandy, and port were plentiful, too. There were always leftovers in the kitchen, and most nights Franny and the other staff managed to get a good meal—although it wasn't the same as being there as a guest. Patrons dined at candlelit tables while the house band played, and then, as the evening drew on and the plates were whisked away, they would take to the dance floor.

Franny longed to be a customer at the club. Sometimes, when no one was around, she would slip on one of the fur coats, imagining what it would be like to own something so expensive. Even now, she still had her dreams. She just had to figure out a way to make them a reality.

By ten, most people were seated and the show was in full swing. Franny knew from experience that there would be a lull at the cloakroom now until people started to leave around midnight.

"I'm going on my break," she told Hazel. The other girl didn't even look up as Franny left; she was too busy flirting with one of the waiters to notice.

In their free time, most of the girls went out the back for a smoke, but Franny liked to watch the acts. As long as she stood in the shadows at the back of the room, no one seemed to mind. Now she slipped into the huge dining room. With its aged wood paneling and twinkling mirrored walls, it had an air of sophisticated elegance. Her timing was perfect. The saxophonist finished the last few bars of his solo, and as the crowd clapped, the bandleader made his way to the microphone.

"Thank you for your kind applause," he began, his face flushed and brow damp from the heat of the lights. The musicians always put on such an energetic show, clearly loving every minute of what they did. "And now I have the distinct pleasure of introducing the nation's sweetheart . . ." He paused for a drumroll and then declared, ". . . Miss Vera Lynn!"

The clapping had begun even before he finished speaking, and there were cheers as Vera Lynn swept onto the stage. Franny was captivated by her: in a floor-length gown of pink satin, her fair hair styled in an elegant chignon, she looked poised and affluent, everything the young Irish girl longed to be.

The singer waited patiently for the noise to die down. Graciously, she said in her soft, sweet voice, "Thank you, everyone, for such a warm welcome." Then the first piano chords struck up, and she began to sing "We'll Meet Again."

Sometimes during the acts, the audience chatted among themselves. But Vera Lynn had everyone enchanted. A few couples took to the dance floor, but most seemed happy just to watch. Franny lost all track of time as the great lady moved from one number to the next. It was only when Hazel sent one of the waiters to fetch her that she realized how long she'd been away from her post—she'd ended up watching most of the act. And as Franny hurried back to help in the cloakroom, she vowed to herself that one day she would be up on that stage, as famous and adored as Vera Lynn herself.

Over the next few months, whenever Franny had a spare moment, she would sneak in to watch the acts perform. Most weeks, there were big names headlining, and she got to see everyone from Ella Fitzgerald to

Sammy Davis, Jr.; Frank Sinatra to Lena Horne. Alongside the stars, there were other high-quality acts: burlesque performers and high-kicking showgirls; magicians and trapeze artists—a wonderland of color and sound. Franny watched them all, studying their performances while beginning to dream up an act of her own.

The club held open auditions for new acts twice a year. The next one was scheduled for June, and Franny vowed to be ready for it. She continued to study the performers at the club, trying to pick up the big band and jazz numbers that they all sang, and practiced them whenever she could: at home with Cara or while she was doing her cleaning jobs. Before she knew it, the time had come for the audition.

The first Monday in June 1949, Franny sat nervously, waiting to perform. She had turned up at one, which was as soon after her cleaning job as she could make it. Annie had kindly offered to fill in for her that afternoon, so she could have the time off to be there. Now she wondered if she'd made a huge mistake. More people were auditioning than she'd thought possible. It was off-putting, watching all these talented performers. She wasn't sure how she was going to distinguish herself.

By the time Franny got on stage, her confidence had deserted her. She was practically shaking as she took her place in front of the microphone: she wanted this *so* much, was so terrified of failure, that she felt almost paralyzed by fear. She'd decided, after much agonizing, to sing "Copacabana," as she'd seen Carmen Miranda do in the movie. It was an upbeat song, which would disguise any slight weakness in her untrained voice and let her show off some movement too. But now, standing center stage with all these strangers watching her expectantly, the lyrics flew out of her head. As the band struck up, she was so busy swaying to the rumba beat that she missed her cue. She tried to join in on the second line, but the mistake had thrown her, so she held up her hands and the musicians stopped playing.

"I'm so, so sorry," she whispered to the bandleader, Jaime. "For the life of me, I don't know what happened there."

Jaime told her not to worry and agreed to start over. This time, Franny came in at the correct moment, but then her nerves got the better of her, and during the third line, her voice began to shake. She could see people in the audience wincing as she missed a note. She came to a halt. One after another the instruments petered out.

There was silence throughout the auditorium. Franny wanted to run off the stage. It was too awful. This was her worst nightmare come to life. But if she left now, she would never get another opportunity like this. So she forced herself to ask Jaime if she could have another go.

If it had been anyone else, the bandleader would have refused: when someone messed up this much at an audition, it didn't bode well for performing live every night. But he liked Franny and knew how much she wanted this, so he felt the least he could do was give her one more chance.

"All right," he reluctantly agreed. "But just this one last time."

He turned to the band, but before he could instruct them, Franny said, "I think I'd rather sing unaccompanied this time." She smiled weakly. "Maybe it'll help."

Jaime shrugged. "Fine. Whatever you think is best."

Knowing this was her last chance, Franny had decided to abandon "Copacabana": it would be too demoralizing to start over with that again, and she wasn't in the mood to sing a feel-good number. Instead, she wanted to go with a song from the heart, which meant something to her. Closing her eyes, she thought about how much she wanted this. There was an impatient cough from the audience, but it didn't even register with Franny. In that moment, a strange calm came over her, and—unaccompanied—she began to sing the tragic tale of Molly Bán:

> *Come all ye young fellas*
> *That handle a gun*
> *Beware of night rambling*
> *By the setting of the sun*
> *And beware of an accident*
> *That happened of late*
> *To young Molly Bán*
> *And sad was her fate.*

It was an old Irish ballad that she'd used to sing at the weekly *ceilis* back home, as familiar to her as breathing. Telling the story of a young man out hunting who accidentally shoots his sweetheart as she shelters from the rain, it was a haunting ballad, a lament, and it suited Franny's mood perfectly. She poured all her feelings of regret and disappointment into the lyrics, drew on the grief she felt about the mistakes she'd made in her life, the nostalgia for the family home she'd been cast out of, and the foolish girl she'd been.

She was going to her uncle's
When a shower came on
She went under a green bush
The shower to shun
Her white apron wrapped around her
He took her for a swan
But a hush and a sigh
'Twas his own Molly Bán.

Jaime and the stage manager, Callum, exchanged looks. This was what they'd been looking for. Franny's voice soared like an angel's through the auditorium, and if she wasn't pitch perfect, it didn't matter: there was something so pure and genuine about what she was doing that no one watching her could fail to be captivated. Franny was more than just another singer—she was an act in her own right, something that could be a draw to the show.

"Well, you're a dark horse," Jaime remarked afterward.

Franny laughed. She was too thrilled to answer. On the strength of her audition, the club's manager had agreed for her to do a twenty-minute slot on Tuesday and Wednesday evenings, at seven thirty. It wasn't much: the equivalent of the graveyard shift, the warm-up slot when customers were drifting in. But at least it was a start.

6

"Chicken!" Olly Gold made a loud squawking sound to emphasize his point. The other boys laughed and joined in, bending their arms at the elbow to make wings. "Cluck-cluck-cluck! Chicken!"

Color flooded Cara's cheeks. "Am not!" she insisted, trying not to show just how intimidated she was. The boys had formed a tight circle around her, meaning she had nowhere to run even if she wanted to—which she didn't, because if she left now they'd tease her forever after. With four months still to go until her seventh birthday, she was the youngest member of the gang and the only girl. She was also the smallest, apart from poor Timmy Glover, who still sucked his thumb and wet the bed, the stained sheets hung outside the upstairs window each morning for everyone to see. Timmy was usually the one picked on, but because he wasn't around today, it was Cara's turn.

"So you gonna do it, then?" Olly demanded.

Cara instinctively looked toward Danny Connolly, Annie's son, who was now the de facto leader of the group. It had been Olly's role up until a few months ago, but then Danny had fought him for it. Although at twelve Olly was the older and bigger of the two, ten-year-old Danny had come out like a pit bull, refusing to back off. Cara knew that it was only because of Danny that she had been allowed in the gang. Having grown up in the same house, he was like a big brother to her. As such, he usually looked out for Cara, but sometimes the other lads took the mick out of him for it, and she knew he worried that showing her favoritism weakened his position. Now, to her disappointment, instead of stepping in, he gave her an encouraging smile. "You'll be all right."

With her last chance of escape gone, Cara had no choice. "Well, come on, then, and move out of my way," she said bravely. "Let me get on with it, will you?"

Impressed now, the boys parted to let her through.

Cara began to walk forward, surveying the task ahead of her. The children were on Adley Road. The street had taken a direct hit during the Blitz, and it was little more than a pile of rubble now. But if you climbed on top of the bricks and peered down, you could see into the demolished rooms below. The gang played war games there a lot. The last time, Olly had spotted an old gun trapped under some iron supports in one of the houses. Today he had dared Cara to go and retrieve it.

The children were the only ones around. The area was roughly boarded off, hiding a wasteland of rubble and half-demolished terraces. Big red signs had been nailed up, warning in black writing: DANGER—KEEP OUT. Building was due to start soon, and the government was putting up something called "flats," paid for by the council. A lot of people in their street were hoping to get one. Work was supposed to start any day now; this could be one of the last times the gang would play here, so Cara knew she had to get the gun today.

As with every other bomb site, there was a secret entry, where the boarding had been carefully removed, allowing a small body to squeeze through. As Cara eased into the gap, Olly called out, "Watch where you tread in there. I've seen a few dead bodies hanging around."

There was another round of laughter.

"Shut it," Danny ordered, silencing them.

But for Cara, the damage was already done. She wanted more than anything to turn back, but there was no way she could lose face with the others. She just needed to get this over with as quickly as possible.

She scurried across the wasteland, toward the crumbled walls that had once been people's homes. Scrambling to the top of the bricks was easy enough, since she was good at climbing and light enough not to disturb the precarious balance of the rubble. At the top, she saw right away that the hardest part was going to be getting down inside the house, to the floor of the destroyed rooms. She took a moment to decide on the best course of action.

"Get on with it!" a couple of the boys called. "What's the holdup?"

Ignoring the taunts, Cara sat down gingerly on the ruins, dangling her legs into the opening. Then, once she was sure the bricks would hold her weight, she began to edge herself inside. Using her arms for support, she gradually eased her body into the gap, sucking in her breath to squeeze her stomach through. Soon she was hanging on to the side by her fingertips, but there was still about a yard between herself and the ground. That meant she would have to let go and hope that she didn't land on anything sharp. Closing her eyes, she counted to three and then dropped.

To her surprise, she landed almost squarely on her feet. Stumbling a little, she grabbed at the leg of an upturned chair and managed to right herself without incurring any damage. Finally inside, she felt relief wash over her. She was halfway through her ordeal. Quickly scanning her surroundings, she saw that she was in what must have once been the living room: along with a couple of broken chairs, there were a sofa, with the stuffing blown out, and a damaged radio. There were no photos or personal items, so maybe the family had been in a shelter on the night of the raid and had been able to come back later to retrieve them. She hoped so.

Keen to get this over with, Cara began to search for the gun that Olly had seen. Squatting down, she picked her way through the damaged furniture and debris, moving carefully across the room. At first she couldn't see the gun. But then the sun came out from behind a cloud, chinking through the gap above, the light catching on something. Among the wreckage, something that looked like the barrel of a revolver caught her eye. Removing a charred book and an empty photo frame, Cara dug down and grabbed at the gray object. Pulling it out, she emitted a squeal of delight. She'd found it! The gun—and it was a toy gun at that! A plastic water pistol. Oh, she would have fun ribbing Olly about not being able to tell a real gun from a fake!

With prize in hand, Cara straightened up, and started to look around for a way out.

It was then that she saw the dead body. In fact, it was only a coat that had fallen across the floor, but all Cara could hear was Olly's earlier warning. Panicking, she stepped back heavily and knocked into the load-bearing steel beam that was holding up what was left of the building. Even though she weighed very little, the beam had been sufficiently weakened so that the tiniest push was enough to cause it to move. Cara froze as she heard the beam buckle and stretch, trying to right itself as it strained under the weight of the building. Then the joist gave up the fight.

There was an almighty crash, and everything went dark.

Outside, the boys stood frozen in shock. The cave-in had sent up clouds of dust, obscuring the site from view for the moment, so they couldn't see the exact damage. But it looked bad.

It was Olly who reacted first. Swearing under his breath, he said, "I'm out of here."

His words prompted Danny to action. He knew the boys would be scared of getting into trouble, as they shouldn't be there. But if they left, Cara would never get out alive. He was happy to go in and try to save her himself, but he'd need the others to run for the police or ambulance if he couldn't get her out. He grabbed his friend roughly by the collar. "You dare . . ." he growled. Leaving the threat hanging, he turned and ran toward the site.

Danny felt guilty now about sending Cara in there. He shouldn't have let Olly pressure her into doing the dare—after all, he'd known she was frightened. But it was hard being the leader: he had to be on his guard all the time against the other pretenders to his throne. As he raced toward the demolition site, he just prayed that his ambitions hadn't cost Cara more than he could ever repay.

Cara woke up coughing dust. She fought to breathe, but the air was thick with dirt, and every time she inhaled, her lungs filled with noxious fumes. In her panic, she tried to move but couldn't. A wooden cupboard lay across her legs, trapping her. She knew instinctively that if the structure shifted again, the beam would topple and crush her. In the darkness, Cara whimpered. She could hear the brackets creaking under the weight of the rubble. She was terrified. How was she going to get out?

"Cara?"

Danny's voice came from above. Hearing it, Cara felt relief flood through her. "I'm here!"

"Are you all right?"

"Yeah, but—" She tried to move again. "But I'm trapped. I can't get out." She heard the wobble in her voice and felt ashamed.

But Danny was reassuring. "Hold on. I'm coming for you."

With anyone else, it might have seemed like false bravado. But Cara trusted Danny implicitly, and simply knowing that he was nearby and attempting a rescue had calmed her. It was pitch black, so from where she was lying she couldn't see anything. But she could hear the reassuring sounds of him moving through the darkness: scrabbling across the rubble, breathing hard at the exertion, cursing as he lost his footing.

Soon he was by her side, a shadow in the darkness. "Are you hurt?" he wanted to know straight off.

She felt sore all over but didn't think anything was seriously wrong. "No, not really."

"Good." He was brusque and authoritative. "Now, I'm going to try to get this off you."

She felt his hands sliding under the cupboard, and she gritted her teeth as he began to lift the furniture. As one side went up, the other dug into her, and she couldn't help but let out a small moan. Immediately, Danny stopped. "Am I hurting you?"

Cara clenched her fists, and forced herself to say, "Don't worry, I'm fine."

Even though Danny was strong, he was only ten years old, so it took a combination of sliding the cupboard as well as lifting to finally shift it off Cara's legs.

He knelt by her. "Can you stand?"

She tried, but her knee hurt too much. "No," she said, feeling a fresh wave of panic set in.

He smiled confidently, his teeth white in the darkness. "Don't worry. I've got a plan."

By now the other boys had followed Danny over and were at the opening. Danny instructed them to stand by as he passed Cara up to them. Once he was sure she was safe, he hauled himself out. Supported by Danny and Olly, Cara, along with the other boys, stumbled to safety. They were barely ten feet away when the structure groaned loudly and collapsed.

The gang turned and gazed open-mouthed at the hole in the street. Cara was the first to react. She looked up adoringly at Danny and said, with a mixture of awe and admiration, "You saved me!"

Then, like Prince Charming from one of her fairy tales, Danny scooped her up in his arms and carried her home.

* * *

Franny was horrified when she saw the state of her daughter. Cara was covered in dust, there was blood gushing from her leg, and it didn't help that she was crying hysterically, making it impossible to know how badly hurt she really was. In fact, once the surface dirt had been cleaned away in the big steel bath in the Connollys' kitchen, Franny saw it was little more than a graze and that there would be a small scar but no permanent damage.

"You stupid girl," Franny scolded as she bandaged up her daughter's knee. "Whatever were you doing in that place? I've told you time and again not to play there, that it's dangerous. Have you not got a brain in your head?"

As Franny said the last words, she was aware of sounding just like her mother. Suddenly she could understand how Theresa had felt, that the harsh words she'd often spoken had been said out of worry and concern for her child, not simply because she was a spoilsport. In that moment, Franny wished she could tell her mam that she understood.

"It wasn't Cara's fault, Aunty Fran," Danny piped up.

Franny gave him a withering look. "I know that, my boy. I'm sure whatever went on today, *you* were at the center of it." Her accusation was meant to elicit some sort of acceptance of guilt, but instead of looking contrite, Danny simply stared back at her, defiant. Ten years old he was, and with the front of someone twice his age. Suddenly she didn't want him anywhere near her daughter. "Now get out of here."

Danny didn't do as she asked straightaway. First he went over, kissed Cara on the forehead, and said, "You did well today." Only then, with a last insolent glance at Franny, did he saunter out of the room.

Cara murmured a protest as her friend left, but the look on her mother's face stopped her from saying too much.

"It was him who made you go into that house, wasn't it?" Franny demanded. When her daughter said nothing, she sighed heavily. "You're a fool for that boy, aren't you? If Danny told you to jump off a cliff, would you do it?"

Her daughter's mouth set into a line. "Danny didn't *make* me do anything."

Franny shook her head in despair. To Cara, Danny was the hero of the hour. She'd conveniently forgotten that he was the one who'd gotten her into trouble in the first place. Danny was turning into a right little tyke. The only male in the household, he was doted on by his indulgent mother and sisters and could do no wrong in their eyes, which meant he got away with murder. God only knew what he would be like when he grew up.

But Cara was safe, and for now that was all that mattered to Franny. Securing the bandage with a pin, she smiled at her daughter, wanting to show her that she was forgiven. "Come on, then. Let's get you to bed."

Despite being slight herself, Franny lifted her daughter easily. The child was tall for her age, but skinny, too. Around the age of three, Cara had started to outgrow her toddler's potbelly, and now at nearly seven years old, she was as long and skinny as a hare. With her shock of black hair and big green eyes that seemed too large for her gaunt face, even Franny had to admit that she wasn't an attractive child. "She don't look much like you" was a frequent comment from the women on the street. Franny knew what they meant: *you must be disappointed that she isn't prettier*. But she wasn't. It was a strange, instinctive feeling—she loved Cara no matter what.

Now, looking down at her daughter, tucked safely into bed, Franny felt that same rush of love. Pushing the dark mop of hair back from Cara's face, she asked, "Would you like to read for a little while?"

It was a nightly ritual. Franny had encouraged her daughter to read from a young age. Back in Ireland, her mother, Theresa, had always been keen to ensure that her daughters made the most of the education on offer to them, and Franny wanted to do the same for her own child. So every Saturday morning, she would take Cara to Whitechapel library, a beautiful redbrick building over the entrance to Aldgate East tube station, where the little girl would browse the children's section for the books she wanted. Then, each night before bed, Cara would read a chapter or so aloud to her mother, and Franny would help her with any words she didn't understand.

Like a lot of children, Cara loved Enid Blyton, and she had recently discovered *The Faraway Tree* series. Opening *The Enchanted Wood*, she began reading.

Half an hour later, once her daughter was finally ready to sleep, Franny went downstairs, intending to clean out the bath before she headed off to work. Walking into the kitchen, she was put out to find Liam Earley there again. A builder who boarded in one of the lodging houses down the road, Annie had taken up with him a few weeks earlier. Sitting alone at the table, he was halfway through a Spam sandwich—pretty much the last of that week's precious rations.

"All right, Franny?" He belched loudly and made no effort to apologize. "You're looking mighty fine today."

A tall, thickset man, he had a bald head and a big, quivering belly. His face was round and his features squashed and off center, courtesy of the boxing he'd used to do, and he reminded Franny a little of a pit bull terrier. But his most distinguishing feature was his red nose, the mark of a hardened drinker. Liam was a brickie by trade, but Franny secretly thought he was little more than a thug and a drunk. Lately he'd been spending more and more time at Annie's. If Liam was going to become a permanent fixture, she would need to think about moving on.

"How can you put up with the likes of him?" she'd asked Annie once, after coming in to find him slumped on the settee, sleeping off his latest drinking binge, the floor beside him thick and ripe with his vomit.

The older woman, who had already begun clearing away the mess, had answered with surprising honesty. "I missed having a man in my bed. Liam takes some of that loneliness away."

That had thrown Franny. After being burned so badly by her experience with Sean, she had been happy to put romance from her mind. It had never occurred to her that Annie might not feel the same way.

Now Franny gave him a polite nod of greeting. "Where's Annie?"

Liam belched again, and this time Franny was close enough to smell the sour mix of pickled onions, meat, and beer. "She's popped out to the shops."

Franny's heart sank. Liam gave her the creeps, and she hated being alone with him. He hadn't done anything specific to make her feel that way, but she sensed it was only a matter of time.

As she bent to clean the bath, she heard the scraping of the chair on the floor. She'd been hoping that meant Liam would leave, but instead the next minute she felt his strong hand on her bottom.

"Just as I thought, nice and firm," he murmured, squeezing one buttock before slipping his hand into the crevice.

Quick as lightning, she straightened up, turned and slapped his hand away. Her eyes flashed with hatred.

"Don't *ever* do that again!" she hissed, stepping back out of his reach.

But despite the venom of her words, Liam grinned, displaying a set of rotten brown teeth with bits of half-chewed bread stuck between them.

"Come on, love. Take a joke, will you?"

Franny stared at him with utter dislike and contempt, then turned and walked out of the room.

7

It was a Tuesday, usually the quietest time of the week at the Victory Club, but there was a buzz in the air when Franny got to work that night. The dressing room was alive with chatter and excitement, the girls fighting even harder over the mirrors than usual. It didn't take long to work out the reason for all the fluttering: the Hollywood movie star Duke Carter was out in the audience. Debonair, charismatic, and charming, he was a big box-office draw, the kind of actor who set hearts racing.

Peeping out from behind the stage curtain, Franny saw that there were five people at the round table with the actor: three other men, all in white tie, and two very young women, in cheap but revealing cocktail dresses. Paula, one of the showgirls, filled Franny in: Duke was over in England filming a big-budget period drama on the English Civil War.

"The girls are nobodies, hired floozies," Paula said dismissively. Gesturing at the other three men, she pointed out the director, a tall, skinny, intense-looking man named Landon Taylor, and the second male lead, Earl Fox, a poor man's version of Duke. Then she got to the last person, a short, fat man with a receding hairline. "And that's Clifford Walker, some hotshot producer at Juniper Pictures."

"Oh?" Franny's casual tone concealed her interest.

"Yeah, he was the one behind *Brothers in Blood*."

Brothers in Blood was an epic movie set during the American Civil War, about two half brothers who end up fighting on opposite sides, as well as over the same girl. It was Juniper Pictures' answer to MGM's

Gone with the Wind, made more than a decade ago now, and it had certainly been as popular in the cinemas when it had been released the previous year. Hearing that the short, rotund man had been behind it, Franny studied him more closely.

The floozies were all over Duke Carter, but they were wasting their time. He might be the star, but Franny knew where the real power lay: with the producer. While working at the Victory Club, she'd learned a little about show business. The producer oversaw the movie from beginning to end, organizing everything from getting the financing together to hiring the actors and crew and arranging the distribution.

In the dressing room, Franny's mind raced. This could be it, the opportunity she'd been waiting for—the chance to change her fortune.

It was over four years since she'd started performing at the Victory Club, and life had definitely improved for her. The first few months, when she'd just had a short spot, she'd stuck mainly to Irish folk tunes, like the one she'd performed in her audition: songs about love and emigration. But she'd always known that if she were to get more visibility, she needed to come up with a stronger act with wider appeal. After a year or so, she'd decided to combine her singing with her talent for mimicry and create a routine based around impersonating great singers. So she'd asked the bandleader, Jaime, to play a medley of popular songs, each immortalized by a different well-known artist, allowing her to make the most of her charisma and stage presence.

She would always remember the first night she had performed her new act. Taking the microphone, she'd looked over at Jaime and nodded, which was his cue to start playing. As the rumba sounds of "Copacabana" filled the theater, she'd begun to sway to the beat, as she'd seen Carmen Miranda do in the movie, and sang the opening lines.

There had been a gasp from the audience. She wasn't just singing the famous Carmen Miranda song—in that moment, she *was* Carmen Miranda, a perfect mimic. A verse and a chorus in, Jamie had changed the tempo and she'd switched to Marlene Dietrich singing "Falling in Love Again." Then she was Edith Piaf performing "La Vie en Rose." Maybe her voice wasn't always on key, but she had the singers' demeanor and movements down perfectly.

When she'd finished, the audience had given her a standing ovation, and the stage manager had asked if she could increase her hours.

The success of the new routine had allowed her to give up all the menial jobs—cleaning and coat checking—so now she worked six evenings a week, three at the Victory Club and the rest of the time at a couple of other nightspots. They weren't as classy as the Piccadilly supper club, but they allowed her to be an entertainer fulltime.

However, that still wasn't enough for Franny. It was seven years since she had left Ireland. At twenty-four years old, she could feel time creeping on, and she was still waiting for her big break—because however much she enjoyed singing, what she really wanted to do was act. And now, just as she'd begun to despair of ever getting an opportunity, one had finally presented itself to her: there was a Hollywood producer here, someone who could give her a start in the business. She couldn't just let him walk out of the club without making some kind of impression. Unfortunately, her routine tonight was fairly bland: she was supposed to be performing a medley of songs by the likes of Judy Garland and Doris Day, a girl-next-door act, complete with a frumpy floral dress. It was hardly going to attract the attention of a flash producer.

As Franny dwelled on her problem, her eyes alighted on the next dressing table. A black lace cocktail dress hung over the mirror. It belonged to one of the club's best singers, Dawn Morris. She was very precious about her costumes and wouldn't let anyone near them. But she worked only on weekends, which meant she wasn't here tonight, so she'd never know if Franny borrowed the gown for the evening.

An idea began to form in Franny's head. She was the next act up, so she had to work fast. Quickly slipping on Dawn's dress, she teased out her hair and vamped up her makeup. Then she headed to Jaime and asked him to change her music. Instead of the chirpy medley she was supposed to sing, she opted for a sexy Mae West number. As the saxophone drawled the opening notes, she sashayed out onto the stage, taking her place at the microphone.

The dress was a size too small for Franny, and it seemed to be molded onto her body like a second skin. It was meant to be a demure outfit, with a high Victorian neckline and full-length sleeves, but as the lace material clung to Franny's curves, it meant that the dress ended up being quite see-through when she stood in the direct spotlight.

Standing center stage, Franny knew that every man in the audience was watching her. But the only one she cared about was Clifford Walker. Locking eyes with him, she began to sing "I'm in the Mood for Love."

Her performance was all for him, a long seduction. After the first verse, she picked up the mike and went down into the audience. So it wasn't too obvious who her target was, she stopped along the way, picking on men as she passed, snaking her feather boa around their necks. As she came to Clifford's table, she could see he was captivated by her and delighted by all the attention. Perching on his knee, she began to sing the third verse directly to him, as though he were her lover and she meant every word, looking up at him from lowered lashes, giving him a secret little smile.

With the song coming to a close, she trailed her fingers across his cheek, then stood up and glided back to the stage. As she came to the final line, she made sure to meet his gaze again, running her hands suggestively over the microphone stand. Seeing the look that crossed his face, she knew that she'd nailed it.

Sure enough, she'd been back in the dressing room for only five minutes when one of the stagehands came over to her. "A guest at table one asked for you to join him. Some American chap."

"Good." She felt a surge of triumph, followed by a rush of nerves. It wasn't in the bag yet. "Tell him I'll be right there."

Franny didn't hurry out. Instead, she retouched her makeup, not wanting to look too desperate. By the time she entered the dining room, the rest of the party had discreetly taken to the dance floor and Clifford was sitting alone.

Clifford Walker watched as the girl sashayed toward him. She had a quality about her. She was sexy without being slutty; a classy broad, worth waiting for.

"Mr. Walker?" Franny kept her voice low and breathy.

He stood to greet her. He was an inch or so shorter than she, with a round belly that his jacket could hardly close across. She could see dark hairs coming out of the top of his shirt collar. No wonder the other girls were making a beeline for Duke instead.

"Miss Healey." His eyes swept over her and he nodded appreciatively, as if to confirm that she looked just as good as he remembered. "Thank you for joining me."

"It's my pleasure," she said.

He waited for her to be seated and then sat down himself. Franny had never been allowed at one of the tables before—the performers weren't supposed to fraternize with the guests. But she tried to look as though this were something that happened to her all the time. A waiter brought over a bottle of Dom Pérignon and poured them two glasses.

It was Franny's first taste of champagne. She wasn't expecting the bubbles to go up her nose, and she choked a little but hid it with a cough. She thought she saw amusement in the producer's eyes, but if he noticed her faux pas he didn't mention it. Instead, he sat back and regarded her with keen, professional eyes.

"I have to tell you," he drawled, "I was damned impressed with your performance tonight."

"Oh?" Despite the way her heart was hammering, Franny tried to play it cool.

"Yeah, you were real good up there; knew how to work it. I couldn't take my eyes off you. And neither could any other man in the room." The professionalism slipped for a moment, and there was the faintest hint of a leer.

Franny dropped her gaze and tried to look modest. "I'm glad you enjoyed the song."

"I more than enjoyed it." He rubbed his belly contemplatively. "Hell, I've been in this business a long time, and I know talent when I see it. And I reckon I just might be onto something here with you."

"Really?" Again Franny tried to appear nonchalant.

"That's right." He waited a beat and then said, "Course, it's always hard to tell how good someone's gonna be until you have them up there in front of the camera."

"I see."

"But I guess it might be worth putting you forward for a screen test, see if you've got what it takes." He looked at her slyly. "How does that idea grab you?"

Suddenly all Franny's poise deserted her. Without thinking she grabbed his hand, wanting to show him how much the opportunity would mean to her. "Oh, sir, Mr. Walker—I want this so badly. You have no idea. I'd do anything to get that screen test. Anything."

"Anything?" Clifford seized on the word. Something in his expression changed, his eyes narrowing and growing predatory, as though he were a lion tracking a gazelle from the undergrowth. His grip tightened on Franny's hand, his palm hot and clammy against hers, and it took all

her willpower not to pull away. "In my experience, that's very easy to say, much harder to mean."

He was watching her intently, a calculating expression on his face. "So, Franny Healey, I guess my question is: what do *you* mean by 'anything'? Exactly how far are you willing to go to get what you want?"

The sick feeling in the pit of Franny's stomach stayed with her all the way back to Clifford's hotel. She kept thinking that at any minute she would find the courage to tell him that she'd changed her mind. Instead, she found herself being helped out of the taxi under the bright lights of the entrance to the Savoy, walking past the liveried doormen and entering the grand lobby filled with impeccably dressed guests. Sensing her hesitation, Clifford took her by the arm.

"Come along, darling," he said loudly, as though they were like any other couple.

As he led her toward the elevator, she kept her head down, unable to meet anyone's eyes, certain everyone could tell exactly why she was here. They rode the elevator together in silence, and Franny tried to forget the task ahead of her and concentrate on her surroundings instead.

The hotel was beautiful. Clifford had a suite of rooms to himself. It was bigger than the whole of Annie's house, which regularly accommodated at least twelve people. The suite itself was elegantly decorated, with Regency striped wallpaper, a thick carpet, and solid wooden furniture that looked as though it had taken months to carve. A huge fire burned in the grate, welcoming them. The hotel staff lit it every evening at six, Clifford explained.

He went over to the drinks cabinet, poured a tumbler of what looked like whisky, and then hesitated over a second glass. "Drink?"

"Please." Franny needed the Dutch courage.

Despite the fire, she couldn't stop shivering. Hearing her teeth chatter, Clifford frowned. "What's up? You cold or something?"

There was a note of irritation in his voice. Franny could tell he wasn't happy with her lack of enthusiasm. Spotting the bathroom, she saw an escape route. "Just give me a minute to freshen up."

Inside, she managed to turn the taps on full blast to mask any noise, before collapsing in front of the toilet bowl and throwing up several times. Once she was sure there was nothing left in her system, she got up and went to the sink. Staring at herself in the mirror, she was alarmed at how pale and shaky she looked. Her only currency was Clifford's desire for her, and what man would want her like this?

Pull yourself together, she scolded herself. *You want to be an actress? Well, think of this as your first audition.*

That helped. Quickly washing out her mouth, she tried to approach this as if it were a role in a movie. First she reapplied her makeup: mascara emphasized her emerald eyes, a little rouge gave color to her cheeks, and dark red lipstick brought out the vamp in her. Already she was starting to feel better. Next, she unpinned her hair—Sean had always preferred it that way—until the rich auburn curls spilled around her shoulders. But it still wasn't enough of a transformation. When she stepped outside, she needed to be a different person, at least for the duration of her time with the producer. Taking a deep breath, she began to unbutton her dress.

Clifford was growing impatient when he heard the key turn in the lock of the bathroom door. "Finally! What the hell have you been doing in th—"

The final word died on his lips as Franny stepped into view. Along with her clothes, she had removed her brassière and panties, and now she stood there in the doorway, wearing nothing but a black lace garter belt, sheer stockings, and four-inch heels. She struck a pose.

"Well?" she demanded, in a breathy imitation of Marilyn Monroe. "Was I worth the wait?"

Clifford's eyes ran over her, taking in her full breasts, the nipples carefully rouged with lipstick; moving down to her tiny waist, then onto the red triangle of hair between her legs. He was pleased to see that the naïve ingenue had disappeared and the vamp who had sung to him earlier was back. He patted the bed. "Why don't you come over here and let's find out."

When it was over, Franny dressed quickly in silence, trying hard not to think about what she had done, and then stood uncertainly, watching Clifford. He was lying on his back on the bed, a sheet pulled over his waist and legs and his hand thrown over his face, so she couldn't tell if he was asleep or not. She opened her mouth to speak once and then a second time but eventually settled for clearing her throat to remind him that she was there. He opened his eyes. "What?" he grunted.

"I . . . er . . . just wondered about . . . well, about the test."

Clifford didn't answer right away, and for a horrible moment, Franny thought he was going to renege on his promise. But then he said, "I'll leave word at the club," before closing his eyes again, signaling that she should go.

Franny felt dirty all the following day. Although Clifford had promised to be in touch about the screen test, she kept wondering what would happen if he didn't do as he'd said. She had no guarantee that he would keep his word, and it wasn't as if she could take back what she had done.

But she began to feel a bit better the next evening, when she went into work and found a note from Clifford, saying that she was to come out to Juniper's studio in Hertfordshire for a screen test the following Monday. She had her opportunity—now all she had to do was prove that she had what it took to be a star.

8

"So what do you think?" Clifford leaned back in the soft green velvet couch and regarded the attractive redhead intently.

He hadn't expected to be in this position. When he'd seen this Franny Healey perform her Mae West number, he'd wanted her badly and had been prepared to use his pull with the studio to get her into bed. In his wildest imagination, he hadn't expected her to be any good. But she'd pulled off the screen test: she was one of those rare people who looked even more beautiful on film than in person—and boy, could she act! With the growth of television and government deregulation, times might be hard for the big Hollywood studios, but they were still always on the lookout for new talent, and Clifford had a feeling he'd found someone who had a real future in the business.

Sitting across from the producer on an identical couch, Franny didn't know what to say. How many times had she read magazine articles about the way stars had been "discovered" and longed for that to be her? And now it was.

It was two weeks since her screen test. Along with other Hollywood giants, Juniper had a studio out near Elstree, a nondescript village in Hertfordshire, about a forty-minute train ride from London. The sheer size of the place had amazed Franny: it was like a little village, made up of a series of anonymous low-rise rectangular buildings of varying lengths. Franny had been escorted to one of the empty lots, a little like an aircraft hanger. An assistant director, a low man on the totem pole, had taken charge, giving her instructions. There was a plain stage with nothing but a blank backdrop, where she'd had to read lines from a short scene about a woman who has just found out that her husband is dead.

After the screen test, she'd had a tense two-week wait until she heard from Clifford. He'd left word at the club for her to meet him at his hotel room this afternoon. She hadn't known what to expect. But as soon as she'd reached the room, she'd known it was going to be different this time. He'd ordered tea for them; the bedroom door was firmly closed. This was altogether more professional. And once she'd sat down, he'd spoken those magic words: "Honey, you might just have what it takes to be a star."

He'd loved her screen test, he told her; absolutely *loved* it. He'd shown it to Juniper's head of casting, Lloyd Cramer, and he'd loved it, too. So much so that they'd decided to fly her out to Hollywood. They had her in mind for a project that was due to start filming in the next few weeks. All she had to do was get on a plane. Franny couldn't believe it. This was exactly the news that every girl dreamed of hearing.

Except now, as she looked down at the airplane ticket Clifford had handed her, she bit her lip and frowned.

Seeing the change in her expression, Clifford frowned, too. "There's no problem, is there? I was under the impression that you had no ties here."

When she didn't answer at first, he went on, a little sharper this time, "I am right in thinking you have no husband, no sweetheart?"

She looked up at him and then back down at the plane ticket. "It's just there's only one ticket."

"So?"

Franny waited a beat, certain she was about to say the wrong thing, but knowing she had to get it off her chest. "Well, you see, I have a child. A little girl called Cara. And I really can't go anywhere without her."

On the way back to Whitechapel, Franny couldn't stop looking at the plane ticket that Clifford had given to her. It was as if someone had handed her a wonderful, once-in-a-lifetime opportunity and then snatched it away. Because Clifford had been very clear on one thing: there would be no additional ticket for her daughter.

"It was hard enough persuading the studio to fly *you* out. If Lloyd finds out that you've got a kid, he'll blow a fuse." The fat man had shaken his head in exasperation. Hell, there was only so much he was prepared to do in return for a quick roll in the sack. "Look, I've gone out on a limb here. You've got your shot. It's up to you whether you take it or not."

He had stood up then and opened the double doors that led through to the bedroom, and she'd been expected to show him how grateful she was for his help. Two hours later, she'd finally been allowed to leave the hotel. Now she was trying to forget everything that had happened, how cheap and degraded she felt, and instead concentrate on her dilemma. There was no way she could afford another ticket, which left two choices: either give up her dream or leave Cara behind.

The thought of being apart from her daughter was like a fist in the chest. It might be six months before she could afford to bring Cara out, which would feel like a long enough time to her, but to the little girl it would be a lifetime.

I can't leave her.

She just couldn't do it. What kind of mother would she be, to leave her child because she wanted to go off gallivanting in Hollywood? But as the bus drew into the gray bowels of Whitechapel, she thought suddenly of the days and weeks and years of drudgery that lay ahead and felt a wave of defeat wash over her. Could she really give up this chance to fulfil her dream? It wasn't as though opportunities like this came her way often. This might be her only shot at fame.

What if she left her daughter in Annie's care? The idea suddenly struck her. Annie and her girls were pretty much like family anyway. And it would only be temporary, Franny assured herself—just until she'd made a name for herself. Once she had some money and a nice place to live, she could fly Cara out to be with her. In fact, far from abandoning Cara, this would benefit her daughter in the long run. Maybe it would mean a brief separation, but it would also make it possible for her to finally get her child out of the East End. Franny felt excitement rush through her. She *could* make this work; it would just take a bit of planning.

With a solution found, Franny sat back and began to daydream about a film set, complete with a director, cameramen, and crew, and everyone's eyes were on the beautiful red-haired star as she came out of her dressing room . . .

As soon as Franny stepped into the hallway, she heard a commotion coming from the sitting room: the sound of a man shouting and a child crying. There was something about the child's cries—more like howling, really, the sound of an animal in pain—that sent a shiver through her. Without pausing even to take her coat off, she rushed to see what was going on.

Pushing open the door, Franny stood frozen as she took in the scene. She'd been right about the child crying out in pain: it was Danny, and Liam—Annie's lover—had clean picked him up off the ground and was holding the struggling boy in one meaty hand. He'd tugged the boy's trousers partway down, and in his other hand he had a belt, with which he was hitting Danny, hard. Cara was crouched in the corner, watching the whole scene as she sobbed.

"That'll teach you to cheek me, lad," Liam muttered, bringing the strap down on the boy's exposed red buttocks again. Danny let out another strangled cry.

For a moment Franny simply stared in silence, too shocked to move. No one else in the room had spotted her yet. She was about to call out to Liam to stop, but before she could say anything, Cara got to her feet and, with an almighty bellow, put her head down and charged at the man like a bull. It all happened so fast that he didn't see her coming, and when she struck him he let out a yelp and promptly released his grip on Danny, who dropped to the ground.

But that wasn't enough for Cara. Clearly intent on, as she saw it, saving her friend, the little girl started to pummel Liam's right leg with her small fists. He turned to swat her away like a fly, pulling his hand back to strike her. It was only then that Franny recovered sufficiently to act.

"Don't you dare!" she shouted, storming over to put herself between Cara and her attacker.

Liam glared at Franny, irritated by the interruption. "*She* attacked *me*."

"Only because you were killing Danny!" The man was breathing hard, his face red with anger, but Franny refused to be intimidated. She knelt down in front of the little boy, pushing his dark hair back from his face. A purple bruise had already started to form on his forehead, and his lip was split and bloody. "Are you all right, love?"

Danny rubbed his stomach, where Liam had kicked him. "Yeah," he said. To prove it, he struggled to his feet. He swayed a little at first but managed to stay upright.

Satisfied that he didn't need to go to the hospital, Franny turned back to Liam. "What in God's name was all that about?"

"The kid was giving me cheek."

"And that gave you a right to hit him, did it?" Franny breathed in deeply, trying to calm herself. There was no point getting into an argument; that wouldn't help anyone. She needed to try to reason with Liam so that this didn't happen again. "For heaven's sake," she implored, "Danny's just a child."

But if she'd hoped to shame Liam into seeing the error of his ways, she was wasting her breath. "What business is it of yours?" he sneered. "I'll soon be the man of the house, and I'll do what I damn well please if I see one of the kids defying me. So if you don't want that animal of yours getting hurt, make sure she stays out of my way!"

With one last glare at Cara, he stormed out of the room, slamming the door shut behind him, so hard that the whole house shook.

Later that night, when Liam went down to the pub, Franny tried talking to Annie about what she had witnessed that day. But her friend didn't seem to want to hear it.

"Ah, you know what Danny can be like," she said dismissively. "Sometimes I think the Devil and all got into that boy of mine. He could use a man like Liam around to knock some sense into that thick head of his."

"So you're planning to have him move in here?" Franny did nothing to disguise her horror. She'd hoped Liam had just been trying to get her worked up earlier when he'd mentioned soon being the man of the house.

Annie shrugged. "Nothing's settled as yet."

Franny felt a chill pass through her. It upset her to see her usually sensible friend being so blinkered over a man. But it didn't seem there was anything she could do to make a difference, and if Annie was determined to ignore Liam Earley's quick fists and hard drinking and have him live with her, there was no way that Franny could leave her daughter here alone, without any protection against that brutal pig of a man. It seemed she would have to give up on her Hollywood dream after all. A wave of disappointment washed over her. It was too awful— to be handed what she wanted more than anything else in the world and then to see it snatched away from her so cruelly. Hot tears sprang to her eyes. There *had* to be another way.

Then the solution came to her. There *was* someone else who could take care of Cara for her—someone whom she might not like but whom she could trust. It wasn't ideal, but it would serve as a temporary fix until she found a way to bring her daughter out to live with her.

That night, Franny sat down and wrote to her mother. Aside from giving birth to Cara, it was the hardest thing she'd ever had to do. There was so much to say, and it was hard to explain in a letter. Telling her about Cara and their lives together over the past seven years, then explaining about the job offer, before finally asking if Theresa would agree to care for the granddaughter she'd never met.

Franny drafted and redrafted the letter before finally deciding to tell the story in the simplest way possible, with no embellishments or pleas for either understanding or forgiveness. At the last minute, she got Annie to address the envelope, since she feared her family might destroy the letter before reading it if they realized it was from her. Her friend was good enough not to ask any questions.

"Lord knows what scheme you're cooking up, Fran, but best leave me in the dark" was all she said.

Once the letter was addressed, Franny mailed it and then waited anxiously for the reply.

9

Forget the English and the famine, thought Franny as she huddled down with her daughter in the open cart. The bitter wind that blew across the bogs of Connemara was God's curse on the Irish.

Franny might have sung nostalgic songs of home while she was in London, but the reality of her country of birth was nothing like the romanticized version she'd created in her head. And if there was one place that she hated even more than her hometown of Glen Vale, it was Connemara in Galway. A remote region of the country, famine and emigration had made it one of the most sparsely populated areas of Ireland. It was at the heart of the *gaeltacht,* the Irish-speaking part of the country. To Franny, it was the most backward place in a backward land and one she would have happily never seen again, if it hadn't been for her mother.

The mail took around five days to get from London to Ireland, and it had taken nearly three weeks for Theresa to reply. Franny had almost given up hope. But then it had arrived: a brusque, unforgiving letter. There had been many changes in the seven years that Franny had been away: most significantly, her father had died four winters ago, after his tractor overturned into a ditch. It was hard for Franny, discovering that her father had gone and that she would never be able to get his forgiveness. Whatever their differences, she'd still loved him. She'd always imagined that one day she would go home in triumph, having made her fortune, and that he would be able to see that she'd come good in the end. Now it was too late, and she hated herself for not having gotten in touch sooner.

Once she'd dried her tears she'd read on, and found there'd been other changes, too. After Michael Healey had died, Maggie and Conrad had married, and he had moved to the Healeys' farm. Theresa had lived with them, along with Conrad's mother, until her elder sister, Agatha, had caught a chill that developed into pneumonia. Theresa had traveled to Agatha's isolated cottage in Connemara, staying with her until the end came. Feeling that she was a burden on Maggie and Conrad and their new family—for they had two daughters now—Theresa had decided to stay put in Agatha's house for the time being.

"That's why it took me a little longer to reply," she wrote. "Maggie had to forward your letter to me here."

The tone of Theresa's letter had been cool, but she had agreed to take in Cara, and that was all that mattered. The one condition was that they should come to Connemara, allowing Cara's existence to remain a secret from family and friends. Although Franny didn't like the idea of hiding her daughter away, it would be only for a few months, until she could get Cara out to America, so she'd decided to go along with her mother's plan. What other choice did she have?

It had been a long day for Franny and her daughter. They had been traveling for eighteen hours now: eight hours by train from Euston to Holyhead, then four hours crossing the rough Irish Sea to Dun Laoghaire docks, followed by the train journey to Galway. Outside the station, Franny had found a horse and cart to take them to the village of Recess, the closest point to where her mother now lived. Remembering just how cold the open valleys could be, she had made sure that both she and Cara wrapped up warmly for the journey. But now, as the trap trundled along the rocky path that took them through the blanket bogs that typified this mountainous and rainy area of western Ireland, Franny realized that two sweaters and a coat were still not enough to keep out the Galway winter.

It was after midnight by the time they got to Recess. By then the streets were empty, the houses all in darkness.

"Here we go." The driver pulled his horse up in the square. Assuming mother and child were staying in town, he pointed out a couple of bed-and-breakfasts. Franny pretended to take it all in.

Cara had fallen asleep during the journey. Now her mother turned to her. "Sweetheart?" Franny peered down at her sleeping child. Cara stirred, mumbling indistinctly, reluctant to wake. "Come on now, darling," her mother urged. "Be a good girl and do what yer mam wants."

Throwing her bag down onto the cobbled street below, Franny got down from the carriage, then turned back to lift her daughter out. Franny buckled a little under the girl's weight. Cara was a skinny little thing, but at almost seven she was still heavy enough that her mother rarely carried her these days.

"*Slán leat,*" the driver said in Gaelic.

Franny glared at him. "And good-bye to you, too," she replied, deliberately speaking in English. That was one of the things that irritated her most about Connemara, its inhabitants' obsession with using the outdated Gaelic language.

Taking her daughter's hand, Franny picked up the suitcase. She didn't want the driver to know where they were going, so she made a show of heading in the direction in which he'd pointed. But as soon as the horse had clip-clopped around the corner, she turned and headed in the other direction, out of the village.

Typically of the Connemara nights, there was no one about. During the day, if you walked for long enough, you might come across locals out cutting turf or farmers herding cattle or sheep, but now, in the dead cold of the winter's evening, the place was deserted. With no one of whom to ask directions, Franny had worried that she might get lost. But to her surprise, even in the dark she easily remembered the way out to her aunt's. Memories of childhood holidays floated back on the five-mile walk. There had been some good times, such as when her brother had taught her to swim. Maggie had been too cowardly to join in, so it had been left to her and Patrick to have diving competitions, daring each other to climb to a higher rock and dive into the choppy waters below.

At first Franny and Cara passed by houses and cottages at regular intervals, but they gradually thinned out the farther they got into the countryside, until any abodes they did pass were ruined and overgrown, their inhabitants long since departed for America. With the path lit only by the pale glow of the half-moon, it was hard to see. Franny had to take care where she stepped so she didn't end up knee-deep in a watery marsh. Connemara's most distinguishing feature was its dramatic and varied landscape, and the walk took them up over a mountain and down into a wooded, boggy valley;

even in the dark, Franny could make out the white of the bog cotton, blowing gently in the breeze. She wondered what Cara would
think of all the fresh air and space after a life lived in the confines
of Whitechapel.

An hour and a half later, they finally reached their destination—the
cottage where Franny's aunt had once lived. The house was, if anything, in worse condition than Franny remembered. Made out of uneven gray stones, its best feature was the carefully thatched roof. At
the front there was a scratched wooden door, the knots showing its
age, and four small, ragged windows—no bigger than two hand spans,
or the cold would get in; one didn't even have any glass in, no doubt
because a strong wind had blown it out. The oil lamps were on in the
downstairs portion of the house, which meant Theresa had received
her second letter, with their planned arrival date, and had decided to
wait up for them. Did this welcome mean that she had been forgiven?
Now that Franny was here, about to confront the mother she'd abandoned, she suddenly felt nervous. Steeling herself, she knocked on the
door.

She heard shuffling inside and then a round of mumbled curses before the light went on in the porch. A second later, the front door flew
open.

Franny stood frozen in shock. The past seven years had not treated
her mother kindly. The death of Michael, her husband, had taken its
toll on Theresa, turning her hair completely white and leaving her with
a stoop, as though she was burdened by the hand that life had dealt to
her. At sixty, she was already an old woman.

Franny felt tears gather in her eyes. "Oh, Mammy." She took her
mother's thin, bony body in her arms, wanting to make up for the years
she'd missed.

But Theresa, never one for big emotional displays, held her daughter
for just a few seconds before pulling away. "Now, don't be getting silly
on me, child." Her tone was low and gruff.

It wasn't exactly the greeting Franny had been hoping for, but she
hid her disappointment.

"Here, Mam," she said with forced joviality, trying to pretend this
was some happy family reunion. "It's about time you met your granddaughter." She turned to where her child hovered a little way behind.
"And here she is, hiding. This is Cara."

Cara stood shyly by her mother's side, happy to be hidden by her skirt. The old woman looked down at her with disinterest.

"So this is the girl." It was said dismissively, a cold statement of fact. There was none of the interest and curiosity that Cara had been expecting. On the train and the boat over, strangers had petted her and given her sweets. She'd expected more of the same from her grandmother. But instead the old woman simply stood back and said, "You'd best come inside out of the cold. The last thing I need is a week nursing a sick child."

Feeling frightened, Cara looked up at her mother, hoping that they could leave now and go home. Instead of being warm and welcoming, her grandmother was old and mean. With her wild white hair, hard eyes, and slight stoop, she reminded Cara of a witch from one of her fairy stories. The thought made the girl give an involuntary shiver, and she gripped her mother's hand tighter. If she'd known that it was going to be like this, she never would have agreed to come.

It had been a little over a week since her mother had asked if she'd like to go on a little adventure. Cara had listened with interest as her mother outlined the trip. They were going to Ireland, she explained, to visit her grandmother. Cara, who had always wondered what it would be like to know more of her relatives, thought it sounded like a fine idea.

The one drawback was that it meant being away from Danny for a little while, but Cara's sadness about that was compensated by her excitement over the impending trip. And there was so much to see and experience along the way. Euston station was busy, noisy, and hot. Then there was the long train journey from London, with all its sights and sounds and smells. For a curious child like Cara, it was Heaven.

Now, though, having arrived at their destination, the excitement had waned. Even though her mother kept smiling, Cara sensed that deep down she wasn't very happy about the whole situation either.

As soon as they got inside, Cara wrinkled her nose. The house had that distinctive smell of old people and cats. As if on cue, a thin black cat wound its way around Cara's legs. She bent to stroke its back, but the animal drew back in anger. Green eyes flashing, back arched, it hissed a warning to stay away.

Hearing the noise, her grandmother turned and glared. "Leave her alone, child. She's for catching mice, not playing."

Cara wanted to say that she hadn't done anything to the cat but decided not to.

Franny frowned at her mother's harsh words. "Do you want us to go?" she demanded. "Say the word, and we'll be out of here."

"I said I'd take care of your child," Theresa said evenly, "and I won't break my promise."

Cara looked between the two women, her eyes round and large like saucers, taking everything in. She didn't understand a lot of what was being said, but it was clear that her mother and grandmother didn't get on.

Aware of Cara's eyes on her, Theresa looked over sharply. "And what would you be staring at?"

Cara swallowed hard, too scared to answer. Her mother put a protective arm round her, drawing her close. "Leave her, Mam," she said wearily.

The old woman gave a loud "Humph" and then shuffled from the room. Once she was gone, Cara looked up at her mother.

"You're leaving me here?" Her voice was little more than a squeak.

"Oh, Cara." Franny sighed deeply. "Yes, I'm sorry, my darling—you're right, I am leaving you." Seeing the distressed look on her daughter's face, she added quickly, "It's just for a little while, though, I promise. And"—she glanced toward the kitchen—"and your grandmother isn't as bad as she seems." The last part wasn't said with much conviction.

From the kitchen, there was the sound of saucepans being knocked together, followed by muttered cursing. The turf on the fire hissed and crackled. Cara felt her heart beating faster. "Mummy?" she said in a small voice. "I don't think I want to stay here."

Cara watched as her mother's eyes filled with tears. She dropped to her knees and hugged her child tight to her breast. It almost hurt, but Cara didn't want to say so. "I know," she said at last, her words muffled against her daughter's hair. "I don't want to leave you here, either. But I have no choice." She released Cara and looked into her eyes. "You do understand that, don't you, my darling?"

Cara didn't understand. But she hated to see her beloved mother upset, so she tried to be brave as she said, somewhat solemnly, "Yes, Mummy."

She was rewarded with a smile. "Thank you, sweetheart," her mother said, a few tears leaking out again. "Thank you for making this easier."

*   *   *

It had been a long, hard day, so it didn't take long for Cara to fall asleep. Franny sat for a moment in the tiny bedroom, watching her daughter slumber. Exhausted herself, she longed to climb into bed beside her child, but she needed to speak with her mother. Theresa's hostility had been apparent tonight, and Franny knew they had to clear the air, if only to make sure that the old woman didn't take her resentment out on Cara these next few weeks. With a heavy heart, she went to face her mother.

Downstairs in the tiny sitting room, Theresa was dousing the last embers in the hearth. Already the room was growing cold. Franny drew her shawl around her shoulders and prepared to make peace.

"Would you like me to make some more tea, Mam?"

Theresa grunted. "If I drink another drop, I'll be out in the privy all night."

Behind her mother's back, Franny rolled her eyes. She didn't particularly want any more tea herself—it had simply been a pretext to get them to sit down together. But it was just like her mam not to notice an olive branch. She decided to be more direct. "Can you stop tidying up for five minutes and talk with me?"

"What's there to talk about?"

Franny felt her hackles rise. "Well, it might at least be nice to hear a little about my father."

Theresa rounded on her. "Your father? You want to know about your father? It broke his heart, you leaving like that. It killed him, sure as if you'd put a bullet between his eyes." Franny drew in a sharp breath, but her mother wasn't finished. "Eight years and not a word from you, then when you want a favor, you get in touch. You've always been the same, haven't you? A selfish so-and-so."

Tears stung Franny's eyes. "And you haven't changed either, Mam," she said bitterly. "You're still having a go at every chance you get."

"Someone needs to get through that thick head of yours."

Mother and daughter glared at each other, as they had many times over the years.

It was Franny who looked away first. She was wasting her breath, she realized, with a pang of disappointment. There would be no bridges built here tonight.

She got to her feet. "It's late, and I need to get some rest. I'll be gone early tomorrow, before you're awake, no doubt."

She'd added that last part to make her mother understand that this was the last time they'd see each other for a while, hoping to prompt her into some kind of reconciliation. But all her mother said was, "Fine. Just make sure that brat of yours knows to behave herself once you're gone."

Franny bristled on behalf of her daughter. "Cara's a good girl. She'll give you no trouble."

Theresa gave a crooked smile. "Then she's less like you than I feared."

10

For the first time that she could remember, Cara woke alone in bed the next morning. At first, she didn't know where she was. Usually she awoke to the sounds of the busy East End streets. Then she remembered everything about the day before—the long journey and meeting her horrible grandmother, who seemed to hate her. Looking around, she saw that her mother's belongings had gone. The girl suddenly panicked. She couldn't stay here alone. Maybe if she hurried, she could catch her mother before she left . . .

Pulling on her clothes, Cara hurried from the bedroom and downstairs, where she could hear the sounds of breakfast being prepared. But when she got to the kitchen, she found her grandmother there alone, setting the table. Hearing her, Theresa looked up. The two stared at each other for a moment: the old woman and the girl. Cara was too scared to ask where her mother was. But the old woman must have sensed what she was looking for, because she said, "She's gone already."

It was the curt tone of her voice that set Cara off. She felt hope leave her. She was stuck here now, with this horrible person, far away from the two people she cared about most in the world: her mother and Danny. She wasn't even aware that the tears had started until her grandmother tsked. "Stop sniveling, child, and eat your breakfast. All this fuss over a few weeks . . ."

Mindful of not showing her mother up, Cara did her best to stop crying. Taking one last large sniff, she dug her nails into the soft palm of her hand and then sat down at the kitchen table. The floor was uneven and the table wobbled a little, but Cara didn't dare complain. A bowl was dropped in front of her, and Theresa began to spoon hot porridge into it.

Cara looked down in dismay. The one thing she hated most in the world was porridge, with its gray color and slimy consistency. "Can I have bread and jam instead?"

"Why?"

"Because I don't like porridge," Cara said in a small voice.

"You'll eat what's put in front of you or not at all."

Her grandmother sat down at the table and started shoveling her own porridge into her mouth, signaling the end of the discussion.

Cara had been considering not eating as a protest at the woman's harsh treatment, but she was so hungry that she reluctantly picked up her spoon and, scooping up a small bit of porridge, tried a little. She'd been bracing herself for the usual watery sludge, but to her surprise it tasted different: creamier than she remembered. She took another mouthful, bigger this time.

"It's good," she said. "It doesn't usually taste like this."

Her grandmother didn't look up. "You've probably had it with water. This is made with milk. There're plenty of cows round here and no shortage of milk and cheese."

"I like it," Cara declared.

She wasn't sure if it was her imagination, but Cara thought she saw her grandmother smile. It might have been a mistake, though, because a split second later it was gone. Instead, the old lady pushed a pot of honey across the table.

"Stir some of this in if you like. It sweetens the taste."

Cara did as she was told and found that her grandmother was right: it did taste sweeter. "Thank you. It's really lovely."

But this time her enthusiasm was met with a grunt. Whatever had caused the brief lull in the atmosphere was over, and the rest of the meal passed in silence.

After breakfast was finished, Theresa gave Cara a tour of the cottage and its surroundings, explaining how she liked things done and what chores she expected Cara to complete. In the light of day, Cara could see how close they were to the cliff's edge. There was a big Irish community near them in the East End, and she had heard people speak of what they called "The Old Country" as somewhere with green fields and lush countryside, but there was something desolate and abandoned about this place.

The cottage was largely self-sufficient, Theresa explained. "I rarely go into town. Everything I need's right here." She pointed out the vegetable garden, where she grew potatoes, leeks, and cabbages, and showed the fascinated Cara how to dig carrots from the ground.

There was a goat tethered at the side of the house and a chicken coop where they could collect eggs. She let Cara pick one up, and the girl's eyes widened as she felt the warmth of the freshly laid egg in her palm.

If Theresa's plan had been to distract Cara from brooding about her mother, it had worked perfectly. With all the new experiences, she hadn't had time to think about being left behind. But once they were finished with the tour, Theresa announced that she was going into the village. "I only go in once a week, for flour and the like, and to catch up on what's going on in the outside world. I also go to the post office. That's where your mother's letters will come, and if there's any messages for me, that's where they'll be."

As no one was to know of Cara's whereabouts, she would remain behind at the cottage.

"It's a shame to leave you here alone, it being your first day and all. But it's my day to go in, and they'll send someone out here for me if I don't make an appearance. But don't you worry—I'll leave you some chores to do while I'm gone, to keep you out of mischief."

Half an hour later, just before nine in the morning, the old woman set off for the village, and Cara started on the housework. She was to wash up the breakfast dishes, make the beds and tidy away, and then she was meant to fetch and prepare vegetables for the evening meal.

Cara worked hard all morning. By midday she was starving. It was lunchtime, but her grandmother still wasn't home, and she didn't dare risk taking any food without being invited. An hour later, with all the chores finished inside the house, she went outside and started to dig up the carrots for their supper that night. She did it the way that the old woman had showed her, but it was harder than it looked.

By two she was almost faint with hunger, her back hurt, her fingers were red and sore with cold, and her grandmother still wasn't home. Thinking a glass of water might help, Cara went through to the kitchen. She sat at the table to have her drink. Five minutes later, feeling a bit better, she decided to head outside again. But as she got back up, blood rushed to her head, the dizziness causing the glass to slip from her hand and smash on the floor. Looking down at the mess, she knew she ought to clear it up. But she felt so ill and tired. Maybe if she could just lie down for a moment.

Stumbling through to the small sitting room, she lay down on the two-seater sofa. The wool material was scratchy and uncomfortable, but Cara was too tired to care. A blanket lay across the back of the couch, no doubt placed there to cover up the shabby appearance of the furniture. Now she pulled it down on top of her. Curling up into a ball, she slept.

A rough hand shook Cara awake. For the second time that day, she woke confused and dazed. It took a few seconds for her eyes to focus, and then, seeing the furious face of her grandmother, she was suddenly wide awake.

"You wicked, wicked child!" Theresa thundered. "How dare you sleep when you've hardly dug any vegetables and left the kitchen in such a state?" Cara wanted to explain, but the old lady gave her no chance. "I was right about you, wasn't I? You're a lazy, selfish girl, just like your mother."

That was too much for Cara. She might have been able to accept the attack on her own abilities, but she wouldn't let Theresa get away with that dig at her mam.

"How dare you say I'm lazy!" she burst out. "You're working me like a slave. I'm going to write to my mother and tell her everything you've done, then she'll come and take me away from here, because she's worth a hundred of you!"

But her grandmother simply shrugged. "Do what you want. I'm not stopping you."

She walked out of the room. Cara stared after her, feeling lonely and trapped. Surely her mother would never have left her here if she'd known how bad it would be?

The next few days passed much the same as that one had. Any slight thawing in the old lady that Cara had seen on the first morning had passed. Even though she tried to behave herself—doing all her chores, saying grace at mealtimes and prayers before bed—her grandmother seemed to have already made up her mind that she was not to be trusted.

At the end of the week, Cara wrote her mother a letter telling her just how bad everything was at the cottage. With her limited spelling and writing skills, it was a rudimentary attempt. But it managed to convey how she felt.

Once the letter was finished, she read it over. Then she tore it up and threw it in the bin. If her mother read how unhappy she was, she would simply worry. And, however miserable Cara might be, she didn't want to add to her mam's troubles. So instead she wrote another letter, telling her mother all about the new things she'd been doing and seeing. When she looked back through it, she decided it sounded more as though she was having a good time. Worried then that it might sound like she was having *too* much fun, she added a comment telling her mother how much she was missing her. "Write to let me know when you're coming back," she said in closing. "I hope it's soon!"

With that she sealed the letter, putting one of the stamps her mother had given her on the front. Then she handed it to the old lady to mail.

"I didn't write anything bad about you," she felt obliged to say.

Her grandmother snorted. "I couldn't care if you said I was the Devil himself."

As the elderly woman set off for the village, Cara could only cross her fingers and hope that she would keep her promise to send the letter.

11

Guilt gnawed at Franny all the way back to England. She'd left early, before Cara woke up, fearing that she would break down and change her mind if they said good-bye in person. Standing on the bow of the boat, the icy Irish Sea spraying up into her face, she thought seriously about turning back. But deep down Franny knew that she couldn't bring herself to give up on her Hollywood dream. However hard it was to be apart from her daughter, this was the opportunity that she'd always longed for, to be a movie star, and she couldn't just walk away from that. And it wasn't as if she was being entirely selfish, she quickly assured herself; if she was successful, then she would be rich, and that money would mean that she would be able to change their lives forever, allowing her to give Cara everything she'd ever wanted.

Franny had just one day in England before leaving for America, but it was a lonely twenty-four hours for her. She had moved out of Annie's house, telling her friend that she was off back to Ireland. Franny had hated lying, but she wanted to keep her good fortune secret. People could be jealous, and she didn't want anyone from her past to start coming forward with tales of her life as an unwed mother. By the time a movie came out with her in it, no doubt she would be forgotten in the East End. She was banking on the fact that if people weren't expecting to see her face, they probably wouldn't guess that it was her.

It had been hard to say good-bye to Annie and her kids. Franny would be forever grateful to the woman who had helped her when she was so desperately in trouble, and the Connollys had been like family to her and Cara these past years. But there was no point dwelling on what had once been. Both women had felt their bond loosening over the past few months, and it would never be the same. A man had come between them, and Annie had made her choice to be with Liam. He had moved in the day that Franny and Cara had left.

Franny spent her last night in London at a grubby little bed-and-breakfast near Euston train station. The following day, as she left for London airport, with all her worldly possessions contained in one small brown case, she resolved to work as hard as possible to make it to the top.

Franny's first taste of Hollywood was every bit as glamorous as she'd imagined. She was booked on Pan Am's D6 Clipper Liberty Bell, and though the tourist-class flight might not offer the same standard of luxury as the company's Stratocruiser airplane, she found the whole experience mesmerizing: from the roar of the engines on takeoff to the beautifully coiffed stewardesses strolling up and down the aisles in their powder-blue uniforms. At Los Angeles airport, the glass-and-chrome building seemed the height of modernity to her. Stepping outside, she felt the warmth of the evening on her skin, saw the palm trees lining the sidewalk, and knew that she was as far from Ireland and the East End as she could ever hope to get.

After that, though, things started to go downhill. She hung around for a while, feeling increasingly hot in her wool twinset, until she finally realized that the studio hadn't sent a car for her, so she would have to get a cab instead. The driver was overly friendly and, when he heard that she had come out to try her luck at being a star, had insisted on taking her past the Hollywood sign. He took great pleasure in telling her that it was where the failed starlet Peg Entwhistle had committed suicide back in 1932.

"Jumped off the H, would you believe?" He shook his head as though the incident defied any explanation. "Now, don't you go doing anything stupid like that, will ya, dollface?" In his rearview mirror, he winked at Franny. "Things don't work out, a fox like you can always find some schmuck to take care of her."

After that he dropped her at the Sunset Lodge. It was only when he tried to charge her a small fortune that Franny noticed he hadn't been running the meter the whole trip. She gave him what she could, and he went off happy. Franny knew she was being ripped off, but she couldn't be bothered to argue; she was just relieved to have reached the hotel. Except it wasn't a hotel—it was a rundown motel. Franny's room contained a single bed with a lumpy mattress and sheets that seemed dusty and were stained with what looked like blood. Even with the window closed, she could hear the traffic on the three-lane freeway that ran past the front of the building. Out back there was a pool that had been drained months ago, the bottom now lined with beer bottles and brown paper bags.

Even though she was exhausted, Franny had difficulty sleeping. Everything was so different from England. It was hot, for one thing, even at night. There was a small, noisy ceiling fan, but it didn't help much, and she didn't dare open the windows, because she was on the ground floor and there were people walking by all the time, chatting and laughing overly loudly, as though they'd been drinking. The people were different, too; they were curt, dismissive, as though they didn't have time for her. And the food—well, that was strange as well, but in a good way. It was also cheap. For dinner, she went next door to a diner, sat in a booth, and was handed a plastic-laminated menu with a dazzling array of dishes, all accompanied by little pictures. She ordered deep-fried chicken with fries and a strawberry milk shake. For dessert she had a huge dish of apple cobbler and vanilla ice cream, along with another milk shake. After the shortages in England, it was like being in Heaven. The first thing she'd do when Cara came out would be take her out to dinner, she decided.

The next morning, Franny took another cab over to Juniper's vast studio. Juniper was located on Gower Street, just south of Sunset Boulevard and a block down from Paramount. Passing through the gates, she thought of all the stars who had come this exact route before her and felt her excitement about being in Tinseltown return. The sheer size of the place left her breathless. If Juniper's studio in Elstree had been like a village, the one in Hollywood was more like a city. Her first meeting was in the executive building—but she couldn't just walk there, a driver had to take her through the back lots in a golf buggy. As they drove by the sets, they moved from the pyramids of Ancient Egypt to the tenements of New York; from the bistros of Paris to the saloons of the Wild West. Franny gazed in wonder at the changing scenery, although it was a little disappointing to see that the buildings were just empty shells, with walls missing and no furnishings. It spoiled some of the magic.

The executive building had been built in the 1920s, in the Art Deco style. It was tall and made of white marble, with perfectly curved turrets and long, narrow windows. Inside, it was smart in a traditional way: all mahogany furniture and fresh-cut flowers. Intense men in sharp suits rushed around importantly, followed closely by pretty girls in pencil skirts and tight sweaters clutching clipboards to their ample bosoms. Everyone looked busy and important.

Before coming out to Hollywood, Franny had written to Clifford Walker, the producer, reminding him of her imminent arrival in town. He had left word at the Sunset Lodge for her to come in to the studio to meet Juniper's head of casting, Lloyd Cramer. Lloyd had been at Juniper all his life. A sharp, no-nonsense man who looked a little like a fox, at fifty he was one of the most powerful people in the studio. He was known for being scrupulously fair but unsentimental. If an actor wasn't performing, he or she was out—no matter how much money he or she had brought in for the studio in the past.

In the comfort of his office, Lloyd studied Juniper's newest recruit, trying to get the measure of her.

"You're one of Clifford's girls, right?"

Franny nodded eagerly. Though she wasn't in any hurry to see Clifford again, he was her only contact and for that reason she was happy to name-drop. "Yes, he was the one who sent me for a screen test."

"Hmmm." In fact, the head of casting was unimpressed. Clifford had a reputation around the studio for using his position to get laid. A family man himself, Lloyd had no time for the casting-couch system. He'd reviewed the footage of Franny Healey, and though she might have *something*, he wasn't about to push her until she proved herself. "Well, let's see if you got what it takes to make it in this town."

Lloyd made it clear that becoming a star wasn't going to be easy. There were many things that Franny needed to change about herself—the first being her name.

"It's all wrong. Franny Healey isn't going to stick in anyone's mind." He considered the problem for a moment. "Franny can't be your real name. What's it short for?"

"Frances."

His face brightened. "Frances. Mmmm—that's better. Now, what goes with Frances? Something Irish, but maybe with a bit of class . . ." He thought for a second. "How about Fitzgerald?" Without waiting for a reply, he said, "*Frances Fitzgerald* . . . yes, I like that. What do you think?"

"Sounds great." It wasn't as though she was going to object. She was prepared to listen to him about everything. Next on the agenda was her looks. He made her stand in the middle of the room as he walked around, appraising every inch of her. There was nothing sexual in the way he surveyed her: it was almost how her father would have examined a heifer when deciding whether to buy it. She half expected him to come over and check her teeth.

After a thorough inspection, Lloyd declared that he thought aesthetically everything was pretty much fine—"maybe the nose could be smaller, but I think we can get away with it for now"—but that she should definitely dye her hair.

"Blond?" she asked hopefully, imagining herself as cool and sophisticated as Grace Kelly. But even as she said it, she knew that she could never pull that off—she was too buxom, too obviously earthy.

"Hell, no!" He mused for a moment. "A deeper red would be better, a more vibrant color than you are now, so we can bring out that Maureen O'Hara look. So, yeah, red would be good. I'll send you to the hairdresser we use. And we'll have to do something about your clothes, too."

Franny looked down at herself, surprised by his comment. She was dressed in her very best outfit: a neat suit in racing green with a matching pillbox hat perched on her head. It was a castoff from one of the headline acts at the Victory Club.

"That green color is perfect on you," Lloyd explained, "but it's clearly a cheap knockoff. We'll have to get you into something better before you're in any of the papers."

Next to go was her accent. He might want her to look Irish, but he couldn't have her sounding that way, since "half the people won't understand a word you're saying." Instead, he wanted her to sound more neutral, hard to place, like Audrey Hepburn. "Is that a problem?"

Franny, always a good mimic, replied in what she thought was a perfect mid-Atlantic accent. "No problem at all."

He nodded seriously. "Good. But our speech coach will make it better."

Last, he wanted to know about her personal life, if there was anything noteworthy or special about her. "It's always good if our press agents have something to work with, some angle to go out with to the media. So is there anything special about you that I should know?"

"I don't think so."

Lloyd sighed, clearly irritated at having to do all the work. "What about family? You must have someone back home?"

"Well . . ." Franny hesitated, not sure whether to share the information on Cara after Clifford's reaction. But what else did she have to say? "I have a little girl. She's about to turn seven."

Lloyd's smile faded a little. "Oh?" He started searching through his papers, as though looking for a crucial piece of information he'd missed. "You married, then?"

"No."

He looked more hopeful. "A war widow?"

"No."

"Then . . . ?"

"It was back when I was seventeen." She dropped her gaze, feeling embarrassed to be confessing her past indiscretions in front of this important man. "I thought he would marry me, but . . ." She trailed off.

"I see." Lloyd sighed and put down the notebook he'd studiously been writing in. "Look, honey, I'm going to be honest with you here. We're pitching you as a young romantic lead. A kid—well, that just won't work." There was a pause. "Where is the child now?"

"Back in Ireland. With my mother."

Lloyd relaxed a little. "Well, that sounds good. Hollywood . . ." He puffed his cheeks out. "Hell, it's no place for a kid. I'm sure she's much better off with her granny. Don't you think?"

Franny knew the answer he wanted to hear. "You're probably right," she said miserably.

"And that means there's no reason to mention the girl to the media. Or to anyone else. Gossip has a way of getting out in this town. You tell one person in confidence, and suddenly everyone knows your business." He waited a beat. "And then you're on the next plane back to England, dream in tatters. Now, you don't want that, do you?"

A cold fear took hold of Franny. That was what she dreaded most— this whole opportunity being snatched away from her. But if she agreed to his suggestion, what would that mean for Cara? She was going to have to deny her own child. It didn't bode well for bringing her daughter over here if she was going to have to lie about her existence.

But it wasn't really a lie, she comforted herself. It was just an omission of information. And Lloyd was probably right: Hollywood was no place for a child. At least not at the moment, while she was starting out. Once she was famous, that would be different. She could do anything then.

"No, I don't," she said finally.

"Good." Lloyd's tone was brisk. "Then that's all settled. You're a young, single woman, newly arrived in Hollywood, chasing your dream to be a star. Not exactly original, but it'll do." He regarded her with keen eyes. "And talking about being young—you said you were seventeen when you got pregnant and the kid's now . . . ?"

"Seven."

"So that makes you, what, twenty-four?"

"Twenty-five next month."

There was another frown. "Again, that's just not gonna work. We need you to be young, say . . . twenty-one." He squinted at her. "You can pass for that, can't you?"

Yes, she agreed; of course she could. After all the other lies, that seemed the least of her worries.

Following that meeting, Franny was signed by Juniper to a contract at a hundred dollars a week, becoming one of its stable of starlets. The movie that Clifford had originally had her in mind for had been postponed, which was a bit disappointing, but Lloyd said they had something else lined up for her instead. It was just a bit part, not as meaty as the role she'd been promised, but it was a start and her chance to prove herself. Filming was due to begin the following week, and she couldn't wait.

12

Cara sprinted along the makeshift path, forging deeper into the forest. Behind her twigs snapped and leaves rustled, telling her what she'd already guessed: someone was following. But the girl wasn't worried. She was as fast as the hares that dashed through the Galway countryside, as cunning as the foxes that hunted them. Over these past few months she had gotten to know every inch of the Connemara woods, as she came out here every day after her chores and lessons were finished. No one could catch her.

Ducking under the low-hanging branches of a sycamore tree, she turned to look over her shoulder. The split-second distraction meant she missed a recently fallen log and stumbled across it. She righted herself quickly and flew on, but the momentary lapse had cost her precious time, allowing her pursuer to catch up. With the footsteps drawing closer and no more corners to dart around, she had no choice but to hide behind the trunk of an oak.

Sure enough, a second later her anonymous shadow's footsteps began to slow. Cara resisted the urge to peep out.

"Hello?" the voice rang out in the silence of the woods, startling some birds from their trees.

It was a female voice, and belonged to a child, not an adult. Cara felt herself relax a little.

"Hello?" the voice called out again, with a tinge of desperation this time. "Are you there?" A pause. "It's just—well, I don't know this area very well. I followed you, you see, which means that I have no idea how to get back unless you show me." Another pause before the girl said, somewhat tearfully, "So if you are there, could you show yourself? Please."

Confident that she had the upper hand now, Cara stepped out from behind the tree. She could see right away that the newcomer was about the same age as she, but that was where the similarity ended. The stranger was a girly type, wearing a pretty pink-and-white gingham dress, shiny black patent shoes with white socks, and her fair hair in ponytails, tied with ribbons to match her outfit. In contrast, Cara looked more like a boy now. In the two months since she had come to Connemara, she'd grown almost wild: she wore trousers whenever she liked, and her hair was cut short. She was like one of the boys from Danny's gang back home, and she was proud of that fact. This girl was no match for her in strength or speed.

"Who are you?" Cara demanded. "And why were you following me?"

"I'm Alysha, and I'm from Dublin," the girl explained. "My mam's having a baby soon, and as it's school holidays I was getting under her feet, so she sent me to stay with her sister and her husband for a while. They don't have any children, so I'm bored on my own. I saw you out here yesterday and the day before. I thought we could play together."

The last part was said as a plea. Cara knew how the girl felt—she missed Danny and her friends back home and would love to have a new playmate. But something made her hesitate. No one was supposed to know about her, which meant she wasn't allowed to talk to anyone. It was one of her grandmother's rules, like having to stay out for the afternoon today because Theresa had a guest coming over. Cara wasn't allowed back to the cottage until the stranger had gone. Not that she wanted to be in that horrible, musty place, but it was awful to think that she was such an embarrassment that no one could know about her.

"So?" the girl pressed. "Can we play together?"

"I'm not sure."

"Why not?"

Cara bit her lip. "Because no one's supposed to know about me," she said in a small voice.

Alysha frowned, confused. "How come?"

"I can't tell you. It's a secret." Cara felt suddenly miserable. It was horrible being alone, and although she read a lot and made up games to keep herself amused, it wasn't the same as having a real friend. And now this girl would be off out of it, thinking she was odd or something.

But instead of being put off, Alysha looked impressed. "I can keep a secret," she said. "If it means we can play together."

Cara couldn't help being tempted. It meant breaking the rules, but she was so lonely. And what would it hurt? This girl was here on her holidays, it wasn't like she had anyone to tell.

Aware that Alysha was watching her, waiting for a decision, Cara finally nodded. "All right, we can play together. As long as you swear an oath not to tell a soul?"

The girl's eyes were solemn. "I swear. But you have to tell me your name first."

"It's Cara. And I'll show you the way out of the woods now. The path is easy enough to find, and we can meet there again tomorrow."

"I heard from your sister."

It had taken Theresa all afternoon to build up to telling Maggie about Franny's reappearance in their lives. Her eldest daughter usually came to visit once a month, but because her children had come down with chicken pox, one after the other, this was the first time she'd visited since Cara had been left here. Theresa had debated long and hard about whether to tell the rest of the family about Franny's daughter. Eventually she'd decided that it was something that she couldn't keep to herself.

It took a moment for Maggie to work out who her mother was talking about. Theresa knew when she'd gotten it because her eyes widened with surprise. "Franny?"

"That's right," Theresa said. "She wrote me a little while ago."

Maggie sat back in her chair and folded her arms. "Oh, yeah? And what would *she* be wanting after all this time? Money, I'd bet."

"Maggie!" Theresa scolded. "Don't speak about your sister that way."

"Why not?" her daughter demanded. "She disappears in the middle of the night, and we don't see hide nor hair of her for the best part of eight years. I *saw* the grief she caused you and Da. You cried every night for months after she left. So I think I've got every right to say what I like now."

"Oh, come on now, love." Though Theresa might be hard on Franny to her face, behind her back she wouldn't have a word said against her youngest child. "Whatever Franny's done, she's still my daughter and she's still your sister."

"She's no sister of mine." Maggie's face curled into a sneer. The years had done her no favors. Whereas most women were mellowed by motherhood, she seemed to have grown more shrill and harpy-like. "But trust you to defend her. You always favored her most, Mam. Pretty, talented little Franny—so *special,* that's what everyone thought. Even my husband. But she turned out to be the little tart I always knew her to be. Running off with that laborer. She found her level, all right."

Theresa stared at her eldest daughter, stunned by the bitterness in her voice. She'd been planning to tell Maggie about Cara, hoping that she might be able to help with the burden of raising the child. But now, realizing how much Maggie hated her younger sister, she knew that she could never tell her. Maggie wouldn't stand for her looking after Franny's daughter. She'd probably go to the authorities, and the next thing Theresa knew, Cara would be taken from her.

The knowledge depressed Theresa. She would have to keep this se-cret to herself. It was a lonely position to be in.

Theresa looked at the clock. Cara would be back soon, and she needed to get Maggie out of there.

"Franny just wrote to say that she's in London and doing well for herself, that was all," Theresa said quietly. "Now it's late, and no doubt you want to be on your way. You've got a long journey back."

13

"You." The assistant director pointed at Franny. "Come with me."

Her stomach churning with excitement, Franny followed the man onto the movie set, a re-creation of a nineteenth-century Wild West saloon. It was her first day working for Juniper, and she had a bit part in *Preacher Man*, a lighthearted western about a preacher who falls for a brothel madam and the trials they go through before finally getting together. The majority of the movie had already been filmed on location in New Mexico, but the director wanted to shoot a couple of extra scenes back in the studio.

Franny's scene was at the end of the film. By that point in the story, the preacher has been run out of town, and the madam is in the saloon with her girls, drinking and playing cards and trying to forget the man she loves—not realizing that he's secretly ridden back to claim her. As he comes through the bar doors, Franny—playing one of the saloon girls—is the first to spot him, and it was her job to nudge the madam and say, "Looks like you got a visitor." Then the madam turns around, sees the preacher, and goes to join him.

It wasn't much of a role, Franny knew, but at least it was better than being an extra or just having a walk-on part. And she would be credited, too, as Saloon Girl One. Not bad to begin with.

The scene had been set up so that a group of saloon girls were sitting round a table, laughing and joking with a handful of customers. Like the others, Franny was wearing a black-and-pink-striped cancan dress, the skirt ruffled up at the front, accessorized with long, elegant gloves and a headband with a pink feather in it. She loved the costume, even if it had been made for someone two sizes bigger than her and the wardrobe mistress had spent twenty minutes taking it in with safety pins at the back. Franny was so excited just to be on a real movie set, to have had her hair and makeup done and gone through the wardrobe fitting, that she didn't even care that one of the pins was digging into her flesh.

The other extras were already at the main table: three girls, dressed like Franny, along with four cowboys. The assistant director pointed at the best-looking of the men.

"Sit on his knee," he ordered.

Franny dutifully did as she was told. There was a bit of fussing around to make sure that she was facing exactly the right way to be in line of sight of the saloon doors. Then, once the assistant director was finally satisfied, he went off to fetch the stars.

The cowboy whose knee Franny was sitting on was a sandy-haired, all-American type, fresh off the bus from Ohio. He introduced himself as Brad and confessed that it was his first film, too.

"Gotta start somewhere, don'tcha?" he said.

Brad was pleasant and friendly and clearly trying to strike up a conversation, but Franny was too interested in everything else that was going on to be anything other than polite. She was surprised at the number of people on the set. Alongside the actors with speaking parts and the walks-ons and extras, there were dozens of crew members, everyone from lighting and sound men to camera operators and continuity photographers. As they waited for the stars to emerge, the hot, bright klieg lights burned down on Franny, making her sweat under her makeup and hurting her eyes. But she didn't care about the pain—this was the most fun she'd had in her entire life.

Finally, after another twenty minutes, the stars came onto the set. The female lead was Lily Powell, who was perfect as the madam. Originally from Texas, she had a sweet southern drawl, and with her platinum hair and killer figure, she was Juniper's answer to Marilyn Monroe. Like Monroe, she'd made her name in screwball comedies, playing the dim-witted blonde. Franny had seen all of Lily Powell's movies and couldn't believe her luck at finally being in a film with one of her heroines.

Franny watched as the director talked Lily through her shots and then walked her over to the set and got her settled. The star smiled at the table of extras.

"Morning," she greeted them. "Hope y'all haven't been waiting too long."

Once Lily was settled, Makeup, Hair, and Wardrobe flocked round her again to tidy up the details before filming began. And then, just as in the movies, the director called, "Action!" and everything went silent.

Franny's part went off without a hitch and was over in one take. The section between Lily and the preacher took a little longer to get, as both forgot their lines a couple of times, and then the director asked them to run the scene again with a different emphasis on certain parts of dialogue. Most of the bit players got bored and wandered off outside to chat and smoke, but Franny stayed to watch, transfixed by the whole process.

An hour later, the director finally seemed happy and called it a day. He came onto the set to congratulate Lily. "Well done, sweetheart." He embraced the star warmly. "You're a true professional."

Laughing, the blond actress playfully pinched his cheek. "I just do what you tell me. You're the one who knows all that fancy camera stuff."

Franny looked on enviously as Lily Powell swept off the set.

"A few of us are going for ice cream at Schwab's," a man's voice interrupted Franny's thoughts. It was the handsome blond cowboy, Brad, changed back into ordinary clothes. "Wanna join us?"

Franny was tempted. It would be lovely to have some company, rather than going back to her lonely motel room. But she'd had her fill of good-looking, happy-go-lucky men with no prospects or money.

"Thanks, but I'm beat. All I want to do right now is go home and get some sleep."

Ignoring the disappointed look on his face, Franny went to get her bag. She knew she was doing the right thing. From now on, she was focusing on her career. She'd come to Hollywood to be a star. And she wouldn't be happy until she had everything that Lily Powell did—including her own dressing room with her name above the door.

Preacher Man was just the beginning for Franny. The following week, she started work as a chorus girl in a lighthearted musical comedy. After that, she was given a bit part on a western, then a small speaking role as a coffee-shop waitress in a film noir. Nothing big as yet, "But that will follow," Lloyd assured her. Since their initial meeting, Juniper's head of casting had taken a shine to Frances Fitzgerald, and he was going to do everything to make sure that the claim that she was the studio's next great star—said about so many young actresses—actually came true in her case.

When Franny wasn't on the set, she was being given lessons by Juniper's acting and vocal coaches. She got her hair dyed and even had a consultation about having her nose fixed. She posed for countless publicity shots with other up-and-coming actors in restaurants and clubs throughout the town. Early on, Lloyd gave her a lecture on what a big part publicity played in any aspiring star's career. The studio staged the outings, took pictures, and then tried to get the papers to print them along with a suitable accompanying story. Franny thought of how she'd always gobbled up the photos of her favorite stars out for the evening. Now she felt so naïve!

It was difficult to crack the papers, Lloyd explained, but if you got one of the major gossip columnists on your side, that was half the battle. "Hedda Hopper still likes to claim responsibility for giving Elizabeth Taylor her first break," he told Franny.

The *Los Angeles Times* gossip columnist, Dolores Kent, was currently one of the most influential people in Hollywood. As revered as Hedda Hopper and Louella Parsons, Dolores could make or break a career with her pen. Originally married to the head of one of the Big Five studios, she'd lived the life of a lunching lady until a week after her fortieth birthday, when her husband had dumped her for a younger model. With his assets neatly tied up where she couldn't get to them, Dolores had been forced to find work. Her insider knowledge of the movie business had led to a job as a showbiz reporter at the *L.A. Times,* and she'd quickly discovered a talent for scooping her rivals. Her weekly column was now followed religiously, and she was feared and revered in equal measure by the industry.

Lloyd happened to be good friends with Dolores. Over lunch at the Brown Derby, he took the opportunity to have a word with the gossip columnist about his newest protégée.

"She's someone to watch," he told Dolores.

"Aren't they all?" She laughed cynically.

"No, no, I mean it in this case. She's something special."

That piqued the columnist's interest. "Tell me her name again?"

"Frances Fitzgerald."

The next day, a small piece appeared in the *L.A. Times,* announcing the arrival of "a new talent at Juniper, Frances Fitzgerald." It was accompanied by a lovely publicity still of Franny, all big eyes, luscious hair, and creamy skin. Franny tore it out and pinned it to the grubby wall of her motel room. She stood back to admire the cutting. It was going to be the first of many—she would make sure of that.

In the midst of all this hard work, Franny still made sure to keep her promise and write her weekly letter to Cara. However tired she was, however late home from shooting, she always wrote a couple of paragraphs about her day. And however much of a hard time she was having, Franny made the whole experience sound amazing, as if she were just on the verge of great riches, and that any day now she would be able to bring Cara to live with her. And if sometimes Franny wondered whether it was cruel to lie, she would reassure herself that it was only a little fib and that everything would come together soon enough, and then she *would* at last be able to send for her daughter.

During those first three months in L.A., Franny's acting appearances were limited to a series of walks-ons and bit parts. Though she was content with this at first, soon she was itching to be given a shot at a bigger role. She'd heard about a new project called *My Fake Wedding,* a romantic comedy about a perennially single playboy who, finding that he needs to get married in order to secure his inheritance, asks his secretary to pose as his fiancée in order to appease his elderly father. Inevitably, the disapproving spinster secretary begins to thaw toward her rakish employer, and, after a series of misunderstandings, he falls for her, too.

Franny had hoped to be cast as the main female lead, but instead she'd been given the role of the villain—the father's vampish nurse, who is next in line in the will. Determined to get her hands on her patient's money, the nurse does what she can to break up what she believes to be the happy couple, but her actions just bring them closer together. Although it wasn't the lead, it was by far Franny's biggest part to date, and it would mean she'd get fourth billing on the cast list.

"Don't screw this up," Lloyd warned her before shooting started—as though she hadn't realized how important this opportunity was!

Lloyd's words kept echoing in Franny's head once filming started. She knew this was her big break and that if she performed badly, she was unlikely to get another shot. Unfortunately, the pressure was getting to her, and she kept messing up her lines. The director, a short-tempered bull of a man named Emery Brecht, wasn't happy. Every time she got something wrong he would tut loudly or snap out a sarcastic comment, which only made it worse.

By the third day of filming, Franny was already a nervous wreck. When she forgot her lines for the fifth time, Emery finally exploded.

"Frances Fitzgerald!" he roared. Rocketing out of his chair, he stormed across the set, his heavy footsteps making the whole crew visibly wince. "Five words!" He held up his hand right in front of her face, spreading his fingers and thumb to illustrate the number. "That's all your tiny little birdbrain needs to remember—five little words. Do you think you can do that?"

Franny was so upset that she couldn't speak, so she settled for nodding.

"Good! Because if you don't get it right next time, then you're fired!"

Franny's eyes filled with tears. She felt so humiliated in front of her fellow actors, particularly Lily Powell, who was playing the lead. What must she think of this new girl, getting everything wrong?

But, to her surprise, Lily spoke up for her. "Can it, Emery. This isn't her fault, it's yours. With you bitching at her every five minutes, it's little wonder the poor lamb's screwing up."

Emery stared at his female lead, enraged. "Excuse me?" he spluttered.

But Lily was unimpressed by his posturing. "You heard. Now why don't you call lunch, we'll all take five, and I bet you'll see a big difference later."

Without waiting for an answer, Lily linked arms with Franny and led her off the set and to her dressing room. Franny expected the other actress to maybe give her some tips to help her through the filming. But on the contrary, when she tried to bring up the subject, Lily refused to discuss it with her or let her look at a script.

"It's called a break for a reason, honey. We're just here to eat and relax. No work talk—and that's an order!"

Although Franny didn't realize it yet, Lily was one of the few genuine people in Hollywood. Though a lot of the big-name actresses feared the new starlets, Lily was happy to help. She sat with Franny through lunch, deliberately keeping up a constant stream of chatter, so the redhead didn't have time to think about Emery's threat. By the time Franny got back on set an hour later, her head was miraculously clear, and she got the scene in one take.

At the end of filming that day, Franny went to Lily's dressing room to thank her for her help.

"Oh, it's no problem," Lily said breezily, as she cold-creamed her face. "We've all been there, honey. Let's talk about something more important. What are you up to tonight?"

"Nothing," Franny answered honestly. Most evenings she went back to the motel and wrote to Cara. Apart from the obligatory publicity shots that she posed for on a regular basis, her nights were spent alone.

Lily tutted. "Wrong answer, sugar. You're coming out with me."

With her makeup successfully removed, she went over to a large rack with two dozen outfits hanging on it. Franny followed her.

"Where to?" she asked.

"Ciro's."

"The nightclub?" Franny could hardly keep the excitement out of her voice. That was where Hollywood's royalty went to party.

Lily stopped hunting through the dresses and turned to stare at her. "You've never been?"

"No."

"Oh, honey!" Lily looked genuinely appalled. "If you haven't been to Ciro's, you haven't lived." Her cornflower-blue eyes sparkled. "Trust me, sweetheart, you're in for a real treat tonight. But first we need to find you something simply sensational to wear."

14

It was Thursday morning, and Theresa was in the grocer's, waiting for Mr. Quinn, who owned the shop, to measure out flour and a bit of bacon, when Mrs. Murray came in with her little niece. The Murrays were Theresa's nearest neighbors, their cottage half a mile away from her own. Theresa knew them to say hello to and exchange the odd piece of gossip. But she had no interest beyond that. Noreen was in her thirties and had never been blessed with children, and she'd told Theresa all about looking after her sister's child for a few weeks. She was obviously spoiling the kid something rotten: dressing her in that fancy outfit just to come into town.

Theresa watched disapprovingly as they walked over to the candy counter, and the child ordered half a pound of hard candies. As they waited for Mrs. Quinn to measure them out, the child began chattering away, continuing a conversation that they'd obviously been having outside.

"I'm not making it up," the girl insisted. "I followed her into the forest and talked to her."

"Oh, Alysha, will you ever give over making up these stories?"

"But it's true. There was a girl in the forest, and she said no one was meant to know about her."

"Did she say why?"

"No. She said it was a secret."

Theresa's ears pricked up. "What's this?" she interrupted.

Noreen Murray rolled her eyes at Theresa. "The girl reckons she met someone in the woods yesterday." She lowered her voice and tapped the side of her head meaningfully. "It's all in her mind, you know."

This time, Alysha stamped her foot. "It's not! I saw her! I did! Her name's Cara, and we're going to meet later today. If you don't believe me, you can come along this afternoon and see for yourself."

Cara whistled to herself as she went about her chores. She was looking forward to meeting with Alysha that afternoon. Boredom and loneliness had been the most difficult things to deal with these past months. She could put up with her grandmother's moods and harsh words, but it was hard having no one to talk to. Apart from Theresa's eldest daughter, whom she wasn't allowed to meet, there were never any visitors to the cottage; the closest neighbor was half a mile away. She hated having nothing to do once the housework and her lessons were finished. Roaming the countryside was her only escape. Meeting Alysha yesterday had been a stroke of luck. Now she had a potential playmate, and she could hardly contain her excitement. For the first time since she'd arrived at the cottage, she had something to look forward to.

She'd already finished all her chores by midday. She was just thinking about making lunch when the front door banged open, signaling that Theresa was back from town. It was earlier than usual, and the change in routine made Cara uneasy. Her suspicions were confirmed a moment later, when her grandmother came into the kitchen, bristling with anger. She was breathing hard; her white hair was wild from the wind, her nostrils flared, and her eyes burned with fury. Cara instinctively shrank back.

Theresa took two giant steps across the kitchen and grabbed Cara by the arm. Although she was older now and frail, she was still stronger than the seven-year-old child.

"What did I tell you? What was the one simple rule you had to follow?"

Cara simply stared at her, mute and frightened. She had no idea what was going on.

Theresa shook her none too gently. "You are *not* to speak to anyone! You know that, don't you?"

Cara nodded.

"So what's this I hear about you arranging to meet Noreen Murray's niece by the woods this afternoon?"

Finally Cara realized what had happened. Alysha hadn't been as good at keeping a secret as she'd said.

"I told her not to say anything," she said in a small voice. It was her only defense, and she knew it wasn't a good one.

Now that she'd admitted what she'd done, Theresa released her. "Stupid girl," she muttered. "Don't you realize this is for your own good? While you're here, no one can know about you. Understand?"

Cara nodded because she knew that was what was expected, but really, she didn't understand. It seemed to her that her grandmother was just mean and trying to spoil her fun.

Theresa sighed deeply. "Well, that's it, then. You can't go out the rest of the day now."

Cara let out a little moan of protest.

But her grandmother had no sympathy. "Don't complain to me, girl. Until you prove to me that you can be trusted, you'll have to do what I say."

The child stared at her grandmother and felt dislike and anger rise within her. It wasn't *fair*. She hated the old witch. Thank God her mother was going to come back for her soon. After that she would never have to see her grandmother again.

Theresa and Cara didn't speak the rest of the day. They moved around the cottage as though they were there alone, studiously ignoring each other's presence. Cara saw the time when she was meant to meet Alysha come and go and felt her frustration growing.

After a silent dinner, Theresa settled in the kitchen to listen to the wireless. Cara decided to go upstairs to read. She was in the sitting room, trying to find where she had left her book, when she knocked over her grandmother's handbag, which was lying on the floor. She bent to pick up the contents and spied an envelope that had fallen out. She knew immediately that the letter was from her mother, because she always wrote on lilac writing paper.

The mailman didn't come out this way, it was too far, and so when Theresa went into town she would pick up all the mail. Usually once she got home, she would give the letter straight to Cara. They would read it together, Theresa helping her with any words she didn't understand, and then Cara would write back, again with her grandmother's assistance. But after finding out about Alysha, Theresa must have decided to keep the letter from her as punishment. That wasn't fair, Cara thought. She had so little to look forward to; now she couldn't even get her precious letters!

She bent to retrieve the letter. But just as she stood up, Theresa appeared. "What are you doing?" she demanded, stalking over and snatching the envelope from her granddaughter's hands.

So far, in the eight weeks that she had been here, Cara had tried hard not to answer back. But after the terrible, disappointing day, she was moved to anger. "That's mine! Give it back!"

Theresa looked unimpressed with her outburst. "That's where you're wrong. It's not yours. Your mother wrote this to me."

"Oh." Cara was shocked into silence. "So she didn't write to me?"

That made her even more depressed. She lived for her mother's letters: they were her windows to the outside world. Usually the envelopes were addressed to Theresa, but the letters inside were to her. Why was it different this time?

Theresa hesitated for a moment. "Yes, she included a letter for you, too," she said carefully. "But she wanted me to speak to you first."

Cara heard the tremor in her voice. "Why?" She was beginning to feel scared. Something wasn't right.

Theresa's eyes softened. There was something in her expression that Cara had never seen before: compassion. "Because she wanted me to tell you that she won't be coming for you as soon as she'd hoped."

"No!" The word came out as an anguished cry.

"She has the chance of some more work, you see," Theresa explained gently. "And money's been so tight for her. She wanted you to know that she's doing all this for you."

But Cara wasn't interested. She didn't care about the money—she just wanted them to be together again.

"How much longer before she comes back?"

When her grandmother bit her lip, Cara knew it wasn't going to be good. "Three months. Maybe four."

Cara was already shaking her head. "No! I can't stay here! I don't want to! She said she wouldn't be long—"

At that Theresa's expression hardened. "And were you expecting anything more from your mam? She's a selfish so-and-so, and the sooner you learn that the better!"

"No, she's not! She's wonderful, and I can't wait for her to come for me so I never have to see you again!" Cara ran from the room.

*   *   *

After a moment, Theresa heard Cara's bedroom door slam shut. Then the crying began. Hearing her, Theresa felt bad. She wanted to comfort her granddaughter, but she wasn't sure how—it simply wasn't in her nature. The woman had had a hard life, filled with much sorrow, and there had been little room for displays of affection.

But despite her outward hard exterior, she liked the girl. Cara seemed smart and willing to learn, and took a genuine interest in the different vegetables and herbs that Theresa grew. She never minded helping out with chores, and she had inherited none of her mother's vanity or selfishness. Theresa had never thought much of her other grandchildren, Maggie's offspring; they were a slovenly lot who had no interest in anything. Cara wasn't like that. Whatever Franny had done wrong in her life, she had raised her daughter right.

So Franny's letter today, saying that she wouldn't be back for a while, had been a godsend for Theresa. She was pleased to be getting more time to spend with her granddaughter. And it upset her to see that something that had brought her so much pleasure obviously caused Cara such pain.

Theresa knew it was difficult for the girl to understand why she imposed the rules that she did. But there was in fact a good reason for keeping Cara a secret. Here in Ireland, unwed mothers still had few rights. It was considered that a child would be better off without the influence of someone with such loose morals. So if the authorities found out about Cara, that she was an illegitimate child staying with her elderly grandmother while her mother waltzed off for months at a time, they might very well take her away. *That's* what all the secrecy was for. But how could she begin to explain that to a child?

Theresa was trying to do her best with Cara. She had a little money put by—enough to ensure her granddaughter was fed and clothed. But she was most worried about the girl's schooling—she seemed bright, and Theresa didn't want to see her fall behind. So she'd been forcing Cara to sit down for two hours every morning, to practice her writing and do some rudimentary sums. Luckily, the girl liked to read, so she'd get out books from the local library for her, encouraging Cara to ask if there were any words she didn't understand.

She was a clever little thing. Inquisitive, too. The other day she'd asked whether Theresa had known her father.

"What's yer mam told you about him?" the old woman had asked warily.

"That he was a nice man who loved us both very much and that he's in Heaven, like Danny's dad."

"That sounds about right," Theresa had lied. It seemed better than telling her the truth—that Sean had run out on Franny and that the last Theresa had heard of him, he had been drinking his way through the bars of Cork.

Upstairs, the girl was still crying. Theresa wished there was a way to stop her hurting, but she had no idea how to comfort her. There was no way she would ever be able to share her thoughts or feelings with her granddaughter—it wasn't in her upbringing or her nature. Instead, she went to the foot of the stairs and called up to Cara. "Will you get yourself down here?" Her voice was gruff. "I need help with the dinner."

In the kitchen, they began to silently prepare supper together. Theresa watched her granddaughter struggling to peel a potato, removing half the vegetable as she tried to take off the skin. Theresa tutted. "Not like that, you eejit." The older woman snatched the knife from Cara. "Like this." Then she began to quickly and expertly scrape away the outer layer under running water in the sink.

Once she was finished, Theresa handed the knife back to her granddaughter. "Now you have a go."

Frowning in concentration, Cara attempted to mimic her grandmother's actions. After a couple of minutes, she held up the potato. It was jaggedly cut and not as proficient as Theresa's effort, but it was an improvement on before.

"Not bad," Theresa said.

Then, after a moment's hesitation, she patted her granddaughter on the shoulder. It was an awkward gesture, unfamiliar to the older woman, but it seemed to work. Cara smiled up at her grandmother, her earlier anguish forgotten, for now at least.

Theresa quickly withdrew her hand. "Come on, then," she said brusquely. "You need to do two more of those."

But she was secretly pleased with herself for having finally done something right for the child.

15

That first night at Ciro's was Franny's initiation into the Hollywood party scene. Lily insisted on loaning her an outfit, and the two young actresses left the studio in matching wiggle dresses: Lily's in sinner's red, Franny's in emerald green. With their similar builds—they were both five foot five and voluptuous—they could have passed for twins, distinguishable only by their hair color: the blonde and the redhead, out looking for trouble.

Outside in Juniper's garage, Lily had her own reserved space, where she parked her white convertible Corvette.

"Don't sweat it, honey," the blond actress said when she saw Franny looking enviously at the car. "You'll have wheels like this in no time. I'm certain of it."

It was a short drive from the studio to West Hollywood and the Sunset Strip, the mile-and-a-half-long stretch of Sunset Boulevard where the rich and famous went to party. The area owed its existence to the fact that it fell outside the Los Angeles city limits, so during Prohibition, nightclubs and casinos had moved out there to escape the harsh regime of the LAPD. Since the thirties, its glamorous clubs and expensive restaurants had become a magnet for movie stars and the industry's power brokers. Now, at ten on a Friday night, the Strip—as Lily called it—was buzzing. Ciro's was busier than most. At the moment, Herman Hoover's nightclub was *the* place to be, the clientele made up of A-list stars. It was Lana Turner's favorite hangout; Mickey Rooney had chosen the venue for his birthday party; and earlier that year, Frank Sinatra had hosted Sammy Davis, Jr.'s, comeback there.

Lily joined a line of Cadillacs and Lincolns all lined up for valet parking. At the front she tossed her keys at a liveried young man who barely looked old enough to shave, and then she turned to Franny.

"Let's go, sugar. We're not getting any younger sitting here."

Franny needed no further encouragement. She stepped out of the car and into the warm evening, trying to take in every detail, hardly able to believe that she was actually *here*.

Ciro's exterior was one of understated elegance: a low-rise building painted black, with a white neon sign announcing the club's name. Inside, though, was another story. This was old-school Hollywood glamour, the baroque decor overdone and luxurious: the walls covered in silk drapes, the bandstand a raised dais fringed with velvet, tiny colored lights turning and sparkling in the moody darkness. Everyone was done up to the nines, a sea of sequins and fur, long evening gloves, and cigar smoke. Scantily clad waitresses smiled and sashayed their way through the crowd.

In the lobby, a leggy girl in a short skirt and heels took their fur shrugs. That could be me back at the Victory Club, Franny thought. It was nice to be on the other side. Before she could dwell too much on the past, Lily grabbed her hand. "Come meet the gang."

Lily's "gang" turned out to be some of the most famous names in the movie business at the moment. A genuinely fun party girl, she was now the queen bee of what had become known in the press as "the hive," an elite group of young, hot actors who were always pictured partying together. Stories about the group's incestuous romances and rivalries mysteriously circulated whenever one of them was about to release a movie.

Franny recognized the four faces already at the table. There were two women: Emily Apple, a formerly chubby, curly-haired child star, now a half-starved, wistful-looking brunette, and the raven-haired Helena Harris, a sharp-faced, serious character actress. She was currently a hot property, having taken the Oscar for best actress earlier in the year for playing the headmistress of an all-girls school whose strict discipline begins to border on psychopathic. Emily and Helena both acknowledged Franny with a brief hello, but neither of them looked terribly interested in her—they were more preoccupied with each other. The two men were another matter. Both were equally well known: the handsome, suave Duke Carter, who had been at the Victory Club in London with Clifford Walker, and Hunter Holden, one of the new breed of brooding young male stars who seemed to be all the rage since James Dean had appeared in *East of Eden.*

It was Duke, all charm and good manners, who stood to greet the two newcomers. "Good evening, ladies. And who do I have the pleasure of meeting?" The comment might have been addressed to Lily, but his eyes never left Franny.

"Frances Fitzgerald," Lily announced. "Fresh meat at Juniper." She winked at her new friend to show that the last part was a joke. She seemed to be thoroughly enjoying her role as Franny's mentor.

"How wonderful," Duke murmured, bending low to kiss Franny's hand. He obviously didn't remember her from the Victory Club, which was a relief.

Watching them, Hunter gave a snort of disapproval, although Franny wasn't sure if it was aimed at her or Duke. Slouched moodily across the leather banquette, a glass of bourbon in one hand and a cigarette in the other, his bow tie hanging loose around his neck, he looked as meanly handsome as in his movies—and also bored out of his mind.

"Oh, don't mind Hunter," Lily told Franny. "He never says much. He just likes to act all mean and moody."

True to form, Hunter just glared at Lily. She ignored him. "Come on now," she ordered. "Scooch up and make room for Frances."

Despite the obvious attitude, he did as he was told, and Franny soon found herself squeezed in between Hunter and Duke, two of Hollywood's greatest heartthrobs. In that moment, she finally felt she'd arrived.

A tuxedo-clad waiter came over to take their order. "Martini, straight up," Lily said. The waiter turned expectantly to Franny.

"Make that two," Franny added quickly, trying to look as though she ordered drinks like this all the time and wasn't simply copying her new friend.

But if anyone suspected that she didn't know what she was doing, they didn't seem to care. Duke in particular wasted no time in getting to know Franny. His arm slid round the back of the booth as he leaned over toward her.

"So come on now, gorgeous." He flashed his trademark megawatt smile. "I want to know *everything* about you."

Franny went into the standard spiel that the studio had made up: how she was a poor Irish country girl who'd gone to London to make her fortune; how she'd been discovered there and gotten whisked off to Hollywood. It was a familiar story, nothing particularly special, but Duke seemed fascinated by every word.

"I'll talk to Lloyd," he said, his hand finding hers on the table. "See if he can't find a project for us to do together. I'm sure we'd have great onscreen chemistry. Don't you agree?"

"Oh, yes!" Franny nodded vigorously. She couldn't have been more thrilled. The evening was turning out to be far better than even she'd expected.

Drinks kept arriving at the table. One martini turned into two and then three. Franny, who wasn't used to alcohol, was soon feeling light-headed and giddy with happiness.

"I can't believe how lovely he is," Franny whispered to Lily when Duke got up to go to the restroom. "Do you think that, well, maybe he's interested in me?"

"Oh, sweetheart." Lily laughed, but not unkindly. "Duke's interested in anything with a pulse." She lowered her voice conspiratorially. "Take it from me, he's a great lay, but don't expect anything more than that."

It took all of Franny's acting skills not to show how shocked she was by Lily's words. The waiter had just set down more drinks. She reached for a fourth martini. Hunter, who had been silent throughout the conversation, stayed her hand.

"Be careful," he growled. He fixed dark, frowning eyes on Franny, nodding over at the drink she was holding. "Them things are lethal. And there ain't nothing worse than a drunk broad."

Flattered by his interest, Franny's natural coquettishness surfaced for the first time that night. "Well, aren't I the lucky girl," she teased, lowering her lashes flirtatiously, "having someone like you looking out for little old me?"

Reaching for a glass of water instead, she raised the tumbler in a silent toast to his chivalry. By the time Duke got back from the restroom, he had some serious competition for Franny's attention.

The rest of the night passed in a blur. As the evening wore on, people kept dropping by their table: fellow actors, directors, and producers. Some pulled up chairs, and by one in the morning there were at least a dozen people crowded around. For Franny, the highlight of the night was when *L.A. Times* gossip columnist Dolores Kent stopped by.

Lily had shrewdly cultivated Dolores's friendship over the years, ensuring that her name was rarely out of the papers. Now, as the gossip columnist neared the table, she leaned over to whisper a few words of advice to Franny: "Make sure to suck up to the old cow. She loves that."

The gossip columnist had been primed by her good friend Lloyd, the head of casting at Juniper, to watch out for the studio's new starlet tonight. Juniper's PR machine had been sending her releases about Frances Fitzgerald for weeks, but so far, apart from that small initial mention, she hadn't seen any reason to give the new girl any additional coverage. Now, seeing her in such illustrious company, Dolores came over and introduced herself, extending a bejeweled hand to Franny.

"You do know who I am, don't you, dear?" she said, peering at the young actress.

"Oh, gosh, yes." Franny was on her feet, at once the wide-eyed ingenue. "I make sure to read all your columns, Miss Kent. It's such an honor to meet you." Although it seemed as if she was following Lily's advice, in fact she genuinely meant every word.

Dolores beamed. She liked respect and loved having her ego flattered even more. The pretty redhead had won her over.

By three the nightclub was closing, and the party moved on to Lily's home in the Hollywood Hills. The two-story, Spanish-style villa was a typical movie-star pad, expensively furnished with William Haines furniture and filled with little luxuries like cream silk sheets on the bed. Franny thought of her poky little room in Sunset Lodge and vowed to move out as soon as possible. *This* was what she wanted.

All around the room, couples were pairing off, some of them disappearing into darkened rooms behind closed doors. Franny noticed Emily and Helena going off into one of the bedrooms, hand in hand; she frowned, wondering what that was all about. Outside, Lily was holding court by the pool. Franny spotted Hunter by the bar, mixing drinks. She went over.

"Can you handle another martini?" he asked.

"Why not?" After spending three hours drinking water, Franny felt she deserved one.

Hunter poured himself a bourbon, and they clinked glasses. He didn't say much, just watched Franny moodily over his drink. She was beginning to get used to his silences.

From outside on the veranda, a girl screamed. Franny looked around just in time to see Duke push Lily into the pool. There was an almighty splash, and she disappeared beneath the water, so all that could be seen were ribbons of blond hair floating in the pool, before she finally resurfaced, coughing and spluttering.

"You bastard!" She gestured down at her dress. "That's a Balenciaga you just ruined!"

But there was no real anger in her voice, only outrage and a trace of amusement. She was enjoying this, Franny realized. In fact, instead of getting out of the water, as Franny had expected her to, she slithered out of her dress, and threw the sopping material onto the terrace. A moment later, her underwear joined her clothes, making a soggy pile.

"Hey, Duke!" Lily called. He moved closer to the edge and crouched down, to try to hear what she was saying. Franny had already guessed what her new friend was about to do. She was right: grabbing him around the ankle, Lily pulled him into the pool. He surfaced laughing and was already unbuttoning his shirt as three others—two starlets, whose names Franny couldn't remember, and a well-known screenwriter—began undressing, too.

Franny felt a blush rising in her cheeks. She looked over at Hunter to judge his reaction. But he seemed relaxed, as though this were something that happened all the time.

Nodding outside, he said, "How about it?"

"Oh, I don't know—"

But Hunter wasn't listening. He grabbed her hand and pulled her onto the terrace. Clearly unaware of how uncomfortable she felt, he began to strip. Naked, he turned to her.

"Coming?"

She averted her eyes. It wasn't that she considered herself to be particularly prudish. She'd already crossed a line that most people never would, having slept with Clifford to get what she wanted. But somehow this felt like a whole new level of decadence.

"Maybe in a bit."

Shrugging, he went to join the others in the pool, leaving Franny alone on the side. Part of her wondered if she should call a cab and leave them to it. But for some reason she couldn't bring herself to go. There was a lure about the party that kept her here. She snuck a look at the pool. Steam rose from the water, creating a dreamy feel to the night and preserving everyone's modesty. They were treading water, five faces looking up at Franny expectantly, all calling out to her to join them.

"Come on, Fran!"

"The water's lovely!"

"What're you waiting for?"

From the edge of the pool, Franny stared down at the swimmers. They all looked like they were having such *fun*. And that's why she was here, wasn't it? So she could finally live rather than just exist. She was twenty-five years old: if she didn't grab this moment now, who knew when she would have the opportunity again? They were right—what *was* she waiting for?

With a chorus of clapping, cheers, and wolf whistles egging her on, Franny stepped out of her shoes, unzipped her dress, and then, after a moment's hesitation, began to unhook her brassiere. Standing there, completely naked, her ivory skin glinting in the pale moonlight, with five strangers staring up at her, Franny was surprised to find she wasn't embarrassed or shy, not even of the tiny little silvery marks that had appeared on her stomach and thighs since having Cara. Instead, she felt strangely liberated. This was her time, and she was going to start making the most of it.

Taking a running jump at the pool, she dived in headfirst.

PART 2

1956–59

Good Intentions

The road to Hell is paved with good intentions.
—WELL-KNOWN PROVERB

16

Franny pressed her foot down on the accelerator, enjoying the roar of the engine as the car sped along the Hollywood Freeway. There was nothing more liberating than driving at night, opening up her Pontiac convertible on the empty roads. She loved the feeling of the warm California air against her cheeks, the wind rustling the scarf that held her hair tightly in place. Right now, she felt on top of the world.

That evening at Ciro's had signaled a change in Franny's luck. In the two years since then, she had become a star. It was *My Fake Wedding* that had set her on the road to fame. Although the veteran Lily Powell garnered most of the attention, Franny's comic timing as the gold-digging nurse had also ensured she was singled out for praise, being variously described as "a notable newcomer" and "one to watch."

On the strength of those reviews, Lloyd gave Franny her first shot at a lead. It was only a monster movie, a ridiculous story about a giant snake terrorizing New York, but Franny played her part as the damsel in distress well. Seeing how good she looked on-screen, Lloyd decided to test her for Juniper's epic western *The Gunslinger*. She was perfect for the role of the plucky, passionate daughter of a reverend, forced to hire an ex-convict to defend her father's water-rich lands from the greedy local landowner. When *The Gunslinger* was a box-office success, much of the credit went to her.

From there, Juniper negotiated a personal contract with Franny, raising her salary to one thousand dollars a week. With her red hair, green eyes, and buttermilk complexion, comparisons to Maureen O'Hara were inevitable. The studio capitalized on this, casting her in roles that required a spirited heroine with a high moral compass. Her characters were fiery but sensitive, passionate and sensual without being slutty, proving themselves to be the match of any man without losing their femininity.

With the salary increase, Franny moved out of the roach motel and into a duplex on Wilshire Boulevard. It was a typical starlet apartment, a glitzy, glamorous place filled with lacquered furniture, crystal chandeliers, and ornate mirrors. She also treated herself to the Pontiac convertible in a pretty silvery blue. Although the studio provided a car and driver, she preferred the independence that came from being behind the wheel and soon became a familiar sight driving east on Wilshire Boulevard, top down and red hair flying out behind her, toward the bright lights of downtown L.A.

You're about to miss the exit. The thought broke into Franny's reminiscences. Making a sharp right, she turned onto Hollywood Boulevard and began to slow down as she saw her destination: Musso & Frank Grill. The famous restaurant had become a regular hangout these past two years. Pulling up outside, Franny switched off the car engine and took off her leather driving gloves. Opening her handbag to pop them inside, she paused. There, nestling next to her Chanel compact, was a letter from Cara that she'd picked up on her way out that evening. Seeing the envelope, with its scratchy handwriting, Franny felt the familiar rush of guilt that hit her whenever she thought about her daughter.

The only blight on Franny's otherwise perfect life was that she was living it without Cara. Franny hated being away from her child. She missed Cara dreadfully, and she could tell from her daughter's letters that she was unhappy, too. As the months went by, the little girl had begun to complain more about life at her grandmother's, saying that she was bored and she missed Danny and the Connollys—and her mother, of course. At the end of every letter, she would always ask when Franny was coming back for her.

Franny never knew how to answer that. She hadn't intended to be apart from her daughter for so long. But two years had slipped by without her noticing. Life moved so fast out here in Hollywood—there was always so much going on, what with filming and all the parties and public appearances. And she'd gradually realized that she couldn't just broadcast the fact that she had a daughter. The McCarthy witch-hunts had created a climate of conservatism in America: given that her whole career was built on being a morally upright heroine, she was worried the papers would crucify her if they found out the truth about her past. Her career would be over, and she couldn't stand the thought of giving up something for which she had fought so hard.

Because, when it came down to it, she *loved* being an actress. Though she might like the trappings of success—the apartment and the car, the furs and the jewelry—they weren't why she stayed in Hollywood. She stayed because she still got a flutter in her stomach every time she stepped onto a film set. And not only did she love acting, she was *good* at it. For the first time in her life she had respect, and she didn't want to give that up.

But she also didn't want to go on living here without Cara. She just needed to find a way to have everything—her career and her child.

As she got out of the car, Franny resolved to put the matter from her mind for now. Tonight she had a date with Duke Carter—and she wanted to put all her energy into that.

Aside from her career success, Franny had become something of a party girl. After that night at Ciro's, she'd started to go out regularly with Lily and her crowd. She'd become a fixture at swanky Sunset Strip nightclubs like Mocambo and Trocadero, spending her evenings drinking, flirting, and laughing, always surrounded by male companions. The press adored her, and most weeks she made the *L.A. Times,* usually pictured arm in arm with a well-known actor or wealthy businessman, with an accompanying paragraph speculating about a budding romance.

But although she'd had plenty of male attention and had enjoyed her share of lovers these past two years, nothing ever seemed to develop into a serious romance. It was something that had been on Franny's mind a lot recently. Perhaps it was her age—she was, after all, twenty-seven now, even if the rest of the world thought she was only twenty-three—but she was tired of being single.

Then, earlier that year, in May 1956, she had been cast alongside Duke Carter in a swashbuckler, *The Princess and the Pirate.* Since that night in Ciro's, the two stars had flirted on and off, but this was the first time they'd ever acted together. It turned out to be a perfect pairing. Duke was born to play the dashing, devil-may-care hero, and Franny was a delight as the prim but feisty princess, alternately appalled and intrigued by his rough charms. On-screen, Duke and Franny smoldered. Their verbal sparring was quick and witty, the sexual chemistry between them palpable. Viewing the rushes for the first time, Lloyd saw an opportunity: what better way to publicize the movie than to have a romance between the two leads played out in the papers?

The studio's publicity machine had gone into overdrive, and soon Duke and Franny were being seen everywhere together. Dolores Kent, of the *L.A. Times*, was among those eagerly following the courtship.

"Don't they look adorable?" Dolores cooed in print below a staged photo of Duke helping Franny on with her coat after a dinner at Chasen's. "I predict an October wedding."

Reading the article earlier today, Franny found she liked that idea more than she'd thought possible. *Mrs. Duke Carter*—it had a certain ring to it. Perhaps it was because of this that she'd found herself dressing more carefully than usual for her date with Duke tonight. Because although Franny knew that it was the studio that had arranged for her and Duke to be seen together, as she walked into the restaurant she couldn't help hoping that it might turn into something more.

Musso & Frank was one of Franny's favorite places in Hollywood. The grillroom, famous for attracting the likes of Raymond Chandler, Charlie Chaplin, and Rudolph Valentino, had a wonderful old-school feel, with its oak beams and mahogany furnishings. As a waiter escorted her to the table, she saw that Duke was already seated in his favorite red leather booth. In a dinner jacket, he looked suave and debonair.

He rose as she approached. Already smiling, he took Franny's hands to hold her at arm's length, as though to inspect her.

"Well, don't you look wonderful tonight," he said appreciatively, bending to kiss her hand. It was a typical Duke compliment—he was always so smooth, especially around the ladies—but Franny lapped it up anyway.

It helped that she knew how good she looked tonight. Right now she was at the height of her beauty. Her ivory skin was free of lines and blemishes, and her rich red hair—which had been painstakingly styled by her maid—fell in soft barrel curls around her shoulders. Poured into a midnight-blue cocktail dress, she looked as sensual as Lana Turner. Between the nose job, the grooming, and the different accent, she was unrecognizable as the girl she'd once been. She'd even stopped worrying about someone from her past coming forward to spill her secrets.

There was no way anyone would guess that Frances Fitzgerald was Franny Healey.

Duke stood back to let her slide into the booth. "I reckon every guy in the joint wants to switch places with me right now," he said smoothly.

Franny smiled. "And I'm sure every women would love to be in my shoes," she returned.

They settled at the table, and the waiter brought over two martinis.

"I hope you don't mind," Duke said, "but I took the liberty of ordering drinks."

"Fabulous." Franny lifted her glass. "Here's to a wonderful evening!"

Duke smiled politely as Franny threw her head back and laughed. It took all his willpower not to look at his watch. They'd been here for about an hour now, and he was wondering when it would be all right to leave.

It wasn't that he didn't like Franny. He'd be the first to admit that she was beautiful and amusing, but the fact was, he simply wasn't interested. As a rule, he didn't like dating actresses—well, not successful ones. He'd preferred Franny the first time they'd met at Ciro's, when she'd been just starting out in Hollywood and was still fresh and naïve. There was only room for one fragile ego in a relationship, and he'd found that he preferred to be the one who was adored.

Looking past Franny, he spotted the cigarette girl who'd sold him a packet of Chesterfields earlier. At first glance she was pretty enough, but close up you could see her eyes were a little too close together and her nose had a large bump on the bridge. He would bet anything that she was a failed starlet: sweet, adoring, and grateful for his attention.

Feeling his eyes on her, the girl looked up. She blushed prettily as she realized that he was staring at her. That made up Duke's mind.

"Excuse me," he told Franny, getting to his feet. "I'll be right back."

Franny sipped at her martini and tried to amuse herself with people watching as she waited for Duke to return. She flicked a look at her watch. He'd been gone for about twenty minutes now. Where on earth had he gotten to?

Assuming that he'd been waylaid at another table, Franny twisted around in her seat to see if she could spot him. But as she scanned the restaurant, she saw instead that he was sitting up at the long mahogany bar, talking avidly to the rather plain-looking cigarette girl. It took Franny a moment to work out what had happened—that she'd been dumped by Duke in favor of a nobody.

Her cheeks burned with humiliation. Before she could think about what she was doing, Franny picked up her martini glass, walked across the room to where Duke was sitting, and threw the drink in his face.

The following morning, Lloyd Cramer, the newly promoted head of Juniper Studios, stared down at the latest issue of *Confidential* magazine. There, on the front cover, was a picture of a furious Franny shouting at a perplexed Duke in front of an entire restaurant. The studio head was appalled. Not only had her behavior undermined his carefully staged romance between his two stars, but he certainly couldn't have his leading lady behaving in such an unladylike manner.

Sighing heavily, he asked his secretary to get Frances Fitzgerald on the phone. "Tell her to get her butt in here," he growled. "ASAP."

Sitting in Lloyd Cramer's office later that morning, Franny was feeling somewhat contrite. It was the first time she'd been told off by Lloyd, and she didn't like how it felt. She'd listened attentively to the studio head's lengthy lecture on her conduct and felt herself go cold with fear as he told her that if *anything* like that happened again, he would invoke the morals clause of her contract and drop her from the studio's roster.

"Once you start getting negative press, it's hard to get back in the media's good books," he warned.

"But the papers love me!" she interjected, unable to stand the criticism any longer.

"They won't if you keep carrying on like this."

Hearing that, fear again gripped Franny. Falling out of favor with the press would spell the end of her career. Lowering her gaze, she tried to focus on appeasing Lloyd. "Again, I'm really sorry. I promise, this is the first and last time we'll be having this conversation."

"Good. Well, we'll draw a line under this. Although I have no idea what to do with you next. I was going to put you on another picture with Duke, but that's blown out of the water now."

Franny mumbled another apology, but Lloyd carried on as though she hadn't spoken. "I don't have much else for you at the moment," he said. "There's *The Black Rose,* of course . . ."

At that, Franny's ears pricked up. She'd heard all about *The Black Rose,* a film noir set in London during the Second World War. The main female lead was a nightclub singer who might or might not be a double agent. Usually that type of role wouldn't have interested her, but this one did for one reason alone: the movie was going to be filmed in England, which meant she would finally get to see her daughter.

"Oh, yes." She tried not to look too eager. If Lloyd guessed that she had a hidden agenda, he would veto her involvement in the movie. "That's right. The lead sounds amazing."

"Not really the type of role we'd usually cast you in," Lloyd mused. The studio head looked at her sharply. "You know it's going to be filmed in London?"

"Yes." She gazed at him impassively. "That's why I thought it'd be ideal for me. It would give me a chance to get away from here for a while, until all the gossip dies down."

Lloyd couldn't deny that her reasoning made sense. Frowning, he said, "Let me think about it."

17

Being back in London was a strange experience for Franny. Before, it had been a place of poverty for her. Now she had returned in triumph: she was the one staying in the Savoy, going out to supper clubs.

She was there for six weeks. Despite the weather—the incessant rain and thick, pervading fog—filming on *The Black Rose* was completed quickly, and she felt it had gone well. She was tired of being typecast as the noble female and relished playing a character with a little more bite to it. The director seemed delighted with how the dailies had turned out, and the London fog—which seemed to have worsened since she was last there—gave extra atmosphere to the outside shots.

And then it was time to see her daughter again.

Franny had organized every detail of the reunion perfectly. Given the limited time she had in Europe, she'd asked Theresa to bring Cara over to England to meet up. Of course it was crucial that the rendezvous remained secret. With that in mind, Franny had decided it would be best to get away from London, so she had booked the Grand Hotel in Brighton for a week's stay. It would be lovely, she thought, for Cara to have a proper seaside holiday. She made the reservation in Theresa's name and brought enough cash to pay in full. This week she wanted to be anonymous, to be a normal person again.

With that in mind, she bought some dowdy old clothes, reading glasses, and a wig of mud brown hair—nothing that would draw attention to her. On her final day at the Savoy in London, she brought her disguise down to breakfast, and then, halfway through her meal, she disappeared off to the ladies' room and changed. She altered the way she walked from her usual graceful glide to a brisk stride, more commonplace in a prim middle-aged spinster. As she left the hotel and got into the cab the porter hailed for her, no one gave her a second glance. On her way to Victoria Station, where she would catch the train to the seaside town, she felt exhilarated. It was like playing a spy in a movie.

The Grand Hotel in Brighton was sufficiently discreet to ensure that no one paid any attention to the schoolmarmish woman checking in that afternoon. At the beginning, Franny had planned to book the best suite, but then she'd realized that that was a bad idea—she didn't want to draw too much attention to herself. So instead she'd settled for one of the deluxe family rooms: two adjoining bedrooms with a shared bathroom.

Her first impression of the Grand was favorable. Built in the Victorian era, originally for upper-class visitors, the formidable white building looked gracious and dignified. Situated on the seafront, it had pretty views and would be convenient for all the amenities.

The rooms were lovely, exactly what she'd been hoping for. The bedrooms had high, corniced ceilings, huge French windows, and a view out to the gray English Channel. It might not be as welcoming as the azure-blue California ocean, but the bellhop had told her that on a clear day they would be able to see straight across to France. The bathroom was huge if somewhat drafty. But they could always dry themselves by the fire.

Her mother and Cara weren't due to arrive until five, which was another three hours away. Already impatient to see them, Franny needed to keep busy. She hung up all her clothes and then ordered some tea and sandwiches and sat by the huge window to eat them, thinking of all the fun things she would do with her daughter this week. After that she took a nap.

A tentative knock woke her an hour later. She knew immediately who was there.

"Coming!" she called, quickly checking her appearance in the mirror. She had discarded the disguise, wanting to show off how well she was doing to her daughter, to make her proud.

Hurrying over to the door, she threw it open. There, standing in front of her, was an elderly woman holding the hand of a dark-haired little girl. Franny stared at her daughter, aware suddenly of the changes that the two years had brought. Cara had grown at least two inches taller, and she seemed thinner, too: she was all arms and legs. Her wide green eyes seemed to take up most of her face, and her sooty hair was like a mop, sticking out in different directions. She looked like a little urchin. Franny stood in shock for a moment. Her daughter had grown up, and she'd missed all of those changes.

With tears gathering in her eyes, she crouched down so she was face-to-face with Cara. "Darling! It's so wonderful to see you!" she said with feeling. Then she held out her arms and waited for her daughter to rush into them.

Cara made no move. Staring at the glamorous woman in front of her, she felt an overwhelming shyness. This wasn't her mother. This was a beautiful stranger, too perfect to touch. Her hands were soft and perfectly manicured, and Cara was suddenly ashamed of her own callused skin and dirty, bitten nails. Her grandmother had insisted that she dress in her Sunday best for the occasion, but still she looked crumpled and messy compared to this elegant lady. What if she got the woman's pretty blue dress dirty? What if she messed up the lady's carefully curled hair? She hung back, feeling uncertain.

The red-haired woman frowned a little. "Well? Don't you have a hug for your old mum?" It was said with gentle teasing, but even nine-year-old Cara could hear the disappointment in the lady's voice. But that still didn't make her want to hug the woman. This couldn't be her mother: the hair was too red and perfectly styled, the nose smaller than she remembered. She even *sounded* different.

Theresa gave her a little shove. "Come on, girl. Do what yer mam says."

Dutifully, Cara stepped forward into the woman's arms. "Oh, sweetheart," her mother murmured, "I've missed you so much."

And Cara wanted to ask, "Then why didn't you come back for me?"

Franny couldn't understand what was happening. She'd looked forward to seeing her daughter so much, remembering how well they'd used to get on back when they'd lived at Annie's house. But instead of being pleased to see her again, Cara seemed so shy around her; it was as though they had never met before. Franny had spent time shopping before she came over to England and had brought several sets of new clothes for the little girl—but they all turned out to be too small. It made her painfully aware that she was a stranger to her daughter.

Late the first night, after Cara had gone to bed, she drank a little too much brandy and confided her fears that they had grown apart to Theresa. The older woman smiled knowingly. "Course she's acting different round you. She was only a nipper when you went away. Two years is a long time at that age." She gave her daughter a sidelong look. "What did you expect—for nothing to have changed? You're not that naïve, are you, love?"

In fact, that was exactly what Franny had expected. But when her mother put it that way, it did sound silly. "No," she lied. Sighing, she took another drink. "I suppose you're right, this is only to be expected. I just hope it gets easier."

Theresa made no comment.

After a good night's sleep, Franny woke feeling more positive. As her mother had said, it was bound to be a little strange for Cara at first. But they would be reacquainted in no time.

So that she would have to wear her disguise as little as possible, Franny had breakfast sent up to their room. "Isn't this a feast!" she declared as they sat down to bacon, eggs, and sausages.

But Cara didn't seem interested and settled for nibbling at a piece of toast and jam. It took all of Franny's willpower not to show how upset she was. Instead, she said, "I hope you're looking forward to today. I've got lots of fun things planned for us to do." And if her tone was a little forced, a little overbright, Franny tried not to think about it.

An hour later, they were dressed and ready to go out for the day. Cara looked at the strange clothes and wig that her mother had put on. "Why are you wearing those?"

Franny giggled. "Oh, these? It's like a game, darling. Well, don't look so blue. It's meant to be fun!"

Cara couldn't bring herself to smile back. She wasn't fooled for a moment. She knew what was really behind the disguise: this woman didn't want anyone to know that she was her daughter. Cara was her dirty secret.

Franny was determined to pack as much fun as possible into the day. On her request, Theresa agreed to stay behind at the hotel, leaving her to spend some time alone with her child. She wanted to win Cara over, to get back to the way they'd used to be together, when they'd been as close as a mother and daughter could be. She hated this distance that had come between them and knew that it was her fault—and that it was up to her to put it right.

Franny crammed the morning full of activities. It was too cold to swim, but they took their shoes and socks off and paddled in the shallows. After that they played minigolf, ate a fish-and-chips lunch, and then walked along the promenade. Franny insisted on buying Cara sticks of candy-striped rock and toffee apples.

"How about some candy floss?" she asked, pointing over at the stand.

"No, thanks. I don't feel very well."

Franny looked at her daughter's unhappy face and felt a surge of disappointment. The day wasn't going as she'd have liked. She had hoped the activities might thaw her daughter a little, but still she didn't seem able to connect with Cara. It was horribly frustrating, and she had no idea how to put things right.

They walked in silence along the pier. The silence was unbearable to Franny, so when she spotted a bumper car track, she felt a surge of relief.

"Let's go on a ride!" she cried, grabbing Cara's hand and pulling her over.

"My tummy hurts," the little girl said. But Franny was already buying the tickets and didn't hear her.

Franny wanted them to go in separate cars, but her daughter didn't seem keen, so they shared the same one. "Do you want to drive?" Franny offered.

Cara shook her head.

As it was midwinter, they were the only ones on the ride. Franny tried to make it fun, bumping into the sides and the stationary cars, but the little girl didn't smile or laugh as she was hoping.

When they finally got off, Cara was promptly sick.

"Oh, for heaven's sake!" Franny snapped. Some of the vomit had gotten onto her dress.

Hearing the irritation in her mother's voice, Cara burst into tears. Franny was immediately contrite. "Oh, darling, I didn't mean it." She knelt down to hug her daughter, to show her that it didn't matter, but Cara wriggled out of her grip.

"I want Granny!" she sobbed.

Staring down at her daughter, Franny felt a wave of sadness wash over her. The time apart had created a distance between her and Cara, and she had no idea how—or if—she was ever going to be able to bridge it.

"There you go." An hour later, Theresa tucked her granddaughter into bed. It had been left to her to clean Cara up, help her into a clean nightdress, and settle her down with a cup of tea. The child seemed a little better now, and the color had returned to her cheeks, but she still looked unhappy.

"Do you need anything else?" Theresa asked.

Cara shook her head.

"Then I'll leave you to sleep."

The old woman was about to get up, but Cara grabbed her arm. "Wait!" she said in a low, urgent voice.

Theresa turned back and saw her granddaughter looking up at her with wide, worried eyes. "What is it?" When Cara didn't say anything, she said more impatiently, "Well? I don't have all day. Spit it out, girl."

"Does Mum hate me?" she asked in a small voice.

Theresa felt her heart contract. She could kill Franny for upsetting the child like that. Sitting back down on the bed, she said, "Of course she doesn't hate you. Now, why would you think such a silly thing?"

"Because I ruined her day and she was cross."

Silently cursing her daughter, Theresa shook her head. "She wasn't cross. She was just upset because she was worried about you." She pulled the sheet up to her granddaughter's chin. "Now go to sleep. You'll feel better after you've rested, I promise."

Feeling reassured, Cara closed her eyes, and Theresa left her to it. Out in the shared sitting room, Franny was standing by the window, smoking. Even now she looked elegant and posed, her red curls falling around her shoulders. No wonder Cara found it hard to connect with her. Theresa knew that when her career had started to take off, Franny had worried about someone from Glen Vale or the East End recognizing her in a movie. But she needn't have fretted. These days Franny looked so different that even she, her own mother, wouldn't have seen the connection between the beautiful, poised actress called Frances Fitzgerald and the wayward daughter she had raised. The realization saddened Theresa a little.

"How is she?" Franny asked, oblivious to her mother's thoughts.

"Better. Her stomach's settled."

"That's good." Franny waited a beat and then said, "Do you think I should go in and see her? Or should I let her sleep?"

Theresa had no idea what to say for the best. She remembered how well Franny and Cara had gotten on when they first had come to her house in Connemara, and she could see the gulf that had emerged between them. She could appreciate both points of view—that Franny was trying her best to bond with her daughter but that it was hard for a nine-year-old child to let the mother who had abandoned her back in. She thought of telling Franny that Cara would rather see her than sleep; that right now she was confused and upset; and that she needed to be reassured that she was still loved despite what had happened that day. But there seemed little point. Soon Franny would be gone. What was the point of encouraging Cara's attachment to her mother, only to see her heartbroken again?

"Probably best to let her rest for now," she said finally.

Franny looked disappointed. "Of course," she said, having decided it was best to accept her mother's advice. "You're probably right."

She poured herself another drink and tried not to feel bad that Theresa knew her daughter better than she did.

The rest of the vacation was much the same. When it got to the end of the week, Franny still felt no closer to Cara. Her train left first, on the Friday evening. She would then catch a plane back to L.A. first thing the next morning. Cara and Theresa's passage was booked for the following day, so they would stay one more night in the hotel without her.

They went to see Franny off at the station. It was a sorry little farewell. It was already dark, and the platform was empty. The only other passengers were in the waiting room, the wooden structure providing a little shelter from the chill night. Huddled together on the platform, their breath turning to condensation in the cold, Franny, Theresa, and Cara waited in silence. In the distance, the steam train chugged toward them, puffing out small white breaths of hot air from its chimney.

Franny crouched down in front of her daughter. "Be good for your grandmother, won't you?"

Cara looked solemnly up at her mother. "I will."

It seemed like such an inadequate end to a frustrating week. Franny couldn't let them part without making some kind of last overture to her daughter, to show her that she cared. "I *will* come back for you," she said impetuously. "I'll find some way for us to be together. Soon. I promise."

Her daughter stared back at her impassively, and Franny could see that Cara didn't believe her. And a large part of her didn't blame the girl for feeling that way.

With that Franny turned to leave. The train had come to a halt in the station a few moments earlier; passengers had already started to get on, slamming the wooden doors shut behind them.

It was as though in that moment Cara finally realized what was happening—that she wouldn't see her mother again for a long time. Suddenly she rushed at Franny, clinging to her skirt. "Please, please don't leave me! Please!"

She was sobbing now. The unexpected display of affection, which Franny had been longing for all week, brought tears to her eyes, too.

"Oh, darling." For a long moment Franny hugged Cara to her. Then, finally, she gently disengaged herself. "I'm sorry, but I have to go."

The train journey back to London was bleak. The reunion with her daughter had made Franny face up to some harsh realities. During these past two years she'd missed out on so much of Cara's life. She could never get that time back. The choice she'd made, to follow her dream of being famous, had been at the expense of her relationship with her daughter. It was a sobering realization. As Franny looked out of the window, into the darkness of the English countryside, she felt a tear slip down her cheek.

18

In the weeks following her trip to Brighton, Franny felt very low. Her failure to reconnect with her daughter had left her feeling miserable and guilty. And she kept thinking back to her promise—made hastily on that ice-cold platform in Brighton—that they would be together soon. Knowing there was no chance of bringing Cara out to L.A., she'd even begun to wonder if she should throw up her whole career and go back to be with her daughter.

That feeling had become even more acute when, back in Hollywood, Franny had found that the media were beginning to turn against her. Her former supporter, Dolores Kent, was the most vocal of these critics. The gossip columnist had taken the news of Franny and Duke's breakup personally. Enraged by what she saw as Franny flagrantly ignoring her well-meant advice, she used the split as an opportunity to stick the knife in. Under the headline "Frances and Her Men" appeared a photograph of Franny at Club Alabam, sprawled across Hunter's lap, laughing delightedly while being fed an olive by up-and-coming leading man Logan Wainwright. In case the picture wasn't damning enough, Dolores's accompanying text in the paper that morning had left the reader in no doubt as to what she thought of the movie star's behavior: "Since her split with Duke Carter, Frances Fitzgerald has continued to flit from one man to the next. Be careful, my dear! You're rapidly becoming the girl that men have their fun with but never marry."

Franny was shaken when she read that. Not only because the blame for their breakup had been unfairly put on her but also because she didn't like the idea that people saw her that way. Growing up, she had always seen marriage and babies as a trap for a young woman. But now, already twenty-seven and having had nothing close to a serious relationship since Sean Gallagher more than a decade earlier, she suddenly felt less like a fun-loving party girl and more like an old maid.

Faced with her failings as a mother, her stalling career, and fears of impending spinsterhood, it was fair to say that by late 1956, Franny was feeling more vulnerable than she had in a long time. It was perhaps for this reason that she proved so susceptible to the advances of Maximilian Stanhope.

Like most of the studios in Hollywood at that time, Juniper was struggling to stay profitable. With the growth in television, cinema audiences had decreased. Revenues had also been hit hard by the Competition Commission's decision that studios were no longer allowed to own movie theaters. With profits dwindling, shareholders had begun to grow restless, and Woodrow Milton, Juniper's long-standing studio chief, had been removed the previous spring. Lloyd Cramer, head of casting, had been appointed in his place.

The promotion was undoubtedly a poisoned chalice. Juniper's problems were to do with business conditions, not any one employee. It was for that reason that in late 1956 Lloyd Cramer began to look for a new financial backer, someone prepared to give the studio a much-needed injection of cash. That person was Maximilian Stanhope.

The billionaire businessman Max Stanhope was well known around town. Scion of a newspaper dynasty based on the West Coast, he had taken his father's company and grown it, diversifying into areas such as mining and paper production. He had the Midas touch—every business he took on turned to gold. He'd even dabbled in moviemaking in the thirties, when Hollywood was at its peak, and although he'd exited in the late forties, just before things began to get tough in the industry, he still had strong links to L.A.: he owned three newspapers in town and had a mansion in Holmby Hills. Now, with this eleventh-hour investment in a failing studio, Max no doubt hoped to make another killing, as Howard Hughes had at RKO.

On the morning that they were due to sign contracts, Max arrived at Lloyd's office at eleven on the dot. At forty-five, he was a tall, imposing man. In the dozen or so times that Lloyd had met him, he'd said little, allowing their lawyers to hash out most of the details. He'd sat through the meetings, quiet and watchful—but the times he did speak, it was obvious he had a razor-sharp mind and knew exactly what was going on.

Lloyd, always somewhat flamboyant as his job required, greeted Max like an old friend. "It's great to see you again, buddy," he said with a smile, pumping Max's hand.

Max said nothing. It was an unnerving tactic he'd used throughout the negotiations, one that Lloyd had never gotten used to. Considered a powerful man in his own right, Lloyd always felt something of an amateur in Stanhope's presence.

Today, as always, Max declined the offer of coffee and eschewed chitchat, making it clear that he had come in for the sole purpose of signing the contract. Max had told Lloyd that he had no interest in getting involved with the creative side of things. He just wanted to see his money-saving initiatives implemented, which meant cutting down the number of movies made each year and no longer having so many staff under permanent contract.

It was the one concession that Max was making, and that was only because it suited him to leave the day-to-day running of the business to someone else. Lloyd knew he was selling the studio at a knockdown price, but he didn't have much choice—it was that or bankruptcy. Max had the upper hand, and both men knew it.

Lloyd signed first. When he'd finished, he passed the papers to Max and held out his fountain pen.

"You might as well keep this," he joked. "You've already pretty much had the shirt off my back."

Max fixed him with a cool look. "I'm sorry you feel that way." Then, ignoring the pen that Lloyd offered, he took out his own solid-gold Mont Blanc—custom-made, with a diamond-encrusted nib—and signed with a flourish.

With the formalities over, Lloyd indicated the liquor cabinet. "Sure I can't tempt you to a celebratory drink?"

"I have another appointment to get to," Max demurred.

The response left Lloyd in no doubt that though this might be a big deal for him, it was just a small part of the other man's day.

With their business concluded, Max rose to leave. Lloyd was just showing him out when Franny turned up for a meeting they'd arranged to discuss her latest bad press. Dressed in a blue-and-white polka-dot swing dress, wearing little white gloves and with her red curls spilling out from under a pretty bonnet, she looked as fresh as a spring day.

"Frances Fitzgerald!" Despite his cooling regard for his leading lady, in that moment Lloyd was delighted to see her. It felt like something of a coup to be able to introduce one of his most beautiful actresses to the new owner of Juniper. "Max here has just agreed to buy us," he told her.

"Really?" She raised an eyebrow. "I didn't realize that I was for sale." She posed coquettishly. "So what do you think, Mr. Stanhope? Did you get your money's worth?"

Lloyd gasped. "Franny—"

But Max, who'd appeared so humorless earlier, seemed amused by her comment. "I can't think of any other asset that I'd rather have in my portfolio." He grasped Franny's hand, his grip strong and powerful, which was a perfect word to describe him, she decided. "It was lovely to meet you, Miss Fitzgerald."

She smiled prettily up at him. "You too, Mr. Stanhope."

At the time, Franny gave little thought to the exchange. But the following evening, she was out with Lily and the rest of the gang at the Cocoanut Grove, the Ambassador Hotel's elegant nightclub, when someone sent over a bottle of vintage Krug for her.

Seeing the unexpected gift, Franny clapped her hands together in delight. "Oh, how lovely! And who . . . ?" She raised a questioning eyebrow at the tuxedo-clad waiter.

"With the compliments of Mr. Maximilian Stanhope."

It took Franny a moment to work out who he was referring to: Maximilian Stanhope—the new owner of Juniper Studios.

As the waiter uncorked the champagne, Lily nudged her. "Looks like *someone* made quite an impression on our new boss."

Franny, who had told her friend all about running into Max outside of Lloyd's office, batted her eyelashes theatrically. "Don't I always?" She turned then to the waiter. "And where's Mr. Stanhope sitting?"

"Over there, Miss Fitzgerald."

Franny looked past the dozens of palm trees that gave the Cocoanut Grove its name, and sure enough, there was Max, looking right at her, clearly waiting to see her reaction. She hadn't been able to recall how he looked exactly—all she'd remembered was that aura of power around him. Now she saw that her first impression had been correct. Maximilian Stanhope wasn't exactly a good-looking man, not compared to the likes of Hunter and Duke, with their matinee-idol looks. But he had something about him—a charisma and confidence that all powerful men seemed to possess. He was older than her, of course; she would place him in his midforties. Tall and broad-shouldered, he had intelligent eyes and dark hair that was graying at the temples, adding to his distinguished demeanor.

Sitting at the best table in the place, he looked commanding in the requisite black tie. His party consisted of four other men of similar age and attire—other money men, Franny guessed—and they were all in the midst of drinking brandy and smoking cigars. Their dates were good-looking starlets, no doubt there to provide the necessary glitz to the evening. Instinctively, Franny knew Max wasn't serious about any of them. She raised her glass to him in thanks, and he mirrored the gesture in acknowledgment. Their gazes remained locked as they both took a long sip of their drinks.

Unfortunately, the waiter chose that moment to return to Franny's table to serve their meals, blocking her view across the room. She waited impatiently for him to move, but by the time he finally left, Max's attention had been diverted and he was deep in conversation with his dining companions.

Well, Franny wasn't about to pass this moment up. She got to her feet. Guessing her intention, Lily caught hold of her wrist.

"Where do you think you're off to, missy?"

Franny nodded at the bottle of champagne. "To thank the gentleman properly, of course."

"Now, honey, do you really think that's wise?" Lily said in a voice that made it clear she didn't.

"Why wouldn't it be?"

"Because, my dear, sweet thing, our humble fates now rest in the hands of that very gentleman you are about to go and make eyes at."

Franny gave a knowing smile. "That's exactly why I'm going over." If the studio's new lead investor had taken a liking to her, she wasn't about to ignore him. On the contrary, if she played her cards right, she might be able to use his interest to her advantage. Gently tugging her wrist free, Franny set off across the room.

She had come out tonight in all her defiance, determined not to let her recent bad press get to her. In an ice-blue strapless gown, she had dressed to be noticed. She had gotten her maid to pull the corset especially tight, Scarlett O'Hara style, to emphasize her hourglass figure. Her long red hair was pinned up in an elegant chignon, and she'd left her neck unadorned to keep all the emphasis on her figure.

Franny had always known how to draw the eyes of a crowd. Now, as she glided across the marble floor, she could feel everyone watching her—everyone apart from Max. He had his back to her, and it wasn't until she drew closer, and his companions told him that she was approaching, that he swiveled around to look at her.

"Miss Fitzgerald." He rose to greet her, and she was struck again by how tall he was. He took her small pale hand in his and brought it to his lips. "What a pleasure to see you again."

"I wanted to thank you for the bubbles." She lowered her eyes, knowing that was how she looked her most charming. "It was a lovely gesture."

"It was my pleasure," Max returned.

There was a pause as Franny waited for Max to make a move. But he simply held her gaze, as though he wanted to see what she'd do next. She realized then that it was going to be up to her to take matters into her own hands.

"And," she said boldly, "I also wanted to see whether you'd like to dance."

He regarded her with amused eyes. "You're very forward, aren't you, Miss Fitzgerald? Can't you see I'm here with a date?" He nodded toward a pouting brunette.

Franny shrugged carelessly, refusing to be made to feel ashamed of her behavior. "Did your date mind you sending over the champagne, Mr. Stanhope?"

"Touché." He inclined his head in acknowledgment of her point.

"So," she said, with a touch of impatience, "are we going to dance or not? Because I can find someone else to partner me easily enough—"

She made to turn away, but he reached out and grabbed her wrist. "Don't go." He spoke softly. She turned back and found herself looking directly into those intense dark eyes of his. "Of course I'd love to dance with you."

Offering Franny his arm, he led her through the sea of tables to the dance floor in the middle of the room. A quickstep was playing.

Franny was a good dancer, and she was pleased to see that Max was, too; so many men stared at their feet or concentrated on counting the beats, but he took the lead and moved confidently, spinning Franny effortlessly around the floor.

They stayed another two hours, and if Franny felt a little guilty about abandoning Lily and her other friends, she managed to put it from her mind. After everything that had happened lately, she needed an evening like this to cheer her up.

At the end of the night, Max insisted on driving her home. The valet brought out his car, a Cadillac Series 62, a four-door sedan in silver. It was a status symbol, a proclamation of serious wealth. Franny was impressed but tried not to show it. Instead, she said, "No chauffeur?"

Max's eyes met hers. "Not tonight. I've got a whole fleet of cars and several drivers who work for me, but this is my newest toy and I'm not done playing with it yet." He shrugged. "I like driving."

Franny nodded approvingly. "Me, too."

At her apartment block, he parked and walked her to the door. She stepped into the marble foyer and turned to him. "Thank you for seeing me home."

He leaned against the porch brickwork. "No invite in?"

"Of course not," she said, affecting primness. "What kind of girl do you think I am?"

"The kind I'd like to get to know better."

"Then call me sometime and ask me out on a proper date." Smiling sweetly, she closed the door in his face.

That night, for the first time in ages, Franny had something other than her failure as a mother to think about. She kept rerunning the evening's events through her head. She hoped that she hadn't played too hard to get.

But she needn't have worried. The next morning, she got up to find that Max had sent her six dozen long-stemmed Avalanche roses. Ten minutes after they arrived, he called.

"I think I shouldn't have sent those flowers."

"Oh? Why's that?"

"Because my P.A. tells me that white roses are meant to represent innocence and purity. And my intentions toward you are certainly neither of those."

Franny laughed. "Well, that's good to hear."

"Really? But I thought last night you said that you weren't seducible."

"If you impress me enough, anything's possible."

"So let's get this straight—if I impress you, *then* you'll let me take you to bed?"

"Perhaps."

"Well, that sounds easy enough."

"Oh, I wouldn't be too sure," Franny warned. "I'm very hard to please."

"And I'm used to getting what I want, and right now I want you." Up until then the tone of the conversation had been lighthearted. But Max sounded so deadly serious with that last line that Franny didn't know quite what to say.

It was a whirlwind romance, a sophisticated courtship. Max was in town for only a few more days, and he insisted on spending every spare moment with Franny. On Monday, he took her for dinner at Musso & Frank's; on Tuesday, they met at the Brown Derby for lunch; and on Wednesday, they went dancing at Mocambo. He sent her daily gifts of champagne, flowers, and jewelry. In the past few years, Franny had dated her fair share of wealthy men, but none of them had ever made so much effort for her, nor had they chased her quite so aggressively. Max made her feel special, adored, and that was something she liked more than anything else.

When it came time for him to leave—"I have to travel to San Francisco and then Chicago"—he promised her that he would be back in L.A. on the first Friday of the month. "You'll be free, won't you?"

She didn't bother to answer, mostly because it sounded like a command rather than a question.

Lily was less than enamored with her friend's new romance.

"I never see you anymore," she complained when Franny finally returned her call. In the two years that she'd known Franny, Lily had never seen her friend so smitten with a man before. She could understand the attraction, of course—Max was rich and important, the power player who all the rest looked up to. Almost unnervingly composed, he was notoriously standoffish and elusive, which only made him more desirable. Although it pained Lily to admit it, part of her was a little jealous that Franny had managed to capture such a man's interest. But mostly, she just missed seeing her partner in crime.

"I know I haven't been around much." Franny tried to sound contrite. "It's just—"

"What?" Lily pressed.

"Well, I think I'm falling in love with him."

The last part was said in a confessional rush. But if she'd been hoping for her friend to show some interest, she was sadly mistaken. Lily gave a derisive snort. "You're always falling in love."

"That's not true!" Franny was hurt, in the way that people are when someone tells them a home truth.

"It is, too," Lily said, oblivious to her friend's feelings. "But I'm not worried," she continued. "I'm sure this will go the way of all the others. I give it two more months, and you won't even be able to remember who Maximilian Stanhope is."

Franny, wounded by the implication that she was flighty, decided it was best to end the conversation.

Lily wasn't the only one who worried about Max and Franny. Lloyd wasn't sure what to make of the romance between one of his female leads and the new majority financial investor in his business. Part of him was slightly concerned that Franny would lose interest in Maximilian Stanhope and spurn him. Who knew how the powerful man would react? Max was something of an enigma: a smart man, a charismatic man, but above all an elusive man. Since the death of his wife fifteen years earlier, he had stayed resolutely single. He had dated his fair share of women, all high-profile socialites or beautiful movie stars. But he'd never seemed so serious about one of them before.

It was a month after Franny and Max had danced at the Cocoanut Grove that Lloyd realized exactly how serious his chief investor was about Juniper's leading lady. At the end of a routine catch-up call, the businessman mentioned an item he had seen in *Variety* that day: a small announcement saying that Frances Fitzgerald was to take the lead in a movie about Queen Elizabeth I. Her love interest, Robert Dudley, was to be played by Duke Carter.

"Duke and Franny, they were an item?" Max wanted to know.

"Yes," Lloyd said carefully.

"And they broke up quite recently?"

"That's right."

"I imagine it must be very difficult to work with someone with whom you've been romantically involved."

Lloyd was a little puzzled by the conversation. Max had claimed that he didn't want to interfere in creative matters; was he now making an exception to this? To be on the safe side, the head of Juniper made the change, sidelining Duke for the time being. But even as he did so, he couldn't help hoping that for Franny's sake, she wouldn't ever do anything to anger Max Stanhope. He could clearly be a powerful enemy.

"So have I impressed you yet?" Max asked when he dropped her back from another dinner at Musso & Frank.

Franny shrugged carelessly. She'd learned today that Duke wouldn't be playing Dudley in *Elizabeth* after all; the good news had made her even giddier than usual.

"Let's see. Dinner at Frank's, lunch at Derby's," she ticked off activities on her fingers. "Dancing at Ciro's. Nothing I haven't done before. I'm still waiting for you to impress me."

Max looked thoughtfully at her. "I'll have to see what I can do about that."

The next day he took her to Paradise Cove, a secluded piece of beach one and a half hours' drive from L.A. It was early March, and an unexpected storm meant it had turned colder: the sea churned black, and they were the only two people there.

"Why here?" she asked as they walked against the bracing wind.

"I heard you liked beaches."

Her eyes widened. "How did you find that out?"

"I have my sources," he said, tapping his nose.

Franny threw back her head and laughed. "You're unbelievable!"

"So—does that mean I've finally impressed you?"

Instead of answering, Franny called out suddenly, "Race you to that rock!"

She was off before he could digest what was happening. He shouted something about her not playing fair, but she only laughed in response, refusing to turn and lose her advantage. Running along the beach, the wind blowing sand into her face, she felt happy and carefree.

She could feel him gaining on her, his footsteps thudding on the sand as he closed the gap between them. She practically ran into the boulder, her hands slapping the rough, gray face.

"I won!" she called out, her voice carrying on the brisk wind.

She turned just in time to see Max draw up in front of her, breathing hard. "You didn't play fair," he panted.

"I never promised that I would."

"And neither did I."

Before she could ask what he meant, he grabbed her by the shoulders and backed her up against the hard rock. Then he bent his head and kissed her, right there on that cold, empty beach, his warm body stretched across hers, her soft breasts crushed against his chest.

Franny felt her breath catch, making her gasp. Whatever Lily might think, she was truly falling for Max. Perhaps she'd started off thinking that being with him might help her career, but that was no longer her motivation. Her other love affairs paled in comparison to this. Max was in a different league. He wasn't weak like Sean; he wasn't self-obsessed like Duke or any of the other actors she'd dated. It was a heady thing, to be able to capture the attention of this powerful, sought-after man. For the first time ever, Franny felt that she had met her match.

Max must have felt the same way, because when he finally broke from their kiss, he drew back a little, so that he was staring straight into her eyes. "No more games, Frances Fitzgerald," he murmured fiercely. "I just want you to answer one question—will you marry me?"

19

Cara kicked a stone as she wandered along the rough path that ran through the woods. Usually she would run and jump as she went, but today she wasn't feeling up to it. It was May 4, 1957, six months since the trip to Brighton. Cara still felt awful about what had happened that week. She'd looked forward to the holiday so much, to finally seeing her mother again, and it had all been a disaster. She kept wishing she could go back in time and relive that week—she would do everything differently then. She hadn't meant to behave badly, but obviously Franny hadn't been happy with her; that was why she'd left her behind. Since then, her mother hadn't written much either. Cara knew she was being forgotten. She'd learned to cope with the loneliness, of missing Danny and Aunt Annie, of having only her grandmother to talk to. She'd learned to lose herself in books and make-believe adventures, but the realization that her mother didn't want her was the hardest thing to bear.

Cara felt a tear slip down her cheek. Today the feeling of abandonment was more acute than usual, because it was her tenth birthday—something her mother had obviously forgotten. Franny hadn't even sent her a card. Her grandmother had tried to make the day special, in her own way. That morning, Cara had gone down to breakfast to find a card and a box of chocolates. In previous years, Franny had sent over several beautifully wrapped gifts, but in their absence Cara had been touched by her grandmother's gesture. It was a frugal present, in keeping with Theresa's austere manner. Although Franny sent plenty of money, old habits die hard, and she preferred to take only what she needed, saving the rest for when Cara grew up.

Along with the card and present, Theresa had made a cake when Cara was out of the house yesterday and presented it to her after lunch. Over the past three years, their relationship had developed into one of fondness. Cara knew her grandmother was never going to be the most demonstrative person, but she had come to realize that Theresa's small, understated kindnesses meant more than all of her mother's grand gestures.

Cara was wrong. Her mother *did* remember her birthday—except not until three days after the date. Franny felt wretched when she realized. She guessed it was because she had been in the middle of filming, reworking some scenes on *The Black Rose*. Back in Hollywood, the director had been less than pleased with how things had turned out on the film, particularly with her performance, and the stress from that had obviously distracted her.

With no time to go out to the shops herself, Franny made a hasty list and passed it to her P.A. to organize. "It's for my niece back in Ireland," she explained. Then, her conscience soothed a little, she went back to her movie.

The parcel for Cara's birthday finally arrived a month after the actual date. She was so delighted to receive the present that she pushed aside any unkind thoughts she'd had about her mother and tore the paper open. At first all she saw was a flutter of pink and white, ribbons and lace. Then she realized—it was a princess dress! Something so beautiful that she hardly dared touch it.

But as she took the gown out of the package, her initial delight turned to frustration. Why had her mother bought her something so pretty? It was totally impractical in the rough surroundings of the cottage. Where on earth did her mother think she was going to wear this?

Cara stared at the dress for a moment, feeling the luxurious material in her hands. Then, without warning, she started tearing it apart, ripping at the seams and pulling off the bows and pearls.

She was still attacking the material when her grandmother, who'd come to see what all the noise was about, hurried into her room. "What in the name of God is going on here?"

The shock in her grandmother's voice pulled Cara up short. Pausing in her decimation, she stared up at Theresa, tears streaming down her face. "I hate her!" she burst out.

The older woman took in the scene, the torn wrapping paper and ripped dress. She frowned for a moment, and then her expression cleared. Walking over to Cara, she eased herself down into a kneeling position, so that she was at eye-level with her granddaughter.

"Now, hush, child," she said, frowning. "Don't ever say something so wicked." Though Theresa understood her granddaughter's frustration, her belief in having respect for one's elders prevented her from denigrating Franny.

"But I *do* hate her," Cara insisted.

"No, you don't," Theresa pointed out reasonably. "You're just upset because she forgot your birthday and your present was late and maybe not what you wanted. You love your mother, you know you do, and that's how it should be."

Cara thought about this for a moment. "Maybe. But she doesn't love me."

Theresa sighed. "Of course she does."

"Then why doesn't she come back for me?"

It was the question that Theresa had been dreading—and one to which she didn't have an adequate answer. "You have to understand your mother," she said carefully. "She isn't like you or me. She can't just settle for an ordinary life. She's always wanting something more. She *needs* people around her, telling her how wonderful she is. But she still loves you, even if she can't be here with you. You understand?"

It was the longest speech that Cara had ever heard her grandmother make.

"Now, come on, enough of this silliness." She gave Cara an affectionate pinch on the cheek. "I saw some strawberries on the bushes earlier. Go out and see if you can collect enough for us to make some jam later."

Cara did as she was told, happy to get away from the remnants of her disastrous birthday present.

Later, when she got back, feeling strangely happier, the strawberry picking having distracted her, she found that the mess had all been cleared away. The little act of kindness meant so much to her. Her grandmother might be a strange, brittle woman, but underneath, Cara knew that she cared. Whereas her mother, for all her pretty words and promises, didn't seem to love her one bit.

20

Like their courtship, the marriage of Frances Fitzgerald to Maximilian Stanhope was a whirlwind affair.

After his proposal on the beach, Max took her back to his gated white marble mansion in Holmby Hills, the most exclusive neighborhood in Los Angeles, naturally. In his wood-paneled study, he removed a Renaissance-style painting from the wall to reveal a safe—from which he produced a six-carat square-cut diamond ring in a platinum setting. He hadn't had it with him at Paradise Cove because he hadn't planned on proposing to her today, he confessed with a sheepish laugh. He'd wanted to wait for the perfect moment before asking her to marry him, but then out there, on that windswept beach, he'd felt so overwhelmed with emotion that he'd *had* to ask her right then and there. He seemed almost embarrassed by the admission, and Franny thought how out of character it was for him to seem so unsure of himself. It felt good to think that she had the power to do that—to unsettle this strong, commanding man.

Sitting on the leather Chesterfield couch, Franny looked on delightedly as Max knelt down and slipped the ring onto her left hand, hardly able to believe that this was happening. A few short months ago, she'd felt so rejected by Duke, so criticized by the press. Now it seemed everything was going her way again. Because Max was a million times the man that Duke was. He was handsome and powerful and rich, and he treated her like a queen. What more could she want?

She looked down at him then, feeling more overwhelmed and

touched than she'd imagined possible. "I didn't expect this," she said quietly. "Not so soon."

He smiled up at her. "Well, why wait? We're both free and single. My children are old enough to understand. We only have each other to worry about."

Franny stared at Max for a long moment. She'd been on the verge of telling him about Cara, thinking that once they were married, she would be able to bring her daughter out to live with them, certain that Max's clout would provide shelter against any bad press. But the mention of his children had drawn her up short. He'd told her early on about his son and daughter, Gabriel and Olivia, by his first wife. Wouldn't he think it strange that she'd never mentioned her own child before now? It might seem as if she'd been—well—a little less than honest with him.

Unaware of the dark turn in her thoughts, Max came to sit beside Franny. He reached up to cup her face in his hands, his cool fingertips pressing against her bare skin as he looked deep into her eyes, just as he had done on the beach earlier. "You're everything to me, my darling," he said fiercely. "I need you to know that. I never imagined it would be possible to feel this way about someone again. And now I have you, I won't ever let you go."

He pulled Franny to him then, his lips seeking hers, kissing her hungrily, greedily, as though he couldn't get enough of her. As he tugged down the zipper of her dress, pushing the straps down off her shoulders, she dragged the white shirt over his head, her ardor matching his in its intensity. Franny's last cogent thought was that she wouldn't tell him about Cara *quite* yet. She needed to find the right time to broach the subject, once the initial excitement about the engagement had passed.

Lily wasn't happy when she heard about the engagement. Franny had gone over to her house to tell her in person and to ask her to be chief bridesmaid.

"Well!" her friend said, sitting down heavily on her cream-colored couch. "I wasn't expecting that."

Franny noticed the distinct lack of congratulations being offered. "You're not happy for me?" she asked, hurt.

Lily sighed. "No, it's not that. It's just . . ."

"What?"

"I'm just sad to be losing my partner in crime, that's all."

"Oh, darling." Laughing, Franny hugged her friend. "Don't be so silly. Just because I'm getting married, it doesn't mean anything's going to change."

"Really?" Lily sounded skeptical. "Max might not agree with that."

"Max?" Franny scoffed. "He loves me the way I am. He wouldn't ask me to give up anything for him."

Lily just looked at her friend. "Are you so sure about that?"

Max's associates were equally surprised by the match. Since the death of his wife fifteen years earlier, Max had been out with dozens of women, yet he'd never gotten close to marriage. What made Frances Fitzgerald so special? If they'd imagined Max with anyone, it would have been an elegant society lady, born with a silver spoon in her mouth and reared to be a good hostess at his parties. Franny was a good-time girl who loved being in the limelight. Surely she would never be content to be just Mrs. Stanhope?

"But why *marry* her?" Frank Brewer III asked. The head of a Boston banking dynasty and as wealthy as Max, he was the only one brave enough to say such a thing.

"Because I love her," he replied simply. "Isn't that the usual reason?"

No one dared argue with that.

Max himself couldn't explain his feelings for Franny—his *obsession* with her, as he'd come to see it. He knew she was a party girl and that she had something of a reputation. But still, he couldn't get enough of her. After what had happened with his first wife, he'd never thought that he would marry again. He'd dated plenty of women over the years who would have liked to get him to settle down, mainly movie stars and socialites, all of them attractive, witty women. But Franny was different. It wasn't *just* that she was beautiful—although of course that didn't hurt, he admitted ruefully—it was her spirit, her zest for life, that he found so fascinating. He wanted her with him, and he didn't give a damn what anyone else thought.

The impending marriage brought up other issues—namely, meeting Max's two children, Gabriel and Olivia. While Franny and Max had been courting, they had been able to keep everything lighthearted, and the past had seemed like less of an issue. But now they had to make the effort to integrate into each other's lives.

Franny knew just the barest details of Max's first wife, Eleanor, the beautiful only daughter of a wealthy Bostonian financier. Max had been twenty-seven when they'd met at a fund-raiser, and they'd married six months after that. Their son, Gabriel, had been born the following year, and a daughter, Olivia, two years after that. That was when the problems had set in. Eleanor, plagued by depression after the birth of her second child, had committed suicide when Olivia was just three months old.

In his grief, Max had blamed Olivia for his wife's death. Unable to look at or hold his baby daughter, he'd arranged for his children to be brought up by a series of governesses, while he'd immersed him-self in work. Everyone had assumed that as time passed, Max would relent. But unfortunately, as Olivia grew older, she began to resemble her mother, a permanent reminder to Max of the wife he had lost. Not that he'd treated his son any better. It was as though on the day his wife died, Max had decided to withdraw from fatherhood completely. As soon as Gabriel turned seven, he'd been packed off to an exclu-sive boarding school outside San Francisco. Once she was old enough, Olivia had suffered the same fate. The result was that even though Gabriel was now seventeen and Olivia fifteen, Max hardly knew his children.

"I'm afraid they lost two parents the day that their mother died," Max confessed to Franny. "I haven't been a very good father to either of them. But now that I've found you, I want all that to change."

That came as news to Franny. She hadn't reckoned on becoming a stepmother to two teenagers, and she wasn't sure how kindly they were going to take to her marrying the father they hardly knew.

Max warned her that his children had reacted very differently to the distance he'd put between them. Though Gabriel had grown into a tough, independent young man, Olivia was much more fragile. "I hope in time you may come to be a mother to her. Or at least a friend. At her age, she needs some guidance from another female."

Franny wasn't entirely sure she would provide the best role model for an impressionable young mind. But she kept her thoughts to her-self.

The following week, Max arranged for her to meet his children over dinner at his mansion in Holmby Hills. When Franny arrived, Max was on a call to Europe, so she went into the drawing room to wait. She walked in to find a tall, slender young man, with dark hair and intense dark eyes, lounging across one of the couches, reading *The Catcher in the Rye*. He glanced up as she entered, a look of amusement crossing his face.

"Ah! So you must be my new stepmom." He got up and sauntered over to her, planting a kiss on each of her cheeks. He smelled of cigarettes and too much aftershave. His years at boarding school had clearly made him self-sufficient, and he had a confidence about him that bordered on arrogance. Dressed in blue jeans and a black leather jacket, his hair worn long and floppy, he looked as though he had stepped out of *Rebel Without a Cause*.

"It's good to finally meet you," Franny said. "Your father talks about you all the time."

Gabriel gave a disbelieving snort. "I somehow doubt that." His eyes swept over her in a way that made her feel distinctly uncomfortable, which she suspected was his intention. She wondered if there was something strange about feeling so unnerved by a seventeen-year-old boy. Except maybe that was her mistake, to think of him as a boy when he was far closer to being a man.

"Now," he pretended to muse, "have you given much thought to what I should call you? I have. Personally, I think 'Mother' seems a little too formal. Then there's 'Frances,' but that just seems a little . . . well, impersonal."

He took a step forward. Franny instinctively tried to move back, but she'd forgotten the marble statue that was there and stumbled a little. Reaching out to steady her, he continued talking. "So, after much long, hard thought, I decided on 'Mummy.'" He emphasized the word, affecting the accent of an upper-class English schoolboy. "What do you think?"

"Gabriel!"

Hearing Max's voice, relief flooded through Franny. With Gabriel momentarily distracted by his father, she took the opportunity to step away from him and hurried over to her fiancé's side.

"Darling." She put her hands on Max's shoulders and reached up to kiss his cheek; suddenly her acting skills had kicked in. For some reason she wanted to show this presumptuous young man that she was firmly attached to her husband-to-be—his father, she reminded herself. Taking Max's hand, she said, "Gabriel and I were just getting to know each other."

It was then that Franny noticed the girl standing a little way behind Max. Olivia, she presumed. She was as beautiful as her brother, tall and slender like him, with the same fine bone structure and perfect porcelain skin. But whereas Gabriel had dark hair and dark eyes, like his father, Olivia had long fair that fell straight to her waist and pale blue eyes, Franny assumed like her mother, Eleanor.

Franny gave the girl what she hoped was a winning smile. "Hello, Olivia. It's lovely to meet you at last."

But the girl stared blankly back at her. Inwardly, Franny groaned. It was going to be a long evening.

Over dinner, she tried hard to include both Gabriel and Olivia in the wedding plans. "Perhaps you'd like to be a bridesmaid?" she said to Olivia. "I have eight already, so one more won't matter."

Instead of Olivia answering, Gabriel did. "Olivia hates being the center of attention," he told Franny, swinging back in his chair. "You'd be better off finding someone else."

"Oh, I see." Franny tried not to feel hurt. "And what about you?" She turned to Gabriel. "Will you perhaps be doing a reading?"

"I'll do whatever you want me to." With the main course finished, Gabriel turned to Max. "Would you be so kind as to excuse us from dessert, Father?" His formal words sounded faintly mocking. "We both have homework to do."

It was only after they had gone that Franny realized Olivia hadn't spoken once throughout the meal.

"Well, that didn't go quite as well as I'd hoped," she said once they were out of earshot.

Max sighed. "I know." He reached across the table and squeezed her hand. "But they'll come around eventually, darling. I'm sure of it."

Franny wasn't so certain.

Upstairs, Olivia was surprised when Gabriel came into her bedroom. They didn't have the kind of sibling relationship where they sat around chatting. She assumed that he wanted to gossip to her about Franny, but instead he headed straight for the window, opened it, and started to climb out.

"What're you doing?" she asked tentatively. Even though he was her brother, Olivia found Gabriel slightly intimidating—but then again, she found most people intimidating.

"What does it look like I'm doing? Getting out of here."

Of course; that's why he'd come in. Her bedroom was on the second floor and outside the window, she had a flat roof next to an old oak tree: perfect for climbing down.

He held up a set of keys. "I'm planning to liberate the Mustang and go meet some people. Want to come?"

It was typical of Gabriel. He was always out and about. He made friends easily, and wherever they were, he could always find someone to hang out with. To Olivia's frustration, she was very different. She was shy around people and found it hard to open up. As children they'd played together a lot, seeking comfort in each other in the face of their father's lack of interest. But since they'd become teenagers, Gabriel had been off doing his own thing a lot. This invitation was an unexpected treat. But although Olivia would have loved to have gone with him, she didn't dare.

"I'd better not," she said with regret.

He shrugged. "Your loss." He was halfway outside when he turned back. "Oh, just make sure to leave the window open a bit before you go to sleep."

"Why?"

"So that I can climb back in later, stupid."

With that, he was gone, leaving Olivia alone. It was something she was used to. At school she was known as a loner. She pretended to be happy with her own company, but secretly she wished that she were more like her outgoing brother—or her father's fiancée, the movie actress Frances Fitzgerald. She was so beautiful, confident, and glamorous—everything that Olivia was not.

Sighing deeply, the girl went over to her dressing table and opened the top drawer. There, hidden within the pages of her diary, was a picture of her mother. She had to keep it secret, as her father had taken down all reminders of his wife after she died. Looking at the picture, she could see why he hated seeing her so much: the resemblance between her and her mother was uncanny. Unfortunately, there was nothing she could do about that. As with most things in her life, Olivia had no say in the matter.

Aside from dealing with Max's decidedly standoffish children, Franny had her own daughter to worry about. She kept meaning to tell her fiancé about Cara. But somehow she was never quite sure how to broach the subject. She'd rehearse what she was going to say in her head, but nothing ever sounded quite right. What would he think of her, she wondered, for hiding her child for so long? It made her seem, well, somewhat callous. What if he was never able to look at her in the same way again? What if he called off the wedding?

And then *The Black Rose* finally came out, to bad reviews and even worse box-office numbers. Franny had hoped it would be her break-through role, but her performance was labeled as "unconvincing."

A couple of weeks later, Lloyd summoned Franny into his office to say that filming on *Elizabeth* had been postponed. Although he assured her that it had nothing to do with *The Black Rose*—"we still have every faith in you"—Franny couldn't help feeling that professionally she had suffered a bit of a setback.

In light of that, her marriage to Max couldn't have come at a better time. The papers loved the story, so it was keeping her in the news, and it provided a face-saving excuse for why she wouldn't be filming that summer: "Maybe it sounds old-fashioned, but I take my responsibilities as a bride and a wife very seriously," she told the delighted Dolores Kent. "For the time being, I want to concentrate on looking after my husband. My career comes second to him."

And given everything that had happened, Franny decided it would be best to wait until after they were married to reveal the truth about Cara and her past to Max. After all, she didn't want to risk ruining their wedding.

The wedding took place on June 3, 1957, less than four months after that night in the Cocoanut Grove. The day itself was everything that Franny had dreamed it would be—a fairy-tale wedding, notable for its adherence to tradition. The service was held at the Good Shepherd Church in Beverly Hills, a full Catholic Mass as the bride was a devout attendee. Franny herself was a storybook bride: she wore a Cinderella-style gown of raw silk, hand-embroidered with thousands of seed pearls, and a full-length veil. Perhaps the effect was a little more virginal than she would have liked, but it was what her fans—more than a thousand of whom gathered outside the church to wish the newlyweds well—expected.

Eight bridesmaids were in attendance—all blond and so perfectly proportioned that they could have come straight out of Central Casting—and they wore ballet-length dresses of dusky pink. Franny's bouquet of tea roses matched the color perfectly, as did the six-tier strawberry-frosted wedding cake. A reception for six hundred guests was held at the Bel-Air Hotel, like that of Elizabeth Taylor and Nicky Hilton had been seven years earlier.

The reception ended by six in the evening, and the newlyweds waved good-bye to their guests, Franny having changed into her going-away outfit—a beautiful baby-blue silk suit—before setting off for their honeymoon. Because of Max's work, he'd been able to take only a few days off, so instead of going on an extended trip to Europe, he had suggested that they spend a few days alone together at his other home, Stanhope Castle.

Stanhope Castle was located in the heart of the Big Sur, a beautiful but sparsely populated region of the central California coast. Max had been keen for Franny to see it for months, but their schedules hadn't allowed time for the trip. A five-hour drive from Los Angeles along Highway 1, it might as well have been another world: the terrain was rough and untamed, a hundred miles of rugged cliffs, rocky coves, and crashing surf. There were no large towns in the area. Hearing that, Franny wasn't sure it was going to be her kind of place. She supposed it would be fine for a second home—somewhere they could go out to on the odd weekend.

On the long drive, Max told Franny all about the history of Stanhope Castle. He had purchased 30,000 acres of land back in 1938 and had spent a year working with a Paris-trained architect, Julia Morgan, who had designed William Hearst's Hearst Castle in San Simeon, a little farther along the coast. Like the latter, Stanhope Castle had been built in a medieval-Gothic style, Max explained. To Franny, it looked like a huge cathedral—in fact, its weathered dark gray stone turrets, decorated with carved gargoyles, reminded her of pictures she had seen of Notre Dame in Paris.

Max was obviously immensely proud of Stanhope Castle. He took great delight in telling Franny details about the estate. As they drove along the winding road that led out to the house, he told her that sometimes at high tide, the track was completely covered in water.

Franny was fascinated and a little horrified. "It must feel very isolated."

He gave her a brief smile. "That's what I like about it."

"But doesn't that worry you?" she pressed. "Being stranded out here?"

"If the tide comes in, it will always go out again. It's just a question of waiting."

Franny thought that sounded somewhat tiresome, but she decided to keep her feelings to herself.

It was midnight by the time they reached the castle. The staff had been informed of their arrival, so lights shone through the narrow slits of windows. Flaming torches lit the long driveway to the main house. As it was so late, there was no time to explore—"We'll do that tomorrow," Max said. But even just seeing the main building, Franny could get a feel for the vastness of the estate.

They were greeted in the hallway by Max's housekeeper, a reed-thin, stone-faced spinster named Hilda, who looked a little like one of the gargoyles carved into the parapets. She was about forty but looked older—her high-necked gray wool dress wasn't doing her any favors. She greeted Franny with a practiced formality.

"Welcome to your new home, Mrs. Stanhope." She bowed her head a little. "I hope you'll be very happy here."

Franny murmured her thanks. She felt somewhat overwhelmed by her new surroundings. Luckily, Max took control. Taking her hand, he said, "I think a drink is in order, don't you, darling?" She nodded gratefully.

As Max led her through the castle, Franny could see that the rooms were huge and had high ceilings and the walls and floors were made out of stone, giving a permanent chill to the place, even though it was summer now. The decor was sumptuous, all tapestry wall hangings and thick animal-skin rugs; the furnishings were much the same, with lots of intricately carved dark wood and gold candelabras.

Hilda followed the newlyweds through to one of the reception rooms and poured a glass of brandy for each of them. Franny took it gratefully. The rest of the staff were waiting downstairs for instructions, the housekeeper informed them. She was happy to assist in any way they needed.

"I presumed you'd want to dine after the long journey," she said. "Cook's preparing duck."

Franny's heart sank. It seemed they would have to put up with the stern-faced woman for another hour or so at least. But Max must

have sensed her feelings. "Thank you, but dinner won't be necessary," he said, his eyes fixed on his bride. "I would like to be alone
with my wife now. After all, I believe it's traditional on the wedding
night."

Hilda flushed at the implication and dropped her eyes. "Yes, of
course. I understand. Good night to you both," she murmured, withdrawing from the room. "And again, let me offer my congratulations."

"Well, that was rather rude of you," Franny teased after the housekeeper's footsteps had faded.

"Would you have rather she stayed?" Max challenged.

Instead of waiting for Franny's answer, he walked over and took the
glass from her hand, setting it down on the nearby occasional table.
Reaching up, he unfastened the grip that held her chignon in place.
Franny shook her long red hair out around her shoulders. Max nodded
approvingly. "That's better."

Then he bent his head and kissed her. As the kiss deepened, she felt
all her earlier misgivings about the somewhat isolated, creepy castle
slip away. His lips grazed her neck, his fingers opening her jacket and
pushing it back to expose her collarbone. His mouth moved to the tender flesh, and she squirmed and gasped against him.

Sensing her reaction, he drew back from her a little. Before she had
time to protest, he bent and scooped her up in his arms.

"Max!" she protested. "What on earth do you think you're doing?"

He looked down at her with amusement. "Didn't you mention once
that this was a fantasy of yours?"

At first she didn't understand what he meant. Then, as he carried
her out into the hallway and up the sweeping staircase, it clicked: he
was re-creating the scene when the drunk and frustrated Rhett Butler
takes Scarlett O'Hara to bed in *Gone with the Wind*.

She laughed delightedly. "You remembered!"

"Of course." He looked down at her in all seriousness. "I told you
before—I'll do whatever it takes to make you happy."

By then they had reached what she assumed to be his suite. Instead
of putting her down, he pushed the door open with his shoulder. Inside, the decor was rich and magnificent, the space dominated by a
huge canopied bed. Dozens of candles had been placed around the
room, so that the lighting was soft and romantic, quivering flames
casting shadows across the walls. Over on the bed, red rose petals had

been laid across the cream top sheet, spaced evenly apart, in exact symmetry, to form a perfect heart. It must have taken ages for the staff to prepare—under Max's orders, of course.

"Oh, it's so beautiful!" Franny gasped, her arms tightening around his neck.

"I'm glad it meets with your approval," her new husband replied.

And with that he kicked the bedroom door closed.

21

When Cara read about her mother's marriage, she felt almost relieved. She had been waiting for something like this—Franny's next excuse for not being able to come back for her, knowing that it was inevitable. Now that the worst had happened, she could finally accept it and stop hoping, in the knowledge that she had been abandoned here forever.

Not that her mother admitted as much, not even in this letter. The usual excuses were still there: "The wedding was so spontaneous that I had no time to sit Max down and tell him about you," along with the accompanying assurances: "As soon as things are more settled, I shall talk to him. Rest in no doubt that we will send for you then, without delay!" But at ten Cara was too old for fairy stories. It crossed the girl's mind to wonder if her mother believed the web of lies that she regularly spun. Probably, she decided. Franny never intended to do anything harmful—it was just that her actions were so thoughtless that they often caused pain to others without her even realizing.

So, with that very grown-up understanding, Cara tucked the letter under her bed, along with the others, and penned a suitably thoughtful and bland "congratulations" letter back. She then resolved not to think about it any longer.

There was another good reason why she didn't dwell on the news for too long—because there was a far more pressing problem at hand: clearly something was very wrong with her grandmother.

*　　　*　　　*

Cara would be the first to admit that Theresa had always been a little odd. But lately she was acting even stranger than usual. It had started a few weeks after they'd returned from England. Cara had spent the afternoon tending the little vegetable patch. As she entered the kitchen, the yeasty odor of baking bread came wafting toward her. Theresa, bent over the stove, looked up. "Ah, there you are, Franny. I was wondering where you'd got to."

It wasn't the first time Theresa had mixed up the names of her daughter and granddaughter. As always, Cara answered patiently, "It's not Franny. I'm Cara. Remember?"

Usually it would take just this one simple correction to jog her grandmother's memory. But this time, instead of righting herself, her grandmother frowned. "What's this, child? Some new, wicked game of yours?"

"No, of course not—"

But Theresa cut her off. "Well, you can stop it right now, I tell you. Go and get your father and Maggie in for their tea."

Cara stared at her, uncertain of what was happening.

"Well?" Theresa said. "Don't just stand there gawping at me, girl. Get a move on with you."

"But I don't know who you're talking about," Cara said helplessly. "There's no one here but us."

It was the wrong thing to say. Theresa crossed the room in two strides, raising her hand as she did so. Cara let out a yelp as the blow struck.

"Enough of your cheek!" Theresa's eyes blazed with anger. "There'll be no supper for you tonight, Frances Healey. Instead you can go to your room and think on what you've done."

Deciding there was no point trying to reason with her nan, Cara went upstairs, rubbing her bottom as she went. Whatever had happened to make Granny forget her name, one thing was for sure: she still remembered how to hit.

"Do you need some help in there, Mam?" Maggie called from the parlor. "Mam? Did you hear me?"

Maggie waited a moment, but there was still no response. Sighing, she went through to the kitchen, where her mother was meant to be making tea. Instead, Theresa was standing by the sink, staring absently out of the window. Maggie walked over and put a hand on her mother's arm. "Mam? Are you all right?"

At that Theresa turned to look at her daughter, but there seemed to be no recognition in her eyes. Maggie frowned, unsure how worried she should be. Her mother had always been somewhat eccentric, and living alone these past few years she seemed to have gotten a little housebound, never wanting to leave the cottage, even for a night. They would ask her over for Christmas and Easter, and she would agree at first but then make some excuse at the last minute and end up not coming. It seemed a little strange that she never wanted to see her family, but she was old and stuck in her ways, Maggie always reasoned.

But lately her mother's strange behavior had seemed to be more than simple eccentricity. Whenever Maggie saw her, Theresa appeared strangely absent. Maggie had first noticed it on one of her visits a few months earlier. She'd talked it over with her husband, Conrad, and it had been agreed that she would come to see her mother more often, to keep a closer eye on her. Then, if things really got worse, they could deal with it.

Seeing Theresa looking so vacant now, Maggie wondered if the time had come for her to take action. But then, glancing around the kitchen, it occurred to her that perhaps she was overreacting. Though her mother might be a little off these days, she still seemed perfectly able to look after herself. The house was spotless, if a little shabby, and there were sandwiches and cake sitting on the kitchen table, all freshly prepared today. Theresa herself looked clean and well fed. If she'd really been losing her mind, surely there would be some more outward signs?

It suited Maggie to think that way. Because the only alternative was for her mother to come to live with her, and she wasn't in any hurry for that to happen.

As Maggie went to put the kettle on, there was a creak from the floorboards upstairs. Instinctively, she looked up.

"What's that?" she asked.

Theresa seemed not to have heard. Maggie listened out for a moment, but everything had gone quiet. It was probably just the cat, she decided, and went back to making the tea.

*   *   *

An hour later, Cara finally heard the woman leave. She breathed a sigh of relief. Most times, she tried to be out when Theresa's daughter came round. But today it was too cold, so she'd hidden upstairs, trying to stay quiet. Her grandmother had warned her when she'd first come to stay that it was imperative that Maggie never find out that she was here. It seemed they had gotten away with it for another time. Cara just hoped their luck didn't run out.

22

Franny dozed contentedly in the comfort of the four-poster bed, reveling in the delicious feeling of having nothing to get up for. Stretching languidly, she rolled over onto her back, the cool silk sheets tangling around her naked limbs. A stream of light chinked through the heavy drapes, just enough to illuminate the grandfather clock that stood across the room: it was nearly midday.

With a soft sigh, Franny pushed back the covers. Slipping from the bed, she pulled on her ivory satin robe and padded across the room to the French windows, which led out onto the forty-foot terrace that ran the length of Max's suite of rooms—*their* suite, Franny quickly corrected herself. She wasn't at all surprised to find her husband sitting outside, reading a copy of *The Wall Street Journal*.

Hearing her step out onto the terrace, Max looked up from his paper and smiled.

"Good morning, sleepyhead." Getting up, he walked over to Franny and kissed her, before giving a pointed look at his watch. "I was beginning to think I'd married Rip Van Winkle."

Franny laughed. "Remember, darling, I *am* an actress: I *need* my beauty sleep."

His hand reached up to touch her cheek. "That's one thing you don't need."

Franny thrilled under his words. Max had been like this every morning since they'd gotten here: sweet, attentive and loving. This was how they'd started every day: breakfasting on the terrace, drinking Buck's Fizz to toast the start of their married life. These past four days at Stanhope Castle had been magical. Franny had been well off as an actress, but not rich in the way that Max was. This was wealth on a scale that most people couldn't even dream of. There was an army of staff, with maids to do everything. It seemed amazing to Franny that in a few short years, she had gone from cleaning up after other people to becoming the mistress of the house.

And what a house it was!

The morning after their wedding night, Max had taken Franny on a tour of Stanhope Castle. With more than a hundred lavishly furnished rooms in the main building alone, it was like exploring a museum. It was all about excess, a demonstration of wealth: from the bowling alley to the fifty-seat cinema to the series of Roman-style plunge pools in the basement. The grounds were equally impressive: a hundred acres of flower beds, fruit trees, and fountains, a veritable Garden of Eden. Alongside the main castle, there were four guesthouses scattered throughout the grounds, mansions in their own right.

The tour took four hours, and they still hadn't seen even a quarter of the estate. With lunch about to be served, Max had insisted on showing his new wife one last room before they sat down to eat. He took her up to the fourth floor, where there was a door that led to a spiral staircase. It was a steep climb, but finally they reached a lookout post at the top of the house. It had been part of the old lighthouse that had once stood there, Max explained. He'd asked the architect to incorporate it into the design of the house.

Max and Franny lingered there for a long moment in the little room with its glass walls and ceiling, looking out across the vast ocean. And then Max said, "This is where it happened."

Franny felt a chill pass over her. She had a feeling that she knew exactly what he meant, but she needed to ask anyway. "What do you mean?" she asked nervously. "What happened here?"

"This is where Eleanor climbed over the railings and jumped to her death."

The words were said almost matter-of-factly, which Franny supposed was only to be expected when talking about a tragedy that had happened well over a decade ago. She was still trying to think up an appropriate response when Max turned and walked out of the room.

Franny stared down at the waves breaking on the black rocks below and thought of what it must be like to feel so desperate that *that* seemed to be the only way out. An involuntary shiver ran through her body. It was almost a relief when Max called back to her, "Are you coming?"

She forced herself to look away. "I'll be right there."

She'd hurried from the room, thinking how little she still knew about the man she'd married. It had been the one blight on an otherwise perfect four days.

"Hungry?" Max asked now, interrupting the memory.

Franny was pleased to have her attention diverted. "Starving," she told him.

Max turned back to the wrought-iron table, where there were a pot of coffee, fresh orange juice, and a bowl of fruit. Reaching down, he plucked the biggest strawberry from the dish.

"Here." Holding on to the stalk, he fed the strawberry to her. As she bit into it, some of the red juice escaped from the side of her mouth. Reaching up, he wiped it tenderly away with his thumb.

"So what else takes your fancy this morning?" he asked. "Eggs? Pancakes? Waffles?"

"Um . . ." Franny hesitated for a moment. He had a cook on standby, and she only needed to mention a dish and it would magically appear within twenty minutes.

"Don't take too long to decide," he chided gently. "The children will be here soon, so I guess you'll want some time to get ready."

At that, Franny felt her heart sink. It was four days since their wedding, and Max's children were due to join them at the house that morning. She had tried to befriend them in the lead-up to the wedding, but her overtures had been continually rebuffed. She sensed that Olivia was a little more open to getting to know her, but whenever Franny tried to talk to her, Gabriel would appear and find some way to intervene. It was all horribly frustrating, but she was prepared to make an effort because she knew how important it was to Max. Plus, at the back of her mind, she kept thinking that if she got along with his children, surely it would be easier for him to accept Cara into his household, too.

"Oh, yes! It'll be wonderful to see Olivia and Gabriel again," she said with forced enthusiasm. "And of course I want to look my best for them." But even as she said the words, she knew that she wasn't quite ready for the honeymoon to end. So loosening the ties of her robe, she said huskily, "But let's skip breakfast. I think it's more important that we make the most of these last moments alone together. Don't you?"

Max didn't need any further invitation.

Gabriel's scowl deepened as the chauffeur pulled the Lincoln through the gates of Stanhope Castle. Max's son had insisted on setting off early from L.A. that morning, wanting to make the journey before the midday heat kicked in. He hadn't spoken to his sister much along the way, preferring instead to entertain his own dark thoughts. Now, as the car stopped in the driveway, Gabriel glanced up at the house and spotted his father and stepmother up on the balcony, locked in a clinch. Even from this distance, he could see his father's hand disappearing beneath the folds of Franny's robe. Gabriel nudged his sister.

"Looks like our dear stepmother is working hard to earn her keep," he said dryly.

Olivia followed his gaze. "Gabriel!" she scolded as she caught his meaning. Unlike her brother, she couldn't find it in her to hate their new stepmother. "I thought you promised to at least *try* to get along with her."

Gabriel snorted in reply. Throwing the car door open, he got out. It wasn't that he disliked Franny, exactly. He just didn't particularly want her in their lives. When he'd pictured what his stepmother would look like, it certainly wasn't this young, beautiful creature, who was closer to his age than his father's. He was tired of hearing his friends' lewd jokes about her and of how uncomfortable he felt whenever she was around. And though he understood that none of that was her fault, it was easier to direct his anger at her than the person he considered to be the real villain of the piece—his father.

He held out his hand to help Olivia out of the car. Seeing her downcast look, he suddenly felt bad. His sister was such a sweet, gentle person—very delicate and ladylike, almost in an old-fashioned way. So different from the fast girls he usually hung out with. She was so uncomplaining that sometimes he had to remind himself that this was even harder on her than him, and as the eldest, he should be trying to make things a little easier for her. After years of neglecting Olivia, maybe it was time to be a good brother.

Gabriel forced a smile. "Come on, squirt." He picked up her case. "Let's get you settled in your room."

Franny was right to be apprehensive about seeing Max's children again. Her new husband had organized for them all to sit down to a formal lunch in the refectory, Stanhope Castle's imposing dining hall, which came complete with tapestries on the wall and a long dining table decorated with silver candelabras. Four places were set at one end, and they sat there as a maid served them course after course, hovering to one side while they ate. Franny found the formality a little uncomfortable, but that was nothing compared to the awkwardness around the table. It was as bad as the first dinner in Max's Holmby Hills mansion, with Gabriel taking every opportunity to make snide remarks while Olivia just sat quietly, hardly saying a word unless asked a direct question.

It was a relief to Franny when Gabriel and Olivia went off to their rooms and she was finally alone with Max. But unfortunately that wasn't the end of the unpleasantness. Swept up in the wedding, they had had little time to discuss the finer details of what their life would be like once they were married. Franny was therefore more than a little surprised when, during their stroll through the grounds that afternoon, Max asked when the rest of her belongings were going to be delivered.

"Delivered *here*?" Franny asked. It had suddenly dawned on her that Max intended for them to reside full-time at Stanhope Castle. "But I thought we'd be living in Holmby Hills?"

"That would mean too much commuting for me," he told her. "I divide my time mostly between L.A. and San Francisco. Stanhope Castle is between the two places." Max must have seen the horrified look on his wife's face because he said, "That is all right, isn't it, darling?"

In fact, Franny couldn't think of anything worse than living in this isolated place all the time. But she didn't want to object now and ruin their first few days of marriage. She was sure it was something she could twist Max's arm about later.

"Of course it's fine." She forced a smile. "I just hadn't given it much thought, that's all. But you're right, living here does sound like the most sensible idea."

Max was due back at his office in San Francisco the following day.

With no movie roles on the horizon, Franny had decided to officially take a three-month break from work, to settle into married life. But without Max around, she wasn't sure what she'd do with her time. The household pretty much ran itself under the watchful eye of Hilda.

"I have no idea how I'll keep myself amused," she confessed to Max as they got ready for bed that evening.

"Perhaps it'll be a good chance for you to get to know Olivia and Gabriel," he suggested.

He was right, Franny admitted to herself, as she drifted off to sleep. It was the school holidays and they would be living at Stanhope Castle until the fall. It was an excellent opportunity to bond with them.

So the next morning, Franny made sure to be up in time to have breakfast with her stepchildren. They were already in the breakfast room, a large conservatory at the back of the house that caught the sun in the morning, when she got downstairs. Their conversation stopped as she walked in the room.

"Good morning, you two," she greeted them cheerfully, determined to ignore the awkwardness. "I slept so well last night. Must be because it's so quiet out here."

She was rewarded with silence. The only sound was Gabriel continuing to noisily eat the plate of ham and eggs in front of him, occasionally slurping at his black coffee, while Olivia stared unhappily at her half-finished bowl of cereal.

But Franny refused to be put off. They were part of a family now, whether they liked it or not. So she walked over to the platters of fresh fruit and pastries that had been left out on the side and began to help herself. This was her house as much as theirs, and it was about time Gabriel realized that. With a full plate and a glass of fresh orange juice, she walked over to the table and sat down.

"Well, this all looks lovely, doesn't it?" Franny said. Olivia looked up briefly and rewarded her with a small smile. A glare from Gabriel made the girl drop her gaze quickly, but it was enough to encourage Franny. "So do you have any plans for the day?" she persevered. "If not, perhaps we could go for a drive somewhere? Your father said the surrounding area is lovely. Maybe you could show me some of your favorite places—"

"Sorry. Can't." Gabriel was curt. "I'm meeting some of the guys from school."

"Oh." Franny wasn't exactly surprised by his reaction, but she was a little disappointed. "I see." She turned to Olivia. "And what about you, sweetheart? Do you have plans?"

"Olivia's coming with me," Gabriel answered before his sister had a chance to speak. "We agreed on this last night, didn't we, sis?" He turned to Olivia, who was chewing at her lip.

"Yes, that's right," she said apologetically, unable to meet her step-mother's eye.

Franny guessed it was a lie. She suspected Gabriel hadn't intended to take Olivia with him today and was just doing it to spite her. She also had a feeling that Olivia would have happily spent the day with her but that her first loyalty was to her brother.

"Of course," Franny said, not wanting to upset the obviously fragile girl. "I understand."

"It seems so mean to leave her here all alone."

It was an hour later, and Olivia was feeling awful about what had happened at breakfast. Franny had only been trying to be friendly—it seemed unfair to abandon her like this.

"Don't worry about it," Gabriel said. "I'm sure she's forgotten it al-ready."

"Perhaps." Olivia was doubtful about her brother's assessment of the situation.

Gabriel gave an exasperated sigh. "Oh, for God's sake, I don't have time for your conscience. We're already late as it is. If you'd rather stay here with our dear stepmother, then just say. I won't mind."

It was said in a way that let Olivia know that he would mind very much. She was torn. She knew the right thing to do would be to go and see Franny, but she also knew it would annoy her brother. She had been looking forward to today, and she didn't want Gabriel going off without her. He usually didn't invite her along to spend time with his friends, but since their father had announced his marriage to Franny, he seemed to be attempting to include her more. She wasn't sure whether it was because they were both getting older, so he was finding her less irritating, or if he was just doing it to spite their stepmother. But whatever the reason, she didn't want to do anything to jeopardize their new relationship.

"I guess you're right," Olivia said reluctantly. "Let's get going."

She knew very little about the plan for the day, apart from that they were meeting some of his friends at the beach. They drove along Highway 1 in the direction of San Francisco for about forty minutes, before Gabriel slowed his Mustang down and pulled over onto a patch of gravel. Apart from two other cars parked there, it seemed to Olivia that they were in the middle of nowhere.

"Where are we?" she asked.

"You'll see," Gabriel said mysteriously.

They got out of the car and walked to the edge of the cliff, and it was only then that Olivia saw the secluded cove below. Gabriel's friends— two girls and two boys—were already there, lounging under giant pink-and-white-striped umbrellas.

"How did they get down there?" Olivia wanted to know. There didn't seem to be any obvious path.

"This way."

She followed Gabriel through some bushes to a makeshift trail cut out of the rock face. It was steep in places, and the stones were covered with slippery moss. Gabriel, who'd obviously done the walk hundreds of times, took the lead and carried their bags down, while Olivia went more carefully. But finally they reached the beach.

Gabriel's friends ran over to greet them. "You made it, buddy!" one of the guys greeted him, slapping him on the back.

He was a tall, muscular young man, with dark hair and eyes. Gabriel introduced him as Teddy. Then there was the more studious-looking Brett, who had sandy hair, a wiry build, and glasses. The two girls were named Trudy and April, both blond and bouncy in their polka-dot bikinis.

Olivia hung back, feeling shy and very young. She wasn't even used to hanging out with people of her own age, and they were all at least two years older.

"I'm baking," Trudy, the prettier of the girls, said. "Let's go for a dip." Her words might have been to the whole group, but her eyes were on Gabriel.

"Sure! I'm in!" April said, taking her hand.

The two girls ran off toward the sea, leaving Olivia with the three guys.

"You up for a swim?" Gabriel asked his sister.

"I didn't bring a bathing suit," she said apologetically.

"Don't let that stop you," Teddy said with a wink.

Gabriel punched him on the shoulder. "Hey! That's my sister."

"Sorry," Teddy apologized. He looked over at where the girls were splashing in the water. "Why don't I go over there and cool off?"

He ran off then. Olivia could see her brother staring enviously after him.

"Don't worry about me," she said. She reached into her bag and pulled out a book. "I'm happy to read."

Gabriel hesitated, not sure what to do for the best. He knew how sensitive Olivia could be, and he didn't want to leave her here alone.

Brett must have sensed his dilemma. "You go," he piped up. "I'll stay here and entertain Olivia."

Gabriel looked between his sister and Trudy, who was calling out to him from the water. He didn't like the idea of abandoning Olivia, but if Brett said he was happy to look after her . . . there were certain friends of his whom he wouldn't have dreamed of leaving alone with his little sister—Teddy, for one—but Brett was a good guy. She'd be safe here with him.

"Well, if you're sure . . ." he said to Olivia.

"I'll be fine," she assured him, not wanting to ruin his day.

He didn't need any further encouragement. She watched him run off toward the sea, swimming out to join the others. Trudy squealed delightedly as he came up behind her and dragged her down into the water, and soon the foursome were splashing and play-fighting, and challenging one another to races up and down the coastline.

Olivia and Brett walked over to where the group had set up their umbrellas. She sat down on the blanket, and he followed suit. Another scream of delight came from the water, and they both looked over.

"You can go join them if you want," Olivia told him. "Don't feel obliged to babysit me."

"It's not an obligation, it's a pleasure," he said gallantly. He nodded at her book. "What's that you're reading?"

"Oh, it's a Victoria Holt novel. Just a romance. But she writes historical books as well," Olivia added, not wanting him to think she only read trash, "under the name Jean Plaidy."

"Oh, right." He lay down on his side, propped up on one hand, and looked up at her. "Do you like history, then?"

The question surprised her, as did his level of interest. "Yes, I do."

"What period?"

As Olivia started to tell him, she was surprised at how easy it was to talk to this person she hadn't even known half an hour earlier. The day was turning out better than she'd expected.

After her stepchildren had left, Franny busied herself writing thank-you notes for the wedding gifts. By one, she had written only ten, and was already bored with the whole process. Hilda, the housekeeper, with an impeccable sense of timing, came to ask what she'd like for lunch. Even though Franny wasn't especially hungry, she ordered food anyway—it gave her something to do at least.

Unable to face writing any more thank-you notes, she spent her afternoon exploring the grounds, before swimming fifty laps in the Olympic-sized outdoor pool. Back in her room by four, she slept for two hours. Waking, she was excited to see that it was nearly six—Max should be home soon. Now, with renewed purpose, she began to rush around, preparing for his return. She washed and styled her hair, picked out a striking cocktail dress. By seven, she was seated in the library enjoying a vodka martini, listening for his arrival.

Hilda came in at half past seven. "I just wanted to check—what time would you like dinner to be served, Mrs. Stanhope?"

"I'll wait until Max gets home," Franny said airily.

The housekeeper looked surprised. "Perhaps it would be better for you to have your meal now. Mr. Stanhope may be some time. He often works very late."

Franny bristled. She didn't like being told what to do by this super-cilious woman. "I told you, I'd prefer to wait," she said firmly.

"Very good, Mrs. Stanhope," the housekeeper murmured. If Hilda was irritated by Franny's snappy tone, she didn't show it. Instead, she quietly withdrew. As soon as she'd gone, Franny went to fix herself another drink.

Gabriel and Olivia returned around eight, laughing and talking as they came through the door. They said a quick hello to Franny, explained that they'd already eaten, and went off to their rooms, leaving her alone to wait.

It was nearly midnight by the time Max got home. Hearing his car, Franny ran down to the hall to greet him, throwing herself into his arms.

"Oh, darling, I missed you!" she said, aware that she was more than a little tipsy. She'd given in at ten and eaten the lukewarm meal, but the food hadn't even begun to soak up the four vodka martinis that she'd drunk.

"Me, too." He hugged her briefly, before pulling away. He looked tired, she saw. Well, he would, of course, having been out since six that morning. With the two-hour drive each way into San Francisco, he'd spent fourteen hours working and four hours traveling, she calculated.

To Franny's disappointment, he was so exhausted that he wanted to go straight to bed.

"Is it always like this?" she asked as they lay together in the darkness. But Max didn't answer. He was already asleep.

23

"Who are you? What are you doing in my house?"

Theresa's eyes were wide and frightened; she had a poker in her hand. Cara eyed it warily. Her grandmother had been getting worse lately, her mounting frustration at her condition making her violent.

Cara smiled gently, trying to show that she meant no harm. "I'm a friend of your daughter's . . . of Franny's." She'd quickly learned that there was no reasoning with her grandmother when she was in this state. At first Cara had tried, patiently explaining to her grandmother who she was and how they were related. But when Theresa was having one of these episodes, it was impossible for her to see anything clearly.

Theresa looked with suspicion at the girl in front of her. "I don't believe you. If you're a friend of Franny's, then where is she?" Cara had no idea what to say. Taking her silence as an admission of guilt, Theresa snorted. "Trying to rob the place, are you? Well, you won't get past me." Brandishing the poker, she stabbed at her granddaughter. Luckily Cara had been keeping an eye on the makeshift weapon as they talked, so she was able to step out of the way in time, and it grazed her harmlessly.

It's not her fault, Cara reminded herself. She doesn't mean any of this. She held out her hands to take the poker.

"Please, Granny. Give it to me, and then I'll make you a nice cup of tea."

Theresa stared at her for a long moment, and suddenly something seemed to change. She looked down at the poker that she was holding. "Why do I have this?" she asked wonderingly. Then she let the poker drop to the ground.

Relief coursed through Cara. Disaster had been averted—for now, at least.

24

The first month of marriage was more difficult than Franny had imagined it would be. Max was either at the office or away on business, which meant she rarely got to see him, making it hard to find an appropriate time to tell him about Cara. Gabriel and Olivia spent most of the time out of the house, too, seeing friends—which left her alone and feeling strangely useless. Her attempts to befriend Max's children had met with no success, mainly because her stepson continued to resist her overtures. So when one morning at breakfast Franny learned that her stepdaughter was going to turn sixteen that August, she knew that it was the perfect opportunity to get to know the girl better, while also giving her something to occupy her time.

"You must let me throw a party for you," she declared.

"A party?" Her stepdaughter tested the unfamiliar word out. "Where? Here?"

"Would you like that?"

"Yes, of course." The girl's enthusiasm was palpable, but then her eyes clouded over. "Except . . ."

"Except what?"

"I don't think father will like the idea."

"She's right, you know." Gabriel's voice came from the doorway.

Damn, Franny thought. She'd hoped to have the conversation before he came downstairs. Turning, she found her stepson smirking at her.

"Oh?" She tried to sound unperturbed. "And why's that?"

"From what I hear, our father used to love entertaining here. But ever since our mother died, he hates having people round. Trust me," Gabriel said with authority. "He won't be pleased."

And you'd just love that, wouldn't you? Franny thought. But, not wanting her stepson to think that he'd won, she forced herself to appear unconcerned.

"Oh, what nonsense. It's his only daughter's Sweet Sixteenth. Of course he'll want to celebrate." Seeing the worried look on Olivia's face, Franny gave her hand a reassuring squeeze. "Don't worry—leave your father to me. You just start planning what to wear."

Gabriel shrugged. "Suit yourself. But remember—I did try to warn you."

Max was away in Geneva. When he called that night, Franny broached the idea to him. But it seemed that Gabriel was more attuned to his father's wishes than his new young wife was, because he told her in no uncertain terms that he didn't want her to organize any party.

"But why not?" Franny wanted to know.

"Because Olivia's a very private person. I don't think she'll enjoy being the center of attention for the night."

"But, Max!" Franny couldn't believe how disappointed she felt. "It's her sixteenth! Of course she should have a party to celebrate."

"That's hardly up to you to decide, is it?" Max sounded irritated. "Olivia is my daughter, and I really don't think it's a good idea."

"Oh, for heaven's sake," Franny said crossly. First he'd told her to connect with his children, and then, when she finally came up with a way to do that, he shot her down. "It's too late to back out, anyway. I've already promised that she could have the damned party, and it's not fair to let her down."

"Then perhaps you should have discussed it with me first."

There was a click on the end of the line. It took Franny a moment to realize that Max had hung up the phone on her.

Later he called back. They were both calmer then and equally contrite.

"I should never have interfered with your children," Franny rushed to say.

"No, it was my fault." Max sighed heavily. "And maybe you're right—we should go ahead with this party."

Franny was delighted. If this was a success, perhaps it would finally be the right time to tell him about Cara.

*   *   *

Franny threw herself into the preparations for the party. Olivia was due to turn sixteen on August 18, which gave her less than a month to plan everything. It was easy enough to hire caterers and a band for the night—the Stanhope name was enough to make anything available. But the guest list was a little more problematic. Olivia had frighteningly few friends. The list of names that she did put forward for invites was written in Gabriel's handwriting, which told Franny everything. Of course, it was easy enough to make up numbers. There were business acquaintances of Max's to invite, along with Juniper's executives and stars, to add some glamour to the night. And if it felt a little sad that most of the guests had never met Olivia before, Franny had to admit that the girl didn't seem to mind. She just seemed excited that a whole evening was being planned in her honor.

Franny tried to make the event as special as possible for her step-daughter. The week before the party, she took Olivia on a shopping trip to San Francisco. After a night in the Fairmont, they spent the next morning trying on dresses in the White House before lunching in the venerable department store's tearooms. As Franny sat watching Olivia happily tucking into an ice-cream dessert, she couldn't help wondering if she was making all this effort for Max's daughter because she wasn't able to do so for her own.

The thought of her Sweet Sixteenth filled Olivia with both excitement and tremulous uncertainty. As her father had said, usually she shied away from being the center of attention, but only because she felt awkward and unsure of herself. Secretly she'd always longed to be the kind of person who was popular, who could hold a crowd—as her brother Gabriel could. In the past, that had always seemed like the stuff of fantasies, but lately she thought that she was getting better at being around people, thanks largely to her brother.

Life for Olivia had improved immeasurably that summer. Although her father remained an elusive figure, she and Gabriel were getting on much better. Beneath the sarcasm and the air of ennui, her brother was really quite sweet. Since that day on the beach, he had taken to including her whenever he went out with his friends, and that had slowly helped build her confidence. And now a party was being held, in her honor—the single greatest and most terrifying event in her young life.

The night of her Sweet Sixteenth, Olivia spent hours getting ready. Franny had helped her pick out a dress for the occasion. It was beautiful, the loveliest thing Olivia had ever owned—a ballet-length gown made of layers of white lace, with little cap sleeves and a sweetheart neckline. She had never felt so pretty. And her stepmother had done an amazing job organizing the event. As it was summer, Franny had insisted on holding the party outside in the grounds of the castle. She'd found a pretty glade within the woodlands and transformed it into something out of *A Midsummer Night's Dream*. Fairy lights twinkled on the trees surrounding the clearing, a band played under a canopy, and there was a raised dance floor. That Franny had obviously put so much thought into the whole evening had endeared her even more to Olivia. The shopping trip in particular would always stick in her mind. It was the kind of thing she'd missed out on with her own mother.

Olivia was particularly excited about the evening because Gabriel's friend Brett was going to be there. She had seen him several times since that day at the beach, on other group outings or when he came to the house to see her brother. Most of Gabriel's friends showed no interest in her, but Brett was always so sweet, making an effort to talk to her and ask her opinions.

She was looking out for him that evening, and when he arrived— dateless, she noted with a little thrill of pleasure—he came straight up to her.

"Happy birthday!" He hugged her tight to him, then stepped back, holding out her hands, so he could get a good look at her. "You look great."

It was said in a brotherly way, almost an echo of what Gabriel had said to her earlier, but at least he'd complimented her, Olivia comforted herself.

Before she could respond, Franny came up to them, placing her arm around her stepdaughter's shoulder. "Darling! I just wanted to check that you're having a fabulous time?"

Olivia beamed up at her stepmother. "Yes, thank you, I am," she said, her mind on Brett.

Franny's gaze drifted around the party. "I think everything's perfect, don't you?" Then she looked over at Brett, noticing him for the first time. "Oh, hello there." She turned to Olivia. "Who's your friend, sweetheart?"

Olivia introduced Brett, explaining that he went to school with Gabriel. She didn't think her stepmother would be interested in talking to a teenage boy, but Franny was surprisingly gracious. "Ah," she said. "I think I've seen you around the house sometimes."

Brett nodded a vigorous agreement. "Yes, but we've never met before."

Franny's mouth twisted into a half smile. "Gabriel's no doubt been hiding me away from you. But it's lovely to finally meet."

Olivia was about to say something, but before she could, Brett said to Franny, "I'm such a big fan. I've seen every one of your movies."

Franny put a hand to her chest. "Oh, how wonderful. I never tire of hearing that."

Olivia looked between her stepmother and the boy she liked. Brett was hanging on Franny's every word, she realized. She might as well not have been there.

"I wonder . . ." Brett began and then stopped.

"What?" Franny prompted.

"Well, this may seem a little presumptuous—but would you like to dance?" He said the last part in a rush, as though embarrassed at making such a suggestion.

Franny's eyes sparkled mischievously, enjoying Brett's bashful overtures. "That sounds like a wonderful idea." She tucked her arm through his. "Come on, let's see what you're made of."

Franny was so busy trying to impress her young admirer that she didn't notice the look of distress on Olivia's face as she watched her stepmother walking off with the boy she'd planned to wow that evening.

Olivia had never felt so wretched as she did then. There was the boy she'd set her heart on, unable to keep his eyes off her stepmother. Suddenly the dress that she'd loved didn't seem so special—it felt young and silly, too girlish. How could she hope to compare with her glamorous stepmother? Her beautiful stepmother, who looked ravishing in a silvery gray satin gown, all womanly breasts and hips, while she, Olivia, looked like a little girl in white lace. It was small wonder Brett was enchanted by Franny, she thought bitterly as she watched them whirling around the dance floor. He whispered something to her stepmother, who threw back her head and laughed. Even her laugh was sexy: a deep, throaty sound. She had never looked better, her long, swanlike neck exposed, her rich red hair falling in soft waves down her back. That was it for Olivia. She turned and started to run.

Watching from over by the drinks table, Gabriel saw what had happened and cursed his thoughtless stepmother for the way she'd treated poor Olivia. He'd begun to thaw toward Franny over the past few weeks, seeing the effort that she was making for his sister. But this behavior tonight negated everything.

He caught sight of his father standing a few yards away, a glass of whiskey in hand, his gaze on Franny and Brett. Gabriel could only imagine how much it was annoying him, seeing his new wife all over some teenage boy. Other guests had spotted them too, and there was a ripple of gossip running through the party. Gabriel couldn't resist putting the boot in. Walking over to his father, he said, "Looks like you've been replaced by a younger model." He nodded over at Franny and Brett. "That didn't take long, did it?"

It had sounded so clever in his head, but as his father turned stone-cold eyes toward him, Gabriel suddenly wondered if he'd gone too far.

"I know I haven't always been the best father to you," Max said icily, "but that's no reason for you to insult my wife like that. I've seen the way you've treated her over the past few weeks, and I've let it go, because I know it's more about me than her. But I'd thank you to keep your vicious comments to yourself tonight. This evening is for your sister, not your petty vendettas." He drained his glass. "Now I'm getting back to the party. I'd suggest you do the same."

With that, he walked off, leaving Gabriel feeling somewhat ashamed.

Duke Carter wandered through the undergrowth, away from the other guests, loosening his bow tie as he went. He hated these parties, with the schmoozing and small talk, although no one would ever have guessed it, given that he was so good at both. But the truth was, he hadn't wanted to come tonight. He was only there because Lloyd had let him know that his attendance was *expected* by their chief investor. So he'd traipsed all the way out here to see the same faces and make the same conversation. His date, some stuck-up actress who seemed to think she was *it* after winning an Academy Award this year, was beginning to bug him, and he wanted to go home. But he guessed he'd better stick it out until midnight at least, so he'd decided to take a few moments' break instead.

As Duke made his way farther into the bushes, he spotted an old tree house. It seemed as good a place as any for a smoke. One cigarette and then he'd go back, he promised himself. He walked over and sat down on the third step, but as he reached for his lighter, he heard a noise coming from the tree house above. It sounded like crying. Part of him was tempted to walk away, but whatever was happening had to be more interesting than going back to the party, so he decided to investigate.

As he climbed the rest of the steps, the sounds got louder. It was definitely a female crying, he was sure of it now. "Hello!" he called out, not wanting to startle anyone. As he poked his head up through the trapdoor, he saw that he was right. A girl, Max's daughter, in fact, was sitting on the ground in a sea of white lace, her knees pulled up to her chin, sobbing her heart out.

Duke considered what to do. The girl was so caught up in her misery that she hadn't noticed him yet. He could slip away, and she'd be none the wiser. But even as the thought went through his head, Duke knew he wasn't about to leave. He may have met her only that evening—Olivia, wasn't that her name?—but the poor little thing looked so miserable that he couldn't just walk away. Duke had always been a sucker for a damsel in distress.

"Fancy some company, Birthday Girl?" he asked.

Olivia looked up, startled. She stared at him for a moment, and then, clearly embarrassed, turned her face away. "Thank you, but no," she sniffed. "I'd rather just be alone."

But Duke sensed she didn't mean it. So instead he climbed up and went to sit beside her, resting his back against the wooden wall of the tree house. "Well, you might not want company, but I do. So humor me for a little while—all right?"

She sniffed again. "All right," she gave in.

"Good." He reached into his pocket and pulled out a hankie. "Now, for God's sake, please blow your nose. I can't bear to hear your sniveling."

At that Olivia gave a weak smile.

"Ah-ha!" Duke said triumphantly. "So I got a smile out of you! Does that feel better?"

"Yes, thanks." She wiped her eyes and blew her nose and then looked at her rescuer properly for the first time, realizing only then that it was Duke Carter, the movie star. How embarrassing. She loved his pictures and had all his posters on her walls. She didn't want him to see her like this. "Please don't feel obliged to stay. I'm fine, honestly," she assured him, just wanting him to go away so she could forget the whole humiliating experience. "I'm feeling better, I promise."

But he seemed in no hurry to leave. "I'm glad," he said. "No one should be sad on their birthday, kiddo." He punched her arm playfully, and then he grew serious. "So do you want to tell me what upset you?"

Olivia's smile disappeared then. Her eyes dropped to her lap, and she began to pick at her lace dress. "Oh, I don't know."

"Tell me."

She hesitated, not wanting to burden him with her childish problems. But he sounded so sincerely interested, and it would be nice to have someone to talk to. "It was just this boy I like," she confessed.

"And he didn't like you back?"

"I thought he did. But then I introduced him to Franny, and well . . ." She stopped, unable to finish,

"He started paying her too much attention?" Duke filled in, guessing what had happened.

"Can you blame him? She looks amazing." Olivia sighed enviously. She could never work out how she felt about Franny. Part of her wanted to be just like her stepmother, and the other part hated her guts. "What would he want with boring old me? I'm a wallflower next to her." A sob caught in her throat as she said the last word. Her bottom lip trembled, and she felt the tears threatening again. She looked away.

"Hey, now. Let's have no more tears." Duke moved so that he was kneeling in front of her. Putting his hand under her chin, he tipped her face up so that she was forced to meet his gaze. "I can tell you this for a fact: you are by far the most beautiful woman here."

"You're just saying that," she said, shaking her head.

"No, I'm not." His eyes, for once, were serious. "Franny's an attractive woman, there's no doubt about that. But it's all manufactured: from the coiffed hair to the carefully applied makeup to the expensive dress. You have something far better: a sweet, natural beauty and a good soul. That's going to mean so much more in the long run. Trust me." He winked then. "I know a thing or two about women."

Olivia didn't know what to say. Part of her wanted to tell Duke that he was being stupid, that she could never measure up to her stepmother. But the other part of her could hear the sincerity in his voice and knew that he really believed what he was saying.

"You're being so nice to me." She met his gaze. "Thank you."

It was not often that Duke felt good about himself, but this was one of those rare moments. "That's quite all right," he told her. "It's your birthday, you shouldn't be sad today of all days. And don't waste any more time feeling upset about this boy. Give it a month or two, and you'll have forgotten all about him."

Olivia laughed. "You know, to be honest, I'm not even sure how much I really liked him," she admitted.

"Then why are you so upset?"

Feeling a little silly, she told him how she'd envisioned her evening: that she'd wanted just one dance with someone—and not her father or her brother but someone she could at least pretend had romantic feelings for her. "Now that'll never happen," she said in a small voice.

She'd half expected Duke to tease her. But instead he looked at her very solemnly and said, "Well, let's see what we can do about that."

He stood up then. Bowing from the waist, he said, "May I have the pleasure of this dance, Miss Olivia?"

Even though they were up in the tree house, they could hear the band playing, the music floating through the warm night sky. Duke took Olivia in his arms and began to waltz with her. There wasn't much room to move, but somehow that made it even more special, as though they were on their own private dance floor.

As Olivia closed her eyes and rested her head against Duke's shoulder, she decided that her stepmother was welcome to Brett: Duke Carter was a far better person to have her first dance with.

For some reason Franny couldn't quite understand, her stepdaughter's sixteenth birthday didn't bring her any closer to Max's children. In September, Olivia and Gabriel went back to their respective boarding schools, leaving her alone in the house. But instead of being relieved, Franny just felt more frustrated. The days seemed so long and lonely.

One morning in mid-October, waking to another empty day, Franny decided there was nothing for it: it was four months since the wedding, and she needed to get back to work. She called up Lloyd, without discussing it with Max first. The studio head seemed happy, if a little surprised, to hear from her.

"So how's married life?" Like everyone else, it was his first question.

"Oh, wonderful! Amazing, of course," Franny replied breezily. "But I was actually calling to find out if there've been any new developments on the Elizabeth project?"

There was a silence. Lloyd coughed uncomfortably. "Well, yes, we've decided to go ahead with making the movie—"

"That's great!"

But already she could tell from his hesitation that this wasn't the news she'd been hoping for.

"Uh, yes," he stuttered. "But, um, I have to tell you that we decided in the end to go with Edie Lincoln to play Elizabeth."

Franny was stunned. It took her a moment to recover. "Oh, right. I see. That's good," she said hurriedly. "I was actually only calling to say that I wouldn't be able to do it, anyway. What with being so busy now."

"Great—excellent. That's what I thought." Lloyd sounded relieved. "Obviously you were always our first choice . . ."

The conversation continued politely enough, but Franny got off the phone feeling hurt and dejected. She'd been gone mere weeks, and already she'd been replaced.

When Lily called an hour later, asking if she'd like to go out to Mocambo the next evening, Franny was surprised to find how eager she was to get back to the L.A. party scene.

Franny neglected to tell Max her plans. It wasn't that she planned to hide her outing from him, but he was staying the night in Chicago anyway, so it wasn't as though he would miss her. Franny set off just after breakfast the following day and drove herself down to L.A. She was there by early afternoon. It felt as though she were coming home. She planned to stay the night at Holmby Hills and had alerted the staff to prepare the house for her arrival. Sitting in front of the mirror that evening, getting ready for her night out on the town, Franny felt more like her old self.

The gang had arranged to meet at Musso & Frank. As a waiter escorted Franny to the table, she saw that everyone was already seated in their usual red leather booth—Lily, Helena, Emily, Duke, and Hunter. Hunter stood as she walked over.

"Long time no see," he drawled, his eyes raking over her. "We've missed you."

"Have you, now?" Franny had always been a flirt, and having a ring on her finger wasn't going to stop her doing something that came as naturally to her as breathing. She felt as if she'd been let off the leash for the night, and she was going to make the most of it. Now she held out her arms. "Well, why don't you get over here and show me how much?"

Hunter bent to kiss her on the cheek, but while he moved one way, Franny went the other, so that they ended up catching each other's lips instead.

"Ooops!" Franny pushed Hunter away, laughing. "Lucky Max isn't around to see that." She was so happy to be back with her friends that she never noticed the magazine photographer snapping away in the corner.

It was that very shot, of Franny and Hunter caught in a full kiss, that made the cover of *Celebrity* magazine the following week.

The night the magazine came out, Max wasn't home until late. Franny lay in bed, waiting for him to come up to their room, but he never did. Sometime along the way, she must have fallen asleep, because she woke to see that it was nearly three in the morning—and Max still wasn't there. Certain that he was somewhere in the house, she got up, pulled on her robe, and went to look for him. Sure enough, she found him in his study with a half-drunk bottle of whiskey and a copy of the magazine.

"Oh, Max," she whispered when she saw that he was staring at the picture of her and Hunter together.

He closed his eyes for a brief second, and when he opened them and looked up at her, she could see the pain he was feeling. "How could you?" he said.

It took Franny a moment to realize what he thought had happened. "I didn't!" she exclaimed.

He shook his head. "Please, Franny—"

"Honestly," she interrupted. "Nothing happened between me and Hunter, I swear. That photo—it looks like something it's not."

Seeing the skepticism in his face, she walked over and sank to her knees in front of him, a sign of supplication. "Please, darling." Tears gathered in her eyes. As an actress, she'd learned to cry automatically, but this was genuine. "Nothing's going on, I swear." She took his hand, imploring him to believe her. "Please believe me. You *have* to believe me."

He stared down at her for a long moment, as though trying to decide whether she was telling the truth.

"I would never do that to you," she told him. "I swear I wouldn't."

Finally he sighed, and she could see he was giving in. "All right. I believe you." He still didn't sound happy, but she could tell at least she was halfway to winning him over. "But just explain one thing to me."

"Anything."

"What on earth were you doing at that club in the first place?"

Franny wished now that she'd mentioned her plans to go out in the first place. She could see from his point of view that this lie of omission made her outing seem more sinister than it should have done. "Oh, it seems so stupid now," she admitted. "I only went because I was upset about not getting the part as Elizabeth."

Her husband looked surprised. "That was the reason?"

"Yes," she said simply. "You see, I thought that *I* was the best Elizabeth that Lloyd had seen. And I was hurt when Lloyd said he'd given the role to someone else."

Max reached out and touched her cheek. "Oh, sweetheart, I'm sorry to hear that." And he did sound as though he was. "But there'll be other parts, I'm sure."

A thought suddenly crossed Franny's mind. "Could you have a word with Lloyd?" she asked hopefully. "I'm sure he'd listen to you."

At that Max drew his hand away. "I'm sorry, but I've told you before, I made a promise at the beginning not to interfere in the creative side of things. And you wouldn't want to get a part simply on my say-so, would you?"

"I suppose not." She could see his point; it would be better to be cast on her own merits. But until then she was stuck out here, feeling useless. "But you see—" Franny stopped. This was it, she decided suddenly; this was the moment she would tell him about Cara. If she had no career to get back to, then she wanted her daughter here. She took a deep breath. "Max," she said determinedly. "I have something to tell you." She stopped again, unsure how to go on.

"What is it?"

"Well, if I'm not going to have my career, then I need something else to occupy me. You see, I find it so difficult, being here alone all day . . ."

But before she could broach the subject of Cara, Max cut her off. "Well, I presumed you wouldn't be alone for long," he said, smiling a little.

"What do you mean?"

"I thought we'd start trying for a baby."

Franny stared at him, stunned into silence.

"I know we haven't talked about it before," he continued. "And to be honest, I never expected to feel this way myself. After everything that happened with Eleanor and the way I've treated Gabriel and Olivia, I didn't think I'd want to have another child." He paused, and took her hand. "But with you it seems like the right thing to do. I *love* you, Frances. I want us to be a family. I want us to have a baby."

A baby? The idea of getting pregnant had been farthest from Franny's mind. She wasn't even sure that she *could* conceive, let alone if she wanted to. She already felt like a failure as a mother: having failed to tell her husband about Cara and then not being able to connect with Gabriel and Olivia. Having another child would surely just complicate an already impossible situation.

There was nothing for it. Before they made this decision together, she needed to tell him about Cara. "But, Max—"

He held up his hands, interrupting her again. "I know it's a lot for you to take in right now. I appreciate that. All I ask is that you give it some thought."

Franny stared at her husband. He seemed so excited about the prospect of having a child together. She felt terrible. How could she tell him about Cara now? It would devastate him. So she decided to take the coward's way out and go along with him, for now at least—especially as she was still feeling so guilty about the photo of her and Hunter.

"Well, I already have thought about it," she said, forcing a smile. "And you're right. Starting a family sounds like a wonderful idea."

25

When Cara woke that morning, she knew immediately that something was different. There was silence in the house. Usually her grandmother rose first, and Cara would wake to the sounds of her pottering around the kitchen. It occurred to her that Theresa might be outside, collecting eggs. So Cara got up and, pulling on her housecoat and a pair of boots, she went downstairs to check. But the kitchen was as clean and clear as it had been when they'd gone to bed the night before, and there was no one in the little garden. The door to the outside lavatory swung open in the morning breeze, revealing that it, too, was empty. So, knowing there was only one place her grandmother could be, Cara went back inside and headed upstairs.

Outside Theresa's bedroom door, she paused. Her heart was hammering so hard she could hear it in the quiet of the tiny landing. She was torn over what to do. On the one hand, her grandmother liked her privacy and grew enraged if Cara entered her room; on the other, it was a Sunday and Theresa was likely to miss Mass if she didn't get up now, and that could make her even madder. There was nothing for it, Cara decided; she would have to go in and wake her grandmother. Steeling herself, Cara reached for the handle.

The stench hit her as soon as she opened the door. "Oh, God."

Instinctively she recoiled, her hand going to cover her mouth and nose. It didn't do much good in blocking out the smell; the foul odor was too strong. Instinct told her to get as far away as possible. She was stepping back outside the door when a frail voice called from the bed.

"Franny? Is that you?"

Cara froze.

"Franny?" The voice came again, a little more desperate this time.

Cara made a decision. "Yes, it's me . . . Franny." It was easier than arguing. She moved toward the bed and saw her grandmother lying there, her eyes wide, looking as weak and frightened as a child.

"I think I've had an accident."

Cara closed her eyes. The thought of what she needed to do repelled her. But there was no one else. However long she waited, there would still only be her.

Not wanting to let on to the old lady how repelled she felt, the eleven-year-old girl forced a smile. "Never mind what's happened." She leaned over the bed, within reach of her grandmother. "Here, put your arms around my neck and I'll lift you."

Cleaning her grandmother up was the hardest thing she'd ever had to do. Trying not to think about what she was doing, Cara helped Theresa out of her filthy nightdress. Seeing the old woman standing there naked, her wrinkly body shivering, suddenly made Cara pull herself together. However hard this was on her, it was even less pleasant for her gran.

After that realization, it got a little easier. At the sink, she sponged her nan down and then helped her into the bath, just as Theresa had done for her when she'd been sick in Brighton. Leaving her in the wrought-iron tub, Cara quickly stripped the bed and left the dirty linen and clothing to soak in a bucket outside. Half an hour later, with fresh sheets fitted, the room aired, and her gran in a clean nightie, she helped the old lady back into bed.

Afterward, Cara stood back, feeling relieved it was all over. Now that Theresa was settled, she could clean herself up and then make them both a bit of breakfast.

"There, that's better, isn't it?"

Her gran stared blankly up at her. "Who are you? Why are you here in my house?"

Cara closed her eyes, trying hard not to cry. The situation was getting worse, not better, and she wasn't sure what to do. There was no one to speak to, no friend or family member to call, no kindly neighbor to approach. She didn't want to write to her mother about the situation, certain that she wouldn't care. She just hoped that her grandmother would get better of her own accord.

26

"I have your results back." Dr. Robertson reached out and touched the brown envelope in front of him, as though to prove that he wasn't just making the news up. "And I'm sorry to say that you're not pregnant."

Franny greeted the news with resignation. She was disappointed but not surprised. Not at this stage. She'd already accepted a while ago that she was unlikely to ever conceive again. She just felt bad for Dr. Robertson, putting him through this charade, not being able to tell him the whole truth. After all, he'd been so kind to her. A tall, slim man in his early sixties, he had an almost fatherly way about him. Along with being a close personal friend of Max, he was also an excellent general practitioner—and a much-sought-after one. His exclusive San Francisco office, with its understated decor and mahogany furnishings, felt more like a gentleman's study than a doctor's office. Franny had gotten to know it far too well these past months.

"So what now?" she asked, because it seemed as though she should.

Dr. Robertson consulted his notes. "You've been trying for—what—about six months?"

"That's right."

"Well, it's still too early to start worrying." He gave a reassuring smile. "Let's give it a little while longer, and if nothing's happened then, I would suggest running some tests to determine if there's any actual medical problem stopping you from conceiving."

Franny kept nodding as he spoke, pretending to be comforted by his understanding platitudes. But as she walked out of his office, she had no intention of keeping her next appointment. She couldn't go through this sham again.

Later that afternoon, Franny took a walk through the grounds of Stanhope Castle. It was a beautiful spring day, but she took little joy from the warm weather. It had been a horrible six months. From the beginning, she'd suspected that she would struggle to conceive. She'd been so sick with that infection she'd contracted after giving birth to Cara, and the doctor who'd treated her had warned that it might affect her fertility. But she'd gone along with trying for a baby anyway, because it seemed to be what Max wanted more than anything else. The thought of telling him again today that she wasn't pregnant filled her with dread. Let alone coming clean about *why* she couldn't ever give him children. That only made it so much harder to tell him about Cara—because how, after confessing that she'd robbed him of the chance to have a family with her, could she then expect him to accept her illegitimate daughter?

Sometimes Franny wondered how she'd gotten herself into such a mess. Putting off telling Max the truth at the beginning had made everything so much worse, so much more complicated. She was a coward, she knew that. With all her lies and secrets, she was hurting the two people she loved most—her daughter and her husband. But somehow, however much she tried, she couldn't see any way out of her situation.

But it wasn't this alone that was making Franny miserable. It didn't help that she still felt so lonely and isolated at Stanhope Castle. She'd talked to Lloyd a few times, but there were no movie roles on the horizon for her. Without her career, she really didn't know what to do with herself. Now that she wasn't acting, her friends from before had all disappeared. Lily was the only one who bothered with her.

Franny had confided in her friend about wanting to get back to work.

"Can't Max sort something out?" Lily asked. "Surely he can have a word in Lloyd's ear?"

Franny had thought about that, too. But her husband always insisted that he had no input on the creative side. She told Lily that, and she could sense how skeptical her friend was. Franny felt unconvinced sometimes, too. But what possible reason could he have for wanting to stop her from working?

Of course she still had some contact with the Hollywood set. As Mrs. Maximilian Stanhope, she inevitably had dinners and award ceremonies to attend. But Franny was very aware of being there as Max's wife and nothing more. She was no longer a player in her own right, and that bothered her. She also had far too much time on her hands. To go from a full-time career, where she was surrounded by people and used to being the center of attention, to empty weeks with seemingly endless hours waiting to be occupied was hard to cope with.

Whole days passed when she spoke to no one apart from the staff. Franny tried to strike up friendships, but there was always that divide of mistress and servant. Sometimes she would overhear the maids laughing together and almost envy them their freedom. Back when she was cleaning in London, she'd never realized how precious that was.

Part of her felt that she should be standing up for herself, taking control of her life—wasn't that what she would normally have done? But lately she'd lost all her fight. It didn't help that she was having trouble sleeping. Franny didn't know why—perhaps because Max was away so much and she found it hard to sleep alone. But the upshot was that she felt tired all the time, completely exhausted, as though she had no energy. And sometimes she got a little confused and forgetful—and overemotional, too. She didn't feel like herself anymore. Sometimes she wondered what was happening to her.

Glancing over at the driveway, Franny saw that Gabriel's car had gone. Max's children were home for the Easter holidays, although she hadn't seen much of them. Over the past few months they seemed to have accepted her a little more, but they were both young and off doing their own thing. Gabriel had friends in L.A. whom he liked to visit, and this morning he had gone down to stay at the house in Holmby Hills for the weekend, taking Olivia with him. She was young to be out of the house overnight, but Franny had persuaded Max to let her go, saying that though Gabriel might be a bit reckless, he was also street-smart and well able to look out for his sister. Franny knew it was the right thing to let them go, but it also left her here alone again.

Sighing deeply, she continued on her walk. She was so lost in thought that she wasn't paying too much attention to her surroundings, but as she passed one particular flower bed, an unusually striking bloom caught her eye. It was in hues of deep orange and red. Spotting one of the gardeners nearby, she called him over to ask what it was.

"It's a daylily, ma'am," he said. He was a young, handsome black man, part of a team of five who tended to the gardens.

She reached out to touch its velvety petals. "It's so perfect."

"Each flower blooms for only one day," he told her. "It comes out at sunrise, and then by sunset it withers and dies."

For some reason, the fate of the beautiful daylily struck Franny as particularly poignant. She smiled at the young gardener.

"What's your name?" she asked.

"Leonard, Mrs. Stanhope."

"Oh, don't be so formal." She smiled at him. "Call me Franny."

"I'm heading out now. You coming?"

At the Holmby Hills mansion, Gabriel stood in the doorway of his sister's bedroom, car keys in hand.

"Thanks, but I think I'll pass," she told him. "I'd rather stay in and get an early night. I'm kind of tired after the drive."

Gabriel regarded his sister through narrowed eyes. He had a feeling she was lying to him—he'd done it enough times to his father to know the signs. Since Christmas, Olivia had taken every opportunity she could to come down with him to L.A. His father and Franny thought that when they were down here, Olivia hung around with him and his friends, but in fact she'd always make some excuse to go off on her own. Gabriel had no idea where she went. Whenever he asked her what she was doing or who she was going to see, she'd claim to be meeting a friend from school. Gabriel didn't believe that for a second. He suspected it was more likely that she was off with some guy. Not Brett, that was for sure; Olivia seemed to have lost all interest in him since her sixteenth birthday party. But someone else, someone he didn't know. And Gabriel wasn't entirely sure what he thought about that.

Their father was under the impression that he was keeping tabs on Olivia; that was the only reason his sister had been allowed to accompany him in the first place. If Max knew what was really going on, he would never have let Olivia come along. Gabriel felt a little guilty about deceiving his father and stepmother like that. But he kept thinking, *What harm can it do? Olivia's sensible; she's not going to get into any trouble.*

With that last reassuring thought, he went out for the evening, leaving his sister to her own devices.

*   *   *

As spring moved into summer, Franny found herself spending more time outside, and that meant more time with the gardener, Leonard. He was intelligent and soft-spoken, and, most important, he had time for her. She asked him about himself and discovered that he was an aspiring musician. He'd moved from Harlem to L.A., looking to get into show business, but it hadn't panned out, so he'd been forced to take this job at Stanhope Castle instead. Feeling bad for him, Franny found herself promising to put him in touch with some contacts she knew.

He was clearly delighted with the offer. "That'd be wonderful, Miz Franny, if you could do something like that for me."

His gratitude made Franny feel good. Few people seemed to appreciate her these days; it was nice that at least someone did.

One morning she was in the greenhouse, standing on a stepladder, trying to reach one of the hanging plants, a Swedish ivy. She wanted to get a cutting and plant it in a separate plot to see if it would grow. The plant was very high, and even on the stepladder she couldn't quite reach it. As she stretched up, the ladder wobbled a little. She probably should have stopped then and asked one of the staff to get it for her, but she was so close that she decided to try just one last time. Going up onto her toes, she reached out with the shears and succeeded in snipping the shoot that she wanted, but the action unbalanced the ladder. It trembled and quivered, rocking back and forth. She tried to right herself, but it was too late, and she fell forward.

Luckily, at that moment, Leonard was coming into the greenhouse. Seeing what was happening, he dropped the bag of compost that he was carrying and rushed toward Franny, managing to catch her as she fell.

She stood in Leonard's arms, trying to get her breath. His hands were on either side of her waist, holding her up; she felt as though she was going to faint.

"Are you all right, Miz Franny?"

"I—I think so," she answered slowly.

Looking up, she saw concern in his deep brown eyes and felt another rush of gratitude. It was the first time in a long while that she'd felt someone cared.

Reaching up, she touched his cheek. "Thank you for saving me."

A cough from behind disturbed the moment. They sprang apart.

Franny turned, feeling flushed and guilty. It was the housekeeper, Hilda, looking at them with undisguised disapproval.

"I just came to say that there's a phone call for you, *Mrs.* Stanhope."

Franny smoothed down her hair, trying to act natural. "Of course, I'll be right there."

Avoiding Leonard's gaze, she hurried from the greenhouse.

A week later, Lily came out to the house. It was such a lovely day that Franny suggested sitting outside in the garden. The maids tittered as they walked past.

Franny frowned. "I have no idea what's wrong with them today."

Lily gave her a sideways look. "Well, I might."

"What?"

Her friend took out a copy of *Confidential* magazine from her handbag and handed it to Franny. Seeing her name, Franny felt a wave of weariness wash over her. Deciding it was best to know what was being said about her, she forced herself to read through the article, which suggested that she had an unusually "close" relationship with the Stanhopes' black gardener.

Franny closed her eyes. Inevitably she would have to talk to Max about this. She hated to think what his reaction would be.

"You know this isn't true, don't you?" Franny said later that night in earnest to Max.

He turned away from her. "I don't want to talk about it."

Franny knew what the problem was. It was like the old saying, "There's no smoke without fire." There had been so many rumors about her with other men that her husband was beginning to doubt her denials.

"Darling, I swear to you—" she began.

"Franny, leave it."

Her husband's tone was firm, but she couldn't let it go. "It's just scurrilous rumors, you know," she said, feeling her frustration rise. "No doubt planted by your precious Hilda." Something told her not to say that last part, but she couldn't help it. She just *knew* it was that old bag, trying to cause trouble.

Max gave her a sharp look. "Don't accuse someone when you have no idea if it's true or not."

"But—"

"Frances. I've told you already. I do not wish to discuss this any further."

Franny gave up. There was no point arguing with Max when he was like this.

Max might have claimed not to believe the story, but it didn't help save Leonard's job. The following Monday when Franny went out to the gardens, Leonard was nowhere to be found. Instead, an elderly man was trimming the plants.

Over dinner that night, it took all of her courage to ask Max what had happened to their old gardener.

"He resigned," her husband answered briefly, clearly not keen to have the discussion.

"But why?" Franny pressed.

Max shrugged. "I imagine he found a better position elsewhere."

"But that's ridiculous!" Franny could feel her eyes filling with tears of frustration. "He loved it here—there's no way he would leave."

"For heaven's sake," Max said impatiently. "How should I know what made him go? And more important, why do you care so much?"

He went back to eating his soup, signaling that that was all she was going to get out of him. But Franny wasn't prepared to let it go. She needed to know what had transpired between her husband and Leonard. It must have been significant enough to ensure that the gardener hadn't come to say good-bye.

"You told him to leave, didn't you?" she said suddenly. "You forced him to go because he was the only person here who was a friend to me."

Max slammed down his spoon then. "Frances, please." She could see him struggling to keep his anger in. "I'm getting tired of all these accusations. I really have no idea what you're talking about. I told you—I had *nothing* to do with Leonard leaving. Now, can we drop this?"

Franny stared at him for a long moment, not wanting to give in. But what was the point of continuing the argument? she thought wearily. He would just deny everything anyway.

"Fine," she said. "Have it your way." Then, throwing her napkin onto the table, she got up and left the room.

Max came to find her later. She was in their suite, lying on the bed, all cried out. She didn't turn as he came in. He walked over and perched on the mattress beside her, laying a hand gently on her shoulder. "Is everything all right with you?"

No, she thought, everything wasn't all right. She had no idea who she was anymore. Less than a year ago it had seemed that everything was going well for her. And now she'd become irrelevant—a has-been. What had gone wrong? It was something that she'd been thinking about a lot lately, and the answer seemed obvious: it was all down to Max. Everything had been on track until she'd met him.

She turned to look at him, the original argument forgotten as her frustration bubbled over. "It's your fault, isn't it, that I don't get any work these days? I bet you told Lloyd not to offer me parts."

Max looked genuinely confused. "Why would I do that?"

"Because . . ." she stumbled. "Because you want me all to yourself. You think if you keep me here in this—this prison, then I'll just give up on acting and be the obedient wife that you've always wanted."

Max drew back, looking wounded. "How could you think I would do such a thing?"

He looked so hurt, so genuinely upset, by her accusations that Franny hesitated in her attack. Was she wrong about him? Or was he just trying to confuse her?

"I don't know," she said at last. "I really don't know. All I know is that ever since I met you, my life has gone increasingly downhill." And with that she buried her head in the pillow and started to cry again.

There was a silence. "I'm sorry you feel that way," Max said at length. "I certainly never intended to ruin your life." Then he got up and left the room.

No more was said on the topic. Max was due to fly to Chicago that night, and when he got back three days later, he acted as though the argument hadn't happened.

But it had. The hurtful words had been said, and they'd been remembered. A distance had grown between Franny and Max, and she had no idea how to bridge it—or even if she wanted to.

A few weeks later, Gabriel finished school. He was planning to spend two months traveling through Europe before starting at Stanford in the fall. Although her stepson had remained outwardly cool to Franny over the past year, he must have thawed a little toward her, because before he went away he took her aside and asked if she'd look out for Olivia while he was gone.

Franny was already aware that something wasn't right with her step-daughter. After all the progress Olivia had made the previous year, she seemed to have gone backward lately. She was listless and quiet, hardly saying a word. Max was concerned, too. But Franny was feeling so strange and disoriented herself that it was hard for her to look out for anyone else.

Lily waited nervously in the Brown Derby for her friend to arrive. It had taken a lot to convince Franny to meet her there. The restaurant was *the* place for Hollywood business lunches. Everyone who was anyone was there, eating Cobb salads and trying to get noticed.

"Can't we go somewhere less public?" Franny had groaned when they'd made the arrangement on the phone. She knew the whole town was still speculating about whether she had been embroiled in an affair with Max's gardener.

But Lily had been insistent. "You can't hide away forever." She was sympathetic to her friend. Though this wasn't the first time Franny had appeared in *Confidential*, the coverage had been particularly brutal on this occasion. But Lily was a great believer in holding her head up high and weathering a storm. "Show them you have nothing to be ashamed of, and they'll soon lose interest" had been her advice.

Lily had known that it wasn't going to be the easiest lunch, but even she was shocked by her friend's appearance. Franny had lost weight. Her hair looked lank, her complexion was pasty—and her trademark green suit had a stain on the jacket. She had lost her famous sparkle. It took all of Lily's willpower to force a smile as her friend drew closer.

"No apology?" she chided gently as Franny sank into the chair.

Franny looked blank. "For what?"

Lily tapped her watch. "We said midday."

"Oh. I thought it was half past." Franny rubbed her eyes. "I'm sorry, I don't know what's wrong with me lately. I seem to be forgetting things all the time."

Seeing how fed up Franny looked, Lily rushed to comfort her. "Oh, don't be silly. It was probably my mistake."

Franny seemed not to hear her. Lily watched her friend as she flicked listlessly through the menu. She didn't like what was happening to Franny. The exuberant, smart, successful woman she had once known seemed to have been replaced by a tearful, absent stranger—and Lily knew who was responsible for the change in her. Max. Ever since they had married, Franny had become a different person. It worried Lily to think of her friend all alone out there in that isolated house with just Max for company—especially as she had noticed bruises on Franny's arms more than once now. Franny always dismissed them, saying she had bumped into things: "Oh, darling, you know how clumsy I am." In fact, Lily had never noticed any such thing.

It was hard to know what to do for the best. It was a taboo, a cardinal sin, to criticize a friend's husband. There were only so many times that she could meaningfully ask Franny how she was without causing an argument between them. But seeing how unhappy her friend looked today, Lily decided to give it one last go. "Darling, I don't mean to be a pain, but you look ever so pale. Is everything all right?"

"Yes, of course." Franny smiled then, but it looked forced to Lily. "Everything's great, actually. I was going to wait to tell you this but, here goes—I have some news."

"Oh?"

"Yes," Franny seemed to take a deep breath. "You see, I just found out yesterday that I'm pregnant."

Lily choked on the ice water she was drinking. "Pregnant?" she spluttered. It was the last thing she'd been expecting Franny to say. "I didn't even know you were trying."

"Yes, we have been. For a while now."

It was a complete surprise to Lily. Franny had never struck her as the maternal type, and she'd clearly struggled to get along with Max's children. Worried about appearing rude, Lily tried to say the kind of things that she knew were expected in this situation. "That's wonderful news! How far along are you?"

"Oh . . ." For a moment Franny looked thrown. "Three months," she said vaguely. "Maybe four."

"And how's Max? Is he happy?"

"Delighted." Franny's tone was bright, but something didn't quite ring true about the whole thing. If anything, she seemed troubled rather than happy.

Lily thought then of the Stanhopes' recently dismissed gardener. She'd never directly asked Franny if there was any truth in those magazine stories—it was part of an unspoken code among their group of friends not to. But now, with this sudden pregnancy news, she couldn't help wondering if Franny had gotten herself into some serious trouble this time . . .

"Well, that's fantastic," Lily said again, because she had no idea how to bring up the suspicion that had suddenly presented itself. "What an exciting time for you both!"

"Yes," Franny said flatly. "It really is."

Lily tried to be pleased for her friend. After all, in those first few weeks, she seemed to be a little happier than before. Not that she saw Franny much after that. At the end of the fifth month of her pregnancy there were complications—high blood pressure, Franny told her on the phone, and she was confined to bed. Lily tried to visit, but any time she called to arrange to come out, she was told by that awful housekeeper, Hilda, that it wasn't convenient. Allegedly it was Franny who'd said that, but Lily didn't believe it for a second: it was Max, of course. She was sure of it. From what she could see, he wanted Franny all to himself and he was cutting her off from everyone else.

Lily had hoped that once the child was born, she might see more of her friend. But then she received that awful, terrible call, from the tearful Franny, telling her that she'd lost the baby.

4519 01 *******76 84   20JUL2015 10:3∶
Receipt: CB25-732∶
A0000002771010

Account: Chequing   Primary

Withdraw $60.00

67.68

Account Balance   ~~$106.48~~

(20)

27

"Rock-a-bye, baby, in the treetop . . ."

Sitting in the rocking chair, the sleeping baby cradled in her arms, Sister Marie moved gently back and forth as she sang. The motion seemed to soothe the child, something the nun had learned in the month that the tiny girl had been here. It was hard to believe that ten minutes earlier, she'd been screaming at the top of her little lungs.

Anyone watching the two of them together now would find it hard to believe that at first Sister Marie hadn't wanted to take care of the baby. The night that Sophie—as they'd been instructed to name her—had arrived, the reverend mother had taken the child up to the nursery. Sister Marie had followed reluctantly. Once they were there, the older nun had held the baby out to the novice. "Here, she will be your responsibility."

Sister Marie hadn't taken her right away. What with the storm and the way the child was . . . it felt as if there were something ill fated about the baby. She didn't want to be spending time with her every day.

Mother Superior sensed her underling's reluctance and said in gentle rebuke, "We are all God's creatures. Doesn't she deserve as much looking after as the other children here?"

There was nothing Sister Marie could say to that, so she did her duty and looked after the baby. Sophie wasn't a good sleeper. One night she wouldn't stop crying. Happening to pass the nursery, the reverend mother came in and picked up the screaming child from her crib. Taking Sophie to her breast, the old nun began to rock her. "Now, what is it that you want?" she cooed down at the baby. "What will make you stop crying?"

"I've done everything I need to," Sister Marie said sulkily. "She's been fed and changed. I think she's just being difficult."

But as though to prove her wrong, the baby began to quiet down, until she stopped screaming altogether. Peering over, Sister Marie saw that she was fast asleep. "I-I don't understand."

Mother Superior smiled softly. "A baby needs more than food and clean clothes, Sister Marie. Sophie may be different from the other children here, but like them she requires love in order to thrive."

Feeling ashamed, the young nun had resolved then and there to make more of an effort. Instead of simply going through the motions of caring for the baby—feeding, changing, and laying her down to sleep—she had started speaking to her as she went about her duties. At first it had seemed a little strange; after all, it wasn't as if she was going to get a response back. But gradually, as she talked, she began to feel more of a connection with the baby. And once she had overcome her initial reservations, she realized that this child was just like any other.

Now, as she finished singing the lullaby, the baby gurgled in her sleep, and Sister Marie felt her heart contract.

"She seems quite taken with you."

Sister Marie looked up and saw the reverend mother standing in the doorway of the nursery, smiling softly at them. "And I with her," the younger nun replied. "She's a very special little girl."

Mother Superior's smile broadened. "I know."

She left Sister Marie alone then, safe in the knowledge that the small child would always have someone to look out for her, in what was undoubtedly going to be a strange, difficult life.

28

Dr. Robertson smiled gently at the woman sitting in front of him. "I think you need to give the pills a chance to do their work."

Franny felt her eyes automatically filling with tears, as they did so easily these days. "But it's been three months."

"You can't put a time limit on these things, I'm afraid," he said sympathetically. "It's been a difficult year for you, what with the baby . . ."

"I suppose you're right." Franny sighed wearily. It was Max who had first suggested that she go to see the doctor, a few months earlier, when her emotional swings seemed to be getting out of control. She'd described her symptoms to the physician—the constant exhaustion, the forgetfulness—and he'd prescribed antidepressants for her. Dutifully she'd taken them, but they didn't seem to have helped. Something was wrong with her, something *more* than depression, she was sure. This wasn't about being a little blue or a bit down in the dumps. Some days her body just wouldn't work properly. Her hands would shake uncontrollably. "But if anything, I seem to be getting worse," she told the doctor.

"Oh?"

"I'm clumsier than usual. I was having tea yesterday morning, and I dropped my cup. And sometimes I bump into things." She pulled up her blouse and showed the faded remnants of a bruise from where she'd walked into the sharp edge of a table the previous week.

Dr. Robertson frowned. "That does look nasty."

"And I'm forgetting things, too. I took my wedding ring off to have a bath this morning, and when I got out"—she faltered a little—"I couldn't remember where I'd put it."

The doctor stared at her for a long moment. Then he cleared his throat and adjusted his glasses, a sure sign that he was building up to a sensitive question. "Please don't take this the wrong way, Mrs. Stanhope. But have you, uh, perhaps been drinking more than usual?"

Franny stared at him for a long moment. Her first instinct was to utter an outraged denial. But then again . . . was he right? She supposed there were some nights when she couldn't sleep and she found herself taking a drink or two from Max's decanter of brandy.

"Perhaps," she admitted reluctantly.

Dr. Robertson nodded understandingly. "Well, let's talk about that."

Half an hour later, Franny left the office, armed with a prescription for sleeping pills to use instead of alcohol. She had wanted to ask how substituting one drug for another was really going to help her. But she would give it a go. "A good night's sleep can be a great healer," Dr. Robertson had said. Though Franny didn't feel terribly hopeful, she supposed it was worth a try—for her daughter's sake, if nothing else. With everything that had happened these past few months—the loss of the baby, followed by her strange mental state—she hadn't felt able to think about bringing Cara over to America. Communication with Theresa and her daughter had gone from sporadic to almost nonexistent now, and Franny knew that she urgently needed to make things right. Perhaps once she was more rested she would be in a position to finally resolve the problem.

Along with prescribing the sleeping pills, Dr. Robertson had suggested to Franny that it would be useful for her to get out and socialize. "Too much time alone isn't good for you. You need to do something to occupy your mind."

So when an invitation to Hunter's thirtieth birthday party arrived the following day, Franny decided to go. Max was against it, of course. He didn't think she was up to it.

"You seem so fragile, my darling," he said when she raised the subject. But she overrode him.

"I need to get out," she insisted. After all, the party was going to be held at San Simeon, William Hearst's estate, which was only an hour's drive from Stanhope Castle.

The night of Hunter's party, as Franny gazed at herself in the mirror, she felt her spirits lift a little. She looked more like her old self. Her dress, by Christian Dior, was a Grecian-style floor-length gown in midnight blue. Hilda had curled her hair into ringlets, and she had gold bracelets on each arm. She looked a little like Cleopatra, a deliberate reminder of the halcyon days of her career, and she would make a great impression tonight. That was what she wanted, given it was the first time she'd been out in public for such a long while. At the thought of the past few bleak months, her smile faltered a little. But no, she wouldn't let herself dwell on bad times this evening.

Instead, she finished getting ready. Spritzing Chanel No. 5 on her wrists and neck, she grabbed her clutch bag and went downstairs to wait for Max. He had been working in San Francisco that day and had promised to pick her up on the way to the party. As it started at eight, he would need to be home by seven so that they would get there on time. But by half past he still wasn't home. Franny wondered what had happened. Maybe he'd gotten caught up at work. But if they didn't leave soon, they'd be late . . .

Franny thought quickly. There was no way she was going to miss out on tonight. She summoned Hilda and asked her to get the driver to bring her car around. "I'll go on my own, and Max can always join me later," she said decisively.

The housekeeper pursed her lips together. "Unfortunately, madam, the tide has already come in. There's no way out of here for the time being."

With that piece of news Hilda left the room. As soon as she had gone, Franny went over to the drinks trolley and poured herself a brandy.

Franny woke up feeling horrible the next morning—more horrible than she should have had any right to feel, because she was sure that she hadn't drunk *that* much last night. Sure enough, when she made it downstairs, she checked the decanter and saw it was only a little way below where it normally was. Then why did she feel so bad?

She found Max in his study. He looked up as she came in, and she could see him frowning at her appearance: she'd felt too ill to get dressed, so she'd come down in her robe. She pulled the belt tighter, trying to look more authoritative.

"What happened to you yesterday?"

He tilted his head questioningly. "I was going to ask you the same thing."

Franny felt tears come to her eyes, and wiped them furiously away, refusing to give in to her misery. "You said you were going to come back here and get me."

"No, I didn't." His tone was reasonable. "Don't you remember, darling? We arranged to meet at the party."

He got up and walked toward her. She took a step back, shaking her head vigorously. For once, she wasn't going to let this go. "No," she insisted. "You said that you'd pick me up *here*."

"Originally I did," he said levelly. "But then I telephoned to say that a meeting had come up, which meant I wouldn't be able to make it back here, after all. So I told you to make your own way there by car."

Franny frowned. What was going on? Was that really what they'd agreed? No, she decided, it wasn't. He was just trying to confuse her.

"No! No, that's not right," she objected tremulously. "You *said* you'd come back and get me."

Hilda, who had been standing quietly by, stepped forward. "Madam, if you'd allow me. I do believe what Mr. Stanhope said is true. I answered the phone to your husband and, having overheard your side of the conversation, you agreed to meet him at San Simeon."

At that, Franny rounded on her. "Oh, what a surprise," she said sarcastically. "You're taking *his* side over mine."

The housekeeper lowered her eyes. "I assure you I'm doing nothing of the sort, madam."

"Oh, *please*." Franny's voice dripped with scorn. "Don't give me that ever-so-humble act. You've resented me from the first day I arrived. No doubt you believed you should have been the one sharing Max's bed instead of me."

If she was hoping to provoke a reaction out of Max, she was in luck. He stood up abruptly. "Frances, please! There is no need to speak like that to Hilda."

Franny looked from one of them to the other. "Oh, so that's it, is it? You're both ganging up on me." Her eyes settled on Max, and she sounded hurt as she said, "I expected more from you."

She ran from the room and tore upstairs, holding her gown up so that she wouldn't trip. She could hear Max behind her, calling out her name, begging for her to stop, but that only made her run faster. She laughed maniacally as she took the stairs two at a time, hardly aware of where she was heading until she finally reached the glass turret at the top of the house.

Max followed her up the spiral staircase, panting from the exertion of chasing her. "What are you doing up here?"

Staring out of the window, she said in a monotone, "Is this what you're hoping for? That I'll throw myself over like *she* did?"

He blanched. "How could you *think* that?"

It was only then, as she saw his genuine distress, that Franny realized what she had said to her husband. It was a low point in their steadily degenerating relationship. It seemed that they were fighting all the time; the physical side of their relationship, which had once been so passionate, was now almost nonexistent. And she knew that the problem lay with her. She was the one pushing Max away all the time; she was the one saying all these awful things. In that moment, Franny's anger deserted her, and she collapsed onto the floor, sobbing. "What's wrong with me?" she cried. "I don't understand why I'm like this all the time."

Max took Franny in his arms. "I have no idea what's going on, my love." He held his wife to him, stroking her hair. "But we'll get to the bottom of it, I promise."

It was a few months after that lunch at the Brown Derby that Lily began to suspect that Franny was drinking too much. She knew that her friend had taken the loss of the baby hard—in fact, she'd hardly seen Franny since the stillbirth, nearly seven months ago now. But Lily had heard the rumors. Even though Franny wasn't acting any longer, she had remained of interest to the media because of her position as Max's wife. Most weeks, *Confidential* ran an article hinting at Franny's drinking or her increasingly bizarre behavior. It was obvious someone close to the household was leaking the information. Max had sacked one of the housemaids after that business with the gardener—was it possible that he had gotten the wrong person? There were other strange rumors going round about the Stanhope household. Max's daughter, Olivia, who'd always been a fragile person, was said to have been committed to a psychiatric hospital. Only Max's son, Gabriel, had escaped scrutiny. He was at Stanford now, safely away from the drama of Stanhope Castle.

But despite hearing whispers of what was going on, Lily had never seen any evidence of her friend being drunk. Then, one sunny day in that summer of 1959, she turned up at Stanhope Castle for afternoon tea. It was a standing arrangement that the women had for the last Friday of every month, and Franny had never missed one yet. But this time Lily was told, by that dreadful housekeeper Hilda, that Mrs. Stanhope wasn't available.

"She's asleep," she told Lily, who was standing on the front step.

"Well, go wake her, then," the blond actress said pragmatically.

The grim-faced housekeeper clearly didn't want to let her in, but Lily was determined to see her friend, so she pushed past the old bag and insisted that Hilda go up and wake her mistress.

It was half an hour before Lily heard footsteps on the stairs and rose to greet her friend. But the words froze on her lips as Franny came into view. "Dear God!" she exclaimed involuntarily. "What the hell's happened to you?"

Franny looked confused. "What do you mean?"

Lily could only stare at her friend. Her hair, usually Franny's pride and joy, hadn't been styled, and the red tresses were a tangled mess that needed a comb taken to it. She'd obviously attempted to apply some makeup to cheer her appearance up, but her foundation was too heavy, her cheeks too rouged, and instead of adding color, the bloodred lipstick made her appear grotesque. She hadn't bothered to get dressed. Instead, she wore a floor-length lilac satin nightdress and matching lace robe.

But Franny obviously didn't think there was anything wrong with how she looked. So Lily decided to gloss over her shock and instead tried to sound cheerful as she said, "Oh, I just meant that I missed you at Hunter's party the other week. Why didn't you show?"

"Oh." Fran waved her hand vaguely. "There was a silly mix-up."

She stumbled a little, and Lily reached out to steady her. As Franny tipped her head up to thank her friend, Lily smelled alcohol on the other woman's breath.

"Franny!" She was shocked; it was still early in the day. "Have you been drinking?"

"What?" Franny's hand instinctively went to cover her mouth. She looked as though she was about to deny the charge, but then she seemed to change her mind. "Well, yes," she said a little defensively. "Maybe I have had a little drinkie or two. Is that a crime?"

Lily sighed. "No, of course it's not. But it seems to be a lot more than that lately, doesn't it?"

Franny drew herself up, her eyes hardening. "I don't know what you're suggesting, but I think you ought to drop it."

"Oh, sweetheart, please." Lily tried to sound gentle and understanding, not wanting to get into a fight. "Don't be like this. I'm just worried about you."

"I don't need you to worry about me," Franny said haughtily. Then she rang the bell for Hilda. "Now, why don't you drop this nonsense, and we'll have a nice cup of tea together instead."

Lily had no choice but to do as her friend asked.

Officer Rafferty took his job very seriously. A lot of the guys hated highway patrol. They found the long hours tedious and would switch on the radio or have a snooze to pass the time. They especially hated the night shift, when few cars passed along the highway. But Officer Rafferty took note of every vehicle that came by, and if he judged that a car was going too fast or was being driven erratically, he had no qualms about pulling the car over and explaining what the driver had been doing wrong.

It was the late 1950s now, and more and more people were becoming owners of motor vehicles. The postwar boom had seen the rise of the purchasing power of the middle class, and now Ford and General Motors were competing to bring their cars to ordinary folk. But this new phenomenon brought a whole new set of problems with it. His first night on the job, five years ago now, a high school boy had taken his father's car for a drive and ended up wrapping it around a tree. Officer Rafferty had been the first one on the scene, and he had seen the damage that speeding could do.

That night, he heard the vehicle long before he saw it. He was standing outside his patrol car, taking a leak, when he caught the sound of an engine, far off still but eating up the distance quickly. Zipping up, he turned just in time to see the car—a silvery-blue Pontiac—whizzing by. The top was down, and as it sped past, he spotted a young woman at the wheel, a scarf wrapped around her head to keep her hair in place. Looking at the way the automobile was swerving from one side of the road to the other, he had a feeling he was about to witness another fatality.

He went back to the police cruiser, ready to give chase, but before he could get in, the sports car veered out of control and plowed across the road. It was sheer luck that it hadn't gone straight over the cliff edge and plunged into the ravine below. Rushing over to the vehicle, he saw the driver—a red-haired woman, he could tell now that the scarf had fallen away—slumped across the steering wheel. The car was side-on to the cliff edge, teetering precariously. He tried to walk around to the driver's side, but the limestone started to give way. So instead he went back to the passenger door and knelt down.

"Miss?" he called out loudly, but there was no reply. Was she even alive? If she wouldn't wake up, there was only one way to find out. He leaned in through the window and grabbed hold of her shoulder, trying to get her to sit up. She fell back against the seat, her head lolling to one side. There was a nasty gash just above her left eye; it was deep and bleeding badly. But her chest was still rising up and down, so at least she wasn't dead. Having established that the driver was still alive, the officer did a quick survey of the vehicle. It wasn't in good shape. He didn't like to move the woman, but he was worried that at any moment the cliff might give way, so he opened the car door and slid her across the leather seats until he was able to pick her up. As he did so, he smelled the distinctive acidic odor of alcohol on her breath.

He carried the woman across the grass until they were a hundred yards from the car and laid her on the ground. After checking her airway and establishing that she was still breathing on her own, he went to radio for an ambulance.

"Vehicular accident, involving one female driver . . ."

As soon as she heard about Franny's accident, Lily rushed to the hospital. Unfortunately, when she got there, Max was inside with Franny, talking to the doctor, and as she wasn't a family member no one would let her know what was going on.

As she sat waiting in the corridor, she overheard a police officer talking to the receptionist and figured out from their conversation that he'd been first on the scene. Concerned about her friend being exposed to further bad press, Lily followed the officer outside the building.

"Excuse me," she called out as he was about to get into his patrol car.

Hearing the woman's voice, he turned back. "Can I help you, ma'am?" he asked politely.

She hurried over to him. "You were there, weren't you?" she said in a low voice, looking round to check that no one could hear. "At the car accident—the one involving Frances Fitzgerald."

Hearing that, his face closed up. "I can't talk about that," he said, going to get into his car.

But Lily put out a hand to stop him. "Well, that's my point. I don't *want* you to talk about the accident." She held out a hundred-dollar bill. "Not to *anyone*."

The officer stared at the money for a moment. "What the hell's that for?"

"Look," Lily said in a low voice, "I care about Franny, is all. And I'd hate to see any details about this scandal ending up in the papers."

It took all of Officer Rafferty's self-control not to explode. A principled young man who took his job seriously, he would never have dreamed of selling his story to the press and didn't like the implication that he would.

"First, I would never take a bribe," he said stiffly. "Second, I certainly wouldn't go gossiping about any aspect of my job." He watched with satisfaction as the blonde's cheeks reddened. "And last," he said quietly, "if you care as much about your friend as you claim, then bad press should be the *least* of your concerns."

Lily stared at him, confused. "What's that supposed to mean?"

The officer hesitated for a moment, as though he'd said too much.

"Please," Lily pressed. "Tell me."

He seemed to debate with himself for a moment before finally deciding to reveal what he knew. "As standard procedure," he told her, "I looked back at the ground, to see what had caused the crash. There was no oil slick on the road and no skid marks. Nothing there to suggest that she lost control."

Lily frowned in confusion. "What the hell does that mean?"

The officer's eyes were solemn. "To me, it looks like she drove deliberately toward that barrier. I think your friend was trying to kill herself."

The state trooper's words haunted Lily. So later that night, she decided to take Max to one side and voice her concerns. Franny's husband listened silently until the actress finished speaking.

"I would rather you didn't talk about my wife in those terms again," he said at length. "These rumors have a nasty habit of getting out, and I'm sure as someone who cares deeply about Frances, you would hate to see anything negative being said about her. As you well know, the studio doesn't care for troublemakers, and I wouldn't want anyone to think that you are one."

The words were said so mildly that it would be hard for anyone to hear the threat. But it was there: if Lily brought the subject up again, he would see that she was blacklisted.

She got shakily to her feet. "I see. Well, I'm sorry to have bothered you, Max. I'm sure you know better than anyone else how to take care of your wife."

It was said with as much defiance as Lily dared show. Then she left Max alone and went to have a strong drink herself.

Despite Max's warning, Lily decided to go out to Stanhope Castle the following week, once Franny was out of the hospital. She thought about calling to let her friend know that she was on her way but decided against it. That old witch Hilda always answered the phone, and she'd just try to dissuade her from coming. So she drove out to Stanhope Castle without telling anyone. Unfortunately, when she got there, Hilda refused to let her see Franny.

"Mrs. Stanhope's resting," she told her.

"Fine," Lily said. "Why don't I wait?"

The housekeeper's mouth tightened. "There's really no point. Mrs. Stanhope has told me that she'd rather not see anyone until she's fully recovered from her accident."

They were standing in the entrance hall when something caught the corner of Lily's eye, the flicker of a dark shadow, like someone moving across the entrance of the open door to the drawing room. But when she looked over, no one was there. A trick of the light, she told herself. Then she heard a click to her left. She looked back, and sure enough, the door was closed—when she was certain it had been open before.

"What was that?" she demanded, taking a pace in that direction.

Hilda moved with her, placing herself between Lily and the drawing room. "It was just the wind," she said. "Old houses have drafts." She had an answer for everything.

Lily might have believed her, but at that moment she caught a sudden whiff of Franny's perfume, Chanel No 5. It was her signature scent.

Of course, she wasn't the only woman to wear it, but Lily couldn't imagine that anyone else in this household did. Instinct told her that someone was skulking in the drawing room, and she was sure it was Franny. But what could she do? It wasn't as if Hilda was holding Franny here against her will. Mrs. Stanhope was the mistress of the house; she called the shots. If Franny didn't want to see her, there wasn't anything Lily could do about it.

"All right, then," Lily said resignedly. "I'll go."

She looked toward the closed drawing room door and felt the urge to call out to Franny, who she was certain was skulking back there. Instead, as she left, there was one question on her mind: *Why on earth would Franny be avoiding her?*

Later, Lily would wish she had been more persistent that day in trying to see Franny, because a month later she woke to the news that movie star Frances Fitzgerald had lost control of her car on Highway 1, driven over a cliff, and died in the ensuing explosion.

PART 3

1960–62

Hard Lessons

Experience is a hard teacher because she gives the test first, the lesson afterward.

—VERNON LAW, MAJOR LEAGUE BASEBALL PITCHER, 1930–

29

One morning, a few weeks before Cara's thirteenth birthday, Granny Theresa didn't wake up.

It was two months since Franny had died. As no one knew of Cara's existence, she'd found out about her mother's death from a newspaper. It was a small piece, simply reporting on the funeral. To Cara's surprise, she hadn't cried, refusing to mourn for the mother who had first abandoned and then forgotten her. She hid the piece from her grandmother, not wanting to upset Theresa's already troubled mind.

Over their years of living together, Cara and her grandmother had settled into a routine. Theresa invariably woke first, at around five, a habit she had developed during all those years living on the farm. If she was having a good day, she would feed the goat, milk the cow, and light the fire in the kitchen in order to have a frugal breakfast of bread and stewed tea prepared for when Cara rose a couple of hours later. As usual that particular morning, Cara awoke at seven. But she knew right away that something wasn't right. There was no sound coming from downstairs. The house was as still as death.

She went to her grandmother's room. There was no sound of movement inside. She knocked on the door and called through, but there was no response. Instinct told her that something was wrong. Pushing the door open, Cara saw that Theresa was still in bed, lying on her side, facing the window, the patterned quilt pulled up to her neck.

"Gran?" she said tentatively, assuming that Theresa had simply overslept. When there was no response, she took a step closer, and said more loudly, "Granny?"

Again Theresa didn't respond. The girl reached out to touch her grandmother's shoulder. Even through the cotton nightie, Cara could feel that her nan was stiff and cold.

No, she thought. *This can't be happening.*

"Gran?" Cara could hear the panic in her own voice. She shook her grandmother a little harder. "Gran? Wake up!" Tears filled her eyes as she pleaded, "Please, please wake up."

This time she shook so hard that she rolled Theresa onto her back. Cara gasped, her hands coming up to cover her mouth, as she saw her grandmother for the first time: blank eyes stared up at the ceiling; the front of her nightdress fell open to reveal one withered breast.

Falling onto her knees, Cara closed her eyes and began to recite the Lord's Prayer. "Our Father, who art in Heaven . . ." Maybe if she prayed hard enough, God would give her Granny back.

She stayed by the body, praying, for the next two hours. By that time, she realized that God didn't intend to grant her request. It was only then that she allowed herself to cry. Granny Theresa might have been a cold, harsh woman, but she had also been the only person Cara had known over the past few years. A bond had inevitably developed between grandmother and granddaughter, and now that Theresa was gone, she was all alone.

Cara had no idea what to do or who to tell. She was self-sufficient for her age, something she'd been forced to be, but having interacted with no one other than Theresa for the past six years, she wasn't well socialized. Another child might have run to a relative or neighbor for help, but she knew no other adults. And, having been warned so many times to keep her identity secret, she wasn't sure if she should go to a stranger. So she locked her grandmother's room—with the body inside—and went through the motions of living in the cottage, as she had with Theresa.

Over the past few years Theresa's contact with the outside world had been minimal. The only regular visitor was the delivery boy from the grocery store. She had stopped being able to go into the village a few months earlier, and, concerned for her, the shopkeeper had started to send his son out once a fortnight with the basics that she had always bought to supplement what they grew on the farm.

At seventeen, Ryan Quinn was eager to get away from his father, the store, and Connemara. He hated going out to the Healey farm and hated having to talk to old Mother Healey even more. She was getting increasingly strange these days. Although he liked to think of himself as a hard man, he was still young enough to have heard the children whisper stories about her being a witch, and he was also stupid enough to believe them. So when he got to the farm and there was no answer at the door, he was almost relieved. No doubt she was out, although God only knew where. He would have happily dumped the groceries on the step and left, and no one would have been any wiser. Except that his father had introduced a new system, where customers had to sign a slip saying they'd received their goods. So instead of leaving the groceries, Ryan took them all the way home and told his father what had happened.

Seamus Quinn was smarter than his son. Aware of how frail Theresa had grown, he suspected that something might have happened to her and contacted the garda.

Young Police Constable Matthew O'Donnell was the one sent to the cottage. Like most people in the little village, he knew Theresa by sight and to nod a hello to.

Approaching the house, he took in his surroundings with a trained eye, noticing at once that the garden was overgrown. It was a shame that Theresa didn't have family or neighbors close by who would look out for her. He knocked a couple of times on the front door but got no answer. As he stepped away, he happened to glance up and thought he saw the curtain at one of the top-floor windows twitch. Matthew was only a couple of years older than Ryan—although, unlike the shop-keeper's son, he was a sensible, grounded sort—but even he felt a little shiver pass through him as he walked around the house trying to get in. The landscape was empty and silent, apart from the sound of birds twittering above.

Trying the handle of the front door, he found that it was open. Al-though he felt a little bad letting himself in, he knew it was the best thing to do. Inside, the house looked surprisingly neat, but it was so quiet that he knew something was up.

Matthew headed upstairs. He'd been in similar cottages and guessed that the main bedroom would be at the back of the house, overlooking the garden.

As soon as he opened the door, he could smell the stench of death. Covering his nose and mouth, he walked over to the bed. Theresa was gray, and from the stink of her, she'd been dead for several days. Saying a quick prayer to himself, he pulled the sheet over her face.

"Leave her be!"

Terrified, he jumped at the voice, convinced it was a banshee behind him. Then he got ahold of himself. Whirling around, he saw a tall, skinny girl glaring angrily at him.

"I said leave her alone!" she said again before bursting into tears.

It took the police another two days to find a way to contact Theresa's next of kin. During that time, Matt's mother had agreed to look after the girl. Recently widowed and with her own children grown, she was happy to fill her empty nest. She took one look at the thin, blank-eyed waif and wanted to make everything better for her. The child managed to tell them her name—Cara—and that she was twelve years old, but after that she went mute.

"The poor mite's no doubt in shock." Mrs. O'Donnell's eyes filled with tears of sympathy. "Imagine, living all that time with a dead body."

Theresa's eldest daughter, Margaret—no longer going by the name of Maggie now that she was a married woman with children—eventually turned up, a week after her mother's body had been discovered. It was the earliest she had been able to get there, she explained as she swept into the police station. She was a very busy person, a respected member of her community, and she had responsibilities that she couldn't get out of, what with organizing a cake sale for her children's school fete, flower arranging in the church, and leading her prayer group in the Stations of the Cross. "And now there's this to deal with," she said with a martyred sigh.

"So do you know anything about the child that your mother had living with her?" Matt wanted to know, turning the conversation from Maggie's complaints.

Maggie looked over sharply. "Child?" she repeated, just to be sure she'd heard right.

"Y-yes." The young policeman faltered under the woman's piercing gaze. "I found her when I went to check on the house. The best we can tell, she was alone with the body for six or seven days. Strange little thing, she is. Says she's twelve, though she looks younger to me."

Something in Maggie's mind clicked. The age of the child—well, it would fit, wouldn't it? It seemed far-fetched, but . . .

"I know nothing about any girl," she said brusquely. "She must have been some stray my mother took in." She pretended to muse on the problem for a moment. "Can I see her, though? Perhaps something will come to me then."

While the policeman went to fetch the girl, Maggie paced the room. If what she suspected turned out to be true, she wasn't sure what she would do. A moment later, the door to the interview room opened and Constable O'Donnell came back in with a thin, sad-looking girl trailing behind him.

Maggie took one look into the child's green eyes—those huge, pained eyes, which seemed to take up most of her face—and knew exactly who she belonged to. She might not have inherited her mother's good looks, but Maggie would know those eyes anywhere. So *that's* why Franny had left so abruptly all those years ago. She hadn't just run off with that farmhand, she'd been carrying his bastard, too. Maggie wondered when their mother had found out about the child. She remembered Theresa saying that Franny had gotten in touch—it must have been then that she'd dumped her child on their mother. Suddenly the events of the past few years fell into place—Theresa's insistence at being left alone; family visits to the cottage being discouraged; and when Maggie did go there, the upstairs rooms being kept locked.

"Well, would you be able to look after the child?" the policeman asked. "If not, it'll be the orphanage for her. She's too old for fostering."

Maggie needed to make a quick decision. Like everyone else who had known Franny in her pre-Hollywood days, Maggie had never made the connection between the movie star Frances Fitzgerald and her wayward younger sister. That meant she didn't realize that Franny was dead. To her mind, she had no idea where Franny had gone to, but it seemed safe to assume that she didn't check in much on her child. And Maggie had no intention of taking on her sister's mistake. Conrad would be here soon. Once he saw the girl, he would no doubt come to the same conclusion about her parentage and would insist on taking her in. That was the last thing she wanted. If the child was anything like her mother, Maggie didn't want her in their home and their life. She had her own children to consider. They were good, God-fearing girls, and she intended to keep them that way. One bad apple could spoil the whole barrel.

"No, I'm sorry," she said at last. "Believe me, I wish I could take her. But I have five of my own, and we have no room and little money as it is."

The policeman looked at the well-dressed woman, with her new winter coat and handmade leather shoes and handbag, and wondered how she could have so little compassion. He tried not to sneer as he said, "I understand. The authorities will be here in a few hours to take the child. After that, you needn't concern yourself with her any longer."

He looked at the poor, skinny wretch, silent and watchful. His mother would happily have taken her in, but at fifty-five she would be deemed too old. Constable O'Donnell didn't understand it. To his mind, there was something very wrong with a system that would rather send a child to an institution than see her with a loving family. But sadly, there was nothing he could do about it.

30

Cara had barely gotten used to Mrs. O'Donnell's house when she was told that she would be leaving. She accepted her fate without question or complaint, simply doing as she was told and packing up her few belongings. She hadn't said much in the week since she'd been found with her grandmother's body. She was still in shock. The policeman and his family had been kind to her, but she'd known not to get too settled with them.

The following day, Cara sat with Mrs. O'Donnell in the front room, waiting for the welfare worker to arrive. On the dot of midday, a black Mini Metro drew up outside the house. An officious-looking middle-aged woman in a brown suit got out and came to ring the doorbell. With her pinched face and mousy hair tied back in a severe bun, she didn't look very friendly.

"I'm Miss Lynch," she introduced herself when Mrs. O'Donnell answered the door. She glanced down at Cara, who stood a little behind the older woman. "Is this the child?"

Frowning, Mrs. O'Donnell said pointedly, "Yes, this is *Cara.*" Then, realizing it wouldn't help Cara if she got the woman's back up, she tried to smile and be more welcoming. "Perhaps you would like to come in for some tea?"

Mrs. O'Donnell had spent the morning baking, thinking that it would make things easier for Cara if she could get to know the woman a little before they left. But the shrewish Miss Lynch appeared to have other ideas.

"Oh, I don't have time for that," she said, looking down her nose at the little house. "We must be getting on."

It was all happening too quickly, Cara thought, panic setting in; she didn't want to go with this woman. She looked up pleadingly at Mrs. O'Donnell, but the kind lady could do nothing more than give Cara a sympathetic hug good-bye.

"Well, come on with you." The woman took Cara by the wrist and dragged her away.

They were already at the car when Mrs. O'Donnell called out, "Wait!"

Miss Lynch stopped reluctantly and turned back. "Whatever it is, be quick. We don't have long."

The older woman hurried inside and came out again with something wrapped in brown packaging. She pressed it into Cara's hands. "There's some fruitcake to keep you going."

Impatient now to get on, Miss Lynch tried to usher Cara into the car. "Come on now. We must be off."

Suddenly faced with the prospect of going with the unfriendly lady, Cara cracked. Breaking from her hold, she rushed over to Mrs. O'Donnell and threw her arms around the older woman's waist. "Please! Let me stay. I don't want to go with her!"

Mrs. O'Donnell's eyes filled with tears. She wished that she could stop this, but there was nothing she could do. "I'm so sorry . . ."

Storming over to the pair, Miss Lynch wrenched Cara away. "Pull yourself together," she hissed as she marched the girl back to the car. "Any more scenes like that, and it'll be the worse for you."

The drive took an hour and a half. Mostly it was in silence. Miss Lynch seemed to have little interest in getting to know her. From snatches of conversation that she'd overheard between Mrs. O'Donnell and her son, Cara knew she was being sent to live at a Church-run orphanage. Having read *Jane Eyre,* Cara was already terrified about what the institution was going to be like, but the first glimpse she gotten of St. Mary's Orphanage was even more disheartening. Miss Lynch pointed out a gray fortresslike building on the horizon.

"The building once served as a prison," she said.

Erected in the seventeenth century, it had been used to house rebels during Oliver Cromwell's Irish campaign. A huge wall, at least ten feet tall, surrounded a large central building. Cara couldn't help wondering if it was designed to keep the children in or the rest of the world out. A young nun sat in a reception booth at the entrance. Seeing the black car approach, she hurried to open up: Miss Lynch was clearly a frequent visitor. The rusty iron gates heaved open, the hinges squealing, crying out for oil.

As the car drew into the little courtyard, Cara saw that the main building was just as unwelcoming: cold gray stone, gnarled wooden doors, and windows that were little more than slits. There was no greenery to speak of. The other children, who were outside on some kind of break, played on hard concrete, not grass. A distant memory clicked in Cara's mind. After years of being starved of the company of others her own age, she suddenly recalled what fun it had been to play with Danny. But, getting out of the car, she realized this was nothing like how she'd played back then. As girls leaped over jump ropes or played hopscotch and tag, there were no squeals of excitement or shouts of joy. Under the stern gaze of two nuns, who were dressed head to toe in black habits like watchful crows, they clearly didn't feel free to show any enjoyment or frivolity.

Only one or two of the girls glanced in Cara's direction as she got out of the car and followed the social worker into the building. They stared at her with blank indifference. Curiosity didn't seem to be encouraged here, and a new arrival clearly wasn't anything to get excited about.

Inside, Cara trailed Miss Lynch through long, dark corridors, passing children and nuns as they went, until they reached a wooden door.

"Stay here while I talk to Sister Concepta," Miss Lynch instructed, before disappearing inside. Through the door, Cara could hear voices; although she couldn't make out the words, she knew they were talking about her. It was a long wait, and when Cara watched a nun go in carrying a tray of tea and cake, she knew it was going to take much longer. Her legs grew so tired that she ached to sit down, but she didn't dare.

It must have been nearly an hour before the door opened again and Miss Lynch appeared, brushing crumbs from her skirt. She glanced briefly at Cara. "You can go in now."

Cara looked at the closed door and felt afraid. Although she hadn't warmed to Miss Lynch, she'd never met a nun before and didn't want to go in by herself. "Aren't you staying?"

The social worker sighed, as though she felt Cara was forever causing problems. "I have to get on." She hurried off, leaving the girl alone. Steeling herself, Cara went into the room.

*   *   *

Sister Concepta had been at St. Mary's Orphanage for twenty years now, which meant she was considered to be the most senior member of staff below the abbess. It fell to her to greet the new arrivals, and it was a job she relished: she liked to have the opportunity to size them up—certain she could spot a troublemaker straight off. Now, staring at the young, bedraggled girl in front of her, instead of sympathy she felt a wave of revulsion. Nothing was known of this child's heritage, but the nun suspected that her parents had been tinkers or gypsies. With that shock of raven hair, she was clearly from raw, ill-bred stock.

"What's your second name, child?" There was silence. The nun looked up over her reading glasses. "Well? I asked you a question."

The girl still didn't reply. She must be slow, the nun decided; that or she was being insolent. Miss Lynch, the social worker, had said that there had been something of a scene at the house earlier when she'd picked her up. Either way, the nun had no time for this child.

She sniffed disparagingly. "Well, you can be as bold as you like, but we've agreed to take care of you until you're sixteen. Three years will be a long time without speaking. I imagine you'll find your voice soon enough."

She rang a bell, and another nun appeared. She was younger, but no less forbidding.

"This is Sister Jude. She's in charge of your year group." Sister Concepta addressed the younger nun then. "Get her processed, will you?"

From there Cara was taken through to a tiled room and made to undress. The nun turned a rusty handle, and there was the sound of pipes clanking as the shower system went to work. Cara gasped as needles of ice water hit her. She tried to jump out, but Sister Jude used a broom to push her back in. "Stay under until you're clean."

Cara's fingers and toes were blue with cold by the time she was allowed out. Using the small, threadbare towel to dry off, she stood naked and shivering until she was handed a pile of clothes. She looked down at them. This wasn't the nice outfit that Mrs. O'Donnell had given her. Instead, it was a plain dark gray dress, like she'd seen the other girls wearing.

Against her instinct, Cara decided to speak up. "These aren't my clothes."

The nun looked at her with scorn. "There is no room for vanity here. We're all the same in God's eyes, and you will look the same as the other girls."

The woman's eyes challenged Cara to dare to object. She was smart enough not to. Instead, she dropped her gaze and turned away to get ready. The dress was shapeless and the woollen material itchy; she had to tie a knot in the huge knickers to keep them up around her skinny waist. But she knew better than to complain.

By the time Cara had gotten dressed, it was a little before five thirty and already dark outside, the winter evening drawing in quickly. During the day, the small, high windows let little natural light in, while in the evening the few oil lamps were spaced far apart, providing only the barest illumination.

"It's suppertime now for the girls," Sister Jude explained as they walked back along the corridors. "Niamh!" she called out.

At the sound of her name, a small, slight girl turned. Eyes wide with fear, she walked toward the nun. Cara was pleased to see she wasn't the only one terrified of the sisters.

Sister Jude pushed Cara roughly forward. "This is the new girl. I'm putting you in charge of her."

The girl named Niamh, who Cara decided looked around her age, bobbed her head. "Yes, Sister."

For the fourth time that day, Cara's fate was handed on to someone else. The other girl waited until Sister Jude was out of sight and then whispered, "What's your name?"

"Cara."

"Well, I'm Niamh, and I've been here for five years. Do what I do, and you should be all right."

The last part sounded ominous, but before she could ask what Niamh meant, they rounded a corner where there was a long line of girls standing in silence. Cara guessed correctly that they were lined up to go in for dinner. At six on the dot the doors opened, and the girls began to file inside.

The dining hall was a vast room, with long refectory tables and wooden benches on either side. The girls filled one row before moving to another. There was no jostling and no more than a low murmur of voices as they shuffled to their places.

When all the orphans were assembled, the nuns came in and sat at a top table, and then one of the girls began to read grace. Only once this was all finished did they finally sit down to eat. The nuns were served first, and Cara watched as girls came out of the kitchen carrying plates of food.

"Kitchen duty's the worst," Niamh whispered. Cara nodded sagely, although she had no idea what the other girl meant. She guessed that she would find out soon enough.

The whole process had taken ages, and Cara was famished, having not had anything since breakfast. When she finally had food plonked in front of her, she thought that she was ready to eat anything. Then she looked down at her plate. She had no idea what was on it—a stew of some sort, she guessed. The girls around her had picked up their cutlery and were already digging in hungrily. With her fork, Cara poked around the brown sludge until she found a piece of what looked like meat. She tentatively took it into her mouth. It was half cooked and lukewarm, which she could put up with, but it was chewy too, mostly gristle. She felt bile rise up from her stomach and into her mouth. Somehow she managed to swallow it down. Feeling sick now, she pushed the plate away.

Niamh spotted the gesture. "What's wrong with you?"

Cara had been used to preparing her own meals for the past few months, simple dishes of bread and cheese, and at Mrs. O'Donnell's the little food that she had eaten had been delicious. She wasn't usually a fussy eater, but she couldn't consume something so unappetizing.

"I can't eat this," she said. "It's disgusting."

A big-boned girl with a sharp tongue, whom the others called Molly, raised her head. "Do you hear that? Her Highness here thinks she's too good for our supper."

The others sniggered. Niamh was the only one who didn't join in. "You have to eat it," she insisted. "You won't get anything more until you finish. That's the rule. And, believe me, it'll taste a whole lot worse tomorrow morning."

Cara looked down at the plate and felt tears gathering in her eyes. She knew she ought to eat, but she just couldn't. It was all too much: her grandmother's death and now being put in this strange, hostile place.

"I can't," she whispered. Glancing up, she made a silent plea to the other girl not to make her.

Niamh studied her for a long moment, as though trying to determine if her distress was genuine. Then, quickly glancing around to make sure no nuns were nearby, she reached over and took Cara's full plate and substituted it for her own empty one. Almost as an afterthought, she gave Cara her piece of bread—the only edible item on the table.

"I'll do this for you as it's your first day, but after that you're on your own."

Cara looked on in surprise as the girl proceeded to devour every last morsel on the plate. Seeing the look on her face, Niamh smiled wryly. "I told you, I've been here a long time. I know how to survive this place. Listen to me, and you will, too."

After dinner, there were chores to do. For the moment, Sister Jude said, Cara was to remain with Niamh, until her schedule was officially determined. Niamh worked in the dressmaker's along with five others, under the charge of Sister Agnes. They were assigned to make and repair all the nuns' habits and the girls' clothes and also sometimes did dressmaking for locals to bring in extra money for the convent. The orphanage was largely self-sufficient, Niamh explained, run mainly by the children's labor. Other duties included helping tend to the vegetable and fruit patches; scrubbing the floors; cooking or washing dishes. Dressmaking was one of the easiest options for work duties, mostly because of Sister Agnes.

"She's one of the good ones," Niamh told Cara.

Certainly she was the most welcoming. As soon as they got to the sewing room, the moon-faced nun came over to the two girls.

"So you must be the new girl. Cara, isn't it?" she said warmly. "Let's find something for you to do."

She set Cara up repairing hems. The work wasn't hard, and the girls chattered easily under Sister Agnes's benevolent eye. It was the first time Cara had been able to relax a little since she'd arrived.

Soon it was time for bed. Niamh showed Cara to their dormitory. There was a spare bed next to hers, so Cara took that. With half an hour until lights-out, the girls went about their bedtime preparations, talking in low, hushed tones. With no rituals of her own yet, Cara watched as Niamh began to unpin her long, fair hair. It fell in a thick rope down to her waist. Sitting on the edge of her bed, she began to brush out the tangles while Cara looked on enviously. Her own hair was short and dark, and though she'd always liked being a tomboy, she couldn't help feeling a little jealous of the other girl's princess locks.

Niamh must have felt her staring, because she looked over and smiled.

"I have to do this every morning and night, and it takes ages," she explained. "But I don't want to cut it."

Cara could see why.

By ten everyone was in bed.

"What happens tomorrow morning?" Cara wanted to know.

But Niamh hushed her. "Be quiet," the girl warned. Her timing was impeccable. The moment after Cara shut up, Sister Concepta appeared in the doorway.

Eyes tightly closed, Cara could hear the nun making her way round the room, checking that everything was in order. When she got to Cara's bed, the girl could feel her heart beating faster. But she managed to keep her breathing steady and feign sleep. The nun stood there for a long time but then finally moved off. There was a click as the light went out. Only then did Cara open her eyes. She desperately wanted to ask Niamh more questions, but she sensed it was a bad idea. Instead she reflected on the events of the day.

As she went to sleep that night, Cara made a quick assessment of her position at St. Mary's. To her mind, she had made one true friend so far and one powerful enemy. She just hoped the former was strong enough to help her combat the latter.

Record keeping wasn't a strong point for social services at this time. Rushing to get home that day, it was little wonder that Miss Lynch, who felt overworked and underappreciated, misplaced the paperwork of the child found in Theresa Healey's house, which meant that Cara disappeared into the system without a trace. So when a man came looking for her several weeks later, he had no choice but to approach orphanages individually. He still might have had a chance of finding her; it was just unfortunate that when he went to St. Mary's looking for a Cara Healey, he met with Sister Concepta, who, out of spite or sheer devilment, claimed to have no child of that name in her charge.

31

Sister Jude raised the broom high. "There's no worse sin than laziness!"

Cara braced herself for the inevitable blow. The broom struck her clean across the legs, the sharp sticks of the brush grazing her skin. She bit down on her lip, and the metallic taste of blood flooded her mouth. It was better than letting the nun see her cry.

She'd brought the punishment on herself, of course, having been too slow cleaning the kitchen floor. But her knees had been aching, and she'd had to stand up for a minute to stretch her legs. Molly had hissed a warning to her that Sister Jude was coming, but it had already been too late.

"You big, lazy lump!" Sister Jude brought the broom down again. "The Devil makes work for idle hands!"

This time the blow sent Cara reeling facedown onto the hard floor. She landed flat on her stomach, winding herself.

"Let this be a lesson to you."

Satisfied with her handiwork, Sister Jude threw the broom on the floor and made to walk out. At the door, she hesitated for a moment and turned back. Too late, Cara guessed her intention, and she looked on helplessly as the nun kicked over the bucket. Before she could roll away, the dirty water spilled across her legs, the bleach stinging her cuts. Despite her vow not to show any reaction, she couldn't help grunting in pain.

Once the nun finally left, Cara managed to get to her feet. Looking down at the floor, she wanted to cry. She would need to start all over again.

It was May 1961, and Cara had just turned fourteen. She had been at the orphanage for over a year, although it felt like longer. The drudgery of the routine there made the days and weeks bleed together. The girls rose at six during the week. After cold showers, a breakfast of bread and tea was doled out at seven, followed by lessons, with a break for lunch. After school finished at four, there were chores to be done, which resumed again after dinner. Religion played a big part of every day. The priest came from the neighboring parish to hear confession on a Friday afternoon; grace was said before every meal, prayers before bed.

Saturdays were the best. After chores in the morning, the girls were usually taken into town and allowed to go to the pictures. But then there were Sundays: the long Catholic Mass in the morning, followed by an interminable day of prayer and contemplation.

Other than religion, beatings formed a regular part of Cara's life. She wasn't sure why, but Sister Concepta clearly loathed her and took every opportunity to make her life a misery. When she'd found out that Cara was working in the dressmaking room, she'd had her reassigned to scrubbing the floors, the worst duty. Cara hated it. Her hands were permanently raw and stinging from the bleach, her knees sore and bruised from shuffling across the wet floor. She'd come to detest the smell of disinfectant; it hung in the air throughout the orphanage and seemed to seep through her clothes and get absorbed into her very skin.

It wasn't just Sister Concepta who victimized Cara. She had two cohorts, Sisters Jude and Bernadette, who joined in her persecution of the girl. Cara wasn't the only one who suffered at their hands. Beatings and punishments were a regular and accepted part of the regime at the convent. Cara, however, had it harder than most. Today's beating was typical. What made it worse was the way outsiders thought the orphans should be grateful to the Church. When they went into town, people would greet the nuns, pressing money into their hands and saying, "God bless you for looking after the poor children, Sisters." Cara would have loved to tell them exactly what the kind sisters did to their charges every day, but there was no point. The belief that the Church knew best was too deeply ingrained.

It was Niamh who made life bearable. The kindness she had shown Cara on that first day was just the start. During those initial weeks, when Cara had struggled to settle in, the other girl had helped her in any way that she could, particularly when it came to lessons. After years without formal schooling, Cara had found that she was behind in most areas. Though she was highly literate, thanks to the fact that there had been nothing to do apart from read in the cottage, she had little knowledge of arithmetic, geography, or history. Because of this, the nuns had at first labeled her slow. But in reality she was a quick learner, and with Niamh's painstaking help in the evenings, she had eventually caught up.

To Cara's surprise, Niamh was actually only a year younger than she, but she looked less than her thirteen years because she was small for her age. Pretty in a soft, sweet way, she had a heart-shaped face, long-lashed blue eyes, and thick, fair hair that fell Rapunzel style to her waist. Like all of the girls', Niamh's story of how she'd ended up at St. Mary's was a sad one. Her father had died when she was eight, and after his death, her mother had struggled to cope with two children. Deciding to start a new life in England, she'd left Niamh at the orphanage and taken her son with her to Birmingham, promising that once she was settled she'd fetch her daughter. That had been five years earlier. She'd remarried now, but still her promise to come back for Niamh hadn't materialized.

Sister Concepta didn't like Niamh much either, and Cara suspected that was because of her beauty. Niamh did her best to conceal it, always wearing her hair pulled into a bun or tucked under a cap, letting it down only at night, brushing the locks out with a hundred strokes to prevent tangles. Cara sometimes helped when she got too tired to lift the brush.

Sister Concepta had caught them once. She'd stormed across the room, grabbed the brush from Cara's hand, and used it to strike first one girl and then the other.

"Vanity is a sin," she'd said over and over again, as she'd beaten them.

Sometimes Cara wondered if there was anything that wasn't a sin.

After the beating had ended, the nun had confiscated the brush. Seeing how distressed her friend had been at losing her most precious possession, Cara had managed to sneak one of the new scrubbing brushes from the kitchen for her to use as a makeshift comb. Now Niamh was more careful about when she brought it out.

Not all the nuns were mean, of course. In fact, Sister Agnes, who along with heading up the dressmaking group acted as Sister Concepta's deputy, was a gentle, fair woman. But she seemed to be the exception rather than the rule.

The six years that Cara had lived with her grandmother had been hard. But Theresa's initial indifference and later madness could not compare with the cruelty and bullying in this institution. Cara spent a lot of time thinking up ways to escape. The only problem was, she had no idea where she would go if she did get out. Sadly, the orphanage and the girls within it were the closest she had to home and family.

Cara wasn't the only one who dreamed of running away. Molly in particular talked about it all the time. She had been the one hostile to Cara on the first night, but it had quickly become apparent that her anger was a defense mechanism, built up after a lifetime in Church-run institutions. A large-boned girl of fifteen, she suffered nearly as much at the nuns' hands as Cara. She was always coming up with schemes for escape, but it was about a week after Cara's beating in the kitchen that Molly and two of the other girls finally managed to get out. They'd been on laundry duty and had gotten dressed up in the freshly washed nuns' habits and simply walked out through the front gate. All three were large girls, so no one had thought to stop them. It was only later, when the head count was taken at lunchtime, that their subterfuge was discovered.

The garda were alerted right away. It didn't take long for them to find the girls. They hadn't thought their plan through very well; as soon as they got out of sight of the orphanage, they had dumped their habits, making themselves conspicuous by being outside in the middle of the day when other children their age were in school. A local busybody had spotted them walking along the road to Galway and contacted the police. Molly and the others were brought back later that night.

Niamh told Cara what she'd heard of their fate. "They've been put in the Quiet Room."

Cara shuddered. She'd taken her turn in there. It was one of the worst punishments: to be locked in the small cellar with no light and nothing other than water for hours at a time.

First thing in the morning, all the girls were called into the main hall. Molly and the two other escapees stood on the stage, trying their best to look defiant. As Sister Concepta and Sister Jude walked out, the girls' expressions faltered. The mother superior took center stage.

"As you are all aware," she began gravely, "these three ungrateful children repaid our hospitality by sneaking out of here last night. You are here to witness their punishment." She turned to the girls. "Molly!" she commanded. "Step forward."

Holding her head high, Molly did as she was told. Along with all the other girls in the hall, she was clearly expecting to receive a public beating. But instead, Sister Concepta produced a large pair of garden shears. A gasp of surprise and faint protest echoed through the hall as she proceeded to hack off the girl's hair. Lock after lock fell to the floor, until Molly—never the most attractive of girls anyway—stood there almost bald, with just a few haphazard tufts of hair sticking out of her head. Realizing their fate, the other two runaways began to cry.

"See?" Sister Concepta proclaimed gravely as she started in on the next girl. "This is what happens to those of you who disobey us."

As they, too, were shorn of their hair, even the hardiest girls in the audience had to look away.

The whole shearing took fifteen minutes, but Sister Concepta made the girls stand there for another half an hour so everyone could witness their humiliation. Niamh was shaking with fear as they eventually trickled out of the hall.

"What's wrong?" Cara said in a low voice as they headed up to the dorm.

The other girl's hand went instinctively to her head. "I couldn't stand it if that happened to me," she whispered back.

Cara knew why she was worried. Sister Concepta was itching to cut off Niamh's beautiful hair. That was why the girl tried to keep it hidden from view. Adept at staying out of trouble, she made sure not to give the nuns any reason to punish her. But she still feared what would happen if they ever did.

A few weeks later, one Monday afternoon in the midst of summer, Cara was outside the kitchens, emptying dirty water down the drain, when she heard someone calling her name. She looked up to see Niamh running toward her, looking breathless and worried.

"Whatever's the matter?" she asked as the other girl drew level with her.

"Oh, Cara," she panted, holding her left side as though she had a stitch. "I've done a terrible thing."

It turned out that some of the girls, tired of Niamh being such a goody-goody, had dared her to sneak outside and steal half a dozen apples from the orchard adjacent to the orphanage. A fence separated St. Mary's from the farmland, and there was a loose piece of wood in it, so small that the nuns hadn't bothered to have it repaired. Few of the girls could have gotten through there—but Niamh, small-boned and flexible, was just able to squeeze between the slats.

She had thought she could sneak in and out without the farmer, Dennis Brennan, realizing that she was there. Everything had been going well, and she had collected about a dozen apples in her apron, when the farmer came out from one of the barns and spotted her. Dropping her bounty, Niamh had managed to quickly shin down the tree and run back toward the orphanage. He'd given chase, shouting and cursing at her all the way, but she'd managed to slip through the gap in the fence before he could catch her.

"What if he saw my face?" she fretted now. "He might tell the sisters, and then what'll happen to me?"

Wanting to reassure her friend, Cara said, "I'm sure it'll be fine. He probably won't even bother saying anything." But there was no conviction in her voice. Dennis Brennan was known to be a stickler for order and obedience. He wasn't the type to let this go.

Unfortunately, Cara was right. Later that afternoon, Sister Concepta called all the girls into the assembly hall, where they were made to stand and wait in silence. The room was broiling, as all the windows were closed, and none of the girls dared go over to open them. They had been on their feet for nearly half an hour, none of them even daring to talk, when the doors finally burst open and Sister Concepta walked in—accompanied by Dennis Brennan. As soon as she saw him, Cara could feel Niamh falter next to her. She reached an arm around her friend's waist to hold her up.

"Now," Sister Concepta began once she'd taken her place onstage, "who can tell me what the Seventh Commandment is?"

The assembled girls answered sluggishly, "Thou shalt not steal."

The nun nodded. "Exactly. So then why is it that Mr. Brennan here tells me that one of you ventured over to his farm to steal from him?"

This time there was silence.

"If someone doesn't own up," Sister Concepta said, her tone deceptively mild, "then I'll simply punish you all. There will be no going into town on Saturdays for the next six months."

Cara knew then what was going to happen next. Niamh would confess; she'd never let everyone be punished for what she'd done. Then Sister Concepta would use this as her excuse to chop off her lovely hair. Cara couldn't let the nun do that to her friend, so before Niamh could say anything, she put her hand up and said, "It was me, Sister. I was the one who stole the apples."

Sister Concepta glowered down at her. "Cara!" she thundered. "I should have guessed!" She looked over at the farmer. "This girl's a troublemaker, and, trust me, she will be punished." Then the nun turned back to Cara, her eyes glittering with malice. "Come up here."

Walking up onto the stage, Cara tried not to show her fear as Sister Jude went to fetch the shears. As Sister Concepta began to hack off her hair, Cara forced herself to stare defiantly ahead and, meeting Niamh's eyes, saw her friend's gratitude and felt strength run through her. It helped her not to cry even as the sharp blades grazed her scalp.

The dorm lights were out, and Cara was nearly asleep when she felt someone come to sit on her bed. Opening her eyes, she saw it was Niamh. In her hands she carried two apples.

"I had these in my pockets still," she whispered, holding one out for Cara.

Without speaking another word, the two of them bit into the forbidden fruit. They both took small bites, trying to crunch as quietly as possible so as not to wake the other girls. When they'd finished, Niamh wrapped the cores in a tissue, promising to get rid of them the next day so there would be no evidence of their illicit midnight feast.

She was about to leave when she turned to Cara and said, "Thank you for what you did for me today." She reached out and touched the black tufts of hair, her hands running gently over Cara's sore head. "I don't know how I could ever repay you."

"Don't worry about it." Cara looked away, embarrassed by Niamh's obvious gratitude and hero worship. "It was nothing."

Niamh cupped her friend's chin in her hand, gently turning Cara's face toward her so their gazes met. "No," she said solemnly. "It was *everything*."

Then, as though it were the most natural thing in the world, she leaned forward and kissed Cara tenderly on the lips.

It was a soft, sweet kiss, tasting of stolen apples and gratitude. And, as with everything Niamh did, there was a complete innocence about it.

Finally Niamh pulled away. The two girls stared at each other for a long moment.

"Thank you again," Niamh murmured. Then she slipped from Cara's bed and padded across to her own.

Neither of them ever mentioned the incident again, nor was there ever a repeat of it. But the kiss that night sealed their friendship.

32

"Good news, Cara!" Sister Agnes exclaimed. She had pulled the girl out of formation as the children were filing into hall for breakfast, and whatever it was about, she seemed genuinely excited for her favorite charge. "I've got a treat for you this weekend."

Cara listened as Sister Agnes explained the reason behind her enthusiasm. It was to do with the Buchanans, a wealthy young Anglo-Irish couple, who lived in the big house just outside town. James Buchanan had fought in the British army before becoming a diplomat and traveling the world, while his wife, Virginia, was the daughter of a landed gentleman and well known in London society circles. After a yearlong posting in India, they had recently moved back to James's mother's family home. He had taken up a hereditary seat in the House of Lords, which would entail occasional trips to England, but for the most part, the Buchanans would now be permanently based in Galway. The couple were interested in becoming involved in the local community. Sadly, they hadn't been blessed with children of their own, and, having heard about the orphanage, they had decided to invite one of the girls to spend the weekend with them.

Sister Agnes beamed at Cara. "So I've decided to send you. As long as you'd like to go, that is?"

"Of course I would!"

The nun's excitement was infectious. Cara hurried back to tell the dorm. A treat like this happened from time to time. Generous families would agree to take the orphans out for a weekend or would come to visit them. Usually once they had met a girl, they would stick with her, taking the same child out again and again. So far Cara had never been chosen to go, because Sister Concepta was in charge of making the selection. But as she was away at the moment, having taken the elderly and sick nuns on a pilgrimage to Lourdes, the task had fallen to Sister Agnes, and she had decided that Cara should be the one allowed to go with the Buchanans.

It was October 1961, nearly five months since the apple-stealing incident. After the low point of having her head shaved, life had improved for Cara over the past few weeks with Sister Concepta's absence. Though her hair still hadn't grown back properly and stuck out in uneven black tufts all over her head, it at least covered her scalp and looked respectable enough for her to be seen in public without feeling ashamed. This opportunity to leave the orphanage for the weekend was the icing on the cake.

The other girls were pleased for her, if a little envious. They all saw the big house on their way to church on Sunday, and each of them would have loved to be the one selected to go there.

Niamh was her usual fanciful self. "Maybe they'll like you so much that they'll ask you to come and live with them," she said dreamily.

Cara snorted. "Yeah, I can see *that* happening. I'm ripe for a fairy-tale ending."

But although she'd die before admitting it, the thought had crossed her mind. Imagine—getting out of here for good. Maybe she could even persuade them to take Niamh, too . . .

That night Cara sent up a special little prayer, asking God to make the Buchanans fall in love with her and take her away from St. Mary's.

She spent the next few days looking forward to the following weekend. But late on Friday, just when she had everything packed, Sister Agnes came to tell her that the Buchanans had been called away to London, so she wouldn't be going anywhere after all.

"Cheer up," the nun said, seeing how disheartened Cara was. "They'll be back next weekend, and you'll get to go then."

Unfortunately, on the following Friday morning, Sister Concepta arrived back early from her trip. Cara was in her geography lesson when she saw the nun walking across the tarmac into the main building. Immediately, she got a sinking feeling. There was no way the older nun would let her go to the Buchanans'.

Sure enough, after lessons that day, just as Cara was about to go and pack, Sister Concepta came into the classroom, along with Sister Agnes.

"So, Cara," Sister Concepta began, "I hear that you're meant to be leaving us for the next two days—"

"Yes, I am!" Cara burst out, already certain she knew where this was going. "And it's not fair of you to stop me going!" She banged her fist on the desk. "Goddamn you!" she swore, drawing a gasp from the room. "Why do you have to make my life such a misery all the time?"

Cara wasn't aware of how aggressive she sounded until Sister Agnes put a restraining hand on her arm. "Cara, please," she hushed, her eyes pleading. She looked over at Sister Concepta. "I'm sorry, Sister. She didn't mean it."

But the older nun ignored her deputy. "Actually," she said to Cara, "I had just come in here to remind you to be on your best behavior this weekend. But I think after *that* little display it would be inappropriate for you to go to the Buchanans'."

Cara was speechless with anger. She'd played right into the nun's hands. Sister Concepta hadn't had any intention of allowing her to go this weekend. She'd just been looking for an excuse to take this away from her. And Cara had given it to her.

Sister Agnes looked distressed on Cara's behalf. "But they'll be here to collect her soon. Should I just tell them that we won't be sending anyone?"

"Oh, no. We'll still send someone. There's no point denying another girl a treat just because one spoils it." Sister Concepta's eyes surveyed the room. "So I'm looking for volunteers. Who would like to go?"

The girls hesitated. Cara was popular among them because she stood up to the nuns, but there could be no loyalty here—it was every girl for herself. Slowly, they all raised their hands.

The nun's eyes settled on Niamh. She alone had remained loyal and not volunteered to take Cara's place. Sister Concepta's mouth turned up in a cruel smile. "I think Niamh should go instead."

It was the ultimate twist and, Cara suspected, a way to divide the two girls, who were known for being inseparable. Sister Concepta no doubt didn't want to see either of them going to stay with the Buchanans, but though she might dislike Niamh, she detested Cara with a passion.

Once the nuns had gone and the crowd had dispersed, Niamh rushed to her friend. "I'm really sorry. Do you mind terribly?"

Cara forced herself to shrug, pretending not to care. "Why should I?" She was damned if she was going to cry over this. She needed to be tough, not show anyone that she'd gotten to her. It was the only way to survive.

But Niamh wasn't so easily fooled. "I could speak to Sister Agnes, tell her that I don't want to go."

"What's the point? Sister Concepta will just send someone else."

Niamh bit her lip. Even the usually positive younger girl couldn't deny the inevitable truth of the situation, however unfair it might be.

Cara got up to head back to the dorm, wanting to be alone so she could pull herself together. Not taking the hint, Niamh followed her. "Maybe I can go to see Sister Concepta," she persisted, clearly still trying to come up with ways to resolve the situation. "I could try to reason with her. Or maybe I could tell the Buchanans what happened. If I explain what Sister's like, then maybe they could insist that you come out next time. Sister Concepta would have to listen then."

Cara rounded on her. "God, would you ever leave me alone?" she snapped. "I'm sick of you trailing around after me. Haven't you got something else to do?"

Niamh recoiled at Cara's words. "I'm sorry," she murmured, dropping her eyes to disguise the hurt. But she did as Cara had asked and went into the dorm alone.

Cara lay on her bed, pretending not to watch her friend pack. She regretted her harsh words and knew that she ought to apologize. The unfairness of the situation was hardly Niamh's fault, after all; she was as much a victim of Sister Concepta as Cara herself. But something stopped Cara. She was jealous, that was it. Even though she knew that was what Sister Concepta had wanted, to drive a wedge between them, she couldn't help how she felt. She'd been looking forward to the weekend with the Buchanans and had spent the last few days imagining what it would be like to get away from these walls. To have that snatched away at such a late stage was devastating, and her adolescent brain wasn't developed enough to manage magnanimity in the face of such disappointment.

Half an hour later, Niamh came over to see her. "I'm heading off now."

"Right," Cara said shortly, not even bothering to look up from the book she was reading. She could see that her friend was near tears, but she couldn't bring herself to comfort her.

By Sunday night, Cara had calmed down. In fact, over the course of the weekend, she'd realized just how much she missed her friend. It had been a stupid fight, and she wanted to make up with Niamh as soon as possible.

Niamh was due to be dropped off by the Buchanans just before teatime. Cara stood by the window of their dorm, watching out for her return. When she saw the Buchanans' car draw up, she felt a surge of excitement and waited impatiently for her friend to come up. As Niamh appeared in the doorway, Cara wanted to rush up to her, but she wasn't the tactile sort. Instead she waited for Niamh to approach her—big expressions of emotion were much more her sort of thing. But instead of coming over, Niamh went to her own cubicle and began to unpack.

She must think I'm still angry with her, Cara realized. So she got up and went over to the blond girl.

"How was it?" she asked gruffly.

Niamh didn't look up from her task. "It was fine."

The reticence was so out of character that Cara gave a theatrical sigh. "It's all right, you can tell me about it. I won't be jealous, I promise." She sat down on Niamh's bed. "Really, I want to hear everything you did."

But Niamh wouldn't meet her eyes. "Maybe tomorrow. I'm tired now. I just want to go to bed."

Cara stared in surprise, feeling peeved by the lack of response. "All right, then." She got up. "Be like that."

Niamh didn't answer. As Cara walked away, she pondered her friend's behavior. The only explanation she could come up with was that the other girl was still cross about how she'd behaved toward her on Friday, but Cara would be surprised if she bore a grudge. It wasn't like her. Maybe she was just tired. Perhaps tomorrow she'd be in a better mood.

But the following day Niamh was just as reticent about her weekend. And over the next week her mood didn't improve. She seemed, to Cara at least, distant, almost distracted. She stopped eating at mealtimes, leaving the other girls to finish off her food. Even when it was her favorite, honey and lemon carrageen pudding, she had no interest. Cara tried talking to her about it, but she kept insisting that everything was fine.

"She's just up herself after being with the Buchanans. She's got airs and graces now, thinks she's above us all, isn't that right?" Molly teased, prodding Niamh in the ribs.

"Just leave me alone," Niamh said tiredly.

So eventually the other girls did. But Cara couldn't help being concerned. There seemed to be something seriously wrong with Niamh. She had lost her sparkle, and Cara was sure she could hear her friend crying herself to sleep. There were often tears in the dormitory at night, but Niamh's seemed to last longer than most. Cara just had no idea what was wrong.

"I don't want to go."

Niamh's mouth set in a stubborn line. Sister Concepta had come in earlier to say that the Buchanans had offered to have her for the weekend again. It was six weeks since the last outing, and they'd declared it such a success that they wanted her to come back. The nun had said it in a slightly disbelieving tone, as though she couldn't quite understand why they'd want to spend time with *her*. But Sister Concepta was a snob; she didn't want to offend the bigwigs in the area, and she also didn't want to risk them withdrawing the large donations that they made to the orphanage.

"Well, they want you, and you're going," she told Niamh firmly. "And that's an end of it."

Niamh looked so unhappy that Cara felt bad. Things hadn't really been right between them since that afternoon when her friend had gone off for the first visit. Assuming that Niamh didn't want to go now because she was afraid of offending her, Cara said, "I don't mind you going, I promise."

Niamh looked at her blankly. "What?" That confused expression was one she wore a lot these days.

"I know it's not your choice," Cara tried again. "I know that Sister Concepta's forcing you to go. I honestly don't hold a grudge if that's—"

"For God's sake!" Niamh broke in suddenly. "You always think everything's about you, Cara." Without another word, she stalked off.

Cara watched her go, open-mouthed. It was so out of character for Niamh to be angry. She wondered what on earth had gone wrong and why her friend was so reluctant to go back to the big house.

33

Sister Agnes put a hand on Niamh's forehead. "You don't seem to have a temperature." She studied the girl for a moment. Niamh had been complaining of stomach pains all night, and she looked pale against the white sheets. She hadn't been right for weeks now and had grown gaunt and gray. Perhaps it was some long-term ailment—she would have to get the doctor to check the girl out. "But you're clearly too sick to be going anywhere."

Niamh was meant to be going to the Buchanans' that afternoon. It was January 1962, and this was the fourth time she'd been invited to the Big House since the visits had begun three months earlier. The nun had already telephoned the family earlier to let them know that the girl might not be able to make it, and they'd suggested she send someone else in her place. Sister Concepta was at a governors' meeting this afternoon, so that meant the decision rested with Sister Agnes.

"Cara." She smiled kindly at the girl. "I think you should take Niamh's place."

Cara felt a jolt of excitement at the unexpected news. Finally, she'd be able to get out of here and see what life with the Buchanans was like.

Immediately she set about packing her little bag. She'd nearly finished when she felt a cold hand on her arm, making her jump with fright. It was Niamh. She looked pale, almost ghostly, in her long white nightdress.

"You frightened the life out of me!" Cara said with mock irritation.

But Niamh's face was serious. "Please, Cara," she said urgently. "Listen to me. Don't go today."

Cara frowned, confused. "Whyever not?"

Niamh hesitated, and then she shook her head. "I can't tell you." Her eyes were pained and pleading. "But please, just listen to me. I beg of you: don't go."

It was too much for Cara. The gulf between her and Niamh hadn't healed, and she'd felt sad and frustrated these past few months with the situation. Now all that anger finally came pouring out. "Oh, I get it all right," she snapped. "You're probably just worried they'll prefer me to you."

She'd been hoping to provoke an argument, so that she could finally find out what was wrong with her friend. But instead Niamh looked crushed. "I'm sorry you think that," she said quietly, before turning away.

Cara watched her go back to bed, feeling angry and disappointed that their friendship seemed to be over. Stuffing the last of her belongings into the bag, Cara resolved to forget Niamh and have a good weekend.

To Cara's surprise, the Buchanans had insisted on coming to pick her up themselves from the orphanage. It was a touching gesture; if it had been her, with all that money and a nice place to live, the last thing Cara would have wanted to do was come out to the dark, depressing convent.

The couple were waiting for her in Sister Agnes's office. They stood up as she came in, looking if anything even more nervous than she. Both beautifully dressed and holding hands, they were two of the most attractive people she had ever seen, a perfect picture of affluence and good breeding. Virginia Buchanan wore a neat little Chanel suit in candy pink, her expensively colored blond hair pulled back into a neat chignon. James Buchanan looked youthful and dapper in a pin-striped three-piece suit. They were like two bright flashes of color against the gray of the institution.

"Oh, Cara, darling," Virginia gushed, as she pulled her into an embrace. "It's *so* lovely to have you with us. I've been absolutely *dying* to meet you. Niamh won't shut up about you when she's with us."

It was odd to hear that, given how detached Niamh had been acting around her lately. But Cara didn't have time to dwell on the matter, because Virginia was off talking once more.

"It's so perfectly dreadful that she's ill." The English lady's face dropped for a second to show how awful this news was, before brightening again. "But at least it gives us the chance to meet *you.*"

Cara listened in stunned silence as Virginia carried on. She'd never met anyone like Mrs. Buchanan—someone as bright, decorative, and frivolous as a fairy on top of a Christmas tree. At first the girl thought it was simply the excitement of meeting someone new, that Virginia wanted to put her at ease. But she quickly realized that Virginia Buchanan spoke like that all the time, in huge, exaggerated terms: everything was "lovely" and "wonderful." She was someone who clearly loved life, and life loved her right back. It was hard to imagine that anything truly terrible had ever happened to her.

By the time they got out to the car, Cara's head was spinning. Virginia was listing all the activities they had planned for the weekend: tennis, riding, walks through the woods . . .

"And there's a croquet lawn, of course," she twittered on, and then saw the blank look Cara gave her. "Oh! Don't tell me you've never played?"

Cara looked between husband and wife. They were all seated in the back of a beautiful cream car—a Jaguar, James had told her. There was a chauffeur up front, and the three of them had piled into the back, Cara happily sandwiched between the two doting adults, like a proper little family.

"No," she said tentatively in answer to Virginia's question about whether she played croquet. "I mean, I don't think so. I don't really know what it—"

"Oh, well, never mind about that," Virginia interrupted. "We'll soon show you, won't we, darling?" She turned and smiled up at her husband.

"Ginny, please," James scolded good-naturedly, reaching over to pat his wife on the arm. "You're overwhelming the poor girl."

Virginia clasped a dainty, gloved hand to her mouth. "Oops, silly me. I'm so sorry, Cara, I do run on. Feel free to stop me any time—it's the only way to get a word in, James always says . . ."

And she was off again. James caught Cara's eye and shook his head—*she's crazy but I love her*, the gesture seemed to say. They made such a perfect couple. She was elegant and beautiful, with a musical voice and an easy laugh. He was handsome and amusing, not stern like a lot of men of his standing, and so clearly doted on his wife. Cara was delighted to feel part of their happiness.

It took twenty minutes to drive to Castle Glen, the Buchanans' estate. Cara had seen it from a distance before, but close up it was even more impressive. It was typical of all big houses, the country homes of Irish landlords: an elegant white mansion with ornamental gardens set in hundreds of acres of woodland, where game was reared for shooting, all surrounded by high stone walls to ensure privacy. As they stepped out of the car onto the gravel drive, Cara could hardly believe she was here.

"It's amazing!" she breathed.

James bent down to Cara's level and asked conspiratorially, "Would you like the grand tour?"

"Of course she would," Virginia cried. "Come on, darling. Follow me!"

Grabbing Cara's hand, she dragged her through the house, showing her room after exquisitely decorated room. James followed a little way behind, seemingly content to watch the two females enjoying themselves. The bedrooms were located on the first floor at the back of the house, overlooking the manicured gardens below. The Buchanans occupied the master suite, which comprised a separate bedroom and bathroom for each of them, linked by an interconnecting door.

"If you need anything during the night, don't hesitate to come and wake me," Virginia told the girl. "Now let me show you where you're going to sleep."

The guest bedroom was located at the far end of the corridor. Cara gasped as Virginia pushed open the door. The room was every girl's dream: it was all pink, but not in a sickly way. It was pretty and fresh, with its pale pink walls and matching carpet, complemented by curtains and linen in a darker shade of coral.

"A princess room!" Virginia declared.

Cara walked around, hardly daring to touch the beautiful things. An exquisitely carved rocking horse made of dark mahogany stood by the window, its mane and tail possessing the kind of silky quality that suggested they were made of real hair. Then, in the corner, there was a giant dollhouse. When Cara drew closer, she saw that it was a perfect replica of Castle Glen, from the sycamore trees lining the driveway to her pretty, pink bedroom, reproduced right down to the wooden horse.

James came forward and put an arm around his wife's waist. "And we have one more surprise for you, don't we, darling?"

Smiling, Virginia walked over to the wooden wardrobe and opened it. Cara had no idea what was going on until the woman took out a dress—again in pink, with white bows at the waist and on the little capped sleeves.

Virginia smiled shyly at her. "If you don't like it, I'll understand."

Perhaps it was a little too girly for Cara's taste, but she was so touched by the gesture that she was happy to wear it. "I love it!"

The rest of the day passed in a dream. After tea and fruitcake in the drawing room, Virginia insisted on playing a round of croquet in the warmth of the early evening. Then they all went inside to change for dinner. Cara found a bath of warm water waiting for her and afterward put on the new pink-and-white dress.

"Doesn't she look beautiful?" Virginia trilled when Cara came downstairs.

"Beautiful," James agreed.

Cara couldn't believe her luck. How could she ever go back to the orphanage after this? But she wouldn't think about that now—she would wait until Sunday evening, when the reality was upon her; she wouldn't waste her whole wonderful weekend worrying about the future. Cara had no idea why Niamh didn't like coming out here. Perhaps it was simply because it made St. Mary's harder to bear.

After a roast beef dinner, they retired to the library, and James taught Cara how to play backgammon until she grew sleepy. At bedtime Virginia produced a fresh nightdress for her. Styled in the Victorian tradition, it was made of white muslin with lace trimming at the collar and cuffs and had a row of tiny satin buttons down the front. Cara had never owned something so lovely in her life. She said so to Virginia.

"You can take it with you on Sunday if you like," Virginia said generously. "The dress, too."

Cara's gaze dropped. It was a nice idea, but . . . "There's no point. I won't be allowed to keep it."

"Oh." Virginia looked lost for a moment. Then she said brightly, "Well, that's no problem. We'll just have to keep it here for the next time you visit." She kissed Cara lightly on the forehead before saying a final good night.

Cara couldn't believe how lovely these people were. As she knelt down to say her prayers that night, she finally felt as though she genuinely had something to be grateful for. Once she'd finished, she made the Sign of the Cross and jumped into bed. It was wonderful and comfy, the mattress so soft that she sank into it, like nothing she'd ever experienced before. It was the first time in Cara's fourteen years that she had experienced such comforts: she was clean and warm and had a full belly—it was all anyone could wish for. Burrowing down under the warm eiderdown, she wondered if life could get any better.

She was already half asleep when she heard the click of the door handle. She peeped up over the sheets to see James, closing the door.

Smiling, he walked over to her and sat down on the side of the bed. "Did I wake you, sweetheart?"

She shook her head, wondering what he was doing here in her room.

"Good," he said. "I just wanted to check how you were and see if you needed anything."

"I'm fine," she told him, hoping that he would go then. She hadn't minded that Virginia had been in here earlier, even when she was changing, but this . . . well, it didn't feel quite right.

But James didn't seem to have any intention of leaving. Instead, he reached over and stroked her hair away from her face. "You look so beautiful tonight," he said tenderly.

Cara fought the urge to flinch from his touch. After all, he had been so kind to her today, she didn't want to seem ungrateful.

He then fingered the lace collar of her nightdress. "I see you're wearing the new nightie Virginia bought for you." He sounded pleased. "You know, it's so lovely to have a child in the house," he continued, seemingly oblivious to how uncomfortable Cara was feeling. "It's been hard for us, me as well as Virginia, not to be blessed with children. Having Niamh here, and now you, means the world to us both. You do know that, Cara, don't you?"

She nodded, wishing that he'd leave.

"Seeing you in here"—he glanced around the room—"well, it's like having a daughter of my own—someone to spoil, someone to shower affection and love on. Because that's what all little girls want, isn't it? To be given presents and love and . . ." He was watching her intently. "And kisses and cuddles."

It seemed to be a question, so even though she didn't really understand what he was asking, Cara said, "I suppose so."

She watched him wet his lips. "Yes, I thought that was right. That's what you'd like, isn't it, Cara? For me to give you a cuddle?"

Cara felt confused now. She thought it sounded a little odd, but the way he'd phrased it made it very hard for her to refuse. "Er . . . yes, I suppose so."

He moved closer to her on the bed. Instinctively she inched back against the headboard, drawing her legs up protectively. She couldn't quite work out what was going on, but something about the way James was behaving didn't seem right. Cara had overheard some of the older girls at the orphanage whispering about what men and women did together in the privacy of their bedroom, and somehow she got the feeling that this was what James wanted to do with her.

"Mr. Buchanan—"

"Why don't you call me James? Just when we're in here, when it's only the two of us. It'll be our little secret."

As he moved toward her, Cara knew she had to act now. Without thinking, she elbowed him hard in the nose.

"Jesus!"

Blood began to spurt from his nostrils, and his hands came up to cover his face. With James temporarily distracted, Cara leaped from the bed. She looked desperately around the room, trying to find some means of escape before he recovered. Her eyes settled on the adjoining bathroom.

"Damn you!"

Cara's head whipped round, and she saw that James was already getting to his feet, his eyes blazing with anger. With no more time to think, she rushed into the bathroom. Slamming the door shut behind her, she fiddled with the key.

"Cara!"

She could hear James crossing the room. The key wouldn't work, and her heart was hammering so hard she could hardly think straight. What would happen to her if she didn't manage to lock the door? But the key finally clicked, and Cara retreated to the corner, sinking down onto the tiled floor between the wall and the claw-footed bath. From there, she watched the handle turn down. Nothing happened. The handle twisted up and down as James frantically tried to get in.

"Get out here!" he hissed through the door.

He kept turning the handle. When it was clear he wouldn't be able to get in, he tried a different tack. "Please, darling," he wheedled, "come out here and talk to me. This has all just been a misunderstanding. I'm sure we can clear it up."

But Cara covered her ears, refusing to listen or to speak to him. She wasn't going to give him the opportunity to coerce her.

She spent all night barricaded inside the bathroom. James continued to rattle at the door for a while, alternately pleading with her and threatening her, but eventually the noise came to a halt. Cara heard footsteps retreating and what sounded like the bedroom door closing. But even though it seemed as if James had gone, she wasn't about to come out of her hiding place, just in case he was lying in wait for her. Instead, she settled down for a night in the bathroom. She tried to get comfortable, lying down on the mat so she wasn't directly on the cold marble floor. It wasn't anywhere near as comfortable as the bed she'd been lying in, but she was used to the thin mattresses of the orphanage; she could put up with this for one night.

At first she was too scared to sleep, in case James found a way to get in. She thought about Niamh. She realized now what was wrong with her friend. She too had been subjected to James Buchanan's attentions, but unfortunately she hadn't been lucky enough to escape. At least now that Cara knew the whole story, she could finally do something about it.

The next morning, Cara emerged from the bathroom only once she was sure the rest of the house was up. She wore her own clothes down to breakfast, which was served in a beautiful glass room with a view across to the lake. Virginia and James were already there. Virginia greeted her enthusiastically, clearly having no inkling about what had gone on the previous night. James was also cheery, but it seemed forced to Cara. The cook brought in a full Irish breakfast, with black pudding and fried toast. It smelled delicious, but Cara found it impossible to eat.

Virginia noticed and looked concerned. "Not hungry? Are you feeling all right?" She came over and felt Cara's forehead, as Sister Agnes had for Niamh the previous day. "You seem fine."

Cara had been about to use being ill as an excuse to go back to the orphanage. Now, feeling that she couldn't, she said reluctantly, "I'm okay."

Virginia brightened. "Good. Then, what would you like to do today?"

"I don't mind." All Cara could think about was how to get out of here before tonight came round.

"Well, why don't we take you out to see the horses? I'll go up to change."

Not wanting to be left alone with James, Cara followed her out of the room. As she left, she saw the look of hatred that James shot her and knew that she had to escape from here before tonight. Following Virginia through to the hallway, her eyes settled on a pretty blue-and-white china teapot sitting on the occasional table. An idea came to her.

"I like this," she said, picking the ornament up.

"Oh, be careful with that," Virginia warned. "It was left to me by my mother."

That confirmed everything Cara needed to know. Offering up a silent "sorry" to poor, clueless Virginia, she allowed the china teapot to slip out of her hands.

"No!" Virginia cried, rushing forward.

But it was too late. All she could do was watch in horror as the ornament smashed on the floor. And that was when Cara started to laugh.

It was decided that Cara should be returned to the orphanage right away. Virginia was too distraught to travel back with her in the car, and she implored James to stay behind with her. Cara could tell he was furious. She imagined he'd wanted to have some time alone with her, to warn her not to say anything. But Virginia was insistent, so Cara was sent back with the driver. He had been given a note to explain the events of the morning that had resulted in her early departure. Unfortunately for Cara, Sister Concepta was the one who took receipt of the letter.

The nun was so delighted to have had her opinion of the girl vindicated that for once she seemed uninterested in doling out punishment. Cara was equally unbothered by the consequences of her actions. Now that she knew about James Buchanan, all she wanted to do was speak to Niamh.

Up in the dorm, Niamh was there, waiting anxiously for her. As soon as she saw Cara, she rushed over to her.

"What happened?" she wanted to know.

"Nothing. He tried, but I got away."

Niamh's face crumpled. "I'm sorry. I tried to warn you . . ."

"Don't worry about it." Cara was brusque. "At least now we can both speak up."

"What do you mean?"

"Well, we have to tell someone what he's doing."

Niamh looked horrified. "I can't. He said he'd kill me if I said anything." She began to cry then, sobbing as though she would never stop. Cara cried with her, tears of shame for not looking after her friend, mingled with anger at a person who could do something like that to a child.

34

In the two years that she had been at the orphanage, Cara had never seen Sister Concepta so furious. Her face had gone red, and Cara fancied that if she had been a cartoon character, smoke would have blown out of her ears.

"You wicked, wicked girls!" she snarled. Picking up a belt, she began to wrap one end around her hand. Niamh shrank back, but Sister Concepta caught hold of her, pulling her back within reach. "How dare you!" *Whack!* The strap came down and caught Niamh's arm. "Telling lies like that about those lovely people!" *Whack!* This time the blow was to her shoulder.

Cara couldn't stand it any longer. It had taken a long time to persuade Niamh to speak up about what James Buchanan had done, and now not only was the sister refusing to believe them, but they were actually getting punished for what they'd said. She grabbed the nun's arm and pushed her away, coming between her and Niamh.

"Stop it!"

Sister Concepta's eyes blazed. "Don't tell me what to do!" She struck Cara across the cheek. It was a stinging blow, but at least the nun's attention was diverted from Niamh. "I bet you were the one behind all these lies, you little troublemaker!"

Whack! Whack! Whack!

Cara crumpled to the ground, but the beating didn't stop. The pain was almost a relief. At least it kept her mind off feeling guilty.

Cara woke up in her dormitory bed. Her head ached. Sister Agnes was sitting in a chair by her side, reading. She explained what had happened—that Cara had fallen against a wall and blacked out.

"You'll need to take it easy for a while until we know whether you have concussion," the nun said.

But Cara's first concern wasn't for herself. "Is Niamh all right?" She struggled to sit up in bed, looking round for her friend.

Sister Agnes couldn't meet her eyes. "She's not here."

"Where is she, then?"

Finally the nun looked up, and her expression was troubled. "She's gone to the Buchanans'. They called and insisted—"

But Cara was already on her feet. Hurrying to the small turret window that looked out over the driveway, she was just in time to see Niamh walking down the driveway to the waiting car. With her shoulders hunched and her slow, stiff walk, she looked like a condemned woman. Cara put her hand to the glass, aware that her friend couldn't see her but wanting to pass on her strength to the other girl anyway.

The weekend passed even more slowly than usual. When the others went into town on Saturday, Cara decided not to go. She felt too worried about what was happening to Niamh.

On Sunday evening, she waited anxiously for her friend to return. As the hours went by, she grew more concerned, a bad feeling growing in the pit of her stomach. It wasn't helped by the fact that the nuns were rushing around, their faces white and drawn. Clearly something was up.

Cara caught Sister Agnes as she rushed by. "What's going on? Is it to do with Niamh?"

Sister Agnes looked as though she wanted to say something, but hesitated. "I'm sorry, sweetheart, but I really can't tell you right now. Just—just say a prayer for her, will you?" Then she hurried off.

There was no more news that evening. Cara lay awake all night, wondering where Niamh could be.

First thing the next morning, all the girls were called together in the assembly hall. From the grim expressions on the nuns' faces, Cara could guess what they were going to say.

She was right. Niamh was dead. Late Saturday evening, she had found her way out of Castle Glen. From what the police could tell, she'd been trying to make it into town. She had tried taking a shortcut across the lake, and the ice had broken. Sister Concepta kept the details to a minimum, letting the girls know only the bare facts. But over the next few days, rumors began to filter through from the outside world, carried in by the lay workers and delivery boys who came up to the orphanage. One overexcited scullery girl, who was being courted by a young garda, told Cara and a group of ghoulish gossipmongers that Niamh had accidentally fallen into the lake and drowned, but that it had been so cold during the night that the water had refrozen afterward. That meant the police search had gone on for hours before anyone went to look at the lake. When they did, they immediately saw her body, trapped beneath the ice and staring up at them like a frozen Ophelia.

"It's a tragedy, that's what it is," the girl said with fake gravity, delighted to be the center of attention, the thrill of the event providing a break in the monotony of her dull life. "Lord only knows what she was doing out on such a cold night, when she could have been in that lovely house."

"No doubt sneaking out to meet a young man," the cook said sagely.

The others murmured their agreement, marveling at the seeming stupidity of youth.

But only Cara knew the truth. Niamh had been trying to escape from James Buchanan.

The funeral for Niamh was held two days later. Cara was too numb to react: first her mother, then her grandmother, and now her best friend. It seemed as though everyone she cared about had been taken from her. None of Niamh's family bothered to come over for the occasion; instead, they would be having a Mass said for her at their local church in England. What made it hardest was seeing the Buchanans there. Cara glared at them as they walked up the aisle to take their place in the front pew.

The priest stood to say the eulogy. He spoke for a few minutes about the seeming senselessness of a young life being taken and the plan that God has for everyone, telling the congregation to take comfort in the fact that the child was with her Father now. Even though Cara wasn't sure how much of it she believed, she found it easy enough to listen. It was only as he got deeper into his sermon that the latent anger that had been bubbling within her for days began to spill over.

"We will never know what was going through young Niamh's mind

that terrible night," he intoned, from his place in the pulpit. "The Buchanans"—he paused to smile benevolently at the couple who sat in
the front pew as James wrapped a protective arm around his crying
wife—"the Buchanans were generous enough to give the girl a break
from the orphanage. Who knows the vagaries of young minds, but
for whatever reason she chose to spurn their hospitality and go out
into the night alone. If she hadn't, perhaps this terrible accident would
never have happened."

Cara couldn't bear the hypocrisy any longer. "It wasn't an accident!"
she shouted out suddenly, before she could think about what she was
doing. The priest stopped talking and the whole congregation turned
to look at her.

"Cara!" Sister Agnes hissed, putting a restraining hand on her arm.

But Cara knew there was no escaping from her actions now. She
got unsteadily to her feet, determined to get this off her chest. "She
died trying to get away from *you*!" She pointed at James Buchanan.
"Because she couldn't stand what you did to her. Her death is on your
conscience. And not *just* yours." She waved a hand at Sister Concepta.
"It was your fault too, because you wouldn't listen to her. She tried to
tell you what he did, and you sent her back."

She was sobbing now, struggling to speak through her tears, crying
so hard that she didn't notice Sisters Jude and Bernadette sneaking up
behind her. "Niamh wouldn't be dead if someone had listened to her
earlier," she went on. "If *I'd* listened to her. We're *all* to blame here. I
should have tried harder with her—"

The nuns chose that moment to grab Cara by the arms. She was so
drained by then that she hardly put up a protest. As they half dragged
her out of the church, she kept saying over and over again, "It's my fault
she's dead. It's all my fault."

Sister Agnes was worried about Cara. After the incident in the church,
Sister Concepta had ordered the girl to be locked in the Quiet Room.
She'd been in there for four days now, and all she'd been given in that
time was water: one cup three times a day. Sister Jude had been put in
charge of administering the punishment, so this was the first time Sister
Agnes had been able to sneak in to check on the girl. But she could see
that the harsh treatment had taken its toll. Cold sores covered Cara's
mouth, and she was hardly coherent. As she was unable even to lift her

head, Sister Agnes had to hold the cup of water to the girl's mouth. She drank it down greedily, then coughed some of it back up.

The nun was by nature a simple, God-fearing woman who believed in the inherent good in people in general and the Church in particular. But the events of the past few days had shaken her faith in humanity. For whatever reason, Sister Concepta seemed to be hell bent on destroying Cara. The girl was half starved and dehydrated and needed to be seen by a doctor. Sister Agnes had tried reasoning with her superior earlier, but the woman had refused to listen. Which was what had brought her here now.

"You need to leave, Cara," the young nun whispered urgently. "To escape. Tonight. And I'm going to help you."

The plan had been forming in Sister Agnes's mind for a while. She had a brother, she explained now to Cara, who worked as a docker. He'd agreed to sneak Cara onto his ship and take her over to England. As the nun spoke, for the first time since Niamh's death she saw a spark of fire in the girl's green eyes.

"How will I get out of here, though?" She looked toward the locked door.

Sister Agnes took a deep breath. This was the part that required her to have courage. She would come back tonight, she told the girl, once everyone was asleep, and open the door for Cara. It would look as though she'd forgotten to lock it after taking Cara her water. At the back of the cellars, there was a secret tunnel that led out past the orphanage's walls. Cara could escape through that, and then once she was outside the gates, Agnes's brother, Declan, would be waiting for her. From there, they would drive to Cork and then leave on the next boat for Liverpool.

Seeing how weak Cara was, the nun knew that the girl had to leave tonight or she'd never be able to make the journey. Though she was a little afraid of what would happen if anyone ever traced the escape back to her, Sister Agnes was sure she could make it look enough like an accident that no one could ever prove otherwise. No doubt Sister Concepta would have her suspicions and make her life a misery, but the young nun could put up with that as long as she knew that she had done the right thing.

Cara stumbled down the stairs to the cellar, gripping the railing for support. Everything was as Sister Agnes had told her. Although the lack of food had weakened her, the thought of escape had given her an injection of strength. Sister Agnes had managed to slip her some bread, and she'd eaten it before she left. That had given her enough energy to make it.

The tunnel was dark and dank; stagnant water pooled on the floor, and the walls were covered in wet moss. Rats scuttled by, brushing against Cara's legs; she tried not to scream. Emerging into the cold night, she breathed in deep, taking in the fresh air and the freedom. But she couldn't allow herself to relax for too long—she hadn't reached safety yet.

Stumbling away from the orphanage's walls, Cara looked all around. There was meant to be a car here, waiting for her. Her eyes squinted in the darkness, trying to see if she could make out any shapes. But there was nothing. Just as she was beginning to panic, she heard a voice hiss through the night. "Here. Over here."

She followed the sound, each step making her feel weaker and weaker, until a hand reached out and grabbed her. Looking up, she half-expected to see Sister Concepta there, ready to drag her back to the orphanage, but instead it was a stocky man with orange hair and skin that had once been white, but was now burned red from days on the deck of a boat. It was Sister Agnes's brother, Declan.

"This way. I couldn't park close, lest anyone heard the engine."

It was another two hundred yards to the car. Declan kept looking around, as though he was expecting someone to be following them. Cara had a stitch in her side and had to stop to catch her breath. Finally they reached the car. Declan rustled in the backseat and pulled out a bag.

"Here." He threw some clothes at her. "Put these on."

As she changed out of her orphanage uniform, he began to warm up the car.

"Get in," Declan said once she was ready.

So far, all he'd done was bark orders at Cara. She got the feeling he wasn't happy about having to help her. She didn't blame him, of course: he could get arrested for his part in her escape. As they set off, Declan made no effort to speak to her. So instead Cara turned back to watch the dark shadow of the orphanage growing smaller as she got farther away. It was a satisfying sight.

Dawn broke over Cork. A storm began to brew, the dark Atlantic Sea churning, the wind rattling the corrugated roof of Declan's quayside shack, making it impossible to sleep or hold a conversation.

The boat couldn't sail that day. It took forty-eight hours for the storm to dissipate and the waters to become calm enough for the voyage across St. George's Channel. Even then the passage was choppy. Stowed away in the bowels of the ship, Cara was forbidden to come up on deck, lest any of the crew see her. Afterward, all she would remember of the journey was the incessant seasickness. Declan had cooked them dinner before they'd come out, a steak and kidney pie with mashed potatoes, and as the boat lurched from side to side, so did her stomach, and soon she'd thrown up everything she'd eaten until all she could do was dry-heave. By the time the boat docked, Cara was itching to get off. But she had to wait until the cargo had been unloaded, in case anyone spotted her.

The docks of Liverpool were loud, noisy, and dirty. Large, rough men threw bags to each other, carried barrels and crates, told crude jokes, laughed and sang.

As she stood on deck, watching the chaotic scene, Declan came over to her. "You off then?"

He had offered her a place to stay for a few nights, in the boardinghouse where he bedded down, "just until you get on your feet." But Cara had refused. She'd got the feeling that he'd agreed to help her to England only because of his sister, but now that they were here, it wasn't fair to be a burden.

"Yeah, I want to keep moving." She was right, he looked relieved. In a way she didn't blame him. He'd already risked his job and livelihood for her, a stranger. She couldn't ask any more of him.

"Well, good luck then, I guess," he said awkwardly. He dug into his pocket and held out a ten-shilling note, a last-minute attack of guilt making him feel that he should do something for the poor bedraggled creature in front of him.

Cara hesitated. She felt bad accepting the money, but she had nothing else and she would need something for the journey.

"Thank you," she said and then turned away. She didn't want to ask him for directions to where she was going. The fewer people who knew, the better. Somewhere along the way she'd ask a stranger how to get to London.

Because that's where she intended to go: to London, to try to find Annie Connolly and her kids, the people she'd lived with until she was seven years old. With her mother and Theresa and Niamh now gone, the Connollys were the closest she'd ever gotten to calling anyone family, and it was the last place she remembered being truly happy. For Cara, it was the obvious destination to flee to now. And the fewer people who knew, the less likely it was that anyone could find her. She needed to disappear completely.

Growing Pains

Mistakes are the growing pains of wisdom.
—WILLIAM GEORGE JORDAN, AMERICAN ESSAYIST, 1864–1928

35

Gabriel Stanhope walked alone through the souk, ignoring the stalls and traders as he went. After nearly two years in Tangier, he was immune to all the color and noise and smells of the medina, the old part of the city. No one bothered him as he passed. With his darkened skin, long beard, and billowing white robe, he could be mistaken for a local.

Turning off onto a quieter way, he followed the labyrinth of alleys in the direction of the Kasbah. A little way farther, he paused outside one of the low, white stone buildings and knocked on the wooden door. An old man answered, as dark and withered as a raisin.

"As-Salāmu Àlayka." Gabriel offered the standard greeting, "Peace be upon you."

"Wa alayka as-salām," the man responded.

Gabriel pressed some coins into the proprietor's hand and stepped inside, out of the heat of the day. A pretty courtyard, with a trickling fountain, led through to a cool, dark room. The shutters were closed, and the air was heavy with the sweet scent of opium. Gabriel picked his way through, stepping over the reclining bodies of writers and musicians, artists and expat aristocrats, all looking to find inspiration and enlightenment among the fleshpots and drug dens of Morocco. Finding a space away from everyone else, Gabriel lay down against a pile of embroidered cushions and waited for a young boy to bring over the heavy wooden pipe.

After two years in Morocco, Gabriel's routine was as familiar to him as breathing. He'd traveled to North Africa from Spain, and he couldn't see himself ever leaving. The seedy city of Tangier was known as a refuge for bohemians and lost souls, and he fitted right in. No one would ever have guessed that he was the scion of one of America's richest businessmen—which was exactly what he wanted.

Not that the Stanhope name meant much anymore. From what Gabriel understood, his father had never recovered from the scandal surrounding Frances Fitzgerald's death. One dead wife could be seen as an unhappy accident; two looked more like a suspicious coincidence. Not that Gabriel knew any of this for certain. He'd had no contact with his father, and he had no intention of ever speaking to him again. It was easier that way. But occasionally he would pick up a paper and read an account of the tragedies that had befallen his family, the salacious details rehashed for the world to feast on. The journalists always seemed to dwell on Olivia—his poor, poor sister. They reported that she'd never recovered from the electroshock therapy and now lived at Stanhope Castle, being cared for twenty-four hours a day by the housekeeper, Hilda. A sad, terrible fate for a young woman, everyone agreed. Gabriel felt bitter laughter rise in his throat. If only they knew the real truth.

At the thought of Olivia, Gabriel took a long drag on the opium pipe, filling his lungs with the sweet smoke. Outside, he could hear the call to prayer begin. As he fell back onto the cushions, he closed his eyes and felt his guilt and regret drifting away, allowing him to forget everything that had happened and find some peace, for a little time at least.

36

"All right, Mum?" Danny Connolly strutted into the kitchen, planting a heavy hand on his mother's shoulder and a kiss on her forehead.

"Not too bad, son."

Annie, who'd been reading the *Daily Express* over a mug of tea, smiled up at her favorite child. At eighteen, Danny had grown into a strong, handsome man, and she couldn't help feeling proud. Her two girls, Bronagh and Maureen, were married with homes of their own, and by the time they'd gone she'd frankly been pleased to see the back of them. But Danny was still living with her, and she hoped that wouldn't change for a long time.

"Are you in for your tea, love?" she asked him now.

"Nah. I'm just gonna change, then head back out."

She wasn't surprised. He had so many girls on the go; when he wasn't out working, he could be found with one of them. More than half the week he was out, but he did like to come back here for the odd night—even if it was just to have a good kip, get his washing done, and eat a home-cooked meal.

Annie got to her feet. "You can't go out on an empty stomach. I'll make you a sandwich while you're getting ready, and you'll sit down and eat it like a normal human being." Her voice brooked no argument.

"Whatever you say, Mum."

If any of Danny's friends had seen the way he caved in, they'd have been amazed. Out on the streets, even the hardest man wouldn't dare cross Danny Connolly, but when it came to his mother, he was a pussycat. She was his only weak spot and the only woman he'd ever really respected.

It was only out of consideration for her that he'd put up with that bastard Liam Earley for as long as he did. After the man had moved in with them, the beating that Franny had witnessed all those years ago had become a regular feature of Danny's life. Liam had been clever enough to hide the worst from Annie—and what she did suspect, she'd overlooked because she'd become reliant on Liam for money and companionship. But the abuse from his mother's lover had shaped the boy forever, toughening Danny and turning him into the hard man he now was.

By the time Danny reached fifteen, he'd grown taller and stronger than Liam. He'd continued to take the odd beating, but when Liam had turned his fists on Annie, Danny had been ready to act. That night, he'd given Liam the hiding of his life—repaying him for every time he'd been knocked about over the years. After Danny had finished, he'd dumped Liam outside the Royal London Hospital. The doctors and nurses had done their best, but the man had still ended up losing the sight in his left eye, and though the scars on his face had healed, they would never fade: a permanent reminder of the punishment meted out.

Rumors about the young lad's actions had quickly spread through the East End. Annie had worried that he'd end up in jail, although Danny had been ready to do his time. Liam had been spitting blood, determined to shop his stepson, but before the police had a chance to interview him, Finnbar Sullivan, the head of the East End's most influential and feared Irish gang, had sent someone to have a quiet word. When a detective constable finally got around to taking a statement from Liam, he told them that he'd been robbed and beaten up in the street.

Of course Finnbar hadn't done the favor out of the goodness of his heart—he'd seen something in Danny that made him think he'd be an asset to his organization. The following week, he'd asked the young lad to meet with him.

Danny had dutifully turned up at Finnbar Sullivan's boxing club as he'd been told. The gang leader was out the back in the changing rooms, having his hands bandaged up. Twenty years earlier, Finnbar had started off as a bare-knuckle fighter, and he still liked to go a couple of rounds.

Sitting astride a bench, a towel thrown around his meaty shoulders, Finnbar said to Danny, "So you think you've got what it takes to come and work for me?"

"Yes, sir, Mr. Sullivan."

"Cocky little bugger, ain't you?"

In fact, standing before Finnbar, with a couple of the gang leader's henchmen looking on, Danny had never felt more like a scared little boy. But he knew that he needed to stand his ground, so he simply shrugged in answer.

Finnbar chuckled. "That's good. I like a bit of confidence. I think we could get along very well." And then his eyes grew hard. "As long as you remember who's in charge." He jabbed a finger at his own chest. "Me. Everything goes through me, and nothing goes down without my say-so. The minute you start taking from me or thinking you can go off on your own sweet way, I'll come down on you like a ton of bricks. And don't you forget that. So as long as you can live with that, then the job's yours."

Finnbar had his fingers in many pies: everything from debt collecting to running girls. He wanted Danny to start off on protection money. It was a simple enough job. He'd go round to businesses in the area, everything from restaurants to grocery stores, and collect cash from them. In exchange, Finnbar would make sure nothing happened to their business. If anyone refused to pay, it was up to Danny to impress upon them why they needed to cough up. His size was usually enough to persuade them, which was why Finnbar had hired him in the first place.

If Annie had wanted more than a life of crime for her boy who'd been smart enough to pass his Eleven-plus exam and get into grammar school, she knew there was no point saying anything. Like his father, Danny had grown up with little respect for authority. And though Annie might not agree with all of her son's choices, she had to admire his no-nonsense resolve. She realized now that she should have thrown Liam out years earlier, and it shamed her to think that she'd waited for her teenage son to step in. Maybe he wasn't ever going to be a doctor or a lawyer, but he was doing well for himself in his own way—in the East End way. He was a hard man, a Jack-the-lad, who thought school was for mugs. He was smart and he was strong, and he wasn't afraid to act. But best of all, he had the brains to be more than an enforcer. After three years of working for Finnbar, he was making his way up in the organization, and also in the world.

Smiling affectionately at her son, Annie took a hunk of bread and started to cut two thick slices. She got out butter, cheese, and ham from the new fridge—provided by Danny, along with the new television and couches in the sitting room.

"Go on with you, now," she said. "I'll have this ready by the time you get back down here."

"Thanks, Mum." Danny was already halfway up the stairs when the front doorbell rang. "Want me to get that?" he called back down.

"Leave it to me. It's probably Bernie."

But when Annie opened the door, it wasn't her friend Bernadette after all. Instead, in the doorway stood a bedraggled, skinny girl, wearing loose-fitting jeans rolled up at the bottom and a shirt that swamped her. She was no more than fourteen, and with her hair tucked under an old man's cap, she had the look of a runaway.

"Sorry, love," Annie said immediately, spotting the bag in her hand. "I ain't taking lodgers no more."

That was another benefit of Danny's work. He made sure she had enough so that she no longer had to clean up after other people. It was nice to have the place to herself, although sometimes she missed the company. Not that she could ever admit that to Danny.

Annie made to close the door, but the girl put out a hand to stop her. "Wait," she said.

Annie glanced up, feeling irritated. But then she saw the girl's face again, more clearly this time, because her features were illuminated by the hall light. There was something familiar about her: the dark mop of hair peeking out from the cap, the large green eyes, the long, skinny body . . .

She peered closer. "Cara?"

The girl gave her a weak smile. "Hello, Auntie Annie. Mind if I come in?"

Cara sat at the kitchen table as Annie bustled round, making her hot tea and a snack. The house looked more robust than she remembered; there had obviously been some money spent here. She was pleased that the Connollys were doing well for themselves—and that they were still living at the same address. She wasn't sure what she would have done otherwise.

Annie set down a sandwich in front of her. "How's that for you?"

Cara didn't reply; she simply picked up the bread and took one large bite, then another, stuffing her mouth full. After the journey she'd had, she had no energy to talk—she was exhausted and starving.

The money that Declan had given her hadn't been enough to pay for the bus or train down from Liverpool. So she'd had no choice but to hitch a lift. Someone had told her a good place to stand was by the M62 motorway. A man in a Morris Minor had come by first. He'd been well dressed in a suit and tie, the interior of his car spotless. But Cara had hesitated. Maybe she was being oversensitive, but there was something about him that reminded her of James Buchanan. She could see something predatory in his eyes, a reason to feel uncomfortable. So she'd turned him down and waited for another lift. It was half an hour before a bright yellow Mini had pulled up. It was a tight fit— there were four people already inside the tiny two-door car, two boys in the front and their girlfriends squashed into the back. They had been up in Liverpool that weekend to see a band called the Beatles. Now, on their way back to London, they had been more than happy to have her join them.

By the time they'd reached the North Circular Road, it had been nearly forty-eight hours since Cara had last slept. The group had been going to Hammersmith, so they'd dropped her there and she'd made her way over to Whitechapel by tube. As it had been more than seven years since she'd last been to the Connollys' house, it had taken her a while to get her bearings. She'd had to ask three different people how to find the street.

Annie had asked her surprisingly few questions, given that she'd turned up out of the blue like this. And Cara hadn't known herself how much she'd want to share. But now, settled at Annie's kitchen table and feeling as though she'd returned home, she found that she wanted to open up about everything that had happened to her.

She gave Annie an abridged version of the intervening years. Telling her about the way her mother had dumped her at Theresa's was cathartic. Cara saw the outrage in Annie's eyes as she heard about Franny and her broken promises, and felt pleased that someone was as appalled as her about her mother's behavior.

"All these years, I thought you were both living with family in Ireland. That's where your mam told me youse were off to before she left, and I had no reason to doubt her. I hadn't a clue that she was going gallivanting off to Hollywood like that."

The older woman shook her head disbelievingly. She'd heard of Frances Fitzgerald, of course. She'd been a Big Thing for a brief time back in the fifties. Annie recalled seeing her in a film once—but had never even *suspected* that the glamorous movie star was her old friend. The hair, the makeup, the American accent, even the way the actress had held herself—it had all made her unrecognizable as the poverty-stricken young mother she'd once been. In fact, Annie would go so far as to bet that no one who'd known Franny Healey—not even her own relatives—would have guessed that she was one and the same as Frances Fitzgerald.

It was all so much to take in. Annie could hardly believe everything that Cara had told her. With hindsight, perhaps it had seemed a little strange that she'd never heard from Franny after she'd left, but they'd fallen out over that scut Liam, and Annie had just assumed her friend was holding a grudge. To think that all this had happened without her realizing. She reached out and took Cara's hand. "If I'd thought for one minute that she'd abandoned you like that, I'd have done everything in my power to find you. You do know that, don't you, love?"

Annie stopped then, and Cara guessed it was because she didn't want to say anything openly critical of Franny in case she was still upset over her mother's death. Well, she wasn't, Cara thought darkly. She'd hardened her heart to Franny a long time ago.

Cara moved on from there to talk about life at the orphanage. Annie seemed sympathetic but not surprised by the stories Cara told of the nuns—until she got to what had happened to Niamh. With her friend's death still so raw, Cara found herself choking over the words, and Annie's eyes filled with tears, too.

"Oh, God love you." Annie pulled Cara to her. "You've been through the wringer, haven't you?"

Cara breathed in Annie's scent of carbolic soap and cigarettes, surprised that it still seemed so familiar after all these years. It was a huge comfort and relief to be back with someone who cared.

The thunder of heavy footsteps coming down the stairs interrupted the moment. A second later Danny burst into the kitchen. It was seven years since she'd last seen Danny Connolly, but Cara recognized him right away. He was a man now, not a ten-year-old boy, but he still had that same rough confidence. And, Lord, he was attractive, in a strong, thuggish way: at least six-two, with broad shoulders, his dark hair cut brutally short. Wearing blue jeans and a leather jacket, he looked like Marlon Brando in *The Wild One,* which she'd seen posters for during one of the orphanage's Saturday trips to the pictures.

Seeing him, Cara straightened up a little, her hand instinctively reaching up to smooth down her hair, suddenly conscious that she was wearing the same dirty, sweaty clothes she'd been traveling in for three days.

Looking at Cara, he said, "Who's this, then?"

Cara wanted to speak up but found she couldn't. It was up to Annie to explain for her. "It's your old playmate Cara. You remember—Franny's kid? Just turned up on the doorstep now."

Recognition appeared in Danny's eyes. Cara felt unexpectedly pleased, but if she'd been hoping for a grand reunion, she was to be disappointed.

"Long time no see," he acknowledged before turning back to his mum. He seemed to have no curiosity about the reason behind Cara's sudden reappearance after all these years—he was a typical eighteen-year-old guy: completely self-absorbed, with little interest beyond his own small world. "So if the filth come round, you know what to say."

"Yeah, yeah." Annie waved him away. "You were here all evening, playing cards with Big Jim and Denton. I know. You've told me a million times already. Must think I'm thick or something." She winked at Cara. "Look, with young Cara turning up, I haven't had time to make you a bite, but if you give me a minute—"

"No time. I've gotta head off."

"Where?"

He tapped his nose. "Never you mind."

Annie shook her head in mock exasperation. "You'll be the death of me," she clucked affectionately.

Grinning, Danny dropped a kiss on his mother's forehead, and then he was gone, slamming the front door shut behind him.

Still smiling from the exchange, Annie looked over at Cara. "So where shall we put you, then?" she said, half to herself. Cara had already suggested earlier that she find other digs, but Annie wouldn't hear of it.

"What about . . ." Annie began and then stopped, biting her lip, as though she'd said the wrong thing.

But Cara was beyond being sensitive. "About what?"

"Forget it."

"Go on. Tell me what you were going to say."

Annie looked a little uncomfortable. "I was going to say—what about staying in your old room, up in the attic, where you used to live with your mother? But maybe that'd be weird for you."

"Not at all." Cara smiled gently, surprised to feel her eyes moistening. "Actually, it sounds perfect."

It had obviously been a long day for Cara, and by then she was flagging. Upstairs, Annie gave her one of Bronagh's old nightdresses that she'd left at the house and set about finding clean sheets. Once Cara was tucked into bed, Annie couldn't bring herself to leave. Instead she pulled up a chair, so she could watch over the girl until she went off to sleep. The poor mite had obviously been through so much. As if to prove her point, Cara began to twist and moan, clearly in the grip of a nightmare. Annie reached out to stroke the girl's dark hair. "There, there, pet," she murmured. "You're safe now."

The reassuring words seemed to settle Cara, and she quieted down after that, falling into a peaceful slumber.

Annie had led a difficult life and seen a great deal of misery in her time, but Cara's story had unsettled her more than she'd thought possible. Imagine Franny abandoning her own child like that! If she hadn't already been dead, Annie would have cheerfully wrung her neck. What kind of a mother behaved that way? The girl was obviously a tough little thing—she'd had to be, after everything she'd been through. But it was sad to think that, after all these years, she and Danny were the only ones the child could call on when she was in trouble.

Not wanting to leave Cara alone, Annie went over to the cupboard, took out another blanket, and headed back to the armchair to settle down to sleep herself. She stayed by Cara's side for the rest of the night.

37

"I've found her."

Pete Grove wasn't the type to get excited. In fact, most people who knew him would say he was usually a downright miserable chap. But even he felt a thrill run through him as he said those three magic words.

It was two years since he'd first been hired to monitor the house. One of the neighbors had agreed to tip him off about any comings or goings in exchange for a small fee. Month after month, there had been no activity. And now, out of the blue, his contact had called to say that the girl had turned up. It felt as if something big was about to happen. He rocked back in his chair, putting his feet up on his tiny desk, enjoying this rare moment of importance.

"She surfaced," he consulted his spiral notebook, "a couple of days ago now. And it looks like she's staying put."

"Excellent."

The voice that answered him was crisp and well spoken. It belonged to Charles Hamilton, head partner in the law firm founded by his father, Hamilton & Sons. It was Charles who had first approached Pete; Charles whom he always dealt with. Pete had no contact with the client, nor did he have any idea who the client was.

This wasn't Pete's usual type of work. He'd been in the police force for twenty-five years, walking the Whitechapel beat, until he'd finally retired five years earlier. After a month, he'd realized that the retirement he'd spent years longing for wasn't all it was cracked up to be. Bored at home and unable to stand his wife's constant nagging, he'd decided to become a private investigator. He'd always loved Raymond

Chandler novels and fancied that it would be exciting work. So he'd set himself up in a poky room above a bookie's in Bethnal Green and waited for good-looking dames to come through the door.

But as with most things in Pete's life, working as a PI had turned out to be a disappointment. Mostly, he spent his time tailing cheating spouses. That's why this particular case had stood out for him. He'd always remember when Charles Hamilton had first walked into his grubby little office, wearing a Savile Row suit and a look of disdain. Pete had wondered if the posh chap had wandered into the wrong place until he'd heard what Mr. Hamilton wanted him to do. After all his years on the beat, there was no one who had better contacts in the East End. It would be easy for him to keep an eye out for the girl without anyone noticing.

For the first few months, it had been interesting, and he'd enjoyed snooping around, finding out if the girl had turned up at the Connollys'. But as time went on and nothing happened, he'd grown bored. He'd kept on delivering his monthly report and receiving the fat little retainer paid to him through Charles Hamilton. If he was honest, he'd expected the client to have given up by now.

But today that had all changed. The subject had finally appeared.

"So what do you want me to do?" Pete asked, eager to find out where this was going.

The solicitor, usually so sure of himself, hesitated for the briefest second. "I'll have to consult with my client and get back to you." There was a click as he hung up.

Hamilton called back an hour later. He delivered his instructions with brusque efficiency. For now Pete wasn't to approach the subject. Instead he was to step up his surveillance and continue to send back a monthly report on how the girl was doing.

Pete was secretly a little disappointed to learn that despite locating the subject, little in his duties was going to change. But once a new figure had been agreed upon, he began to feel happier. It was a generous amount for his time and discretion, and even though it might be a strange setup, it was by far the easiest and most lucrative job he'd ever had. He just wondered what was so special about the girl that made someone want to keep tabs on her.

38

"Are you serious?" Finnbar gave a short, humorless laugh. "I may be a lot of things, but I'm not about to start using child labor." He shook his head as though the whole idea was too preposterous for him to even contemplate. "Come on, what is the girl—all of twelve?"

Annie just looked at the stocky man seated opposite her. She was one of the few people who wasn't intimated by the gang leader. They were in the Blind Beggar, the pub on Whitechapel Road where Finnbar often held court. It was April 1962, nearly two months since Cara had turned up on Annie's doorstep, and she seemed to be settling in nicely. But now the girl had started saying that she wanted to get a job. Annie had tried to convince her to go back to school, but she wasn't keen on it, saying that she'd had enough of institutions to last her three lifetimes. Instead, she wanted her own money and independence. Unfortunately her lack of qualifications limited her employment options, so Annie had offered to have a word with Finnbar for her, sure that he'd be able to sort something out. She hadn't expected him to be so reluctant to help.

"She's almost fifteen," Annie said quietly. "She may look young, but she's mature for her age, I can vouch for that."

"Fifteen!" Finnbar snorted. "Ah, now, you're messing with me, aren't you? I'm not employing no fifteen-year-old kid. Not in my line of work."

At that Annie bristled. "Yeah? Well, you've got a short memory, then, 'cos that's the same age my Danny was when he started grafting for you."

That silenced him. Usually Finnbar wouldn't let anyone speak to him that way, but he'd always had a thing for Annie, long before Liam had come onto the scene. After her husband had died, he'd offered to set her up somewhere, but she'd turned him down. A good Catholic girl at heart, she'd never wanted to take up with a married man. Plus, she knew and liked his wife, Alice. Finn had understood her position and never held it against her, and even now, after the years had taken their toll on her looks, he still had a soft spot for her, and everyone knew it. Especially Annie—which was why she felt comfortable asking him this favor.

"Come on," she said now. "The girl just needs a chance."

"All right," Finnbar reluctantly gave in. He wasn't keen to take on the dark-haired waif that he'd seen knocking around at Annie's, but it seemed he had no choice. "I'll sort something out."

"Something legit, mind," Annie warned. "Nothing that's going to get her in any trouble."

He rolled his eyes. "Jaysus, you ask a lot, woman. But don't worry, I'll take care of her." He held up his hand, as though he were swearing on the Bible. "You have my word on it."

The following week, Cara started working at a grocery store in Bethnal Green that was under the protection of Finnbar's gang. Mr. Grafton, the store owner, wasn't happy about having a new employee forced upon him, who was going to eat into more of his profits. "Don't expect this to be no picnic," he warned her on the first day. "You'll have to pull your weight, or you'll be out on your ear."

In fact, after slaving away in the orphanage, serving in the shop turned out to be a snap. Cara was so happy to be there rather than back at St. Mary's that she didn't mind the hard work. Mr. Grafton quickly figured out that Cara was trustworthy, smart, and a fast learner. Once he saw how efficiently she restocked the shelves, swept the storage room floor, and served the customers, never getting their change wrong, he upgraded her responsibilities. Soon he set her to work doing stock taking and checking the early-morning deliveries, so he didn't have to get up in the cold with his arthritis. It might not be her dream job, but it was a start.

Cara found it surprisingly easy to settle back into life at Annie's. Of course the East End wasn't quite as she remembered it. There was violence on the streets now, talk in the papers of turf wars between the Krays and the Richardsons. But it was still a lively, vibrant place. Annie was also much the same—still warm and down to earth. She'd aged, of course, lost a lot of weight and seemed stooped, not as robust as she'd once been, but she was genuinely welcoming and seemed to love having Cara around. Danny was out so much that she was company for her.

As the months went by, Cara could say that for the most part, she was happy. She had a little job that she loved and was good at and a place to call home. The one thing she didn't have was Danny.

He was nice enough to her, of course: teasing her, asking her how it was going on the rare occasions when he was around the house. But it was the way he would treat a kid sister.

It didn't help that he paraded an array of beautiful but vacuous girl-friends through the house. At the moment he was seeing a girl named Linda. She looked like a typical dolly bird: the type of woman a man felt proud to have on his arm but wouldn't provide much in the way of conversation. She did her best to copy Diana Dors, with her tight little sweaters and big, fake blond hair. Cara hated her—mostly because it showed her exactly what Danny wanted and reminded her that she didn't measure up.

So far, since turning fifteen, Cara had stayed worryingly flat-chested. How was she ever supposed to get Danny to notice her when he had his eyes firmly glued to the two bumps in Linda's tight sweater?

One afternoon, toward the end of 1962, Linda turned up early at the house for her date with Danny. Cara had the misfortune of opening the door to her.

"Is he back?" the older girl demanded with no preamble. She never wasted her charm on anyone who wasn't male.

"No." Cara was just as short with her.

"Well, I'll come in and wait." Linda pushed past her and went into the sitting room. Cara could have gone upstairs to her room, but she refused to be chased away by that cow, so instead she followed her through. Before Danny's girlfriend had arrived, Cara had been watching *The Avengers* on the new television set. Without asking if Cara minded, the other girl switched the channel to *Coronation Street* and then plonked herself down on the settee, putting her dirty shoes up on Annie's clean coffee table.

"Do make yourself at home," Cara muttered sarcastically under her breath, as she walked by, deliberately knocking the blonde's feet down as she went.

Linda glared at her. "What's up with you?" But it had the desired effect, and she took her slingbacks off, curling her legs up under her instead. They both settled down to watch the show. After a while, Linda got a packet of hard candies out of her bag. Instead of offering any to Cara, she started to eat one after the other herself, balling up the empty wrappers and throwing them across the room at the ashtray on the table. She wasn't a very good shot, so most of them ended up on the floor. Seeing the mess she was making, Cara tutted. "Can't you put those in the bin? Annie just hoovered this morning."

But Linda made no move to pick the wrappers up or apologize—she just gave Cara a withering stare. The Irish girl couldn't help wondering what Danny would make of his girlfriend's lack of respect for his mother.

The girls sat watching the television in uncomfortable silence for the next half an hour, until Danny finally turned up. As he came through the living room door, he beamed at Cara.

"All right, sweetheart?" He ruffled her hair. She was momentarily pleased that he'd acknowledged her first, but then he turned to Linda and bent his head to plant a kiss on her lips.

"Hey, Princess." Pulling away a little, he ran his eyes appreciatively over her. "Who's looking gorgeous tonight?"

Over Danny's broad shoulder, Linda shot Cara a triumphant look. Then, turning her attention to her boyfriend, the older girl lowered her false lashes, made extra thick and long by layers of blue mascara.

"Hello, Danny." Her voice was a breathy imitation of Marilyn Monroe's. It set Cara's teeth on edge, especially since whenever Danny wasn't around she screeched like an old fishwife. All these feminine charms were just an act for his benefit.

But he didn't seem to care that everything about Linda was fake, from her lashes to her dyed hair. Dropping down on the settee next to her, he ran his hand through her hair, coming to rest on the back of her neck. "So what do you fancy doing tonight, darling?"

As she nuzzled against his palm like a kitten against its owner's legs, Cara pretended to concentrate on the television. "Why don't we go up the Palais? Gina, Rob, and the others will be there."

"Okay." He sounded almost absent-minded as he rubbed his nose against her cheek. "But why don't we stay in instead?"

Linda giggled girlishly. "Danny!" She flashed another look at Cara, as if she was embarrassed by what he was implying. "You know I'm not like that."

Cara rolled her eyes. From what the neighborhood gossips said, Linda had been "like that" with quite a few blokes already.

Danny stretched lazily. "Whatever you say." Getting up, he pulled Linda to her feet. "Let's get out of here." He looked over at Cara. "See you later."

He didn't even bother to wait for her reply.

Cara had a miserable evening. Half an hour after they'd gone, Annie got back. As usual, they cooked dinner together, but Cara's hearty appetite had deserted her, and she couldn't concentrate on making conversation.

Annie watched her toying with her food. "What's up with you?" she asked eventually.

"Nothing. Just a bit tired." Cara dropped her fork onto the plate, giving in. "I'll wash up and then go to my room."

It was after midnight, and Cara was just dozing off when she heard the front door bang shut. It was Danny arriving home, and he had Linda with him. His bedroom was directly below Cara's, and through the floorboards she could hear the two of them laughing together. After a while, the sounds softened, and music from Radio Luxembourg came on, but it didn't drown out the telltale noises. Cara covered her ears with her hands and then buried her head under a pillow, but nothing made any difference. However hard she tried, she couldn't get the image of Danny and Linda out of her mind.

In the privacy of her room, Cara sneaked the magazine out of her bag. Today, when she was in the newsagent's, one headline had caught her eye: "Do You Want to Go Up Three Bra Sizes? Well, Here's How!" So she'd spent a precious sixpence on a copy of *Women's Own*, hoping it would solve all her problems.

But disappointingly, there was no magic cure inside: just a review of a new push-up bra, the Model 1300, which was far too expensive for Cara. However, at the bottom of the page there was something of more interest: a little box telling readers how they could get the same look for a fraction of the cost.

After seeing Linda and Danny together the other night, Cara was determined to attract his attention. The next day, she'd taken a long, hard look at herself in the mirror. No wonder Danny never noticed her, when she was such a tomboy: her hair was dark and ragged, having never grown back properly since it had been hacked off by Sister Concepta; she only ever wore loose skirts and baggy jumpers, hand-me-downs from Annie that did nothing to flatter her skinny body and made her look like a child still; and she never used makeup. She needed to become more feminine, more like Linda. So she'd splashed out on hair dye, cosmetics, and a new outfit—a slim-line skirt and a tight sweater—and was planning to spend the afternoon getting ready. After all, it was Danny's nineteenth birthday today, and Annie had a special dinner planned for him. Cara was determined to look her best.

Four hours later, the transformation was complete. Cara stared at herself in the mirror, unsure of the result. Her hair wasn't platinum blond as she'd hoped—it was more orangey; the makeup made her look older, but was the foundation a little dark? Her neck was a different color from her face. She wished she had someone to give an opinion before unveiling the new look to everyone. Well, she looked *different,* that was for sure. She twisted and turned, trying to decide whether she liked the outfit. Something wasn't quite right. The sweater looked, well, shapeless on her. She'd bought a bra—her first—but she had nothing to fill it with. Her eyes strayed back over to the magazine and its do-it-yourself solution.

It took her another half an hour to arrange the balls of cotton wool, but by the time she'd finished she was pleased with the results. The stuffing filled out the conical shapes in her bra, and when she pulled the sweater down it looked good—like Linda did in hers. Maybe the left side was a little bigger than the right. She pulled the straps out and wriggled around, trying to make both sides look equal. But the cotton balls shifted, falling lower. *Damn.* She fidgeted a bit more, until it was as good as she could get. It wasn't perfect, but she was sure no one would notice. Anyway, she had no more time to worry—Annie had already called up twice, asking her to come down. Everyone else had arrived, and they were waiting for Danny's birthday dinner to begin.

The Connollys were all in the kitchen, toasting Danny with some sparkling wine that Annie had picked up. No one saw Cara at first as she hovered in the doorway, wanting to make a grand entrance. It was Annie who spotted her—and promptly dropped the tray of potatoes she'd been carrying.

"Oh, Jesus!" she gasped, her hand going up to cover her mouth.

Everyone looked around.

Bronagh, who'd come over with her family to celebrate Danny's birthday, peered at the girl. "Cara?" she said unsurely.

Aidan, Bronagh's five-year-old son, was staring straight at her chest. "What's wrong with your boobs?"

"Aidan!" Bronagh scolded him.

But he was a willful little boy, a lot like his Uncle Danny, and without any thought he got up and walked over to Cara and slapped at the front of her sweater, where her breasts were supposed to be. The cotton balls caved in. There was a gasp of horror from around the room. Aidan looked up at her. "They're not real," he observed solemnly.

There was a moment of shocked silence, and then—almost as one—the whole table started to laugh.

"Oh, sweetheart," Annie managed eventually. She wiped tears from her eyes. "Out of the mouths of babes, hey?"

Tears of embarrassment stung Cara's eyes. She looked over at Danny, who had his arm around Linda, who was smirking at her. How would she ever get him to take her seriously after this? With that thought she fled from the room.

It was Danny who came to see how she was. He knocked on the door. "Can I come in?" he called through.

"No!" Cara shouted back. She felt so humiliated right now that she wasn't sure she ever wanted to see him again.

But Danny wasn't giving up that easily. He cracked open the door. "Please—let me in, will you?"

Cara was lying facedown on the bed and made no effort to look at him. "Do whatever you want."

He walked over and sat beside her, his hand resting on her shoulder. At any other time, she would have been happy to get this level of attention from him. But not like this.

"Are you all right, mate?" he asked gently.

"What do you think?" she sniffed.

He laughed a little. "Not too good, right?"

"Right."

"What's with all the getup, hey? The clothes, the hair, the makeup?"

Cara didn't say anything at first. How could she explain that she'd just wanted him to notice her? "I just wanted to be different," she said at last. "But it all went wrong." Burying her head into the pillow, she started to cry again.

"Hey, hey. No more of that." Danny eased her onto her side, offering her a big hankie. "Now stop crying. And come back downstairs and have some grub, will you? For me, as it's my birthday?"

"Oh, no, I can't." She turned her tear-stained face up at him, mascara and foundation streaking down her cheeks. "You don't mind, do you? I just can't face them all."

Danny looked like he wanted to argue back, but then he seemed to realize how serious she was about staying put. "Don't worry about it. I understand." He ruffled Cara's hair affectionately. "But cheer up. We all do stupid things at your age. It ain't the end of the world."

He went back down to join the others then. But if his words were meant to be reassuring, they'd had the opposite effect on Cara. She'd never felt smaller or more stupid. No wonder he didn't fancy her.

39

The incessant banging on the front door woke Cara. As the wood smashed, her eyes flew open. She heard the sound of heavy footsteps charging through the house, shouting as doors were thrown open and rooms searched, and realized what was going on. It was a dawn raid.

In the darkness of the early winter morning, Cara pulled on her dressing gown and hurried downstairs, but she was only just in time to see Danny being dragged out in handcuffs by two men in uniform. He'd obviously gotten dressed hastily: he had on old jeans, his T-shirt was inside out, and he needed a shave.

Seeing the state of him, Cara's hands automatically went to her mouth. "Danny!" she gasped, her eyes filling with tears at the sight of the man she admired so much being humiliated like that.

But Danny answered cheerfully. "Don't worry about me," he called over his shoulder. "Just look after Mum, will you?"

She found Annie sitting in the kitchen, smoking a cigarette, her hand shaking a little. Cara went over and sat down beside her. Almost two years had passed since she'd turned up on the Connollys' doorstep, and over that time Annie had been like a mother to her. She couldn't stand to see the older woman upset this way.

"Are you all right?" Cara knew it must have been horrible for the older woman, seeing her son dragged out. But though Annie was still in shock, she was surprisingly matter-of-fact about the whole business. She'd been expecting this for a long time. Men like Danny could get away with it for only so long.

"I'll be fine. It's Danny we must be worrying about." She sighed heavily. "I'd better let Finnbar know what's happened."

She made to get up, but Cara put a restraining hand on her. "Don't worry, I'll do that. Do you want me to stick the kettle on, too?"

Annie smiled weakly up at her. "Thanks, love. You're a real lifesaver."

In the interview room of the local police station, Detective Chief Inspector Bailey sat down opposite Danny Connolly. The heavyset policeman sported a shaved head and a squashed nose, courtesy of an altercation with some drunk during his early days on the beat. At forty, with the wrinkles layering on top of each other on his forehead, he looked a little like a bulldog and had a reputation for being the meanest police constable in the station. The chief inspector always sent him in when he had someone he wanted to intimidate.

Danny knew all this and wasn't about to show any weakness. Bravado was all he had left, and he wasn't going to give that up easily. They'd arrested him for an armed robbery that had taken place at a High Street bank in Enfield earlier that week. Allegedly, there was a witness who'd put him at the scene. It didn't look good for him, but Danny wasn't giving up yet.

Bailey stared across the table at the prisoner, and Danny stared defiantly back. They'd left the lad alone in the holding cell for several hours, without food, drink, or information. The tactic had been designed to shake him up, but it obviously hadn't worked.

"So," Bailey began.

Danny cocked his head to one side. "So?" he repeated mockingly.

"You know the score. We've got someone who puts you at the scene, and you're looking at an eighteen-year stretch. By the time you get out, you'll be pushing forty, and none of those pretty girls you hang out with are going to be interested."

"Yeah—that's something you'd know all about."

Bailey bristled at the disrespect but decided to let it go. There were bigger issues at stake right now than his pride. He had a message to deliver. Ignoring the jibe, the policeman tried another tack: "Look, I'll give it to you straight. We're not after you. You're small fry, not even worth the time of day. But if you give us what we want, then you'll be out of here before teatime."

Danny feigned interest. "So what is it you want?"

"The big guy: Finnbar. We know it's him behind the robbery. You agree to stand up and say that in court, you'll get no more than a ticking off."

"Oh, yeah?"

Bailey leaned across the table; he was practically salivating. "Yeah. Just give us Finnbar. That's all we want."

Danny waited a beat, and then he grinned. "In that case, you'll know what it's like to want, then." He stretched lazily. "I don't know no Finnbar—and even if I did, I'm no grass. So if you've got nothing else of interest to say, then why don't you toddle off and get me a cuppa and my brief? I fancy a kip."

With that Danny put his head down on the cold table and closed his eyes. Bailey had no choice but to leave him to it. He'd never met anyone so cool on his first arrest, and despite himself, the policeman was impressed. In fact, he wasn't at all surprised when he got back half an hour later to find Danny snoring his head off.

Danny's loyalty was rewarded. Finnbar provided one of the best lawyers that money could buy. Of course, it helped that the witness conveniently disappeared, so all Danny could be charged with was handling stolen money. He was tried at Southwark Crown Court and went down for an eighteen-month stretch, which was a good result, considering. The worst part about it was where he was sent to serve his sentence. Instead of ending up close by in Wandsworth Scrubs, Bailey—aggrieved at not getting his man—had pulled some strings and seen that he'd serve his time up north in Durham nick instead. That meant family visits would be limited.

Annie tried to be stoical about the whole matter. "It could've been worse. And maybe this'll be a lesson to him." But even she wasn't naïve enough to believe that.

Cara wanted to know when she could see him, but Annie told her it was best that she didn't. "He don't want no one but me up there, darlin'. It's a long way for an hour's visit, and he don't want people seeing him locked up. He's getting on fine, and I think in a way it's easier for him to do his time without having reminders of home."

In fact, beneath her tough exterior, Annie was worried for her boy. Far from straightening him out, his time inside seemed to be making him more determined to pursue a life of crime. He was like a caged animal in there, pacing the floor, waiting for his chance to spring free. His hatred of the police had increased beyond anything she'd thought possible. It was "the pigs" this, "the pigs" that. Any hope Annie had entertained for her son eventually carving out a better life for himself had now gone.

With Danny away, Annie and Cara had no choice but to get on with their lives. Cara wrote to him every week. He never wrote back, but Annie assured her that he loved receiving her letters, so she kept sending them anyway.

"Oi! Wakey, wakey, love."

The sound of someone snapping fingers in front of her face startled Cara out of her daydream. She'd been leaning over the counter of Grafton's grocery store, lost in thought. Now she looked up to see Melanie Dixon smiling quizzically at her. The buxom redhead lived a few streets away from the Connollys. She was a couple of years older than Cara, and the two girls knew each other well enough to say hello.

"Sorry about that," Cara apologized as she rang up the other girl's bread and milk. "I was miles away."

"Somewhere good, I hope. Like a nice, sunny beach in Spain." Mel glanced out of the shop window at the gray drizzle. "It's peeing it down again. And they call this bleeding summer!"

Cara gave a weak smile.

Seeing her lackluster reaction, Mel peered more closely at her. "So what's up with you, then? You look like you've found a shilling and lost a pound!"

"You're right on the nose there," Cara admitted.

It was June 1964, six months since Danny had been sent down. Cara was now seventeen, and she had been living with the Connollys for well over two years. She was still working at Mr. Grafton's grocery and was thoroughly fed up with it. After her disastrous attempt to change her appearance, she'd started to take more of an interest in fashion and longed to get a job at one of the funky boutiques that were springing up along the King's Road. But without a National Insurance number, she had no chance. So she was stuck weighing out fruit and veg to the same faces every day.

It didn't help that she'd heard from Annie today that Danny's horrible ex, Linda, had gotten hitched. Danny had dumped her a few months before he'd been sent down, and she'd taken up with some other low-level thug. Now they were married and she'd moved out to a new semi in Essex, apparently. It wasn't that Cara wanted any of that, but at least Linda was getting on with her life, while she was still stuck here doing the same thing.

"Well, go on, then," Mel urged her. "Tell me what's up. A problem shared and all that."

Usually Cara wouldn't have dreamed of burdening a virtual stranger. But there was no one in the shop, and Mel seemed so genuinely interested that she found herself opening up about how fed up she was.

Once she'd finished, Mel studied her thoughtfully. "What about coming to work at Eclipse?"

"What, doing the accounts or something?" Last year, Cara had started helping Mr. Grafton with the bookkeeping, and she'd found that she was good at it. She'd helped a couple of other businesses out, and it had become a second source of income for her.

But Mel shook her head. "Nah. As one of the hostesses, like me."

Cara looked at Mel as though she were mad. Eclipse was one of the exclusive hostess clubs situated on Old Compton Street in Soho. Finnbar had set it up a couple of years earlier. It had been an instant success, a place where celebrities got to rub shoulders with the criminal fraternity. It was a glitzy, high-quality place, but Eclipse's real draw was the beautiful girls who worked there. Cara couldn't believe that Mel would even suggest that she could be one of them.

"Me?" She snorted with laughter, assuming the other girl was joking. "Yeah, I can see myself fitting right in. Probably scare half the customers off!"

"Don't be daft. You'd be perfect." Reaching into her handbag, Mel pulled out an elegant black matchbox, which she handed to Cara. It had ECLIPSE written on the front in white, with the silhouette of what appeared to be a naked woman by the side. The club's address was on the back. "Anyways, if you fancy it, pop along tomorrow at six, and I'll get the manager to sort something out for you."

Later that night, looking at herself in the mirror, Cara could see what Mel meant. After that stupid incident eighteen months earlier, she'd vowed never to be anything but herself ever again. But now she didn't need to be. Almost without realizing, she'd finally passed through the awkward adolescent stage that had plagued her for years, and she'd blossomed. She would never be classically beautiful like her mother had been, but with her black hair against alabaster skin, huge green eyes, and cheekbones like knives, she was definitely striking. Instead of being too tall and skinny, she was now long and lean, languid and rangy, and although she couldn't hope to rival the likes of Linda in the chest department, she had enough to get by.

So the following evening Cara did as Mel had suggested and went to Eclipse. The redhead had been as good as her word and had managed to arrange for Cara to see the club's manager, Ronan Carter. A short, stocky man, he had once been an enforcer, but since turning forty and getting hitched, he'd stepped into managing the more legitimate businesses. Wearing an expensive black suit, with a black shirt underneath, he was unrecognizable as the thug he'd once been.

He invited her into his office. Like the rest of the club, it was plush rather than functional, with a deep burgundy carpet and solid wood furniture. A two-way mirror ran the length of one side of the room, with a view down to the club below. Ronan discreetly pulled the blind closed and then went to sit behind his desk, leaning comfortably back in his black leather chair.

He got straight down to business. "So Mel says you're after a job?"

"That's right." Despite herself, Cara felt a little nervous in front of Carter. Mel had lent her a black shift dress for the interview, saying it would make her look more sophisticated, but frankly she felt a little uncomfortable in it. The skirt had come to just below the other girl's knees, but Cara was so much taller that the hem sat midway down her thigh, and she felt out of place showing so much leg.

Ronan watched with amusement as Cara squirmed under his questioning. The truth was, when Mel had told him that the Irish girl wanted to come to work here, his immediate reaction had been "No way." The last time he'd seen Cara must have been a few months ago now, and she'd been nothing more than a skinny little waif—hardly the type he could employ as a waitress at a sophisticated place like Eclipse. So today, he'd been pleasantly surprised when this tall, attractive, dark-haired young woman had walked into his office. Although she wasn't beautiful, she was definitely striking, and she really had the most incredible legs he'd ever seen.

Still, he wasn't rushing into giving her a job. He couldn't imagine the overprotective Annie Connolly wanting her precious charge working here. "And what does Annie make of all this?" he asked.

"She's fine with it," Cara answered quickly.

Too quickly. Ronan could tell the girl was lying. He bet she hadn't even given it a thought. "You sure?" His tone let her know he didn't believe her.

"Yes." Cara's green eyes flashed as she finally snapped, "And even if she wasn't, I'm old enough to make my own decisions." Clearly fed up with all his questions, she made a move to stand up. "Look, if you don't want to employ me, then that's fine. I can always go elsewhere."

Ronan laughed at her uppity tone. "All right, love." He held up his hands in mock surrender. "Keep your knickers on. It was only a simple question." He gave a shrug. "And if you're that keen, then I'll give you a go. At least if you're here, I can keep an eye on you—make sure you don't get into any trouble."

"Thanks, but you needn't bother," Cara said tartly. "I think you'll find I'm able to look after myself."

Ronan laughed again. "I can well believe that." She'd developed a mouth on her, that was for sure—which was good, because he couldn't employ a shrinking violet here. Sometimes the customers got out of hand, and she needed to be able to deal with it herself.

"So," Cara said impatiently. "Have I got the job?"

"Yeah, why not? Just get out of here before I change my mind."

40

"My feet are *killing* me." Putting her hands on the smooth mahogany bar for support, Melanie stepped out of her heels, immediately shrinking three inches.

Cara shook her head in mock rebuke. "If Ronan catches you out of uniform, there'll be hell to pay."

"That's the least of my troubles." Mel rubbed the sides of the corset that she was wearing. "I think Donna pulled this too tight. I don't half feel ropey—like a turkey trussed up for Christmas."

"You and me both," Cara laughed, looking down at her skimpy costume.

There were strict rules at the club, and Eclipse's manager, Ronan, was fastidious about enforcing them—especially when it came to what the girls wore. All the cocktail waitresses were expected to dress identically, and they were forever bitching about how uncomfortable it was, although Cara suspected that, like her, most of them secretly loved the slinky uniform. She always felt sexy just stepping into it in the evenings: the black satin teddy with tuxedo tails, full-length black opera gloves, fishnets, and heels. At the start of being hired, each girl had a meeting with the club's dressmaker to ensure her costume fitted perfectly. Cara reckoned the woman must be some kind of miracle worker, since whenever she put the corset on, she went from looking like an ironing board to having an hourglass figure.

Along with the uniform, the girls were all expected to wear their hair up and to be fully made up at all times. It was a sexy, high-class look, which pretty much summed up Eclipse. Housed in an intimate cellar room of a Soho town house, every detail had been perfectly thought out. The nightclub's low lighting, burgundy carpets, and plush velvet banquettes made it a deliciously seedy and decadent place, full of old-style glamour, which was why it attracted such an illustrious clientele. Looking around tonight, Cara could spot a couple of movie stars, a government minister, and a high-ranking member of the royal family, all without too much effort.

She had been working at the club for six months now, and she'd never been happier. It was an easy gig. As Ronan had warned her during that interview, other than delivering drinks, her main task seemed to be to parade half naked around the place, providing color and company as required. And though Cara could appreciate that it was a little mindless, she liked the idea that men were prepared to pay to spend the evening with her. For someone who had always considered herself an ugly duckling, it was nightly validation that she had turned into a swan.

As Ronan had predicted, Annie hadn't been especially happy about Cara's new job. "What do you want to be doing that for?" she'd asked when she heard.

Even though Cara had had little formal education, she was obviously a smart girl, and the older woman had hoped that one day she would get a good job for herself, marry someone respectable who doted on her, and settle into one of the more affluent London suburbs. That was growing less likely now, and Annie couldn't help feeling somewhat responsible for the girl falling into this underground lifestyle. But Cara seemed happy enough, so there wasn't much she could do about it.

Since coming to work at Eclipse, Cara felt that she'd finally started to grow up. Last month, in May, she had turned eighteen. The Connollys had held a little party for her, and Annie baked a cake. The next night, she'd gone out to the Clapham Grand with a few of the girls who worked at Eclipse and gotten chatting with a boy named Grant. He'd insisted on seeing her home, and that night she'd had her first kiss. Annie had met him and approved. He lived in Surrey and had a good job as a civil servant. They had gone out a few times after that, but Cara sensed that he was more interested than she was, so she broke things off with him as gently as she could. She knew that she could never feel the same way about him as she did about Danny, and it wasn't worth pursuing something with no future. Gone were the days when girls settled down with the first man who asked them. This new decade was about women having choices, and she was determined to make the most of it.

"You still up for tomorrow?" she asked Mel now.

"Yeah, can't wait."

They both had the night off then, and they were planning to go out with some of the other girls. The hostesses all got on well, and Cara had made some good friends at Eclipse, helping the other waitresses out whenever she could. She loved the camaraderie between the girls and that feeling of belonging.

Groaning, Mel slipped her shoes back on. "S'pose I'd best get back to it," she said reluctantly.

"If you're feeling that bad, why don't you go on your break?"

The other girl pulled a face. "I already did, an hour ago."

Cara wasn't surprised to hear it. Mel was notoriously work-shy. The only reason Ronan kept her on was that the customers loved her bubbly personality.

"I'll cover for you," Cara offered, as she so often had in the past.

The redhead's eyes lit up. "You sure?"

"Course." Cara made little shooing motions with her hands. "Now, go on with you. Before I change my mind."

Mel didn't need any further encouragement. She hurried away.

Up in the viewing room, Ronan Carter stood with his boss, Finnbar Sullivan, looking down at the club below. The two-way mirror allowed them to see what was going on, with no one aware that they were watching.

"That kid of Annie's working out all right?" Finnbar's eyes were on a tall, slim, dark-haired girl, standing at the bar.

Ronan followed his boss's gaze. "Who, Cara? Yeah, she's a good little worker."

He watched as Cara picked up a trayful of drinks and started heading toward Mel's section. He immediately guessed what had happened— the redhead was always crying off from work, and Cara invariably picked up the slack for her. She was good like that, always happy to cover a shift if one of the other girls was sick or had a family emergency.

"They're a good-looking bunch, aren't they?" Finnbar mused, casting one last glance over the club room below. Satisfied that everything was running well, the gang leader turned from the window and went to sit down. He took out a cigarette. "Danny's out soon," he said as he lit up.

Ronan nodded. He'd already heard, and he was pleased for the lad. He wouldn't have fancied spending eighteen months in jail. But then, he was a very different person from Danny Connolly. Ronan wanted more than to end up as some low-level thug. Danny, on the other hand, was a hothead, always spoiling for a fight. He had been happy enough to do his time, seeing it as part of the life he'd chosen. He didn't realize how hard it had been on those who loved him.

"Annie'll be pleased to have him back," Ronan commented.

And she wouldn't be the only one, he thought, his eyes lingering on Cara for a moment longer. Everyone at the club knew about her crush on Danny—it was something of a running joke. Of course she'd changed a lot these past few months. Ronan remembered back to the first time she'd come to his office, when she'd been all aggressive and defensive. She'd matured since then, grown into a poised, sophisticated young woman. It'd be interesting to see what Danny made of her now that she was all grown up.

Cara was working at Eclipse the night that Danny got out. Although everyone had known that his release was imminent, they hadn't known the exact date. But around nine that evening the whispers started: *Danny Connolly is back in town.*

Cara greeted the news with the same air of detached nonchalance with which she treated everything these days. Danny had been away for nearly two years, and she liked to think that she'd grown up in that time, that she was no longer the faithful little puppy who had followed him around. Although she'd kept writing to him weekly, that didn't mean she was going to fawn all over him. In fact, she'd been seeing Charlie, one of the bouncers from the club, for the past two months. And even if she did still think of Danny occasionally, she was too old now for stupid infatuations, she told herself as she stood by the bar, waiting for her drinks order to be filled. She was past mooning over Danny Connolly, and she wasn't going to waste time on him any longer.

She froze in midthought. Because just as she'd been vowing to greet his return with the casual indifference it deserved, the man himself walked into the club. Seeing him, with his rough, dark handsomeness, she felt the old familiar tightening in her stomach, and she knew that despite her good resolutions, Danny was still in her system and under her skin.

He didn't see her at first. There were too many people surrounding him, slapping him on the back, offering to buy him drinks. It was as if the king had come home. Cara hung back, unsure how to greet him after all this time.

Mel spotted her skulking at the bar and came over. "Aren't you gonna go and say hello?" the redhead asked. "I thought you'd be first in line. Bloody hell, you've done enough pining after him these past months to last a lifetime."

"No, I haven't!"

Mel snorted a laugh. "Yeah, right."

Ignoring her friend, Cara moved off to deliver her drinks.

It was a good hour and a half before Danny finally insisted on going up to the bar himself to buy a round. Cara knew this was her moment.

Luckily, she was looking good. She always did these days. Smoothing her hands over the black corset, she nervously touched her dark hair, tamed into a sophisticated bouffant, and prepared to meet him.

The crowds parted as Danny came up to the bar. It was Friday night, and as usual the place was being mobbed. He sat up on a stool, waiting to be served. He looked good, she saw: older and worldlier, and he'd bulked up, too. He already had a wallet full of cash and was busy counting out his money when Cara walked over.

"All right, Danny?" she asked softly.

Hearing the familiar voice, he glanced up. He looked confused for a moment, and then, finally working out who it was, he did a double take. "Cara?" he asked in surprise.

She heard his disbelief, tried to stem her excitement, and gave him what she hoped passed for a cool look. "Who else?"

"Blimey!" He guffawed, shaking his head a little in disbelief. "So the ugly duckling finally turned into a swan!"

The comment hit straight in her gut. So he still wasn't going to take her seriously? Well, the old Cara might have pined for him, but the new one wasn't going to be so stupid. "I just wanted to say that I'm glad you're home," she said stiffly.

She made to turn away, but he reached out and grabbed her arm. "Hey, don't be like that," he pleaded. "What I meant to say is—you look great. I think I've been inside for so long I've forgotten how to compliment a lady."

It was the hangdog expression that did it for her, the one she'd seen him use on so many other girls over the years, when he'd been caught doing something bad and wanted to get back in their good books. It was the first time he'd used it on her. She started to soften and caught herself. There were always too many women pandering to Danny; it was time to stand back and let him do the work.

"I don't need your compliments, Daniel Connelly," she said archly, shaking his hand off. "There's enough other men queuing up to give them to me."

With that she walked off. She could feel him staring after her. It took all her willpower not to look back.

41

"How does it feel, then, son? Being back on the outside?"

Finnbar leaned back in his chair, tucking his arms behind his head. Danny stood calmly in front of him, refusing to be intimidated. They were in the back room of Eclipse, which acted as a makeshift headquarters for Finnbar's crew. Danny had been summoned there for a meeting, his first since getting out of prison a fortnight ago.

"It's not so bad." Danny grinned. "There're more birds out here."

Finnbar chuckled. "Yeah, and knowing you, you're making the most of it, right?"

The two men grinned at each other, and for a moment there was affinity between them; they were boys together.

In fact, though Danny had spent the past fourteen days savoring his freedom, now he was itching to get back to work. Danny was an ambitious lad; he'd grown up with nothing and being no one, right at the bottom of the pile. He'd seen his mother waste almost a decade of her life with a loser and a bully, and he was determined to be a better man—and for him, that meant being a good provider, even if that entailed straying outside the law from time to time. His upbringing had made him crave money and status in a way few others could understand. He'd been waiting for the word from Finnbar, and he assumed it would be business as usual. Having done his time and refused to grass the leader up, there were certain expectations that he would be looked after. But then again, you could never take anything for granted.

Now Danny cracked his knuckles, something he always did when he was unsure of himself but wanted to pretend otherwise. "So what's the score? Got anything that needs sorting?" It was his way of asking if he was still "in."

Finnbar smiled at his obvious eagerness. "All in good time." The large Irishman got up then and walked over to the wall safe. Taking out a thick envelope, he handed it to Danny.

"I reckon after that two-year stint you could do with a few more days off. But meantime, this should compensate you for your trouble."

Danny's eyes widened as he saw the wad of twenties. It was far more than he'd been expecting. Finnbar had taken care of his mother while he was away, and that had been enough of a gesture as far as Danny had been concerned. This showed how much gratitude the gang leader felt.

"That's very generous of you, sir."

Finnbar gave a satisfied smile. "As everyone knows, I like to reward those who are loyal to me." Then his expression hardened. "Just as I punish those who aren't."

There was a warning behind his words: *You might be in favor now, but if you step out of line, I'll have you, my son.* But Danny was too chuffed with how the meeting had gone to notice. He was still in with Finnbar, he had money in his pocket and a few days left to call his own. As he left Eclipse, he knew exactly what he was going to do with the cash: get a place of his own.

He hadn't been able to settle back into living at home since coming out of the nick. At twenty-one years old, he was beyond taking orders from an old woman, even if she was his mum. He loved her dearly, but it was becoming a bit embarrassing bringing his friends back. Maybe it wouldn't have been so bad if they'd moved to a better place in a fancier area. But whenever he brought the idea up with her, she didn't seem interested.

"All my friends are here," she'd say, casting an eye out onto the street. "What's the likes of me going to do for conversation somewhere la-di-dah?"

Well, maybe she was happy to stay in their old neighborhood, but Danny wasn't. As of today, he was moving up in the world, and everyone was going to see that.

"Cara! Wait a second!"

Hearing someone call her name, Cara stopped in the street and turned. Her heart sank as she saw that it was one of the customers from the club: a well-spoken chap named Hugo, who was out on his stag night. He was alone, which meant he'd ditched the rest of his friends to come after her.

"What do you want?" Cara asked nervously as he drew level with her. She was pleased at least that she'd changed into jeans after her shift; it would have been horrible standing there half naked in her costume.

"To see if you'd like to go on somewhere." Seeming to sense her wariness, Hugo gave her a winning smile. He was a good-looking guy, only a few years older than her, with sandy hair and blue eyes. Perhaps if she'd met him on neutral ground she might have had a drink with him, but apart from knowing he was about to get married, Eclipse had a strict policy against its waitresses dating customers.

"Sorry, I can't," Cara told him.

She turned to go, hoping that would be an end to it, but he moved in front of her, blocking her escape. Alarm bells began to sound in her head, and she cursed her decision not to get a cab. Usually she got a taxi home, but because it was a lovely warm summer's evening, she'd decided to walk up to Oxford Street and catch a night bus instead. Looking around, she saw that the street was deserted, which meant she was going to have to deal with this by herself.

"Come on, sweetie. Just have one little drink with me." His eyes were pleading.

Cara sighed. This happened a lot, especially with the younger guys. They took the hostesses' flirtation too seriously and assumed that their skimpy costumes meant they were easy. Cara could just imagine the conversation that had gone on between this man and his Old Etonian mates—they'd probably dared him to lay the cheap waitress.

"Look," she said firmly. "I'm tired, and I want to get home. And if you've got any sense, you'll go and see that fiancée of yours—Victoria, isn't it?"

She made to push past him, thinking he'd let her go now. But the drink and the spirit of the evening must have been getting to him, because he grabbed her shoulders and backed her up against a nearby wall.

"Hey, not so fast." His eyes were hard, all his good-natured banter gone. She could smell whiskey on his breath. "After that tip I left, the least you can do is be nice to me."

Cara was just thinking about slamming her knee up into his groin when a voice came out of the darkness.

"Oi! What do you think you're playing at?"

Looking up, Cara saw to her relief that it was Danny, running down the middle of the road, straight at them, his eyes blazing with anger. Seeing him, Hugo released his grip on Cara, but before he could move away, Danny was on him. One punch caught the posh lad across the jaw; the next landed in his stomach, sending him stumbling backward. He probably would have fallen to the ground, but Danny grabbed his lapels and hauled him back up, holding the other man close so he could keep hitting him.

"You like a bit of this, do you?" The East End lad slapped him across the face with the back of his hand, splitting his lip. The wedding photos were going to look a treat, Cara couldn't help thinking. "Not such a hard man now, are you?"

Blood was bubbling up out of Hugo's mouth, but Danny still didn't seem to be relenting. As grateful as Cara was to him for rescuing her, she hadn't wanted this. Seeing two policemen rounding the corner, she knew it was time to get away.

"Danny! Stop!" Cara tugged at his arm, but he didn't let go. His eyes flicked over to her, and she could see a black rage there. She needed to find a way to get through to him. "He's not worth it. Come on, let it go," she urged him. "The coppers are coming, and you'll end up back inside."

Those final words brought him to his senses. "All right, I hear you." He pulled Hugo up, so their faces were level, and hissed out his final warning. "Don't you *ever* touch a woman like that again." Then he gave the other man one last, hard shove so that he fell backward onto the ground.

Cara grabbed Danny's hand. "Come on," she urged him. "Let's get out of here."

They ran down the road, turning onto busy Wardour Street. One of the policemen gave chase, blowing his whistle and yelling at them to stop, but they managed to lose him in the crowd. Once they were away, they hailed a cab and climbed in. Both of them were breathing too hard to speak at first.

"Thanks," Cara said finally. "I'm glad you came along when you did."

"No problem." Danny waited a beat and then asked, "But what happened to Charlie?" He was the bouncer that Cara had been dating. "Why wasn't he there looking out for you?"

"We broke up."

"Oh?" Danny gave her a sideways look. "Chucked you, did he?"

She elbowed him in the stomach. "Mind your own business." In fact, she'd broken things off with Charlie. He was a nice enough guy, but there'd been no spark between them. Not that she'd ever admit that to Danny.

Laughing, he said, "Sorry, love, but you know I'm only kidding." Then, more seriously, "He'd have to be crazy to dump you."

Cara looked away, as always unsure how to deal with Danny flirting with her. Since coming out of prison, he'd been treating her differently, no longer like a little sister, and it still threw her. It was what she had wanted for so long, which made her scared of how she'd feel if it went away. So instead she turned the comment into a joke. "It's too late for apologies," she said, pretending to be offended. "I'm not sure I'll be able to forgive you for saying that."

Danny played along, making his eyes wide with pleading. "There must be something I can do . . ."

Cara considered the matter for a moment. "Well . . . you could buy me some grub," she relented. "I'm bleedin' starving after tonight's shenanigans."

They asked the cab to drop them outside Rock 'n' Roe, which was on their route home. They bought a bag of French fries each, and ate them walking along the street. By the time they got back to Annie's, the salt and vinegar had soaked through the newspaper and onto Cara's hands. Without thinking, she licked her fingers. Danny smiled slyly at her. "Want me to do that for you?"

Cara gave him a wry look. "No, thanks. I think I've had just about enough unwanted male attention for one night."

He took a step closer, so they were practically touching in the darkened hallway. "Is it really that unwanted?"

The breath caught in Cara's chest; her heart began to beat faster. Now the moment was here, she didn't know what to do. "Danny . . ." she began, not quite sure what to say next.

"Danny?" Annie's voice came down the stairs. "Is that you, son?"

The moment was broken. Cara stepped back, away from Danny. "I should go to bed," she told him.

She made to turn away, but Danny put his hand out to stop her. "Wait a sec," he said. "I had something I wanted to tell you."

"What?" She looked at him expectantly.

"I've found myself a flat."

"You're moving out?" Cara was devastated.

"Yeah. It's getting a bit much here." As if to prove his point, they could hear Annie moving around upstairs, muttering about not being able to find her slippers. "Want to come and see the place with me?"

"Course!" Cara said eagerly. The fact that he wanted her to come along more than made up for the thought of him not being around all the time.

It hadn't taken long for Danny to find a place he liked. One of Finnbar's contacts had a flat for rent and gave him a good deal. It was in Notting Hill, a sign that Danny was going up in the world. It was the perfect reward for losing two years of freedom.

Annie tried to share his excitement, but it was hard, knowing that her son was moving out and moving on. Although she was pleased that he was doing well for himself, she was sad to be losing him, too.

"I'm gonna take Cara round there later," he told her. "See what she thinks of the place."

Annie's eyes narrowed. She had known this was coming, sensed the change since Danny had come out of nick, seen the way his eyes followed Cara.

Now she said, "Just be careful, son. Cara's not like all those other tarts you're used to. She's special. Don't mess her around."

Danny spread his arms wide. "Mum!" he protested. "As if . . ."

But Annie wasn't having any of it. "You've been warned" was all she'd say.

Cara looked around what Danny called a flat. She hadn't known what one was before she came here. At first, she'd been a bit skeptical— his new digs were in one of those big white houses near Notting Hill tube station, which Annie would no doubt call "la-di-dah"— but then she'd walked in and seen how beautiful it was. He had the whole of the top floor, and there was a real sense of space and light about the place. It was south-facing, and as it was midafternoon now, light was flooding in through the huge windows in the living room, with their views out across the freshly mown grass of the square.

"Oh, it's lovely," she breathed, taking in the high ceilings with the delicate cornicing, the stripped wood floors, and the magnolia walls. "Is it really all yours?"

Danny puffed out his chest, enjoying her admiration. "That's right. Of course, it needs some furniture . . ."

"But that's the beauty of it." Cara spun around the large lounge, her arms outstretched like the wings of an airplane. "There's so much space!"

He laughed at her obvious enthusiasm. "I'm glad it meets your approval."

Impulsively, she threw her arms around his neck, pleased that the scrappy boy she'd once known had made something of himself. "Oh, well done, Dan." The pride in her voice was unmistakable. "You've really arrived, haven't you?"

He hugged her back. "Yeah," he agreed, and there was none of the usual braggart about him. "We've both done all right for ourselves, ain't we?"

They stood there for a moment longer, her head resting against his chest, so she could hear his heart beating. It was then that she became aware of him: his hands on either side of her waist, the proximity of his warm male body against hers. She pulled away a little, just enough so she was still standing in the circle of his arms, looking up at him. She was about to speak, to make an excuse about it being time to leave, but in that second their eyes locked, and something changed between them.

"I should go," she whispered.

But Danny's grip tightened on her. "Hey, not so fast." He reached up and tucked a lock of her sooty black hair behind her ear. "You've got beautiful, you know that?" he said tenderly.

Cara felt her heart speed up, her mouth go dry. She'd wanted this for so long, but now the moment was here, she was terrified. "Dan . . ." she said warningly, dropping her gaze.

"Shush. Enough talking."

She did as he said and shut up, standing perfectly still as he put one hand under her chin and tipped her face up so she was staring right at him: so close that she could feel his hot breath on her face and see the desire in his dark eyes. Then he bent his head and kissed her.

Cara had imagined this moment for so long, playing the scene again and again in her head, that she'd suspected it could never live up to her fantasies. But it was everything she could have hoped for. His kiss was tender and sweet at first, his lips soft on hers, as though he was testing her out, seeing whether she minded; then something changed, and suddenly his hands were in her hair, pulling her closer, his mouth hungrily, greedily devouring her, moving to her neck, biting at her earlobes, as though he couldn't get enough of her.

To Cara, it felt as if the breath had been ripped from her body. She'd been kissed before, but never with such ferocity. It was as if he'd awoken something in her, and she was kissing him back, pressing against him, her body responding instinctively. His hands were at her waist, moving under her blouse and over her bare skin.

"Oh, God!" She gasped as his fingers found the cotton and wire of her bra, sending unexpected frissons of pleasure through her.

Hearing her, Danny pulled away. "Come on, sweetheart," he said huskily.

Taking her hand, he led her through to the bedroom. She stumbled after him, dazed and weak with desire.

The apartment was still more or less bare, but the bed and mattress had already been delivered. Danny wasted no time pulling off his shirt and undoing his belt. Cara hung back, suddenly unsure of herself. She hadn't had much experience with men—she'd kissed a handful of them, and there'd been some fumbling in the back of Charlie's car, but that was all. She was acutely aware of how much more worldly Danny was and couldn't help wondering how she would measure up against all the other girls, when she had no idea what she was doing. And what would he think of her body—skinny and angular, without the soft curves of Linda?

Oblivious to everything that was going through Cara's head, Danny went over to the record player and put on the new Rolling Stones' album. With his back turned, she took the opportunity to quickly undress and slip under the covers. The sheets were freshly on, and as she lay back she could smell the distinctive floral aroma of washing powder.

Turning round, Danny saw what she had done. It must have clicked then that she was anxious, because he came over to sit beside her. "Are you all right?"

"I'm a bit scared," she admitted.

Seeing her staring up at him, her expression frightened and trusting, Danny felt a surge of exhilaration. He might have had lots of women before, but his mother had been right: Cara *was* different. There had always been a connection between them, right from when they were kids. She was his, she always had been, and this would finally be his way of possessing her.

"We don't have to," he said.

But she shook her head, as he'd known she would. "No. I want this."

His dark eyes glittered wickedly. "Thank Christ for that." He pretended to wipe his brow in relief. "I wasn't sure what I was going to do with this otherwise."

He nodded down at the bulge in his trousers. Cara laughed, and whether it had been Danny's intention or not, she felt herself start to relax. This was Danny, *her* Danny. Everything would be fine.

It helped that he took it slowly at first, waiting for her to catch up. There was none of the bluff casualness that she had feared from him. Instead he was gentle and sweet, as though he sensed this was a big deal for her and wanted to make it special. It was a different side to Danny from the one most people usually saw.

He spent a long time just lying beside her, simply kissing her, stroking her bare shoulders, waiting for her to make the next move. It was Cara who took it further, growing impatient for more, running her hands over the tight muscles of his arms, pushing back the covers because she wanted, *needed*, to feel closer to him.

Danny continued to move agonizingly slowly, working his way down her body, kissing and licking, caressing and biting as he went, seeming to enjoy her growing impatience. She arched and stretched, as his mouth grazed the flat of her stomach; she squirmed, hardly able to stand it, as his fingers trailed across her panties, his touch deliberately, teasingly light. She felt herself moistening, hot desire spreading through her groin.

"Please," she begged, her hips lifting, as Danny pushed the white cotton aside, his hand searching out her slickness.

She was so far gone already that almost as soon as he touched her she began to cry out, her nails digging into his shoulders, as a hot, violent orgasm shuddered through her. She'd been so caught up with her own pleasure that she'd hardly thought about Danny's. But now she was suddenly aware of him tugging off his jeans, his underwear; his breathing rough and ragged. Seeing how big he was, she felt a twinge of fear, unsure how he was going to fit inside her. But it was too late to go back now. She was still shaking, unable to speak, as he pushed her legs open and entered her.

She winced, and his eyes registered surprise, then tenderness, as he realized that he was her first.

"Am I hurting you?" Lying, she shook her head. She wanted to do this for Danny. As he began to move inside her, she held him close and hoped that it would always be like this between them.

Afterward, exhausted, they fell asleep. When Cara woke a little while later, it was dark outside and she was alone. It took her a moment to work out where she was. Then everything that had happened that afternoon came rushing back. In the darkness, she felt heat flood her face, then an empty pit form in her stomach. Where had Danny gone? Surely it wasn't a good sign that he'd left before she woke up.

It was tempting to stay closeted in the bedroom. But the sensible part of her knew that she needed to face him at some point, and she might as well get it over with as soon as possible. Climbing out of bed, she grabbed the first item of clothing she could find—Danny's white shirt—and pulled it on, hastily doing up the buttons before padding outside.

She followed the smell of bacon and found Danny in the kitchen, making a fry-up. He didn't look up as she walked in.

"All right, Cara?" His voice was gruff, and her heart sank. This was it—the brush-off. The afternoon hadn't meant anything to him.

"Yeah, fine, thanks." She tried to sound upbeat, as though she wasn't upset by his behavior. There was an awkward silence. "Look, it's getting late," she said. "Shall I just go?"

Cara had judged the situation well. After waking up, Danny had indeed regretted the whole incident. Knowing how Cara felt about him, he knew he shouldn't have let things go so far between them. He wasn't a one-woman guy; once he'd slept with a girl, he wanted her out as soon as possible. So when Cara offered to leave, he felt a wave of relief, glad that she knew the score and he wouldn't have to deal with an awkward situation.

But then, as he turned to face her and saw her standing there—

wearing his white shirt buttoned up wrongly, her long legs bare, her dark hair disheveled—he was suddenly struck by how sexy she looked. The realization was followed swiftly by another: he didn't want her to go. This wasn't just some girl. This was Cara—his friend as well as his lover, someone he actually enjoyed hanging out with.

So instead of taking Cara up on her offer, he grinned at her. "I bloody well hope you're not going anywhere—otherwise all this grub will go to waste."

Hearing his words, Cara's face broke into a delighted smile. Dragging a stool up to the breakfast bar, she said, "Thank Christ—I thought you were never going to ask. Put some more sausages on, will you? I'm starving."

42

"What're you getting all dolled up for?" Danny came up behind Cara as she was applying her eyeliner in the dressing-table mirror, slipped his arms around her waist, and cuddled her to him.

"For work, stupid," she giggled.

"But I've only just got in," he complained, nuzzling her neck. "Stay here, and let's shag instead."

She pulled a face at him in the reflection. "I can't. If I'm late again, Ronan'll hand me my cards."

"So? Tell him to stuff his sodding job. I'll look after you, you know that."

Cupping her breasts with his hands, Danny pressed up against her bottom, so she could feel how turned on he was. Despite her good intentions, Cara gasped, dropping the eye pencil onto the dressing table with a clatter; she always lost control whenever Danny was around.

Aware of the effect he was having on her, he grinned triumphantly. "See? Isn't this more fun than running yourself ragged in that shitty club?"

It was an argument they'd been having a lot lately. Danny wanted her to stop working at Eclipse—he felt that it took up too much of her time. Spoiled by his mother and sisters, he was used to getting his own way, and that included having Cara at his beck and call. He expected her to be available whenever it suited him, and it didn't matter if she'd arranged to do something else, whether it was going to work or seeing her own set of friends.

It wouldn't have been so bad if there had been some structure to his life, because then she could have planned her own to fit in around him. But he'd come in at all hours of the day and night and expect her to be available, no matter what her plans. Lately her job had become inconvenient to him, so he wanted her to give it up. So far she'd resisted, but it was getting harder to refuse. Danny had a way of getting what he wanted.

It had been his idea that she move into his place, only a week after they'd first slept together. She was there most of the time anyway, so it seemed crazy for her to go back and forth for changes of clothes. That was nearly a year ago now. Cara adored the flat and loved setting up home with Danny. He found it amusing that she seemed so content to tidy the apartment and cook dinner every night. "I can get someone in to clean," he offered more than once. But what he didn't seem to understand was that Cara *liked* doing it. She wanted to create a real home for them, something she'd never had in all her nineteen years. For the first time in her life, she felt settled, and that was a feeling she liked.

The only person Cara felt a bit bad about was Annie. Danny's mother didn't approve of them living together without being married. Not that she'd said anything, but Cara could sense how she felt. But it was hard to worry about that for too long. Danny was such a big personality, he consumed her in every way. She felt proud to be on his arm. People cleared out of her way and treated her with respect now. For someone who had spent so long being nothing, it meant everything.

Now, as Danny began to unbutton her blouse, Cara felt herself giving in to him, as he'd known she would. Pulling her miniskirt up a little, she hooked her thumbs into either side of her panties. If she was going to give in, she might as well be enthusiastic about it. Danny was always urging her to take more control, and this time she was going to give him what he wanted. Kicking her underwear to one side, Cara turned to face him. Perching up on the dressing table, she allowed her thighs to fall open and began to play with herself.

"Hey!" Danny's dark eyes lit up approvingly. "That's new."

He'd asked her to do it before, but she'd always refused. She'd rather have gone over to the bed and lain down together properly, but she knew Danny preferred it like this, something a little different. She'd learned to be inventive with Danny. He had a short attention span, and she knew that however much he liked her, it wouldn't take much to turn his head. At first she hadn't needed to worry; her innocence had been enough of a turn-on for him. Most of the girls he'd known had been around the block a fair few times before he'd gotten to them. Cara had been different, totally unspoiled and eager to learn. After their first time together, he'd seen that she'd gone on the Pill, making her feel very much like a modern young woman. He had taken great delight in initiating her, teaching her how to please him, and helping her learn what she liked, too. But lately that novelty had worn off and she'd had to work harder to keep his interest.

As he watched her fingers darting into and out of herself, he groaned with anticipation, and Cara was pleased that her efforts had been rewarded. She could see the length of him outlined through his jeans, straining against the material.

"Do you want to play, too?" she teased, reaching out to touch the denim, liking the way his cock reared up under her touch.

"God, yes," he choked out.

As he hastily unbuckled his belt, she snapped open the buttons of his jeans. Taking the base of his penis, she guided him inside her, taking in only the tip while she moved one hand up and down the length in slow, sure strokes, just the way he'd shown her to. Gradually she increased the pace, feeling the growing heat of him against her palm, until he was able to stand it no longer. With a grunt, he grabbed her waist, and pulled her onto him, all the way up to the hilt.

"How's that, bitch?" he demanded as he pounded into her, each thrust pushing her back further on the dressing table, until her bare spine was knocking against the cold, hard mirror. "Do you like the way my cock feels?"

Usually Cara hated his crude words, but today she was too intent on her own pleasure to notice, her hand working furiously between her legs as he continued to drive into her.

They came at the same time, Cara feeling her own orgasm pulsing through her seconds before Danny let out a bellow, signaling his own release.

For a moment they stayed locked together, panting loudly, her legs wrapped around his waist, his head resting on hers, supporting each other as they caught their breath. As she stopped shaking, Cara's arms tightened around Danny's neck, hugging him close. She always liked this time the most—in the aftermath of sex, she felt closest to Danny. She was going to suggest going over to the bed to cuddle, but before she could, Danny pulled away a little. His dark eyes looked down at her adoringly, and she felt good about herself. Pushing her damp hair back from her forehead, he said approvingly, "That was hot."

Cara basked in his praise. "I know."

He gave her cheek an affectionate pinch. "Some guy's going to really thank me for this one day."

The words were like a fist in her gut. "Dan!" she objected, pushing him away. Her eyes automatically filled with tears. She hated when he did that—made cracks about them seeing other people. To her, this was meant to be forever. "What's *that* supposed to mean?"

Seeing her reaction, he laughed. "Nothing, darling," he said dismissively. Grabbing his jeans from the floor, he began to pull them on.

Cara bit her lip to stop it trembling. "It didn't sound like nothing."

Danny sighed irritably. If there was one thing he hated, it was women trying to blackmail him emotionally. "Christ, there's no need to get out of your pram. I'm only messing with you."

Knowing she was testing his patience, Cara forced a smile. "Sure, I'm sorry. I was just overreacting."

But the moment had been ruined for her now.

"Sorry!" Ronan looked up from his desk to see Cara rushing by. He tapped his Rolex meaningfully, and she mouthed another apology. It was the third time she'd been late this week, and the club manager knew he ought to have a word with her. If any of the other girls had behaved that way, he would have sacked them by now. But he'd always had a soft spot for Cara. Maybe it was because he knew at heart she was a good person; some of the hostesses took the mick, turning up late all the time, but she'd never been like that. In fact, Cara had been the perfect employee—until she'd taken up with Danny Connolly.

Ronan hated seeing the way Danny was changing her. The guy was a parasite, and he was going to take what he could get and then leave, Ronan was sure of it. But he knew there was no point in saying anything to Cara—she was so in love that she wouldn't want to hear it. He just hoped Danny would prove him wrong and actually appreciate how lucky he was to have her.

Cara burst through the doors of the dressing room, pleased to have escaped a lecture from Ronan. She'd expected him to haul her into his office this time, but he'd let her tardiness slide again. However, though the club manager might have been soft on Cara, her fellow waitresses weren't so forgiving. Walking into the dressing room, she could feel the other girls' sharp eyes judging her.

"Late again?" Mel observed.

Cara knew this was a big sticking point with all of the other hostesses. They felt aggrieved that she came and went as she pleased when they couldn't.

"I got caught up," Cara mumbled.

The redhead smiled sweetly. "Maybe Danny should think about getting a clock installed on his bedroom ceiling. That way you might start making it here on time."

As the other girls tittered, Cara felt herself blush. The jibe wouldn't have hurt so much if it hadn't been spot on.

"Oh, leave it out," she shot back. "Just 'cos you got dumped, don't take it out on me."

The words were out of Cara's mouth before she could stop herself. It was only a few short weeks ago that Mel had cried to her about breaking up with Tony, her boyfriend of six months. And now she was using that information against her friend. Cara knew it was unforgivable, but she'd been embarrassed that Mel had guessed the truth about where she'd been, and that had put her on the defensive.

But the truth was, Cara hated fighting with the other girls. She'd worked long and hard to cultivate their friendship. Now, in a few short months, all her work had been undone. What made it worse was that she knew the blame lay mainly with her. Since getting together with Danny, she hadn't been treating the girls very well. They'd been good to her when she'd needed them, and then as soon as she'd gotten a boyfriend she'd dropped them all. Whenever they asked her to go clubbing, she was always rushing off to meet Danny somewhere. But it was what he expected, and she didn't want to let him down. She was sure any one of the other girls would have done the same, given half the chance to be Danny's bird.

The rest of the evening was awful. Mel was popular among the hostesses, and after the news of the spat in the dressing room had gotten round, the other girls blanked Cara. Mel, who was in charge of assigning the tables, kept giving her the worst customers, the ones who were notorious for not tipping. At the end of the evening, unable to face getting changed in the dressing room, Cara simply put a coat over her costume and hurried home.

She got back to find Danny waiting up for her. He insisted on making her a cup of tea and a sandwich, and she sensed he was trying to make up for their earlier spat. Feeling relaxed, she made the mistake of telling him about what had happened at work.

"That's bang out of order," he said once she'd finished. "Do you want me to have a word?"

"No," she said hastily. That was the last thing she needed—Danny weighing in and frightening everyone into being nice to her. That would be even worse than the cold shoulders. "I can deal with it myself."

He shook his head. "For the life of me, I don't even get why you're still there. How do you think it makes me look, you working in that dump? Everyone'll be thinking I can't provide for you."

"But you've gone out with plenty of other girls who worked there," Cara pointed out. "You never seemed to mind then."

"Yeah, well, I wasn't as serious about them. I don't like the thought of other guys leering over what's mine."

She liked the way he said that—*mine*—as though she belonged to him.

"We'll get wed one day, won't we, Dan?" she said impulsively.

He ruffled her hair. "Course we will, love."

As they cuddled up on the couch, she felt better. She had Danny, and that should be enough for her. He was her family, her friends, her everything—it didn't matter what anyone else thought.

The following day, Cara handed in her notice at Eclipse. Danny was delighted—he'd finally gotten what he wanted—and Cara found that she was happy, too. Before, she'd worried about what she would do without a job, but over the next few months she discovered a new occupation, one that took up all of her time: pleasure. It was something she'd had so little of in her life. Danny had no time for authority or convention; he believed in taking what he wanted when he wanted it. And Cara found it wasn't such a bad way to live.

With her new free time, she started hanging out with the girlfriends of Danny's business associates. Most of them didn't have jobs either, and they spent their days on the King's Road and Carnaby Street, shopping in Biba and Mary Quant's Bazaar, frittering away the fruits of their old men's graft. Cara was more than happy to join them. She loved the new fashion for miniskirts, which suited her long legs and lean body, and soon had a wardrobe stuffed full of clothes and shoes; among her favorites was a black-and-white minstrel shift dress, which she wore with a white PVC mac and matching flat-heeled, knee-high boots. Seeing the popularity of the short-haired, androgynous Twiggy fueled her confidence, and she faithfully copied the mod look of her style icon, even going to Vidal Sassoon and getting her unruly black hair shaped into a pixie cut, which highlighted her big eyes and strong features.

The new image wasn't just for her benefit, though. It was all part of being Danny Connolly's girlfriend. He liked getting dressed up in sharp Italian suits and going out on the town with his little piece of eye candy on his arm. All Cara had to do was look pretty. They spent a lot of time at nightclubs, particularly Eclipse. Cara had felt uneasy going back there, after she'd left on such bad terms, but Danny had insisted.

"It's where all our mates meet up. You can't hide away forever," he'd told her. "Besides, no one's going to say anything to you when you're with me."

The first night she'd gone in with him, she'd felt apprehensive, especially when Mel had been assigned to wait on them. But as usual, Danny had been right—Cara's former friend had been scrupulously polite to them. And though Cara missed the banter she'd had with the other hostesses, she told herself it was just the price of being with Danny, and she knew which she'd rather have.

Although she no longer had a job, Cara liked to think her life wasn't totally without purpose. She spent some time overseeing the redecoration of the apartment, bringing it fully up to date with bold colors and streamlined furnishings. Sometimes she thought it was a shame that they hadn't stuck to more conventional decor, something classic and understated, more in keeping with the building's beautiful architecture. But Danny had vetoed that. "When people walk in here, I want them to know that I've arrived."

If it bothered her a little that he referred to the flat as "mine" rather than "ours," still talked of "I" rather than "we," she tried not to let it get to her. Money and status were important to him in a way that they could never matter to her. And he was the one out earning now, not she.

Of course sometimes Cara's conscience nagged at her a little. She remembered how only two years earlier she'd been so proud of her job at the grocery store, balancing the accounts and taking deliveries, improving the filing system. Now she had no purpose but pleasure. But if she ever felt guilty, she would swiftly remind herself that she'd had many hard years and she deserved a bit of fun now.

It was about six months after she'd given up her job at Eclipse that Cara came across the article—one of those tell-alls on the Golden Age of Hollywood. She'd seen it advertised on the front of *Marie Claire* and hadn't been able to resist picking it up. There had been a brief mention of her mother, naturally. It was one of those stories that always seemed to get dragged out—how Frances Fitzgerald, who for a brief moment had been a rising star of the silver screen, had ended up drunkenly crashing her car and dying in the ensuing explosion. There was a lot of innuendo about an unhappy marriage, her erratic behavior in the months leading up to her death, and the mysterious circumstances surrounding the accident that had killed her.

As always, Cara wasn't sure why she'd made herself read the article. Most of the time, she tried not to think about her mother. But lurking at the back of her mind, there was always a strange fascination with the woman who'd abandoned her that every now and then needed to be satisfied. At the orphanage, during Saturday trips to the cinema, she'd occasionally had to sit through one of her mother's films. It had never upset her. She'd always felt curiously detached—as if the glamorous creature on the screen had little to do with her. Even now, if there was a rerun of an old Frances Fitzgerald movie, she would go to watch it— always alone. She'd never mentioned the outings, not even to Danny. She wasn't sure he'd understand. Frankly, she wasn't even sure she did. Maybe it was the only way she could feel close to the mother who'd left her behind.

Cara closed the magazine and let it drop onto the floor. That was enough now. She didn't want thoughts of her mother ruining her day. She'd spent a lovely morning shopping, and now, lying here on the new white leather couch with the afternoon sun streaming in to warm her face, she was feeling sleepy. She wondered if there was time for a nap before she went out with Danny that night . . .

43

"Excuse me, sir?" Danny looked up to see Nina, one of the cocktail waitresses at Eclipse, smiling down at him. She'd only started the previous week, but already she had made quite an impression, mostly because she was built like the archetypal *Playboy* model. The club's corseted uniform had been designed with girls like her in mind.

She bent over, giving him a full view of her cleavage. "Is there anything else I can do for you?" Her voice was breathy and full of invitation.

Danny leaned back into the couch, enjoying the attention of the perky blonde. "I've already got a full glass. So what else did you have in mind?"

Nina batted her false eyelashes. "Well, Ronan says we should cater to our customers' *every* need."

"Is that so?" Danny drawled.

They grinned at each other, a look of mutual understanding passing between them.

"You're in my way," an angry voice interrupted.

Danny and Nina turned to see Cara glaring at them. In an ivory lace minidress matched with flat ballet shoes, she looked tall and willowy, all long legs and effortless class, the very opposite of Nina's more obvious pinup looks.

"Sorry." Confronted by Danny's girlfriend, Nina had the good grace to blush. Picking up her tray, she scurried off.

Cara didn't speak at first. She sat back down, took a sip of champagne, then asked, "So what was all that about?"

Danny shrugged. "Nothing."

"It didn't look like nothing." Her voice was surprisingly calm, but Danny could hear the edge beneath.

"I can't help it if the poor girl can't keep away from me." He felt bad now. It was just that he was considered important round here, and women liked that. Sometimes it was hard to say no. But he didn't mean to hurt Cara; he loved her and only her. Leaning over, he put his arm around his girlfriend, pulling her to him. "Come on, love. Don't give me a hard time. You know you're the only girl for me."

Cara stared at him for a long moment, and then decided to let it go. "Okay." She forced a smile for the sake of the evening, but deep down she wasn't reassured. She'd only nipped out to the loo, and she'd come back to find Danny practically drooling over another woman. Things like that had been happening far too much lately. She didn't think Danny had cheated on her yet, but she suspected it was only a matter of time.

It was a year now since she'd left her job at the club, and at first everything had been perfect. But lately Danny had begun to grow tired of their domestic bliss. He seemed restless and bored—and not just with her. He seemed fed up with Finnbar, too. Danny wasn't happy with the cut he was taking, and he had said more than once that he wanted to branch out on his own. It was dangerous talk. If Finnbar or one of his associates heard about it, they'd have no hesitation in teaching Danny a lesson. But whenever Cara said that to him, Danny didn't seem to care. As always, he thought he was invincible. And that worried her more than all the Ninas in the world.

The following Sunday, as usual, Cara and Danny went round to his mother's for lunch. Danny wasn't able to settle all afternoon; he looked distracted, and it was left to Cara and Annie to keep the conversation going. The atmosphere during the meal was awkward; no one quite sure what was wrong, making it hard to put right.

They'd hardly finished eating when Danny stood up abruptly. "I'm going out to get some ciggies."

Cara watched him go, a sinking feeling in the pit of her stomach.

Annie gave her a sympathetic look. "I'll make us a cuppa," she said.

The two women sat in the kitchen, drinking tea and waiting for his return, taking it in turns to glance up at the clock. By six, it was obvious he wasn't coming back.

"So much for having a nice, pleasant Sunday." Cara knew she sounded bitter, and she didn't care.

"Oh, sweetheart." Annie looked at her sadly. "You know you're like a daughter to me, and I'd be only too delighted if you and Danny settled down to raise a family. But I know my boy. He ain't the marrying kind. And as much as I like seeing you two together, I can't say in all honesty that I see this story having a fairy-tale ending. Do you?"

Cara knew exactly what Annie meant, but she didn't want to hear it. Not now. "Thanks for the advice," she said stiffly. "We'll just have to see how it goes, won't we?"

She made her excuses then, something about needing to get back. Annie watched her go. It was as close to a warning as she could give to the girl. In a way she hoped she was wrong. But she knew her son well enough to realize that the only person he was ever going to look after was himself. It was just going to take Cara a while longer to wake up to that.

Cara got home to find the flat dark and empty. It was nearly half past ten by the time she heard Danny's key in the lock. Springing off the sofa, she went out to the hall to face him, hands on her hips.

"Where the hell did you get to?" she demanded.

He pushed past her. "I bumped into some people. Ended up going for a drink."

Cara followed him through, determined this time not to let it go. "And was Nina there?" She already knew the answer—she could smell the other girl's perfume: the cheap floral scent stinging her nostrils.

Danny looked at her coldly. "Yeah, she was. As were a lot of other people. Now, why don't you stop being so bloody paranoid? You're giving me a right headache."

He went over and switched on the TV, settled into the armchair. Unable to prove whether he was lying or not, Cara decided to let it go and instead went to the kitchen and took the plate of leftovers out of the fridge. "Your mum sent this back for you," she called through the little hatch. "Do you want me to heat it through?"

He didn't even look up from his program. "Nah, I had some grub when I was out."

It hit Cara then, what she had known deep down for a long time: he had so little respect for her that he could be out with Nina all evening and assume he could still come back here at the end of the night. Now she saw that Danny was never going to change. This was her life, if she wanted it—waiting alone at home, for a man who might or might not come back to her.

In that split second of realization, her mood changed.

"You bastard!" she growled, so low that he couldn't have heard it over the sound from the television. Before she could think what she was doing, she sent the plate sailing through the kitchen hatch and across the sitting room. It smashed against the far wall before falling, broken, to the floor, potato and gravy smeared across the paintwork.

Danny sprang out of his chair, his eyes blazing. "What the hell—"

But before he could finish the sentence, Cara had stormed into the sitting room, crossed the floor, and slapped him hard across the face. "I hate you!" she cried, striking him again.

His expression registered surprise, then irritation. But Cara hardly noticed. All she could think of was how much she wanted to hurt him—as he'd hurt her. And if she couldn't do that emotionally, she'd settle for physically. Suddenly she was pouring all her frustrations out on him. She couldn't stop herself: she was hitting, punching, and scratching at him, her nails raking his flesh.

"Stop that!" he ordered, managing to catch her arms. He cuffed her wrists in one of his strong hands.

But Cara wasn't listening. She was twisting and squirming in his grasp, struggling to break free so that she could hurt him some more. Wrenching one hand out of his grip, her nails ripped down the side of Danny's face. He roared in pain, momentarily loosening his hold on her to put his hand to his damaged face. It was all the time Cara needed.

"It's over between us!" she screamed at him, storming toward the bedroom. "I'm leaving you! Right now!"

She already had her suitcase out and had started throwing clothes inside, as he came through after her. "Oh, no, you're not!" he snarled. "This isn't over until I say it is!"

He came from behind her this time, one meaty arm clamping around her waist and lifting her straight up off the floor. Spitting and clawing at him like an angry cat, she tried to escape as he carried her across the room and dropped her in the middle of the bed.

"Bastard!" she seethed, struggling to get up. But he wasn't about to let her go.

He was a strong guy who made a living from physical violence. Cara had no chance of escape as he knelt over her, pinning her hands above her head, his knee clamping across her legs to stop her kicking out. She looked up then, saw his eyes burning with anger—and something else, too: a raw, base hunger. God, he was turned on. That only made her even madder.

She bucked under him. "Get *off* me!" Guessing his intention, she made one last effort to pull her right leg free from under him and, with all the strength she could muster, kneed him as hard as she could in the groin.

Danny let out a cry of pain. His instinct for self-preservation set in, and before he could think what he was doing, he slapped Cara hard across the face, sending her reeling off the bed, cracking her head on the side table as she went.

The blow stunned her into silence. Pain shot through her head, and for a horrible moment her vision blurred. Crouched against the side of the bed, shaking with fear and misery, she let out a sob.

Busy nursing his sore appendage, Danny hadn't noticed at first that anything was wrong. Now, hearing the noise, he looked over. "Cara?" When she didn't answer, he sat up and moved toward her. "Are you all right, love?" He put his hand on her arm, but she flinched away from his touch.

She turned to look at him then, her eyes filled with hatred. "Does it look like I'm all right?" she hissed.

Danny had no idea what to say. As Cara began to cry then, great, wracking sobs taking hold of her, he stared at his girlfriend, taking in the cut on her forehead, the blood pouring down her face. He looked down at his own chest and arms, covered in bites and scratches. It was only then that he began to fully appreciate what he'd done.

"Oh God, Cara." He was genuinely filled with remorse. He reached out to put his arm around her then, but thought better of it. "I'm sorry. I am really sorry." He waited for her to say something, but she just kept on crying. "I didn't mean to do that."

The excuse sounded lame even to his ears. He couldn't blame her as she sneered, "Well, as you didn't mean to, then that's all right."

He winced at the sarcasm in her voice. Something told him that he'd crossed a line tonight and that it wasn't going to be possible to come back from it. He climbed off the bed then, kneeling down in front of her. "Cara, talk to me, will you? Tell me how to make this right."

Cara looked at her boyfriend. She knew he was genuinely contrite, but it didn't help matters. He wanted forgiveness, and right now she just couldn't find it in herself to give him that comfort. "Just leave me alone, will you?" she said tiredly. "I want to get some sleep."

She lay down on the bed then, curled up on one side in a ball, her back to him. Although she'd made it plain that she didn't want him there, Danny made no move to go. Cara could sense that he wanted to put things right between them but wasn't sure how. That was the thing about Danny—he behaved like a pig and then expected to be able to make amends with a few words.

She wasn't entirely surprised when he lay down next to her. He waited a moment, as though seeing if she would object, and then tentatively put one hand on her shoulder. "Please, Cara," he whispered. "Please forgive me."

Cara didn't answer. The truth was, she was tired of forgiving him. Deep down, she knew that she should leave him, but the problem was— where would she go? She had nothing in her life apart from Danny and his family. And despite everything, she still loved him, even though she knew he was no good for her. So when his arm went around her waist, instead of pushing him away she let him hold her—but mainly because it seemed to make him feel better. Because lying in his arms right then, Cara felt exhausted, troubled, and never more alone.

44

As soon as Cara heard about the bank robbery on Baker Street, she got a bad feeling. It was on the BBC's early-evening news. The armed robbers had hit the bank at midday, just as the security shift swapped over for lunch. One guard had been shot and was critical in hospital. The robbers had gotten away with a quarter of a million pounds. There were four suspects altogether: three inside the bank, while the fourth drove the getaway vehicle.

Cara's thoughts immediately turned to Danny. It was a month since the aborted lunch at Annie's, and he had been twitchy and secretive since then. He had gone out at nine that morning and still wasn't back. She had no idea where he was. Not that there was anything unusual about that. But he'd been wrapped up in something lately, and she'd had a feeling it was something big. At first she'd thought he'd taken up with another woman. Then, once she'd gotten over her initial paranoia, she'd realized the signs were all wrong. This was a new, focused Danny. There was more going on here than chasing skirt.

She slept fitfully that night, keeping half an ear out for the sound of the front door. He still wasn't back the next morning, so she had no choice but to get on with her day as usual.

The front door was open when she got back from the shops, and she could hear voices coming from inside. Cara dropped her bags in the hallway and rushed through to see what was going on. There were half a dozen uniformed policemen going through the flat. The search looked thorough. Drawers had been opened, the contents strewn everywhere, her underwear all over the floor.

She saw them looking her up and down, knowing that all they saw was a dolly bird, content to live off her man's earnings. She felt a flash of shame.

The police had even less clue than she did about Danny's whereabouts. But Cara knew one person who would definitely know where he was: his mother.

"He's gone, love." Cara looked blank for a moment. Then she realized what Annie was telling her. Danny had left, not for a day or a week but indefinitely. And he'd left without her.

"Gone?" she repeated. "Where?"

Annie wouldn't meet her gaze. "I don't know."

Cara didn't believe her for a second. "Ireland?" she demanded. "Spain?"

But Annie wasn't saying. "Really, sweetheart, he didn't even tell me this time."

Cara studied her through narrowed eyes. She had a feeling Annie knew more than she was letting on, but however much affection she had for Cara, it didn't even begin to compare to the love she had for her only son. The police hadn't succeeded in getting her to give Danny up, and Cara knew she wouldn't have any more success.

The security guard who had been shot during the raid had died in the hospital. Annie refused to believe that her son could have killed a man, but Cara wasn't so sure. She thought of the security guard's family, his widow and three children, and hoped that she was wrong. But whatever the truth, she couldn't get away from the stark fact that Danny had abandoned her. Not that she could blame Annie, of course. His mother had warned her that this was going to happen. Cara just hadn't wanted to listen. She'd been too busy enjoying the easy life.

"So what am I supposed to do now?" Cara asked. She couldn't go back to the flat. She had no job, no roof over her head. Danny had cleaned them out of every bit of money. And anything he hadn't taken, the police would seize.

Annie went over to the kitchen drawer and took out an envelope. "He left this for you."

Cara took the envelope from her. She'd half hoped it was going to contain a letter, but she saw it was stuffed full of ten-pound notes. She looked down at the money for a moment, and then slid the envelope across to Annie. "I can't take this," she said quietly.

"Too good for it now, are you?" Annie sneered.

Cara knew what the older woman meant. For months she hadn't even thought about where the money she lived off had come from—she hadn't cared. Why develop a conscience now? But it was the thought of that security guard and his poor family: she couldn't take money earned from that.

She got to her feet. "I should go."

Annie stood with her. "Ah, sweetheart, I could cut my tongue out for what I just said. You know I didn't mean it." She was suddenly contrite. "I'm just upset at Danny going like that. Stay here, don't mind me. You know there's always a bed for you."

"Thanks, but I'll be fine." Cara had a few quid in her pockets and friends who would, she hoped, let her stay on their sofa for a night or two. Annie might regret what she'd said, but her words had changed everything between them and there was no going back. It was probably a good thing, too. Cara sensed that if she stayed now, she'd end up waiting around for Danny forever, pining after someone who had made it clear that she wasn't a big enough part of his life to bother including in something as momentous as leaving the country.

Annie looked as though she wanted to object, but thought better of it. "No hard feelings, though?" she said.

Cara smiled gently at her. "How could there be?" And she meant it. Whatever happened now, Annie had been the closest to a mother that she'd ever gotten.

The two women embraced, holding each other for a long time before Cara finally pulled away. Annie saw her to the door.

"Come and see me sometime," the older woman said as she left.

"Course I will."

Both of them knew the visit was unlikely to happen. But it seemed kinder to preserve the illusion that there was still something left between them.

Danny's leaving broke Cara. They'd been living together like husband and wife for nearly two years, and it just showed how little that had meant to him—how little *she'd* meant to him. And as if abandoning her wasn't bad enough, worse still, when he'd left he'd taken all her stability with him. He'd robbed her of her family, of Annie, of every piece of security that she'd known over the past five years since she'd turned up on the Connollys' doorstep.

During those first few days, Cara found it hard just to get out of bed in the mornings. It was as though Danny had died. She felt numb; she had no interest in anything. She couldn't eat, couldn't sleep. It was only necessity that kept her going: the need to find a job and a place to live. She couldn't go back to their flat, as the police had sealed it off. None of their mutual friends offered a place to crash. Danny had pulled off the bank job behind Finnbar's back, and the gang leader wasn't about to forgive that in a hurry. No one wanted to be associated with Danny or anyone close to him now.

So instead Cara had spent the last of her money on a cheap hostel for women in Stockwell, South London. It was probably better than staying with friends anyway, she told herself. Hanging around with the old crowd would just remind her of Danny. And right now she could hardly stand to think of him.

Getting some cash together was her most pressing concern. After examining her options, she realized she had no choice but to try to get her old job back at Eclipse. Not that she could pass for being glamorous, she thought, staring at her reflection in the mirror as she got ready to go to see the club manager. In the week since Danny had left, she hadn't been taking care of herself, and it showed. There were dark circles under her eyes, and her skin was spotty and pasty from a lack of sleep and proper nutrition. There was a permanently nervous, sick feeling in the pit of her stomach, which made it impossible to eat. Always a thin girl, she was nothing but skin and bone now. The slashed neck of her dress revealed her collarbones protruding in an unsightly manner, and she pulled on a cardigan to cover up just how skinny she'd gotten. She forced herself to put on some makeup, but even she could see that she still looked rough. Nothing could take away the aura of sadness that seemed to surround her.

Unfortunately for Cara, one of the hostesses must have spotted her arriving at Eclipse and alerted the others, because by the time she got upstairs, all the girls were standing in the corridor that led to Ronan's office, lined against the wall, waiting for her.

"Heard from Danny, have you?" Mel asked snidely as she walked by.

Her words set off a string of catcalls. Cara could feel her eyes watering at their nasty words.

"Not so high and mighty now, is she?"

It took all of Cara's self-control to make the last few steps to Ronan's office without crying.

If Eclipse's manager was surprised to see her there after all that time, he made no comment. He was a fair man who didn't bear grudges, and so, despite the way they'd parted, he was good enough to hear her out. But he still couldn't offer her a job.

"You know I'd have you back in a heartbeat, love. But Finnbar wouldn't stand for it." He spread his hands in a gesture of helplessness. "Not with you being so close to Danny."

Though Cara was disappointed, she understood his position. Danny had double-crossed the gang leader, and anyone associated with him was now persona non grata around here.

After that Cara went to four other establishments, each increasingly shabby, but no one wanted to hire her. Everyone knew that she'd been Danny's girl, and they were worried that by employing her they'd offend Finnbar. She was getting desperate by the time she got to Flirt, a sleazy hostess club, the last on her list. Buried in the middle of Dean Street, it was a dive, the bottom of the heap in an already vile industry. The cigar smoke barely masked the smell of sweat and worse. It doubled as a gambling joint, which meant it ran twenty-four hours and had no natural light. Sitting on the stained velvet couch for her interview, Cara felt dirty just being there.

The owner, an aging Lothario in a brown cord suit, with false teeth and a bad comb-over, was eager to take her on. "A babe like you'll get on well here," he leered.

Cara carefully removed the hand that had strayed onto her knee and wished she could slap his face and walk out right now. But it was the only place that would give her a job.

"When can I start?" she asked wearily.

Flirt was nothing like Eclipse. At Eclipse, there had been a bit of class, but Flirt was a grubby, sordid place. Gino, the greasy owner, tried to cheat the hostesses at every turn. He took half of their fee and deducted any drinks they had from their wages, even though the customers were also charged for them. If a customer couldn't pay his bill or objected to the steep prices and hidden charges—something that happened often—the bouncers would take him out the back. The hostesses themselves were mostly older, worn-out types; a lot of them had been on the game, and this was a step up for them. They were a good laugh, though, a cheerful bunch who made the most of their situation.

On her first night, Cara found out that two of the younger girls were looking for someone to share their basement flat in Kilburn, north London. They weren't offering much—a foldout bed in the living room—but at least it allowed her to move out of the hostel. She still felt sad and beaten, and right now it was hard to see any good times ahead. But at least she'd started to get back on her feet.

45

The man put his large, clammy hand on Cara's knee and gave her what he obviously thought was a playful squeeze. "So what do you say we take this back there?"

He nodded toward a heavy red velvet curtain. Concealed behind it were the back rooms at Flirt, where some of the women would take their customers for a bit of extra cash. Half of what they got went to the house. From the beginning, Cara had refused to have any part of it. Instead, she had to put up with the men rubbing themselves up against her. This guy, Frank Ellis, was typical of the clientele. A traveling salesman, he was in town for one night and had wound up at Flirt. He was mostly lonely, which Cara could handle, but as he got progressively more drunk, his hands had started wandering.

He leaned closer now, so Cara got a whiff of his breath, which smelled of nicotine and stale onions. "Come on, sweetheart. I reckon we'd have ourselves some fun."

Cara could stand it no longer. She got up abruptly. "If you'll excuse me for just a minute," she said, as politely as she could manage. "I'm just going to nip to the ladies'."

It was what she always said when she needed a break. The risk was that when she was away one of the other women would swoop in and take her client, depriving Cara of her hostess fee. But right now she wasn't sure if she would care. It would almost be a relief.

But any hopes of unloading him were dashed as he gave her a meaningful wink. "Don't worry. I'll be right here waiting for you."

Cara smiled her thanks through gritted teeth.

Gino, the owner, shot her a dirty look as she went. It was one of his rules—never leave a customer. But Cara was past caring. If she didn't get away from Frank for five minutes, she was going to end up slapping him.

Instead of going into the toilets, Cara ducked to the right and through the adjoining door. It led to the women's dressing room, as the place where the hostesses changed was optimistically known. Cara had been working at Flirt for six months now. Those first few weeks after Danny left were a blank. She'd slept through the days, and at night she'd forced herself to go in to work. It was money. That's what Cara told herself every night, every humiliating night. It was a living, and there was no shame in that. But still there were times, like tonight, when it got to be too much.

Cara headed toward the dressing room. As she walked in, the smell of hair lacquer and cheap perfume was overwhelming, as it was most evenings.

"If one more guy humps my leg . . ." Cara grumbled as she sat down at an elderly dressing table.

There were three other women in there, all taking a break or cleaning up after a trip to the back rooms. Hearing what Cara said, they laughed knowingly.

"Just give him a biff on the nose," Denise Brown, one of the old hands, advised. "That usually works for my dog."

"I swear I'll do a damned sight more than that."

Denise chuckled. "Wait till you've been here as long as I have, duck. Trust me, you'll be delighted to have the attention then."

The others joined in with the cackling. But Cara could only stare at the older woman, a wave of depression washing over her. Denise Brown was in her midforties. Her husband was in the Scrubs, halfway through an eighteen-year stretch for armed robbery. Working at Flirt was how Denise had kept a roof over her kids' heads. With her dyed platinum hair and glittery dress, from a distance she looked attractive enough, but up close you could see the years of hard living on her: beneath the thick makeup, her cheeks were puffy and her nose broken with tiny purple veins; her forehead was etched with deep lines, and her eyes were bloodshot. The dress she wore had been made for a much younger, thinner woman, and when she lifted her arms, the bat wings were plain for everyone to see. Too many years of smoking, drinking, and worry had done that to her.

And now, Cara realized, Denise was telling her that she would end up this way. "A lifer," as the women jokingly referred to themselves—because working here was like being in prison, a place that you got trapped in.

It struck Cara then, in that moment. As much as she liked these women, she didn't want to turn into them. All the pining for Danny had made her go backward. She was twenty—she had her whole life ahead of her. She needed to take control of her destiny rather than waste away here.

That night was a wake-up call for Cara. The following morning, for the first time in months, she woke with a purpose: to decide what she wanted to do with her future. She'd spent years living on the fringes of society. Work had always been casual, cash in hand. If she wanted a good job, she needed to start being legit.

She went down to the Labor Exchange to find out where she stood. It turned out to be surprisingly easy. As her birth had been registered in England, she could get a National Insurance number that would enable her to work.

The next problem was deciding what to do. With no qualifications, her choices were limited. She needed a skill—the only problem was what that should be.

It was on the way to work that evening that the idea came to her. On the Tube, there were ads for secretarial courses: pictures of smartly dressed women, looking bright-eyed and purposeful with their diplomas in hand. Before, she'd never dreamed that she could work in an office, but now anything seemed possible.

A month later she enrolled at the Pitman Training Center in Holborn.

It was a grueling four months. Cara went to classes during the day and then worked at Flirt in the evening to support herself. By the time she got back from the club, it was usually three in the morning. That gave her time for just a few hours of sleep before heading in to college. It was a full-time course over sixteen weeks. Classes started at nine and went on until five every day, so there was time only to grab a quick bite and change before going back to Flirt. But somehow it was easier to do the hostess gig now that she knew it was just temporary. Maybe it was also because the hectic schedule gave her so little time to mourn for Danny.

Apart from learning to touch-type, all the girls were expected to master Pitman shorthand. For those lessons, a new group joined the secretaries. They were unusual in the building for being mostly male and looking more like preppy university types. They wore corduroy trousers, blazers, and brightly colored college scarves and kept to themselves.

"Who are they?" Cara asked Suzie, one of the girls she'd befriended in the course, who seemed to know everything.

"Journalism students."

Cara was impressed. "Bet that takes a lot of work."

Suzie shrugged. "Not really. I know someone who went to work as a P.A. to the editor at *Woman's Own*. She's writing her own stories now."

"Really?" Cara said thoughtfully. "That's interesting."

Cara found she was doing well in the course. Although she'd had little formal schooling, she had good common sense and realized early on that there was no shortcut to mastering the skills—it was all about repetition. Sometimes she thought that if she typed "the quick brown fox jumps over the lazy dog" one more time, she'd go mad.

Shorthand was even harder to master than typing. It was like learning another language.

"It's all about practice," her tutor advised the class early on, as the new students struggled to translate another passage correctly. "You have to get into the habit of visualizing everything in shorthand."

Cara did as she was told and started bringing out a notepad whenever she was sitting in front of the television, jotting down lines of dialogue from the program.

One night at the club, the customer she was talking to stopped in midsentence and frowned at the table. "What're you doing?"

Cara followed his gaze. She'd unconsciously been tracing the words of their conversation onto the table in shorthand. "Sorry. Nothing." She hastily took her hands off the table and clasped them in her lap. "Just a nervous twitch."

The man looked confused but continued talking, and, hidden by the table, Cara started sketching the words on her knee instead.

At the end of sixteen weeks there was a series of tests: typing, dictation, shorthand. Then there was an interview with the head of the college, to make sure that the girls were ready to represent Pitman. Cara passed everything.

Receiving her diploma was a big moment: it was the first time in her life she'd achieved something that she was proud of. Now it was time to look for a proper job.

The secretarial college had links to a couple of recruitment agencies. Cara picked Girl Friday on the Strand, the closest one to Fleet Street. The office was staffed by three girls, all beautifully turned out in neat black skirts and white blouses. Cara was registered by Tracey. She had immaculately blow-dried hair and a perfect French manicure: a nail file and an array of brightly colored polishes sat on her desk.

"Temp or perm?" she asked, blowing on her nails.

"Permanent," Cara said firmly. She needed some stability in her life. That's what this was all about.

After a perfunctory glance at the form Cara had filled out, Tracey ran through the list of positions they were looking to fill. She had a snotty attitude and at the beginning of the interview had looked down her nose at Cara's East End accent, thawing a little only when she saw her test scores.

"Anything in journalism?" Cara asked once she was finished.

The other woman sighed, as though she was already tired of this difficult client.

"Well, we've just sent a couple of girls over to *Boyfriend*. And jobs at the fashion mags, *Marie Claire* and *Elle*, go pretty quickly."

"What about the papers?"

Tracey wrinkled her nose. "Most of the girls want the magazines."

"Well, I'm not most girls."

It turned out that there was a vacancy on one of the dailies—the *Chronicle*. It was a left-wing tabloid, somewhat along the lines of the *Mirror*, known for its strong investigative pieces.

"What's the position?" Cara wanted to know.

Tracey scanned the job spec. "Secretary to the News Desk."

It sounded exactly like what Cara wanted. Within twenty minutes, she was on her way to the interview.

Along with all the other nationals, the *Chronicle* was located on Fleet Street. Cara was met in Reception by an efficient-looking middle-aged woman named Barbara.

"It's my position you'll be filling," Barbara explained as she led Cara upstairs to the paper's offices. After ten years as secretary to the News

Desk, she was moving up to be P.A. to the editor. "It's a promotion, but I'll miss the buzz."

The newsroom was exactly as Cara had expected: large and open plan, loud and busy. Ninety percent of the employees were male. Most were on the phone or talking heatedly with one another; the rest were hunched over typewriters. About half were holding cigarettes. No one looked her way as Barbara ushered her into a free office. Even with the door closed, Cara could still hear the low drone of everyone working to get the paper out.

The interview was brief. Barbara seemed happy enough with Cara's test scores: 60 words per minute typing, 120 Pitman.

"That'll improve with time," she said knowingly.

She ran through Cara's duties—"basically, no day is the same"—and warned her that the hours were long and unpredictable.

"If you're looking for nine to five, then leave now," she advised. "This isn't just a job for that lot"—she gestured at the journalists outside—"it's a calling, and they expect it to be the same for you." She looked sharply at Cara. "You're single, right?"

Cara nodded.

"Well, be prepared for it to stay that way. You won't have time for men."

That suited Cara just fine.

Once Barbara was certain that Cara understood the drawbacks of the job, she gave the girl her tacit seal of approval.

"But before we finalize anything, let me get the news editor in here. You'll be working closely with him, so it's important to make sure you get on well."

Cara watched through the glass partition as Barbara went to fetch the news editor, Jake Wiley. The secretary approached a tall, muscular man, who was standing up, clearly in the middle of a heated debate with one of his team. Seeing Barbara, he turned to her and said something like "I'll be right with you," before resuming his argument with the other man. He kept on yelling as he gathered up his notes and started to head toward the interview room. As he pushed open the door, he was still shouting orders at the other journalist. "Check your sources. Check your facts. And don't even think of moving from that bloody doorstep until you've got a quote out of him!"

With his piece said, he strode into the room, slamming the door behind him. At once his entire focus switched onto Cara. "Good of you to come in," he said, giving her a brisk smile, as though he hadn't been engaged in a slinging match ten seconds earlier.

Close up, he was younger than she'd been expecting—in his early thirties, with short brown hair and sharp eyes. A scar zigzagged across his left cheek, and Cara wondered briefly where it had come from. He was good-looking in a rough, unstudied way, with at least two days' stubble and the look of someone who'd been up all night. At some point, he might have been wearing a suit, but he'd discarded the jacket and tie along the way, and now his shirtsleeves were rolled up and his trousers creased. Everything about his demeanor said that he was far too busy to care what he looked like or what anyone else thought of him. Jake Wiley was the kind of man who didn't need to make any effort in order to be taken seriously.

Like Barbara, he had a no-nonsense approach to interviewing. Time was clearly a precious commodity here, and no one liked to waste it.

"So why do you want to work on a newspaper?" he asked first off.

"I'd like to be a journalist myself one day."

Cara had decided to be honest about her ambitions, even though it was a risk. If the *Chronicle* wanted a straight secretary, it might decide not to take her, but she reckoned it was worth being open. It seemed to pay off, because Jake's eyes sparked with interest.

"Oh, so you fancy writing?"

She nodded.

"What? For one of the women's mags?"

She looked at him coolly. "For the *Chronicle*."

He nodded approvingly. "Ambitious. I like it."

Jake considered the young woman in front of him for a moment. Objectively, he could see she was quite a looker, and that worried him. She'd obviously dressed conservatively today, in a black-and-white wool pinafore with a black turtleneck underneath, and low-heeled patent shoes. But even though she'd tried to divert attention from her looks, it was still impossible to ignore those long, shapely legs and the striking gamine face—and the last thing his all-male team needed was another distraction. Barbara had been the perfect assistant—the guys had been far too scared of her to give her any grief—and Jake would frankly have preferred to hire another middle-aged matron like her. But after three days of interviewing, Cara Healey was by far the best-qualified candidate to walk through the door. And if he was honest, he'd warmed to her, too. She seemed hungry for the job, and as a self-made man himself, that was a quality he admired. He just needed to make sure she was of the right mettle, that she could handle the rough-and-tumble of the place.

"Just so you're clear," he drawled, running his eyes over her body, pointedly checking her out, "we come here to work. It's not a fashion show."

He'd wanted to provoke a reaction, and he succeeded. Cara bristled. "Yeah, more like a jumble sale," she shot back, with an equally pointed look at his crumpled appearance.

The words were out of her mouth before she could stop them. Damn, she thought. Insulting the man who made the decision about hiring her wasn't exactly a smart move.

But before she could apologize, he broke into a smile. "Well done, Miss Healey. You've just demonstrated one of the key qualities I look for in my team: a willingness to talk back." He held out his hand. "Welcome to the *Chronicle*. The job's yours if you want it."

46

THE CHRONICLE, NOVEMBER 15, 1969

American billionaire Maximilian Stanhope is suffering from lung cancer, according to a report in the *Los Angeles Times*. Sources close to the business mogul have confirmed that he recently had a lung removed. He is now recuperating from the operation at Stanhope Castle, his Californian home, before undergoing a course of drug treatment.

Mr. Stanhope has become something of a recluse in recent years. Ever since the death of his second wife, Frances Fitzgerald, back in 1959, he has withdrawn from public life. Following her fatal car crash, which was officially ruled an accident, the businessman has gradually liquidated all his assets and retreated to Stanhope Castle, where he lives alone with his daughter, Olivia. His son, Gabriel, hasn't set foot in America for a decade now. He is believed to be living in North Africa.

No representative of Mr. Stanhope was available for comment.

47

The pub was jammed, completely stuffed to the brim. Red-nosed journalists in worn suits jostled with jeans-clad printers about to start their night shift. Cara pushed her way through the crowd, beer and cigarette ash spilling on her as she went. She'd learned not to mind. Every newspaper on Fleet Street had its own watering hole, usually whichever was closest to their offices. The *Chronicle* and the *Mirror* favored the White Hart, or the Stab-in-the-Back, as it was affectionately known. A legend in its own right, it was where the industry's giants traded war stories, insults, and even punches. It was as much a part of Cara's workplace as the paper's open-plan newsroom.

She'd been sent down to fetch Desmond Haines, the *Chronicle*'s chief crime correspondent. A tip had come in about a double murder in Hackney, and he was needed back to cover the story. One of the many larger-than-life characters in the business, he was a thirty-year veteran with a legendary ability to carry his drink. Cara saw him holding court at a prime table in the corner. He must have gotten there early in the afternoon to nab that spot.

"I'm afraid all the seats are taken," he said as she got near.

"Not to worry, pet," Ben Archer, the sports editor, joined in. "I saved a place for you right here." He patted his lap, to titters and catcalls from around the table.

Cara ignored the sexist remark—she was used to them by now. Fleet Street was an aggressively male environment, and the journalists were as puerile as a roomful of teenage boys. She could see now why Jake had given her such a hard time at the interview. The *Chronicle* was no place for a wallflower. Of its one hundred twenty editorial staff, only two were women. Cara planned to make that three.

Working at the *Chronicle* this past year had changed Cara's whole outlook. At twenty-two, she finally felt that she had a purpose in life. Officially, she'd been hired as secretary to the News Desk; unofficially, she did whatever needed doing. There were the basic office tasks, of course: taking the minutes of the weekly editorial meeting, running proofs from the printers to the editors, and answering calls for the journalists. But there were a lot of unofficial duties, too—nipping over to the nearby pub to find a reporter or assessing which story tip-offs from members of the public were worth pursuing. Barbara had been right: this was no nine-to-five post.

It was a baptism by fire. Within three months, Cara felt that she had the basics of journalism. She also knew for certain that she wanted to be a reporter one day. When she'd first seen the journalism students at Pitman, she'd assumed that they'd all had fancy educations and held university degrees. But there was a real mix at the *Chronicle*. Some of the staff had posh accents and had been to Oxbridge, but there were also a fair few who sounded like her and had worked their way up from the bottom. They told her how they'd left school at fifteen and started off on local newspapers, as mail room boys and office runners, learning the trade there before moving onto a national. That was what she liked most about the *Chronicle*: there was no snobbery. If you were good enough, you'd get your break. A handful of young female journalists were beginning to make their mark. Many had started off as secretaries and had found a way in from there. And that meant there was no reason she couldn't do so, too.

"You're needed back upstairs," Cara told Desmond now. She had to shout to be heard above the pub noise. "The subs have some queries on your copy."

It was code to let him know that a big story was breaking. She couldn't risk a rival hack overhearing the real details and scooping the *Chronicle*. But Desmond got the message.

"Okay. I'll be right with you." He downed the last of his pint and stood up, looking surprisingly steady after an afternoon of hard drinking. Like a lot of the journalists, he could spend most of his day in the Stab and still turn out a snappy page-one lead. That was what had surprised Cara most in her first few weeks: the blatant excess of the

print industry. Long, boozy lunches; unlimited expense accounts; outrageous practical jokes played on colleagues and rivals. Cara loved the
seedy glamour of it all. It was like one big party going on in Fleet Street,
and she was lucky enough to be part of it.

"Now," Desmond said once they were outside and a safe distance
from eavesdroppers, "what's this really about?"

Cara quickly briefed him.

"You coming up?" the crime correspondent asked as they reached
the *Chronicle*.

"Nah. I've got somewhere to be."

In fact, she had her own story to get tonight. And if everything
worked out, it could be her big break.

A couple of weeks earlier, Cara had finally plucked up the courage to
ask Jake for advice on getting her first byline. She wasn't quite sure what
the *Chronicle*'s news editor thought of her. He wasn't in the habit of
complimenting people for simply performing their work competently.
He'd kept her on after her probation period, so she couldn't have been
doing that badly, but the most she'd gotten out of him in the time they'd
been working together was the occasional "Good job, Healey." She'd
been half hoping he might assign her a story at the weekly editorial
meeting. But instead he'd made it clear that she was on her own.

"Find me something good enough, and I'll print it," he told her.

It was infuriating, but Cara wasn't surprised. The *Chronicle*'s news
editor was known for his no-nonsense attitude. He was brusque and
focused. Unlike Desmond Haines and his ilk, Jake Wiley was rarely
found in the Stab. Occasionally, if the news team was celebrating a big
scoop, he'd be there, able to hold his own with the rest, but for the
most part he maintained a distance between himself and his reporters,
which was probably the best way to keep that bunch of rogues in line.
So the fact that he wasn't going to do her any special favors was to be
expected. And, as much as Cara might not want to admit it, she could
see his point. This was a cutthroat business. She needed to prove that
she was as worthy as any of the seasoned reporters.

In the end, it was Jake who inadvertently provided her with the initial idea for an article. It was at the very end of the news team's daily
meeting, and almost as an afterthought he tossed a copy of that morning's *Chronicle* onto the boardroom table.

"Oh, and will someone get me a fresh angle on this." The paper was folded over onto page five, and he'd circled one of the articles in red. "There's a story in here, and I don't want the Screws getting it first."

He was referring to the *News of the World,* or the *News and Screws,* as it was nicknamed. Everyone on the *Chronicle* lived in fear of being scooped by the investigative Sunday paper.

The reporters filed out of the room, leaving Cara to tidy up. Out of curiosity, she picked up the paper to see the article that Jake had circled. It was a small, factual piece, relating to a court appearance by twenty-three-year-old Tobias Fairfax, the youngest son of Lord Fairfax. A few months earlier, two sixteen-year-old girls had been rushed to the hospital following a party at Toby's flat in Chelsea. They'd taken some bad LSD, cut with poison, and when they woke up, they told the police that it had been supplied to them by none other than Toby Fairfax. He'd duly been arrested, but at the end of the trial the jury had returned a not guilty verdict. The girls, from ordinary working-class families, hadn't stood a chance against the Fairfaxes' expensive barrister. He'd gotten them so confused on the stand that it had ended up seeming as though they were addicts, when in fact they'd experimented with cannabis only once or twice before the night in question.

Even though everyone knew Toby was guilty, the papers had been left with little option than to simply report the facts of the trial. It was galling, especially as his father, Lord Fairfax, had recently stood up in the House of Lords to take a stand against drugs, demanding the closure of underground hippie clubs such as UFO, Middle Earth, and Happening 44. Yet he was happy to see his son escape prosecution for a far worse crime. Now everyone on Fleet Street was looking for a way to take Toby Fairfax down.

Standing in the meeting room, Cara felt a rush of exhilaration. This was her chance to impress Jake.

After that, Cara arranged to take a day of annual leave the following week to do some research. She took a train out to Essex to talk to the two girls. Their parents, stung by the accusations that had come out, had refused to let her speak to their daughters over the phone, so she waited for them outside their school. Nicola and Jenny were more than happy to go for a coffee at a nearby café and tell her their side of what had happened.

"Anything to help you nail him," said Jenny, the more outgoing of the two. The police had refused to look into the matter any further after Lord Fairfax had had a quiet word with one of the chief inspectors.

The girls told her that they'd first met Toby at Middle Earth. He was there most Fridays, apparently.

And tonight Cara would be there, too.

Back at her flat, Cara got ready for the evening ahead. With her increased wages at the *Chronicle,* she'd been able to move out of the bedsit she'd been sharing and rent a one-bedroom garden flat in Earls Court. It wasn't much, but having a place to call her own meant a great deal.

She'd thought a lot about what to wear that evening, wanting to fit in with the outrageous crowd who attended the club. Since starting at the *Chronicle,* she'd begun to dress more conservatively, but this was her chance to let loose. In the end, she settled on a bright green smock that barely covered her bottom. With matching go-go boots and her short pixie cut, she looked a little like a female Peter Pan. Her lips were pale and her eyes smoky, and she carried a matching beaded bag, in which she had a Dictaphone and notepad. She doubted the Dictaphone would work with all the music, but she'd learned over the past few months at the *Chronicle* that a set of carefully taken shorthand notes would stand up in a court of law just as well as a recording.

Middle Earth wasn't anything like the places Cara had gone to with Danny. Those had been gangster hangouts, glitzy places where the men could show off their cash and connections. Middle Earth was the other end of the London underground scene: a hippie club, a place of free love and psychedelic flower power. Situated in a large cellar in Covent Garden, it had opened recently after yet another drug bust had closed UFO for good. Now Middle Earth was the center of the alternative scene.

Cara arrived at the club a little after midnight, since there was no point going any earlier. Grant Miller, one of the *Chronicle*'s junior photographers, was already in the line when she got there. Like Cara, he was young and eager to prove himself. When she'd approached him with her idea for nailing Toby Fairfax, he'd been happy to come along with her and try to capture the moment on camera. He was a quiet, deep-thinking young man, and Cara trusted him to keep the news of what they were doing tonight to himself.

He was usually quite a conservative dresser, so she was pleased to see that he'd made an effort to blend in for the evening. In brown leather flares, fringed down the side, and a tight checked shirt, he looked a little like a cowboy.

"Ready for this?"

Instead of answering, he pulled up his Stetson to give her a glimpse of the camera he'd concealed beneath.

"Then let's go."

Middle Earth was made up of a series of dark, cavernous rooms, which reminded Cara of a dungeon. Going inside the club was a little like entering Alice's Wonderland: a strange, exotic place, full of curiosities. The air was heavy with the smell of incense and marijuana, the music so loud that Cara could hardly make out that it was The Who's "Happy Jack" playing.

On the way from the Tube, Cara had felt self-conscious in her outrageous outfit, but now, as she went inside, she realized she was far from being the most exotically dressed. The girls were in everything from tiny hot pants to peasant blouses; some were barefoot, others braless; a few had painted flowers and hearts on their cheeks, while others whizzed by on roller skates. The men had long, flowing hair and full beards and wore velvet bellbottoms and brocade jackets, caftans and hippie beads. Psychedelic swirls clashed with paisley patterns, but nobody cared. A girl wafted by in an Indian-print skirt, clearly tripping, embracing everyone she bumped into. Cara had never seen anything like it before.

It didn't take long to spot Toby Fairfax—she recognized him from his photographs in the papers. He was working his way around the room, going up to strangers and offering them his wares, with seemingly no concern about being recognized. Quickly running a hand through her hair, Cara waited for him to make his approach.

"Hey, pretty girl, you looking for a good time?"

Cara turned at the stranger's voice. It was Toby. Tall and lean, he had the whole bohemian look going on: buckskin vest, flared trousers, and strings of beads around his neck. His sandy hair, held back in a bandana, fell to his shoulders, looking softer and sleeker than that of any of the girls in the room. He was a weekend hippie, happy to use the counterculture to justify his life of lazy pleasure.

Keeping in character, Cara gave him a sweet smile. "What've you got?"

He held out his hand, opened his palm. She looked down at the little white tablet with the pink heart etched into it. LSD.

"How much?"

He named his price. Cara handed over the money and took the tablet from him. Out of the corner of her eye, she could see Grant snapping away. There was so much activity going on that no one was paying any attention to him. She looked down at the pill she was holding, wondering if she dared to risk palming it. After those girls had ended up in the hospital, she really wasn't keen to experiment with whatever Toby was giving her.

Opening her mouth, she pretended to pop the tablet onto her tongue and swallow it, hoping that Toby wouldn't notice.

48

Cara cycled along the Embankment, swerving to avoid a patch of ice on the road. She'd bought the bike a month after starting work at the *Chronicle,* when she'd realized that her hours were going to be so erratic that she needed an alternative to public transport—at least until she was made a journalist and given her own expense account. The only drawback to cycling was the weather. A frost had settled overnight, and after ten minutes in the bright, bitter December morning, the tips of her fingers were pink and numb from the cold and her nose was beginning to drip. But even that wasn't enough to dent her good mood. Because today she was finally going to prove she had what it took to become a journalist.

Toby hadn't noticed her palm the LSD, and she'd managed to skip out of the club unnoticed. Then, over the weekend, she'd sketched an outline in longhand of what had happened at Middle Earth on Friday night. Now she was going in to the *Chronicle* early to type up her article, before handing it to Jake. She was both excited and nervous to hear his opinion. She thought the article was good, but it was hard to be sure.

On the Strand, she weaved around a double-decker bus to get onto Aldwych, before slowing as she reached Fleet Street. Luckily, it was early enough that there was a railing free on which to chain her bike. The *Chronicle*'s offices were almost as grand as those of the *Express,* and she always felt a buzz as she pushed through the glass doors, as though she was part of something important. Waving at the night security guard, she crossed the marble entrance lobby to the lift and pressed the button for the sixth floor.

Upstairs, the newsroom was empty. It was coming up for 8 A.M. and one of the few times in the day that the *Chronicle* was at peace. The printers had come off the night shift, and the journalists wouldn't start to trickle into the office until at least nine. Cara hurried to her desk. Pulling out her notebook, she sat hunched over her typewriter, her cold fingers bashing down on the keys as she began to write her article.

Jake Wiley stood in the kitchen of his Chelsea flat making himself a coffee, his first of the day. He took it black, no milk, no sugar—strong, uncompromising, just like himself. His morning routine was simple. From waking to getting out of the house took him no more than ten minutes. Apart from a quick caffeine injection, breakfast could wait—he'd send someone out later. He rarely ate at home, and a quick inventory of the fridge and cupboards would have revealed that there was no food in the place. He had no time for frivolities. He was wholly focused on work.

Jake had grown up in the respectable suburban town of Tunbridge Wells, the only son of the local grammar school's headmaster, a strict, dour man who talked in a grave tone about responsibility and duty. Jake's mother was a housewife who spent her days arranging flowers at the local church and worrying about what the neighbors thought. It was made clear to Jake from an early age that he was expected to follow in his father's footsteps; it was equally clear to the young boy that there was no way he was going to end up in the living death that passed for his parents' life. Though his sister, Alice, embraced convention, Jake was a rebel: cutting class to go for a smoke behind the bike sheds; sneaking out to meet his girlfriend, the pretty daughter of one of their neighbors.

At sixteen, much to his parents' anguish, Jake left school and found work as a trainee reporter on a local newspaper. He was a natural. There were no lengths he wouldn't go to in order to get his story. His father had always called him lazy because he hated studying at school, but when it came to working as a journalist, he didn't care how many hours he put in. He was always first to arrive in the morning, last to leave at night. He got promoted to senior reporter within eighteen months, a record.

It was inevitable that someone as smart and ambitious as he would move on to a national. He was only twenty when he landed a job at the *Chronicle*. From the first day, he loved it there. Despite his patchy school career, he had always had an aptitude for languages. He was fluent in French and Spanish from a summer spent traveling in Europe, so the paper hired him onto the Foreign Desk. Young and adventurous, he soon found himself out covering the conflict zones. He relished every minute of it. Being a war correspondent was the ultimate freedom. He was first on the scene at the Suez Crisis; he exposed the use of torture on both sides in the Algerian war; he interviewed Che Guevara on the eve of the Cuban revolution and Fidel Castro after the Bay of Pigs; and he reported on the Mau-Mau's retaliation against the British in Kenya. He was away for weeks at a time, finding his own stories, making his job whatever he wanted it to be. It was dangerous, but he couldn't think of anything else he'd rather be doing.

It was 1965 when his luck ran out. He was in Vietnam, doing a piece on field hospitals and the medical staff who manned them. He was on his way back to base camp, trekking through the wet jungle heat with a division of the U.S. 53rd Infantry, when they entered a minefield. He caught the back end of the blast, shrapnel to the gut and face: serious but not fatal. His colleague at the BBC wasn't so lucky.

It took him six months to recover, and even then he was left with a scar across his left cheek, and he still got twinges from where they couldn't get all the debris out. He wanted to go back out in the field, but the newspaper's insurance wouldn't cover it. Instead, Neil Simmons, the *Chronicle*'s editor in chief, asked Jake to head up the News Desk.

Jake hesitated before accepting. It was a plum job but not where he wanted to be. Frankly, he missed the action. But he knew the statistics. War correspondents were adrenaline junkies; they found it notoriously hard to go back to civilian life. Most ended up losing themselves in a bottle. He didn't want that to happen to him.

So he took the position as news editor and threw himself into it. He channeled all his restlessness into running the News Desk. He demanded greatness from everyone he worked with, refused to be scooped by rival papers. His motto was that the *Chronicle* made the news, didn't just report it. And he liked his team to be as focused as he was.

That was why he was pleased he'd hired Cara Healey.

That turn in his thoughts surprised him. Now, why was he thinking about *her*? He took another sip of his coffee, mulling it over. He supposed he saw something there, a kindred spirit. A lot of people said they wanted to be journalists, but few had the stamina to make it happen. To an outsider, it might look glamorous, but after six hours door-stepping a politician for a quote, most people lost their appetite for the job.

Not Cara. He'd sensed in her interview that she was hungry for the position, and she hadn't disappointed. The girl had a raw enthusiasm that reminded Jake of himself when he'd first started out. He knew she was eager to get her first byline, and he'd been waiting for her to bring him something great. He was sure she had it in her.

And maybe there was a little more to his feelings for her than simple admiration. He found her attractive too, he couldn't deny that. But a workplace romance—it was such a bad idea. He needed to keep his distance, stay professional. He was good at doing that.

"Who the hell do you think you are?" Jake demanded angrily an hour later. "Lois Lane?"

Cara had been expecting many reactions from her news editor, but anger wasn't one of them. However, as he'd read through her article, she'd seen his eyes darkening and sensed that all wasn't well.

"You don't like it?" she asked in a small voice.

"That's not the point." Jake sighed. He'd told Cara to get a new angle on the story—not put herself in danger like this. Of all the foolhardy things to do! She'd gone to the club without telling anyone what she was up to. She'd bought LSD, for God's sake. If she'd gotten caught, who knows what Toby and his cohorts would have done to her? Those were serious people.

Except that part of him couldn't help admiring her, too. This was just the kind of stunt he'd have pulled. And he also knew that if any of his male reporters had done this, he'd have been delighted with them. Someone like Cara, who had the balls to go out there and get her story, was exactly the kind of person he wanted on his team. His anger was simply because he was allowing his personal feelings to get in the way, and he'd sworn he wouldn't let that happen.

"It's a good article," he admitted reluctantly.

Cara's chin went up. "Then what's the problem?"

"You should have told me what you were up to. You go into a situation like that, you need to let me know where you are, so I can keep tabs on you. That way, if something goes wrong, I can call in the cavalry."

Cara nodded along as he spoke, but frankly she was finding it hard to care. He'd said it was a good article. That was surely all that mattered. "So do you think you'll run it?" she asked eagerly.

Jake nodded down at her article. "Have you got any proof that all this went down?"

"There are photos. Grant came with me—"

"Grant knew about this little escapade of yours? And he didn't do anything to stop it?" The news editor shook his head in disbelief. "Wait till I see him—"

"Don't blame Grant," Cara interjected. "This was all my idea. Even if he hadn't come with me, I'd have still gone ahead and done it."

"Yeah, that I can believe," Jake muttered to himself.

Cara chose to ignore the barbed comment. "Well, will you? Run it, I mean?"

Jake tried not to smile at her single-mindedness. "There's still some more work to be done. And Legal will need to go over it." He was deliberately cautious. "But I can't see any reason it wouldn't make a great piece."

Cara beamed at him. "That's brilliant!"

He sat back in his chair. "So is this what you want to do?" he asked. "Be a journalist?"

"Yes, of course."

"And what area do you want to go into?"

The question stumped Cara. She hadn't really given it much thought. "I'm not sure."

It sounded like a lame answer even to her ears. But Jake just nodded. "Well, first off, you need to be realistic about what someone like you can do."

Cara bristled. "Someone like me? What's that meant to mean?"

"A woman, of course."

"Hey!"

"Don't act outraged. It's a fact of life round here. But if you want to get on, then you have to find a way to use that to your advantage."

That got Cara's attention. "How?"

He nodded at her article. "Well, stuff like this, for one. There're always stories where we need a woman to go undercover. If that's something which interests you . . ."

"Definitely!"

"Good. Well, I'll bear that in mind in future, and you should feel free to come to me with any suggestions for stories, too."

"I will." She got the feeling that it was the end of the conversation and that Jake wanted to get on, so she gathered up her notebook and made to leave.

"Oh, and one more thing," Jake said as she was going.

"What's that?"

"Good job, Healey."

The following week, after a couple of rewrites, her article was published. It ran as the lead on page three, the spot reserved for entertaining color pieces. The headline was simply "Drug Lord" (Cara's suggestion), accompanied by a picture of Lord Fairfax dozing on the front bench of the House and another of his son handing over drugs to Cara in Middle Earth.

Jake came over to congratulate her. "Pleased with how it turned out?" he asked.

"Yeah—just next time I want a picture byline," she joked.

"Great." He rolled his eyes in mock irritation. "One article, and she's already a prima donna."

She laughed. It was a natural end to the exchange, but instead of moving off, Jake lingered by her desk.

"Did you want something?" she asked.

He hesitated and then said, "Just wondered if you'd heard about to-night?"

It was the staff Christmas party, and everyone in the office had been making a big deal about it. Cara hadn't given it much thought until now, and she was surprised to find that Jake was—it seemed too frivolous for him.

"The party? Yeah, I heard."

"So . . . are you going?"

She shrugged. "I suppose so."

"Good. Well, I'll see you there, then."

Cara watched him walk off, wondering what on earth all that had been about.

"Nice work, Healey," Desmond Haines said, slapping Cara on the back. "Can't believe you caught the old bugger like that."

It was later that night, and the *Chronicle* was in the middle of its Christmas party. Held in the paper's offices—in case a story broke—it was a fairly rudimentary affair, with finger food and warm white wine, but everyone was in a jovial mood, especially Cara, who was still on a high from having her article published that morning. All day, people had been coming up to congratulate her. It felt good to be part of the team. Almost as good as seeing her name in print was the police press release issued that afternoon, saying they were reopening the case against Toby Fairfax.

Belatedly, Cara had worried about her own legal position, as she'd admitted in the article to buying drugs. But Jake had assured her that usually with these sting operations, the Met looked the other way, as long as the police commissioner considered what had been done to be in the public interest.

"Glad you liked the piece," Cara said, biting into a slice of quiche. Desmond had cornered her by the buffet. Despite having her article published, she still wasn't officially a journalist, so along with the other secretaries, she'd been in charge of setting up the party. She'd been running around so much today that she hadn't managed to eat anything since breakfast.

Desmond helped himself to a handful of sausage rolls, balancing them carefully on his already full plate. "Good spread you've put on," he said.

"What can I say? I'm a woman of many talents."

Laughing, he moved off. After he'd gone, Barbara, the editor's P.A., came over to Cara. She was in charge of the party and didn't seem to be able to relax.

"We're running low on wine," she said worriedly to Cara. "I think there's more in the fridge. Will you be a dear and go and check for me?"

"Of course."

Grabbing another sausage roll, Cara went through to the tiny kitchen. She was crouched down by the fridge, taking out six more bottles of wine, when someone behind her cleared his throat. She looked up to see Jake standing there.

"Hi." She straightened up. "What are you doing back here?"

"Looking for you, actually. I have something for you."

"Oh yeah? What's that? A bonus, I hope," she said cheekily.

"Something much better." From behind his back, he produced a present. It was a flat, rectangular shape, wrapped roughly in Christmas paper.

She took the present, weighing it in her hands, and looked up at him, confused. "What is this?"

"Why don't you open it and find out?" He leaned against the Formica counter, watching her expectantly.

She pulled off the wrapping paper and gasped as she saw what he'd done: had a copy of her article blown up and framed.

"It was a tradition on the first paper I worked on," Jake explained. "Whenever a cub reporter got a first byline, the editor would have it framed for them."

"Blimey!" Cara was touched. Now she realized why he'd been checking if she was going to be there tonight. "I wasn't expecting this. Thank you." Without considering whether it was appropriate, she stood on tiptoe to kiss his rough cheek. "It's brilliant of you."

Laughing, he hugged her back. "Don't let it go to your head," he warned. "It's to remind you that all your articles had better be this good."

"Yeah?" She drew back a little. "Well, that goes without saying."

They grinned at each other, and in that moment, something clicked. Cara was suddenly aware of how close Jake was. His hands were resting on the small of her back, her hips meeting his warm thighs. She knew that if she closed her eyes, maybe tipped her head back just a little . . . he would kiss her.

Jake swallowed. "Cara," he murmured. His hand came up, and she could sense that he was about to brush her hair back from her face. She also knew that if she let him, there would be no going back.

Then she suddenly remembered another moment, years before, when another man had looked at her in the exact same way. And see how that had turned out. First her mother had left her, and then her lover. She didn't want to give someone else the opportunity to hurt her in that way. She wasn't sure she could survive more heartbreak.

So as Jake went to stroke her hair, Cara ducked away, stepping back so she was out of his reach.

"I should get this wine to Barbara," she said, turning to where the bottles were still standing on the floor. "She's on the verge of a breakdown out there."

Quickly picking up four of the bottles, she hurried from the kitchen before he could say anything more.

PART 5

1972

Happy Endings

If you want a happy ending, that depends, of course, on where you stop your story.

—ORSON WELLES, AMERICAN ACTOR, DIRECTOR, PRODUCER, AND WRITER, 1915–1985

49

Sitting in the study from which he had once run his empire, his wheelchair pulled up to the large bay window, Maximilian Stanhope looked out across the estate he loved so much. Years of neglect meant that it had fallen into disrepair. Without a gardener, the manicured lawns had turned brown under the California sun, and the flower beds were overgrown with weeds. From here he could see down to the outdoor pool. It hadn't been filled with water for years now, and the mosaic tiles were cracked and covered in moss.

Max knew that no one understood why, with all his money, he lived in isolation like this. He also knew what people said about him: that he was an eccentric, a hermit, a recluse—even a murderer. But he'd never much cared for others' opinions, and they seemed even less important than ever now, with his own mortality closing in on him.

He knew he didn't have long to live. The cancer had returned, and this time it had spread from his remaining lung. He was only sixty but seemed at least fifteen years older. The disease had weakened him to the point where he was permanently in a wheelchair. The contraption came with an oxygen tank attached to the right side, which he used at least three or four times a day. At his last appointment, the doctor had given him six months. Most days, Max felt it was a generous assessment. But whatever the truth, one thing was certain: he had little time left to put things right. What he revealed might cause pain, but he still felt it was the best thing to do.

Pulling his wheelchair around to his Louis XIV oak desk, Max opened the top drawer and took out his custom-made Smythson stationery. Then, with his favorite Mont Blanc fountain pen, he finally began to write the letter that he'd composed so often in his mind.

50

Neil Simmons, the editor of the *Chronicle,* put down the article he'd been reading. Leaning back in his leather chair, he regarded his star investigative journalist with grave eyes. They were in his office, the noise of the newsroom muted by the glass walls and the closed door.

"Legal's going to have a coronary."

Cara shrugged. "So? Every word's gospel."

She could afford to be confident. She knew the article was dynamite—it showed a romantic link between a member of the royal family and an associate of the Krays. There had been rumors about it for weeks, and every newspaper hound in London had been sniffing around for confirmation. But Cara was the one who had managed to get both parties to give an interview.

Over the past two years she had garnered a name for her daring exposés. Now, at twenty-five, she was one of the foremost investigative journalists on Fleet Street. The story that had shot her to fame was on James Buchanan, the Anglo-Irish diplomat who sat in the House of Lords. According to Cara, a secret source had passed on knowledge of Buchanan's sexual deviances to her, and she had relayed the information to the authorities. In exchange for the tip-off, she had been included in the sting operation, where he had been caught trying to procure an underage girl from an undercover policeman. She'd also been given the exclusive on his arrest and subsequent trial. It had been one of the biggest scandals of the decade, running a close second to the Profumo affair.

Work had pretty much become her life. Her flat was somewhere she went to sleep. Her friends were all fellow journalists. Even among a notoriously workaholic group, her dedication was legendary.

"Don't you have a home to go to?" Jake would often tease her.

Jake.

Things had changed between them after that embrace at the Christmas party. She'd tried not to think about what had happened—but it wasn't easy. That night, Jake had become more than just her boss. She'd suddenly felt aware of him as a man. She found herself eavesdropping on conversations about him, wanting to hear what others thought, wanting to find out everything she could about the kind of person he was. If she was out in the pub with other journalists, she'd find ways to steer the discussion round to him.

She suspected that Jake might feel the same way, too. Sometimes she'd look up from her desk and catch him staring straight at her. Their gaze would meet for a couple of seconds, and then they'd both look away.

But even though Cara could feel the attraction between them, she was determined that nothing happen. She still felt so damaged after the way Danny had treated her. She might be attracted to Jake, but she wasn't prepared to let it go any farther than that.

One night, in the early spring of 1970, a few weeks after the Christmas party, Cara had been working late. Although back then she was officially still secretary to the News Desk, since the "Drug Lord" article, she'd begun to write more pieces for the *Chronicle*, squeezing the research in around her everyday tasks. It was just after nine by the time she packed up. By sheer fluke, when she got to the elevator, Jake happened to be there, too. They got to talking about what she was currently working on—a piece about illegal dogfights—and just as they stepped out into the downstairs lobby, he mentioned, as casual as anything, that he was going to grab a bite to eat and asked if she fancied coming along.

Cara hesitated. It wasn't such an unusual request. Their profession had a high divorce rate, and a lot of the journalists lived alone. They worked late and seemed to hate going home to an empty house. Several times Cara had been roped into spending long nights in a restaurant or a bar, keeping some lonely soul company. And yet . . . something in Cara's head was telling her it was a bad idea to go along. After all, she didn't want to give Jake any further encouragement.

So she started to say no, that she'd already eaten earlier. But then her stomach, with impeccably bad timing, decided to let out a growl of protest, betraying her. After that, she'd had no choice but to give in.

Cara had assumed they'd head to the Stab, but Jake had other ideas. It was the one night of the week he liked to get away from Fleet Street, he told her. He insisted on driving them, telling Cara to leave her bike chained up over the weekend and catch a taxi back the following Monday morning. "Charge it to expenses," he told her.

She didn't know much about cars, but she knew enough to tell that he had a great one—a silver sports car. "Very James Bond," she commented, sliding into the buttery leather seat.

They drove to a little pub that Jake knew in South Kensington. Downstairs, in the sawdust-covered cellar, food was still being served. The menu listed hearty pub grub. Jake recommended the shepherd's pie, and they ordered two, along with two pints. Once they had their drinks, Jake sat back in his chair and regarded Cara with keen eyes.

"So," he drawled. "Why don't you tell me a bit about yourself?"

"What do you want to know?" Cara couldn't help being guarded. This whole evening was beginning to feel like a date.

Jake considered the question for a moment. "Something . . . personal." Inwardly, Cara groaned. But he didn't seem to notice her discomfort. "You're a bit of a mystery around the office, Cara. You never talk about friends or family."

"There's not much to say."

"Oh, come on. This isn't an interrogation. I'm just trying to make conversation. We're going to be here for—what—at least an hour. Just tell me . . ." he hesitated, as though trying to decide what he wanted to know. "Just tell me about where you came from," he said finally.

So she did. Not the whole truth, of course; not about who her mother really had been. But she gave him an abridged version, sticking as closely as possible to the facts—saying that her parents had died when she was young and that she'd lived with her grandmother in Ireland, and then about the orphanage and running away to live with Annie Connolly, whom she described as a family friend.

"Ah." He nodded knowingly when she'd finished. "That explains it."

"Explains what?"

"Why you're so tough. You've had to be."

"Am I tough?"

"Yes." His dark eyes twinkled. "For a girl."

Cara reached across the table and playfully punched his arm. "Hey!" she objected.

Their food had arrived while she'd been talking, and between telling him her story, she'd managed to eat it all. Now she nodded at her empty plate. "That was good."

"I know all the best places." He nodded at her empty glass. "Another drink?"

"Why not?" But at the same time as she answered, she was trying hard to stifle a yawn.

Jake saw what she was doing and grinned. "On second thought, let's skip it. It's late and you're tired. Let's get you home."

They were both quiet on the drive to her place, lost in their own thoughts. Somewhere along the way, Cara must have dozed off, because when they pulled up outside her flat, Jake saw that she was sound asleep. He gazed down at her for a long moment.

"Cara?" He spoke softly, not wanting to startle her. When she didn't move, he laid a hand against her cheek and said, a little louder this time, "Cara, wake up."

Cara stirred in her sleep, hearing the voice whispering her name. She could feel something warm touching her face, and she nestled into it. Sighing contentedly, her eyes fluttered open.

It took a moment for everything to come clear—that she was in Jake's car, parked outside her flat, and that he was leaning over, trying to wake her; that it was his hand she had been nuzzling.

"God, I'm sorry." She drew away, her own hand going up to her reddening cheek, embarrassed at her display of affection. But Jake didn't seem to care.

"Don't worry about it." In the glow of the nearby streetlamp, she could see him smiling at her. "I enjoyed myself tonight." He cleared his throat, and that's when she knew what he was going to say. "In fact, Cara—"

"Don't," she interrupted. She said it quietly, but there was no mistaking the urgency in her voice.

Jake seemed taken aback. "Don't what?"

She looked up at him then, quiet pleading in her eyes. "Don't say what I know you're going to."

"What? That I think it might be nice if we did this again?"

She closed her eyes. "I told you not to say it."

"Why not? What's the problem?"

"You're my boss," she said simply.

Jake looked genuinely confused. "So?"

"So how's it going to look if I get promoted now? It'll seem as if it's because we're together."

"Oh, come on," Jake scoffed. "Everyone knows you deserve to be a reporter."

"Perhaps, but there'll still be gossip. People who are jealous will point the finger. It'll start interfering with work. And once Neil hears about what's going on," she said, referring to the *Chronicle*'s editor, "he's going to want one of us gone."

Jake waved away her concerns. "I can handle Neil," he said.

"Maybe," she agreed. "But you know the company's policy on office romances—someone has to go, and it's always the woman." She'd been planning this little speech for a while, sensing that at some point it would come to this. The work angle was the best explanation she'd been able to come up with for why nothing could happen between them—a perfectly reasonable explanation that would invite no more questions or arguments from Jake. "It's fine for you. You're really senior. If there's any fallout, I'd be the one to suffer. And this job means everything to me. I don't want to lose it."

There was silence in the car after she'd finished. She could see that Jake was stunned by the vehemence of her rejection. He'd thought this evening was going to be the start of a relationship, and she'd just told him in no uncertain terms that nothing was ever going to happen between them.

"I should go," Cara said quietly. She made to get out of the car.

"Cara." Jake put out a hand to stop her. Reluctantly she turned back. She could see the confusion in his eyes. "I get what you're saying— really, I do. But . . ." He stopped then, as though realizing that there was no way to convince her. She waited, sensing that he was running through the arguments in his head. Finally he sighed, as though giving in. "Maybe you're right. Maybe it isn't a good idea."

"I'm sorry."

He gave her a rueful smile. "But we can still be friends, right?"

He offered her his hand. After a moment, she took it.

"Of course," she agreed. "Friends sounds good."

And that's what they'd been ever since. Friends. And if sometimes Cara felt a stab of regret that there was nothing more between them, she tried to put it from her mind. It was better this way—she got to keep him in her life and didn't risk getting hurt.

Now, as she left Neil's office and headed back to her desk, she saw Jake walking toward her, as though he'd sensed she was thinking about him.

The news editor perched on the edge of Cara's desk, his eyes automatically sweeping over her. In a midi-length brown suede skirt and French-style cream turtleneck, she looked professional and up to date, but along with most of the men in the office, he couldn't help regretting the demise of the mini, particularly in Cara's case. He missed her legs. Clearing his throat, he looked away, down at his notepad.

"I heard Rachel Travers is transferring to the Scrubs tomorrow," he said, forcing himself to be all business. "Thought you might want to go up there and see if you can get her to talk."

Although Cara was no longer on the News Desk and was officially a columnist in her own right, Jake still occasionally asked her to cover stories, if it was a topic she was interested in. Rachel Travers had become something of a crusade for Cara. She was a forty-year-old prostitute who had eventually cracked after years of abuse and stabbed her pimp to death. Despite the mitigating circumstances—not just the daily beatings she'd endured but the fact that she had the mental age of a child—a lackluster defense had meant that she'd ended up sentenced to life in prison. Cara had taken up her cause and run a crusade in the paper calling for her release or at least to have her transferred to a secure hospital. So far, despite overwhelming public sympathy, Cara had had no luck getting a pardon for her, but she looked for any excuse to bring the topic up again. Jake knew that, which was why he was giving her first refusal on the story.

"Sorry. Can't." Cara sounded as regretful as she felt. "I've got the day off."

Jake raised an eyebrow. "Oh? Is there an apocalypse I don't know about?" He had every reason to be curious. Cara was renowned for never taking any of her annual leave. Christmas, Easter, any public holidays that normal people wanted to spend with their families—she was first in line to man the desk.

"Funeral," she explained briefly. "Of an old friend."

He knew not to press her for details. "Ah. Well, let me know if you fancy going for a drink afterward."

Cara smiled up at him. "Thanks. I might take you up on that."

51

It was Annie's funeral that she was attending. Although Cara hadn't stayed in touch with Danny's mother directly, after starting work at the *Chronicle* she had resurrected some of her East End contacts, which meant that she'd been able to keep tabs on how Annie was doing. Through one of them, she'd found out that the older woman had ovarian cancer. It was aggressive, and she'd gone downhill quickly. By the time Cara had gone to visit her in the hospital, she'd already been near the end, in intense pain. It had been a short visit, as Annie had been too tired to speak for long—just enough for them to make their peace. She'd been so ill that Cara had been surprised to hear she'd held on for another month after that.

The funeral service was held at the Catholic church on Underwood Road, between Whitechapel and Bethnal Green, where Annie had attended Mass every Sunday. Cara stood at the back during the service and at the burial, as she didn't know how Annie's family would feel about her being there. But Bronagh came up to her afterward to thank her for coming.

"It was good of you to come . . . after everything that happened."

Cara shrugged and said with honesty, "Your mother was very kind to me over the years."

"Maybe," Annie's daughter agreed. "But Danny wasn't." She clearly wanted to draw Cara into a debate, but the younger woman wasn't having any of it.

"That's all in the past now," Cara said evenly. She looked around the crowd. "He didn't make it, then?"

Bronagh snorted. "As if. You know Danny, always looking out for number one. Knew the coppers would be waiting for him as soon as he stepped foot here, and this time he'd be going down for an eighteen stretch." It was said in a tone that showed she didn't agree with his choice. "Course, Mum was still asking for him at the end. She always had more time for him than us girls."

Cara gave a noncommittal "Hmm."

After a few more unsuccessful attempts to get Cara to bad-mouth Danny, Bronagh gave up and invited her along to the pub for the wake. Cara declined, not wanting to push the Connollys' hospitality.

An hour later, she regretted her decision. Opening the front door to her flat, empty silence greeted her. It was cold inside, too. The Earls Court apartment was bright and spacious, but she'd rented it for its proximity to central London rather than its south-facing view or any of its other qualities. She hadn't done much to spruce the place up, never spending enough time there to justify making it feel homey. The spare room was filled with books and old copies of magazines and newspapers. It wasn't as if she ever had anyone to stay.

Wanting to distance herself from the day, she changed out of the dark funeral clothes and into a pair of hipster jeans and a rainbow-colored gauze shirt. Walking around the flat, she switched on all the lights and turned the heating up, trying to make the place more cheerful. Instead of feeling relieved that the funeral was over, she felt down, strangely empty and aware of her own mortality. If I died, who would come to my funeral? she pondered. Work colleagues, of course. But other than that, she had few real friends. Her life revolved around the *Chronicle*. That's how she'd wanted it—it was easier than being with people who let you down. She shook her head. At twenty-five, that was hardly the sort of thing she should be worrying about. Except that she could already see how her life was panning out, and it worried her.

Perhaps that was why she'd been taking more of an interest in her mother lately.

It had started with a letter she'd received out of the blue a few weeks earlier from Maximilian Stanhope, her stepfather—or her mother's husband, as she preferred to think of this man she'd never met. The letter had raised more questions than answers. He didn't explain how he'd found out about her existence. Instead, he had simply said that there was a matter he wanted to discuss with her while he was still able, al-

luding to information he had on a mutual acquaintance—clearly referring to her mother. He also included a bankers' draft for £2,000, a huge
sum of money, "to cover your fare out to California, and any additional
expenses that you might incur."

Cara had always insisted that she didn't care about what had happened to the woman who had so callously abandoned her. But a few
months after she'd started working at the *Chronicle,* she'd been in the
clippings library one day, researching a totally unrelated story, and
found herself asking the researcher to dig up anything he could on the
actress Frances Fitzgerald.

From the articles, Cara had been able to piece together an idea of
what the media believed had happened to the former movie star. There
were two theories. First, that Franny had been so depressed after losing her baby that she'd killed herself. Or, second, that her husband,
Maximilian Stanhope, had finally tired of her flirting and killed her.
Two dead wives—it felt like more than just a coincidence. But Max had
been such a powerful person that clearly the papers hadn't been able to
say too much without risking being sued.

After she'd received the letter from Max, Cara had begun tracking
everything on him, too. There were fewer articles in the last decade;
he'd become something of a recluse after her mother's death. But she
had seen a small piece reporting that he'd been taken to the hospital to
have a lung removed. Cancer. It didn't sound as if he had long left.

Cara still had no idea yet if she was going to respond to his letter—
but she knew that, whatever her decision, she needed to make it soon.

The doorbell rang, the unfamiliar sound making her jump. No one ever
came around—correction, she never invited anyone around. She went to
open the door, unsure who to expect, and found Jake standing outside.

"What are you doing here?" Cara couldn't hide her surprise. "Do
you need me at the *Chronicle*?"

His mouth twitched, clearly amused that her first thought on seeing
him would be work. "That's not much of a welcome," he chided gently.

"Sorry. I just wasn't expecting you." She noticed then that he was in
jeans and a sweater, his out-of-the-office uniform. "So, if it's not work,
then why *are* you here?"

He shrugged. "I always feel rotten after a funeral. I guessed you
would, too." He held up a bottle of Jack Daniel's. "Thought this might
help ease the pain."

Cara looked from him to the bottle and then back again. Finally she smiled. "Well, it certainly can't hurt."

Jake stepped inside and followed her through to the little sitting room. He took a pointed look around at the sterile decor: the absence of photographs and knickknacks. "I really like what you've done with the place," he said sarcastically.

"Oh, don't start," Cara groaned, getting some tumblers from the cabinet. "You know I'm too busy to play house."

As she poured the drinks, Jake got the fire going. With the only seating option being plastic chairs, they opted instead for sitting on the rough carpet, by the hearth. Cara was surprised to find how grateful she was for his company. Jake knew a little about Annie and how the Irishwoman had taken Cara in, but now, with the day's events on her mind, she found herself opening up about her romance with Danny and how, after he'd left, she'd fallen out with his mother.

"That wasn't fair of me," Cara admitted. "She was the closest thing I had to a mother, and when Danny rejected me, I took it out on her. I shouldn't have. I let her down."

"You saw her before she died," Jake pointed out reasonably. "You made your peace with her."

"Yeah, but that couldn't make up for all those years I ignored her. I can't take that back."

"She understood that you were hurt. Deep down, I bet she knew that it was Danny you were angry with, not her."

"Perhaps." Cara shook her head. "I don't even know if that was the reason anymore. Maybe it was just an excuse not to see her. Maybe I just don't want anyone around." She snorted in disgust at herself. She was feeling a lot of self-loathing tonight. She downed the hot amber liquid, wincing as it hit the back of her throat before starting to speak again. "I don't know what's wrong with me. No wonder I've got no one, when I keep pushing everyone away."

Cara reached for the bottle of whiskey to pour herself another measure, but Jake put out a hand to stop her. "Wait. Look at me." When she didn't, he said more forcefully, "Cara, look at me."

Slowly, she raised her gaze to meet his. He saw the old wariness in her eyes and felt disappointed that even now, at a time like this, she was acting as if she didn't need anyone. He knew that underneath it all she was vulnerable—she just didn't like to show it. Instead, she put up a defensive front and wouldn't let anyone in. He hated that Danny bastard for hurting her so badly that she behaved like this.

"Don't do this to yourself," he told her now. "You're not to blame for what happened." He put his hand on her right cheek. "You've got nothing to feel bad about."

Up until then, Cara hadn't been able to cry. But something about his words set her off. Hot tears began to fall. Jake's grip tightened on her wet cheek, and her hand reached up to cover his. Swiveling her head, she buried her mouth in his palm. It could have stayed like that, nothing more than a comforting gesture between two colleagues, two friends. But after a second's hesitation, she slowly ran her tongue across his warm skin.

Jake let out a slow breath. Over the past few years, they'd grown so close in many ways, but she'd always kept a distance between them. Since that night he had taken her for dinner, she'd made sure never to let anything remotely romantic develop between them. Was that all about to change?

"Cara?" He murmured her name, a question about what was happening between them.

In answer, she raised her eyes so that she was looking up at him. "Kiss me," she said softly, almost a plea.

It was all the invitation he needed. With a low growl, his mouth came down on hers, his arms reaching round her waist, pulling her to him. And she was kissing him too, falling back onto the floor, dragging him down on top of her. And all the while she was thinking how good it felt being held by him, feeling the weight and warmth of his body, having the physical closeness of another human being.

But even as she thought that, a little voice nagged at her that she was being naïve. This could never be for one night. Not when it was with Jake. They'd go out, fall in love, maybe end up living together. Then one day, just when she was happy, he'd start to lose interest, or perhaps he'd find someone else. And she'd be left alone again, miserable and broken.

She tried to put the dark thoughts from her mind and to concentrate instead on Jake's lips on her neck, his fingers working at the buttons of her blouse. But now, for her, the moment was ruined. She broke away.

"Stop!" she panted. "Wait a moment—"

Jake's eyes flew open. Cara saw confusion there and wished she could think of something else to say.

"What's wrong?" He was still lying on top of her, oblivious to what had been going on in her head. Cara hesitated for a moment, knowing that he wasn't going to like what she had to say. Pushing him off, she sat up.

"God, I'm sorry," she said, unable to look at him. Pulling her blouse closed, she busied herself doing up the buttons. "I shouldn't have done that. I'm upset, I've had too much drink." She knew she was babbling, but she couldn't help it. "I don't know what's wrong with me tonight. The funeral must have got to me more than I realized."

Jake reached out and put his hand on her arm, as though to stop her jabbering on. "Cara—"

"*Don't.*" The tone of her voice was so firm that it brought him to a halt. "I told you before. This can't happen."

"But why not?"

Cara could feel Jake's frustration coming off him in waves. She ventured a look at him, knowing it was the only way he could see how determined she was about this. "Because I don't want it to," she said quietly.

There was a silence. Jake stared at her for a long moment. It seemed to Cara as if he might be about to say something, but then he appeared to change his mind.

"Fine," he said eventually.

He put on his shoes and coat as quickly as he could, clearly eager to get away. It was only once he was at the door that he turned back to look at Cara again, his eyes serious. "You know, I'm not going to wait around forever," he said, and then he was gone.

After he left, Cara poured herself another glass of whiskey and roamed the silent flat, feeling aimless. Somehow she ended up back in her room, drawn to the letter that Max had sent her. A wave of bitterness passed through her. This was all Franny's fault. If she hadn't left, Cara knew her life would have been so different. She might have actually been able to trust someone, to love someone.

It was a moment of clarity for her. She needed to find out what had happened to her mother. Because how was she ever going to move on until she put the past to rest? It sounded as though Max didn't have long left—and once he went, so would her chance to discover the truth.

Feeling surprisingly clearheaded, the drama of the evening having sobered her up, Cara sat down at her desk and began composing a letter to Maximilian Stanhope.

52

Once Cara had made the decision to accept Max's invitation, the need to uncover the truth about her mother consumed her. For years, she'd tried to forget the woman who had abandoned her. Now it occupied her every waking hour.

After writing to Max telling him that she would fly out to see him the following month, she spent the next few weeks planning her trip to L.A. She went back through all the articles she'd collected, painstakingly piecing together a timeline that began with Franny's arrival in Hollywood in 1954. Then she started to make calls to everyone who had ever been associated with her mother, arranging to meet with them. Her journalism background provided the ideal cover for her investigations. She was deliberately vague about her intentions, saying that she was writing a series of articles on the Golden Age of Hollywood that might end up being turned into a book. Most were more than happy to agree to speak with her: having fallen out of favor with the press years before, they were eager to get their names back in the media any way that they could.

With her trip all arranged, Cara went to Neil to ask for a three-month sabbatical. The *Chronicle's* editor wasn't happy about it, especially as she wouldn't give him a straight answer about where she was going or what she was doing, but, seeing that she wouldn't be dissuaded, he finally gave in to her wishes.

She considered telling Jake the real reason for her trip. He was the one person she could usually confide in. But since their aborted kiss, things had been a little awkward between them. Still, he came to her leaving party, hugged her good-bye.

"Keep in touch, Healey," he said at the end of the night. "If you need anything, I'm only a phone call away."

She watched him walk away, feeling sad about how things had turned out between them. She just hoped that by the time she'd finished her trip, she might be able to think more clearly about what she wanted.

Most people stepped off the thirteen-hour flight to LAX feeling bleary-eyed and dazed. But Cara, used to long working hours and nights of insomnia, was alert and ready to go. She'd decided to spend a few days in L.A. before heading up to Stanhope Castle, wanting to get a feel for what Franny's life had been like. So she checked into the Sunset Lodge, the roach motel where her mother had first stayed, the name forever imprinted on Cara's mind from all the envelopes she'd addressed. As Cara ate dinner in the adjacent diner, she looked at the washed-up waitress who took her order and couldn't help wondering if it was the same one who'd served Franny all those years ago.

The next morning, Cara set about exploring. Hollywood had changed a lot since her mother had been there. The Golden Age had passed now, and the places that Franny had frequented were now closed or past their heyday: Ciro's had shut in 1959, as had Mocambo. The Sunset Strip was sleazy now, rather than ritzy. In the afternoon, Cara took a tour of Juniper Studios with the other wide-eyed, gawping tourists. Her mother even got a mention by the guide as they made their way through the backlots: her career might not have been as illustrious as Elizabeth Taylor's or Lana Turner's, but her tragic death had guaranteed her a spot in Hollywood's history.

"And yet another young talent was stolen from us," the guide concluded with fake solemnity after a graphic account of Frances Fitzgerald's death.

Another sleepless night on a hard bed, and then came the interviews. There was the producer who'd discovered Franny in London, Clifford Walker, now retired and needing at least two vodkas before he could get up in the morning; Juniper's ex–studio head, Lloyd Cramer, who spent his days on the golf course; a leading man, Hunter Holden, whose career had miraculously survived and was going through another revival. They all said much the same: that Franny had been beautiful and vibrant; the life and soul of any party. But other than the usual platitudes extolling Franny's virtues, there were no new leads. Cara had tried to track down another of Franny's former beaus, Duke Carter, but he'd faded into obscurity long ago. Like Clifford, he'd become rather too fond of the bottle, and he had died of liver disease a few years earlier.

The most interesting interview was with Franny's old friend Lily Powell. Now in her early fifties, she had retired from movies a decade before but had made a nice life for herself since then. Always careful with her money, she'd opened up a chain of beauty parlors across the West Coast, and business was thriving. She still lived in her Hollywood Hills villa, which she currently shared with a muscular hunk named Rod, who didn't even look old enough to drink yet.

Lily greeted Cara wearing hot pink lounge pajamas, a matching scarf wrapped turban-style around her head. She insisted on fixing margaritas and brought the jug outside so she and Cara could sit by the pool, drinking cocktails and talking while her man-boy swam laps in a leopard-print thong.

Lily spoke fondly of her old friend, reminiscing about the wild times they'd shared together.

"And then everything changed," she said sadly. "It's the old story, isn't it? Two girls getting along fabulously until a man comes into the mix. Well, Maximilian Stanhope was that man."

"Oh?" Cara prompted.

Lily shook her head. "I never understood the two of them together. She was such a social butterfly, and while Max might have been attracted to that initially, it wasn't a quality he wanted in a wife. He hated her going out, hated her flirting—it humiliated him. And Franny just couldn't stop, bless her. Flirting came as naturally to her as breathing." She smiled indulgently at the memory.

"Of course he tried to clip her wings," Lily went on. "She stopped coming out with us because she knew it would just cause grief. It killed her, being out there at the house all alone. I guess maybe that's why she decided to get pregnant: to give her something to do."

"I suppose that explains why she was depressed after she lost the baby," Cara probed. "That's what they say, isn't it? That depression made her take her own life."

Lily snorted. "Oh, please."

"You don't think that's what happened." Cara could feel her heart speeding up, feeling as if she was finally getting somewhere.

"No way did Franny take her life because of the stillbirth. Don't get me wrong, she was sad about it an' all, but there was more going on than that. Franny hadn't been right for months. She'd lost her sparkle and become so sad, so forgetful; like her head was always somewhere else. And"—she lowered her voice meaningfully—"she had these bruises all over her body."

This was a new development. Cara seized on it. "You think Max gave them to her?"

Lily shrugged. "She never said for definite." Her tone was supposed to leave Cara in no doubt as to what *she* thought had gone on.

"But none of this was in the papers."

Another snort. "Little wonder. Back in those days, Max had everyone in his pockets."

"You think there was a cover-up? You think she didn't kill herself?"

Lily looked her straight in the eye. "I can't say for certain what went on up in that house in her last months. But there's no doubt in my mind that Maximilian Stanhope was at least in part responsible for her death."

Despite the heat of the day, Cara felt herself shiver.

Lily was a great source of information. She seemed to know everything about the Stanhope family.

"I've heard Max's son hasn't spoken to him for years. Gabriel—that's what his name is, isn't it?—well, Gabriel went away right after Franny's death. To Europe, I believe. Or was it Africa? I really can't remember now. But what I *do* remember is that he didn't even stay for the funeral. I know he was never a great fan of Franny's, but still . . . he should have paid his respects. But for whatever reason, he left the country, and I've heard he never came back. And that he's never spoken to Max again. Or perhaps Max never spoke to him—no one's ever quite sure who cut whom off. All I know is that they haven't exchanged a word for years. You have to wonder about that, don't you? What could possibly have happened to drive such a wedge between them?"

Cara nodded along, taking down every detail carefully.

"And then there's Max's daughter, poor Olivia," Lily went on. "She was always such a fragile little thing. From what I remember, she spent some time in an institution back then. Whatever *that* was about, she never seemed to fully recover. Since then she's always had to be specially cared for—by that housekeeper of Max's, the one who'd been there for years. Oh, yes, Hilda, that's it . . ." Lily paused. "It's funny, isn't it? And by that I mean *strange* funny. Franny always hated Hilda. And yet she's the one still there at Stanhope Castle, living with Max, while poor Franny's been dead and buried for years now."

Cara set off for Stanhope Castle the following morning in the Ford Thunderbird she'd rented. It was a five-hour drive from L.A., with Lily's words echoing in her mind. If Max had killed her mother, it stood to reason that he would do anything to stop her finding out about what he'd done. The knowledge weighed heavily on her. But her dark thoughts were distracted as she got farther along the route and reached Highway 1, the ninety-mile stretch of road that led through the Big Sur. She'd heard that it was a scenic drive, but nothing could prepare her for the rugged magnificence of the views: on one side, the Santa Lucia Mountains soared up into the azure sky while on the other, the Pacific Ocean crashed against the cliffs below. As she passed VW camper vans crammed with hippies, Cara wished for a moment that she were here with no other purpose than to enjoy the place.

There was something that Cara had known she would have to do ever since deciding to come out to California, something she'd been dreading: visiting the spot where her mother had died. It was a tourist attraction now, featured in guidebooks as a stop-off point along the Pacific Coast Highway; there was even a plaque to mark the spot. Standing by the cliff edge, looking down at the location where her mother's car had burst into a fireball, Cara had no idea what she was meant to feel. And if her cheeks were wet, it was from the harsh wind stinging her eyes, not because she was crying.

As she got farther along Highway 1, the number of cars thinned out until the road seemed empty. There were few properties in the area, so it was easy enough to find Stanhope Castle. From a distance, it could still impress. The sheer size of the place dominated the skyline. But as the car drew closer, Cara could see that the building had fallen into disrepair. During her pretrip research, she had read that Max never allowed strangers onto the estate anymore. After her mother's death, there had been a lot of scandal, rumors about his involvement. Eventually, the gossip had driven him away from the social scene. He had turned into something of a Howard Hughes character, reclusive and eccentric.

Heading carefully down the gravel driveway, Cara parked by a large ornamental dolphin fountain—it no longer worked, and the mammal's nose, which had been a spout for the water to gush out of, had broken off. The marble steps that led up to the entrance door were chipped, and there was a general feeling of neglect about the place.

The front door was opened by Max's housekeeper, Hilda. Cara knew immediately that it was the same person whom Lily had spoken about. She must have been in her late fifties now, but she had the kind of looks that could have put her age anywhere between twenty years younger or older. Though her skin was surprisingly clear and unlined, no doubt due to a life of clean living, her sharp features and iron-gray hair aged her. Her demeanor was very proper, like that of a governess in some creepy Victorian gothic novel.

"Mr. Stanhope sends his apologies for not being able to meet you in person," she told Cara straight off, with formal politeness rather than a hint of welcome. "His illness is taking its toll. He asked that I show you up to your room and make sure you have everything you need."

The interior was in the same state of disrepair as the exterior. Looking around the huge hallway, Cara could see traces of the magnificent place that this had once been; but the carpets were threadbare, the wallpaper had faded in the sunlight, the skirting boards had holes in them as though mice were about to scurry out. There was a sense that whoever owned the place had given up. The only work that appeared to have been undertaken recently was the installation of an elevator. "Mr. Stanhope had it put in after his last operation," Hilda explained. "He's in a wheelchair now."

The housekeeper led Cara up the central staircase, then along a corridor, through a door, and up two more small, steep staircases, until they finally reached the room that she'd been allocated. The musty smell hit her as soon as the housekeeper opened the door. The space was cluttered, a bit like a junk room. Someone had obviously been told to tidy up, but it was a surface clean at best: Cara could see there was still dust under the bed where no one had thought to vacuum. The one winning point was the view: huge double French windows—thrown open in a belated effort to air the room—led out to a Juliet balcony that looked onto the dark ocean.

"I hope this will be all right for you." Hilda cast a disparaging glance around. "Mr. Stanhope employs so few staff for the size of the estate that it makes it difficult to maintain everything the way it should be."

Under Max's orders, Hilda was the only staff member allowed to live on the estate. There was a cook who did the shopping and came in every day to prepare meals, she explained. Other than that, there were two maids, who spent one day a week at the house. The place was too big for them to keep clean, so most of the rooms were shut up.

"And where do you live?" Cara couldn't help asking.

Hilda hesitated for a moment. "Not in the main house," she said carefully. Walking over to the window, she pointed down at a low-rise white building, one of four guesthouses. "Max agreed years ago to let me live out there. It gives me some privacy."

"And that's where Max's daughter, Olivia, stays, too?"

Cara had posed it as a question, but Hilda must have assumed it was a statement of fact, because she didn't answer.

After that the housekeeper left. It was nearly seven by then, and feeling hungry, Cara headed in the direction of the kitchen. It was in the bowels of the house, a huge space, immaculately clean, if shabby and old-fashioned. As the housekeeper had promised, there was food in the oven. Cara pulled the warm plate out, wrinkling her nose as she did so. It had once been coq au vin but now looked dry and shriveled. Throwing the meal into the garbage, she went to the larder and found some slightly stale bread and a slab of cheese. The outside was hard, but she cut that off and managed to make a passable sandwich. The milk at least was fresh and cold, and she poured herself a glass. She ate in the silence of the kitchen, standing by the sink, a quick, informal meal, and then she headed back up to her bedroom.

The house was large and confusing, and it took her three attempts to get there. By then she was finally beginning to feel tired. It was a warm evening and the room was still stuffy, so she went over to the French windows to cool down. As she stood breathing in the fresh air, listening to the distant sound of waves crashing over each other, a movement in the grounds below caught her eye. Looking down, she saw a man in a wheelchair, heading along a path through the overgrown gardens, away from the main house. It was Max. In the pale light of the full moon, she watched as he made his way toward the guest bungalow, where Hilda lived. The housekeeper must have been watching out for him, because the front door opened as he approached. He wheeled himself up the ramp and disappeared inside.

Cara waited for ten minutes, but he didn't come back out. Going over to sit on the bed, she took out her notepad and turned to a fresh page. She put Hilda's name at the top and then wrote down a brief account of what the housekeeper had told her earlier. At the very end, she jotted down a note to herself: "Could M & H have been lovers?" She stared at the sentence for a long time, pondering the implications of her theory. Then she added, "Before or after F's death? Was she in their way? Did they need to get rid of her?"

She looked down at the words and felt a chill run through her. Despite her tiredness, it took a long time for her to fall asleep that night.

53

The next morning, Cara made her way down the corridor to the bathroom that Hilda had pointed out to her. The plumbing wasn't too good, and it took a while to get the shower working, the water clanking its way through the ancient pipes.

Downstairs, the cook, Mrs. Jameson, had arrived. This morning, the kitchen was clearly her domain. She asked Cara what she wanted for breakfast and told her that she'd bring it through to her in the breakfast room. Cara would rather have just grazed through the fridge, maybe settled for some fruit and a yogurt, but she got the feeling that that would be frowned on.

Sitting in the breakfast room eating her pancakes, Cara heard the incessant sound of creaking across the ceiling, as though something was being dragged across the floor above, like a child's bicycle.

"What's that?" Cara asked when Mrs. Jameson came in to clear the dishes away.

"It's Mr. Stanhope's wheelchair," she said matter-of-factly. "Rolling back and forth across the wooden floorboards."

As Cara was finishing her second coffee, the double doors opened and Hilda came into the room. "I'm sorry, but Mr. Stanhope isn't well enough to see you today," she informed Cara.

Cara's heart sank. She wanted to get this out of the way now, not wait around to hear from him. "Do you know how serious this is? Is he likely to be better tomorrow?"

The housekeeper was tight-lipped. "I have no idea. But when he's ready, he'll let you know."

Hilda left then, but the way she'd made that last remark suggested to Cara that Max wasn't actually ill but just didn't want to speak to her. She wondered why. After all, he was the one who'd asked her to come out here. It was so frustrating. She'd traveled all this way on his invitation, only for him to block her now. But it seemed there was nothing she could do about it—apart from wait.

Cara spent the morning in her room, going through all the articles on her mother and Max again. Then, after lunch, she went for a walk through the overgrown grounds. As she headed back to the house, she saw a man in his early thirties standing on the patio. Dressed like a hippie, with long, dark hair and a beard, he looked out of place framed by the aged grandeur of Stanhope Castle, and Cara half wondered if he'd wandered onto the property by mistake.

"So you're the journalist, right?" he called out as she approached, disproving her theory. "Cara, isn't it? I heard you were meant to be coming, but I thought I'd confirm it with my own eyes."

"That's right. And you are—?"

"Gabriel Stanhope," he announced. "Errant son and general layabout."

Cara was shocked to hear that. She had seen photos of Gabriel Stanhope as a young man of eighteen and had been struck by how handsome and charismatic he'd seemed—a dark-haired version of his sister: they both had the same exquisite bone structure, high and sharp, and the same intense gaze. But looking at him now, with his long hair, straggly beard, and waiflike build, he was indistinguishable from any other traveler.

He sat down at the wrought-iron table, took out a packet of Rizlas, and began to roll a cigarette. Cara drew up a chair, assuming that's what he wanted her to do. Even if it wasn't, this was far too good an opportunity to turn down. If Max wouldn't see her, then maybe his son would have something revealing to say.

"So have you spoken to Dad yet?" he asked, not bothering to look up at her.

"He's been too ill to see me."

Gabriel snorted a laugh. "Is that right?" A little smile played around his mouth, as thought he were privy to a joke that she hadn't been let in on. She wondered how much he knew about her and suspected it was more than he would reveal.

"So what brings you back here?" Cara asked. "Are you visiting your sister?"

A cloud passed over Gabriel's face, all the jokiness leaving him. "No," he said shortly.

"Then why . . . ?" She let the question hang.

"I'm here to see my father. I heard the end was near and decided to make the trip back for these last few months. Then, once it's all over, I'm out of here, back to Morocco."

If the callousness of his words surprised Cara, she tried not to show it. "You made up?" she asked instead, thinking she hadn't read anything about a reconciliation between father and son.

The smile was back. "We never fell out."

"But I thought you hadn't spoken for years."

"So?" Gabriel said, and he seemed to be enjoying himself. "That doesn't mean we argued. There are far better reasons for not wanting to speak to someone."

Cara had no idea what he was talking about. It seemed as if she couldn't get a straight answer out of him, and his riddles were beginning to make her head hurt.

The sound of someone tapping on glass made them both turn. An elderly man was sitting by one of the downstairs windows, glaring out at them. He was thin, with a full head of white hair, and wearing clothes that swamped him. It took Cara a moment to realize that it must be Max Stanhope. He looked at least a decade older than his sixty years. Now that he had Gabriel's attention, he pointed at his son and beckoned him inside.

"Ooops," Gabriel said. "Looks like we've been caught."

Cara seized on his words. "Does your father not want you talking to me?"

"Don't be flattered. My father doesn't like me talking to anyone."

Cara nodded toward the room that Max was in. "Where is that?"

"It's his study. He spends most of his time in there."

Gabriel was on his feet now. Cara could see this was her last chance to get something out of him before he disappeared. "Do you think I could get Olivia to speak to me?"

Gabriel's mouth twisted into a wry smile. "I'd like to see you try."

Cara watched as Gabriel disappeared inside the house. She could make out the sound of voices but couldn't catch the words. However, after hearing what Gabriel had to say, an idea had begun to form in her head. If Max wouldn't speak with her, she would have to do some investigation of her own. And she knew just where to start.

The key to everything seemed to be Franny's stillbirth. That was allegedly what had sparked the downward spiral in the last months of her life, so that's what Cara would concentrate on.

It wasn't hard to find out the name of the doctor who had attended the birth of Franny's child: Dr. Robertson, the Stanhope family's personal physician. His name was all over the newspaper articles. He seemed to have acted as the family's spokesperson and was quoted several times, explaining what had gone wrong. Franny had wanted a home birth. Unfortunately, there had been unforeseen complications during the labor, and the baby had been born breech. Without being near hospital facilities, it had been impossible to do the necessary surgery to free the child.

That was one of the strangest things—the idea that Franny would have opted for a home birth. Back in her poverty-stricken East End days, Franny had obviously had no choice but to give birth in Annie's house. But why, when she was wealthy enough to afford the comforts of the best medical care, would she have opted to put herself through that again?

Cara guessed that if Max knew what she was up to, he would make sure that she didn't get within a mile of Dr. Robertson. So she had no choice but to use a ruse in order to access her mother's records. She called up the doctor's office, pretending to be the wife of Harvey Covington, a famous English producer who had recently moved to the area. Cara had read about him and his wife in one of the local papers and knew that though their names were well known enough for the clinic to have heard of them, their faces wouldn't be. In real life Emma Covington was fifty and matronly, but when Cara called up, she was a twenty-something and newly wed. The receptionist accepted her cover at face value and was happy to squeeze her in the following day.

Like most of the exclusive doctors, Dr. Robertson's office was attached to an elegant house in the heart of San Francisco. Cara hadn't turned up with much of a plan, deciding it best to play the appointment by ear. She was aware that if she wanted to go through the doctor's records, she would have to get him out of the room at some point.

She had a vague plan to pretend to faint partway through, hoping that he might go out for a glass of water. But in the event, that wasn't necessary. Instead, he was called outside to speak to a patient who had turned up on spec with a question about her medication.

"Do excuse me for a few minutes, will you, Mrs. Covington?"

After he'd gone, Cara acted quickly. Opening the door a little so that she could hear the voices outside and would know if he was about to return, she went over to the filing cabinets. They were locked. But there was a set of keys on the desk, so she grabbed them and, looking at the lock, tried the smallest. It worked. As quietly as possible, she slid open the middle cabinet drawer. It was for surnames M to P. She quietly closed it and then opened the next one down. That went from Q to T. Quickly flicking through, she found the Stanhope file.

Her ears pricked up. Outside, the conversation between Dr. Robertson and his patient was winding up. "Well, I'll see you next Wednesday afternoon, and if the antibiotics haven't worked by then, I can prescribe something else."

With no time to read the file, Cara quickly folded it in half and slipped it into her bag. Then she quietly closed and locked the cabinet. She was back in her seat, as though she hadn't moved from it, by the time the doctor walked in a moment later.

"Sorry about that," he said, as he came back in.

But Cara was already on her feet. "Actually, I've just remembered that I'm supposed to be somewhere else." She brushed past him and opened the door. "I'll call to make another appointment."

She was already outside before he could say anything. Her heart was beating hard as she hurried to the car, half expecting someone to chase after her and demand she return the file. But why would they? she thought, putting the car into reverse. She bet no one even looked at them anymore.

Once she judged that she was a sufficient distance from the clinic, Cara pulled over into a turnout and took her mother's file out. She flicked through the records, scanning the words as quickly as possible, stumped by the poor handwriting and strange shorthand of a medical professional. There were notes about several visits: an initial consultation and then for pregnancy tests. All were negative. The last test had been in April 1958. That had been negative too, and then after that she hadn't gone back for another visit.

That was odd. In July 1958, Franny had announced that she was already four months' pregnant.

The last entry was on the birth itself, meaning Franny hadn't consulted the doctor's advice during her pregnancy. Again, that seemed curious and against her mother's character. She read on: "Called out at two in the morning to the Stanhope residence to deal with home birth. Mother already in labor for sixteen hours by time arrived. She was delirious with pain. Seventeen-year-old girl not sufficiently developed to cope with the trauma of childbirth."

Cara frowned over that last sentence, not quite understanding what she was reading at first. Did these notes belong to someone else?

As then it dawned on her. There *had* been a seventeen-year-old girl living in the Stanhope household back then, one who could have been pregnant and whose father and stepmother would have covered for her indiscretion rather than risk a scandal.

"Olivia!" she whispered to herself.

The baby had been Olivia's. So why on earth had her mother claimed that it was hers?

54

Franny and Olivia were having breakfast in Stanhope Castle. It was a Wednesday and still term time, but Max's daughter was at home after being suspended for the rest of the school year. The headmistress had called the house the previous Friday to request an explanation for Olivia's continued absence from physical education. Neither Franny nor Max had known anything about it. Franny had agreed to go to San Francisco, to the school. The headmistress had shown her ten notes, all allegedly signed by her, excusing Olivia from PE because of a back complaint. The forgery was surprisingly good.

As Max had observed, it was so unlike Olivia. With Gabriel, he could have understood it, he'd said. But Olivia had a gentle nature and had never been remotely devious before. Franny had no idea what was going on with her stepdaughter. In the year that she'd been married to Max, she'd seen Olivia come out of her shell, but recently she seemed to have retreated back into it.

Franny took a sip of coffee and regarded her sullen stepdaughter. Across the breakfast table, Olivia sat hunched over, spooning cereal and then letting it fall back into the bowl. After the trouble at the school, Max had asked her to try to find out what was wrong with the girl. Now was as good a time as any to start.

"It's lovely out," she said brightly.

Olivia didn't respond.

"You must be boiling in that sweater," she tried again.

This time her stepdaughter went so far as to shrug but still didn't formulate any vocal answer. Franny decided to give it one last try.

"Perhaps we could go out later and buy you some nice new summer clothes."

Another shrug. "If you want," the girl said listlessly.

Franny felt a rush of irritation. It was so hurtful. Here she was, making all this effort, and the girl couldn't even be bothered to speak properly to her. And it wasn't as if Franny didn't have problems of her own. Those rumors about her and the gardener in *Confidential* had put a strain on her relationship with Max. And she still hadn't found the right moment to tell him about Cara. She didn't need any additional stress.

"For God's sake, Olivia!" she snapped. "What on earth's the matter with you?"

The harsh tone of Franny's voice made the girl look up finally. "Nothing," she said sulkily.

"Well, it obviously isn't nothing." If being nice wasn't going to work, then maybe it was time to try some tough love. "You're dragging yourself around the house like a condemned woman. I'm fed up with these moods of yours. We all have problems. If something's bothering you, then tell me about it and I'll try to help. If not, then snap out of it."

"Just leave me alone!"

"Fine," Franny said. "If that's how you feel, then go to your room."

Her stepdaughter sprang to her feet. At that exact moment, the sun came out from behind the clouds and shone directly through the window and onto Olivia, momentarily turning the girl's cotton sweater see-through and showing the silhouette of her body with its protruding belly, which could only mean one thing. Franny gasped, making Olivia turn to her.

"What's wrong with you now?" the girl demanded.

For a moment Franny couldn't speak; the wheels of her mind were too busy turning, trying to make sense of what she knew. She thought of Olivia's strange behavior recently: the withdrawal, the listlessness, the notes excusing her from PE.

It suddenly all made sense.

Franny looked at her stepdaughter closely. "Are you pregnant?"

"No!" The girl instinctively put her hands around her stomach. "Why would you say something like that?"

But even as she denied it, Franny could see the fear in her stepdaughter's eyes.

"Oh, Livy," she breathed.

It was that, the simple mention of her name, that finally got through to the girl. In that moment all the defensiveness deserted her. Her face crumpled. "I'm sorry," she whispered.

Then she did something that Franny had never expected to see. She ran toward her stepmother, threw her arms around her, and started to cry.

"Don't worry," Franny soothed, as once her mother had soothed her. "We'll figure something out. Don't upset yourself."

Olivia looked up at her, wide eyes filled with desperation. "Please—will you tell my father for me?"

Franny could think of nothing worse. But she knew she couldn't refuse the request. The girl looked so young and scared—in fact, she was little more than a child herself. Remembering how she had been in a similar position at Olivia's age, Franny wished that she could share her story with her stepdaughter. She settled instead for agreeing to do what Olivia asked.

"Of course. Leave your father to me."

"Who did this to her?" Max's voice was like steel. It was later that night. After settling her stepdaughter down to rest that afternoon, Franny had called her husband's office and requested that he return home immediately. As soon as he'd gotten through the door, she had taken him into his study and told him all about Olivia. So far, all he had asked was who was responsible for his daughter's condition. It was the one question Franny didn't have an answer to.

"I really don't know. She wouldn't tell me."

Although she'd repeatedly asked Olivia who she had been sleeping with and for how long, her stepdaughter had refused to reveal any details. But from the size of her, Franny would guess that she must be at least four months along.

Max stood up. "Well, she'll damn well tell me."

"Actually, I'm certain she won't." Franny's voice was calm. "I spent a long time with her today, and she was very clear that she didn't want the father involved."

She'd expected Max to argue with her, to insist on speaking to his daughter himself, but he must have sensed that she meant what she'd said. In that moment, the reality of what was happening must have

finally sunk in, because his face turned completely white, and he faltered. He clutched at the desk to steady himself, and then sat down
heavily in the chair. Burying his head in his hands, he let out a sob.
"Oh, God."

Franny felt her heart contract. It was awful, seeing the man she
loved, usually so confident and sure of himself, broken by this.

"It's all my fault!" he cried. "I should have known. I should have
protected her."

Franny could bear it no longer. Sinking down beside him, she pried
his hands away and drew him to her, holding him as he sobbed against
her.

"What are we going to do?" he asked. "What *can* we do?"

It was a rhetorical question, meant to convey that in his opinion
there was nothing that could be done about this situation. But Franny
had an answer ready. She had given this a lot of thought this afternoon,
and the solution seemed, to her at least, really quite simple.

"I have an idea," she said quietly.

He looked up at her then, his wet eyes hopeful. "What is it?"

"I think we should let her have the baby."

"And then what? Have it adopted?"

"Well, yes, in a way." Seeing Max frown in confusion, she took a deep
breath and said, "I think we should raise Olivia's child as our own."

55

The knowledge that Olivia, not her mother, had given birth sat heavily with Cara. Not least because it meant that Franny couldn't have been depressed over the loss of her child. But there was something else bothering Cara. According to Dr. Robertson's notes, he had delivered a healthy baby girl on December 5, 1958. This was no stillbirth, as Franny and Max had claimed. So what had happened that had made him sign a false death certificate two days later? And why had they needed to cover it up?

It was dark by the time Cara got back to Stanhope Castle, and the gothic building looked even creepier than usual. On the drive back, she'd been trying to decide how to proceed. She wished she could call Jake, ask his advice. But recalling how she'd left things with him, Cara knew that she had to do this alone. She remembered Gabriel pointing out Max's study to her the previous day. Surely if there were going to be any clues to what had happened, they would be among his personal possessions.

That night, Cara waited by the window in her room. Sure enough, on the dot of nine, Max came out of the main house and made his way to the guesthouse. Once the door closed behind him, she hurried down to his study. It was unlocked. She didn't know how long he was going to be, so she needed to work fast. Kneeling down behind his desk, Cara switched on the flashlight she'd brought with her and began to search through the drawers. She had no idea what she was looking for, but she was sure there must be something here to give her a clue about what was going on.

The drawers were arranged neatly, so it was easy enough to rifle through them quickly. Mostly there were files of bank statements and legal correspondence relating to Max's business interests. But finally, hidden at the back of the bottom drawer, she found several batches of what looked like personal correspondence. She opened the first envelope and took out the letter. It was an ordinary sheet of white paper, and the handwritten address at the top was for the Sisters of Charity Orphanage in nearby San Francisco. With her flashlight, Cara quickly scanned the contents. It was from the mother superior there, written in early 1959, giving an update on one of the children, a girl named Sophie. Pulling out another envelope, from a different stack, Cara saw that the letter was dated 1962, and it was from the same nun about the same child.

Cara tried three more letters, all from different batches, and each time found the same thing—they were written about the welfare of a child named Sophie; all that differed was the dates. From what she could see, they came up to the previous month. Cara wanted to stay longer, see if she could find anything else, but she was afraid that Max might come back and catch her. Stuffing the letters back into their envelopes, she replaced the bundle in the drawer where she'd found it. She thought it looked exactly as it had before, but it was hard to tell. She'd just have to hope that Max didn't notice.

As Cara hurried upstairs, something was nagging in the back of her mind, something that she half remembered reading. In her room, she reached for the old newspaper clippings that she'd brought with her on Franny, flipping through them until she finally found what she was looking for: a small news item in the *San Francisco Journal* about a large donation that Maximilian Stanhope had made in December 1958, following the death of his child. Sure enough, the donation was to the Sisters of Charity Orphanage.

Sitting on the bed, Cara ran through what she knew. Max had donated money to the orphanage and in return had received monthly updates on the progress of one of the children—the same child every month. It was too much of a coincidence. It *must* be Olivia's daughter. But if, as she suspected, Max and Franny had originally intended to pass the child off as their own, what had happened to change their mind? And what connection did it have to her mother's death?

The next morning, Cara called the Sisters of Charity Orphanage and spoke to the mother superior to arrange a meeting. She concocted a story about writing an article on education in state-run institutions, made it sound as if it could help with fund-raising. She avoided asking to see the kids, knowing that would be where the authorities started to get twitchy.

It was a three-hour drive to San Francisco. Cara set off early the next morning and was there by lunchtime. The orphanage was in an affluent part of town, and as she passed the elegant town houses on Lombard Street, she thought it looked like a nice place to live. Her car struggled up Telegraph Hill to where the orphanage was located near the top. She found somewhere to park, pulled the hand brake up as hard as she could, and prepared to enter the Sisters of Charity Orphanage.

Cara had worried about the memories that coming to a place like this might stir up, but to her relief the Sisters of Charity Orphanage looked nothing like St. Mary's in Galway. Perhaps once upon a time it had been a scary gray stone building, a place of penance and abstinence, but someone had gone to the trouble of making it seem welcoming for the kids. The exterior was now a pretty pale lemon, and a cheerful hand-painted sign hung above the door, welcoming visitors to the Sisters of Charity Orphanage.

Mother Superior was on the steps waiting to greet Cara. She was surprisingly young, in her early forties. A round, cheerful woman, with cheeks like rosy apples and a genuinely wide smile, Cara immediately liked her.

"How wonderful to meet you, my dear!" She took Cara's hand, squeezing it warmly. "Let's go through to my office, and we can talk."

The inside was just as welcoming as the exterior. Multicolored murals covered the walls. Some showed real promise; others had clearly been made by younger children, with more enthusiasm than talent. As they walked deeper into the building, Cara could hear shouts of delight coming from outside. She looked quizzically at Mother Superior.

"It's playtime," the nun explained.

Just then they passed a long, low window, which looked out onto a large central courtyard. Dozens of kids were out there, enjoying their break: there were basketball hoops, girls with skipping ropes, as well as climbing frames, swings, and merry-go-rounds. It was nothing like the orphanage back in Ireland. Cara was pleased; at least Olivia's child was somewhere pleasant.

"We had a sponsored walk last year. It paid for all the equipment," Mother Superior informed her proudly.

Her office contained nothing but a desk, two wooden chairs, and a set of filing cabinets. There were a simple crucifix on the wall and a picture of Our Lady with the baby Jesus. Cara was wondering how to get started in such a way that led round to talking about the child, but Mother Superior got there first. Sitting back in her chair, she smiled at Cara. "So why don't you tell me why you're really here?"

"I'm here about a child," Cara told her. "She would have been left here in early December 1958. And her name's Sophie."

It was strange, the reverend mother thought, that this street-smart Englishwoman should come here now, inquiring about Sophie. Even though she hadn't realized it at the time, that night, fourteen years ago, had changed the course of her life. Back then she had been a hesitant novice, little Sister Marie, unsure if she should even be taking the veil. But the then reverend mother, whose heart had finally given out earlier this year at the age of eighty, had seen the arrival of that strange, mysterious baby as an opportunity to help the novice see her calling in life. The bond between Sister Marie and Sophie had shaped the nun's future.

Sister Marie had changed over that first year that Sophie had been with them, from a flighty girl to a caring young woman who took her responsibilities seriously. Before the reverend mother had died in January, she had made it clear that she felt Sister Marie should be her replacement. The other nuns and Church governors had voted unanimously in agreement.

But this striking dark-haired woman wasn't to know of the momentous impact Sophie had had on the nun's life.

"And what do you want with Sophie?" the mother superior asked.

"I just need to see her, that's all," Cara said. "I want to make sure that she's all right. Do you know where she is now?"

The reverend mother studied the young woman in front of her. Perhaps another person would be suspicious of this stranger's intentions. But she believed herself to be a good judge of character, and she sensed that whoever this Cara Healey was, she didn't mean any harm to the child, so she decided to answer honestly.

"Why, yes, of course I know where Sophie is." The nun nodded toward the window. "She's outside playing."

Cara didn't know what to say. She'd half expected the reverend mother to tell her that the girl had been adopted by a nice, loving family and that it was best to forget her altogether. But to find out that she was *here,* only a few steps away, changed everything.

"Do you think it'd be all right if I met her?" Cara asked.

Mother Superior hesitated for a moment. "Yes, I suppose that would be fine," she answered cautiously. "But before I bring her in, perhaps you should prepare yourself."

"What do you mean?"

"Well, you see, Sophie's not like other children. She's *special.* You'll understand when you meet her."

As the nun went to fetch the child, Cara wondered what on earth she meant by that.

It was ten minutes before Mother Superior appeared in the doorway. "I'm just having a little trouble getting Sophie to come in. She's terribly shy."

She turned back to talk to the child, who was obviously hovering outside, out of Cara's line of sight. It seemed odd to Cara. The girl was nearly fourteen now. It was unusual for someone that age to be so bashful.

"Now, come on, sweetheart," Sister Marie coaxed the child. "There's nothing to be afraid of."

There was a moment's pause. Then, as the door was tentatively pulled back, Cara stood up. She felt strangely nervous, meeting this child for the first time.

A girl appeared in the doorway. A fair-haired, fair-skinned, blue-eyed girl: a perfect replica of Olivia.

Except . . .

Except as the Reverend Mother ushered the child forward, Cara saw that something wasn't quite right about Sophie. She shuffled forward, unable to walk properly, her head lolling from side to side, her eyes refusing to focus. And Cara realized then why her mother and Max had decided not to keep Sophie—because she wasn't the perfect child that they'd longed for.

56

That night, in Max's study, the decision was made. Olivia would have the child in secret, and they would raise it as their own. The solution had seemed obvious to Franny. Max wanted a baby, but it seemed that they would never be able to have one. Olivia was pregnant with a child she could never keep, unless she wanted to be shunned socially. This would be best for everyone. And Franny herself? Well, she saw this as her second chance, her opportunity to do the right thing. She couldn't forgive herself for abandoning Cara—she didn't want Olivia to live with the same burden for the rest of her life. And once the baby was born, Franny would tell Max about her own child. If she helped him with this problem, he'd surely be more amenable to accepting Cara.

The most difficult part was persuading Max. At first he was reluctant, concerned about how hard it would be on Olivia. "How will she cope, seeing the baby every day but not being able to admit it's her own? It's a lot for someone her age to deal with."

Franny was ready for that argument. "But what's the alternative?" she asked. "Forcing her to get rid of it?"

Max recoiled, as she'd known he would. "No, of course not!"

"Then what do you suggest?" Franny asked forcefully. "For her to have the baby—to see it take its first breath and hold it in her arms—only to have to hand it over to a stranger, never to see it again? At least if we raise the child as our own, Olivia will still be part of her baby's life."

Max didn't answer right away, and his silence gave Franny hope. She slipped her hand into his. She knew this was the right course of action—if only she could make Max understand. "It's the best solution for everyone," she said gently. "I promise."

Max ran a weary hand across his face. The whole incident with his daughter had shaken him badly. Right now he was willing to accept any solution. He looked up at his wife with resignation in his eyes. "Perhaps it would be best if you told her what we've agreed to?"

Franny sat on the edge of her stepdaughter's bed. Lying curled up under her bedclothes, Olivia listened as her stepmother explained what had been decided. Tucked up with a hot-water bottle and a mug of hot cocoa, it felt almost like the times she had been ill as a child. It was hard for her to cope with the notion that there was a baby growing inside her. The whole situation felt slightly unreal. She had been ignoring the problem for months, hoping that it would go away. It had been almost a relief today when Franny had found out. At least now there was someone else to share the burden.

"So what do you think of our idea?"

Olivia looked up at her stepmother. She was clearly trying to disguise her eagerness, but Olivia could hear it in her voice. Franny was desperate for her to agree to their suggestion, for her father and Franny to raise the child as their own. She supposed, on balance, that it seemed like the best solution. It wasn't as though she had any alternative to offer. And she was so scared, had been terrified for months of what was going to happen to her, that it felt good to let a grown-up take charge.

"I think you're right," she said slowly. "It would be for the best."

"Oh, darling." Franny took Olivia in her arms. If she was aware that her stepdaughter wasn't returning her embrace, she managed to overlook it. Eventually she pulled away a little. Her expression was earnest as she said, "We'll get through this, sweetheart, I promise. I know it probably seems overwhelming now, but in time you'll see it's all for the best. And I will be here to make sure you have everything you need."

She looked at Olivia expectantly. The girl got the feeling she was meant to say something in reply. "Thank you?"

It was almost a question. Franny beamed. "So, on that note, can I get you anything?" she asked.

Olivia shook her head, trying to think of some way that she would be left alone. "No, thank you. I'm just tired now. I'd like to go to sleep, if you don't mind."

They were, as she would learn over the next few months, the magic words. Franny immediately got to her feet. "Of course you're tired. How thoughtless of me—I'll leave you be. Just let me know if you need anything."

Olivia smiled weakly up at her.

After her stepmother left, Olivia got up from the bed and went over to her dressing table. There, hidden under a pile of neatly folded scarves, was the gin bottle she'd stolen earlier. She'd first started drinking it after overhearing some girls at school say that gin and a hot bath would get rid of a baby. But by the time she'd found that the alcohol hadn't worked, she'd developed a taste for it. If nothing else, it helped her forget for a little while. And after the events of the day, that was exactly what she wanted to do.

The deception required a lot of planning. It was decided straight off that Olivia should be permanently removed from her school. The fact that she had been growing distant from her friends and had gotten herself suspended helped; it was a good justification for why she wasn't going back.

"She clearly isn't thriving under your regime," Max told the headmistress, leaving her in no doubt as to where he felt the blame lay. "So it's been decided that she'll be home-schooled for the time being." They could always get her into another school after the baby was born.

Fooling the outside world was easy enough. There was no reason for anyone to suspect that the baby wasn't Franny's, and she made sure not to give them one. First she declared from the rooftops that she was pregnant. She said that she was four months gone, a little late for an announcement, but she could justify it by saying that they didn't want to jinx it until they were sure.

Luckily Gabriel was away traveling over the summer and would start at Stanford in the fall, so they didn't need to worry about letting him in on what was happening. It would be harder to fool the servants. Max insisted that Hilda be taken into their confidence.

"I know you've never gotten on with her," he told Franny. "But she's worked here for twenty years, and she's always been loyal to me."

Despite her reservations, Franny could see that his suggestion made sense. Hilda could keep the other servants away from her and Olivia. Also, before coming to work for Max she'd had some training as a nurse, so she could monitor the girl during her pregnancy and help at the time of delivery, so they wouldn't need to get Dr. Robertson involved. Knowing that his friend would hear about Franny's pregnancy, Max told him that his wife had decided to go to another practice, saying she felt more comfortable with a female physician. The doctor hadn't questioned the lie.

The most difficult part was telling Lily that day at the Brown Derby. Franny had dreaded the lunch, knowing that she was going to have to lie to her friend's face. She felt uncomfortable throughout the whole meal and knew that her shifty behavior made Lily suspect that something was up. But it had been a necessary part of the plan.

Franny tried to involve Olivia in the preparations for the baby, but her stepdaughter didn't seem interested. When she asked Olivia to choose colors for the nursery, the girl simply shrugged; when Franny produced a book of names, Olivia responded listlessly. "It's up to you."

Franny had a feeling that she was still brokenhearted over whoever had fathered the child. She still refused to reveal his identity. It didn't stop Max asking.

"I won't tell you," Olivia insisted, her mouth setting into a stubborn line. "Whatever you say or do, I won't tell."

So Max, concerned about upsetting his daughter in her condition, had to let it go.

Of course as the weeks moved on, it got harder to keep up the hoax. By choice, Olivia rarely left her room, and when she did, her loose clothing concealed her condition from the staff at Stanhope Castle. Max had access to the studio's props department, so he was able to obtain false bumps for Franny, but by the beginning of October, when she was meant to be seven months' pregnant, she decided it was too risky to continue seeing outsiders. She therefore announced that, due to high blood pressure, her doctor had recommended that she be confined to bed.

Most of her friends were prepared to accept what she said. After all, they were a squeamish bunch and had no desire to make the journey out to Stanhope Castle unless it was for an elaborate party. The thought of sitting in a darkened room, even for an hour, did not appeal to them. Only Lily—loyal Lily—pressed for a visit.

"I can come out whenever you want, sweetheart," she offered. "I'll bring some games, keep you entertained."

Franny had to employ all her acting skills to put her friend off. "Oh, darling! It's awfully kind of you to offer, but I'm a sight at the moment. Honestly, you'll take one look at me and run for the hills!"

But despite Franny's assurances, Lily wasn't able to let it go. "Everything's all right there, isn't it?" she pressed. "Max is treating you well?"

"He's being a doll."

"Well, as long as you're sure." Lily sounded doubtful, but there was nothing more she could do.

It was hard for Franny, knowing that her friend clearly thought Max was harming her in some way. But once the baby was born and they could go out in public and let everyone see that they were a happy little family, everything would go back to normal.

A month before the baby was due, Franny went up to Olivia's room to show her some baby clothes that Hilda had knitted. It was early evening, and her stepdaughter had been in her room most of the day—something that happened a lot recently. Knocking lightly, Franny heard a muffled reply, which she assumed meant to come in. She opened the door, putting on the bright smile that she always did when talking about anything to do with the baby. But as she walked in, Franny froze. Olivia was curled up on the window seat, a bottle of gin in her hand.

Hearing her stepmother, Olivia glanced over in Franny's direction. "I told you—go *'way*," the girl insisted, her eyes unfocused.

She was drunk.

It took Franny a moment to react. Then she charged across the room, snatching the bottle from her stepdaughter. "You stupid girl!" she exploded. "Do you know what this could do to the baby?"

Olivia got unsteadily to her feet. "That's all you care 'bout, isn't it? The baby. Well, I don't. I want it gone." She snatched the bottle back and took another large gulp.

Franny raised her hand and without thinking brought it down across her stepdaughter's face. The girl stumbled backward, tried to grab the occasional table, but lost her footing and fell heavily to the floor.

"Oh, God!" She let out a howl of pain.

Franny clapped her hand to her mouth. What had she done? What kind of person was she to hit a young girl in that condition? "I'm so sorry!"

She held out a hand to help her stepdaughter up, but the girl ignored it. Instead, Olivia glared up at her. "You bitch," she hissed. She opened her mouth to say more but then she doubled over in pain—not the kind of pain that comes from a fall but that of a first contraction.

Franny stared at her stepdaughter in horror. The baby was coming.

Olivia screamed. The sound tore through the house, making the hairs on Franny's arms stand on end. The servants had been dismissed for the evening, and Franny wished she could have gone with them. She wanted to put her hands over her ears to shut out the sound; close her eyes so she wouldn't have to see the blood. So much blood.

Luckily Hilda was there. She'd taken charge. Max was outside, pacing, worried, but content to leave the birthing to the women.

"Quiet, now," the housekeeper shushed the girl. "No need for all this fussing. Plenty before you have done this without such complaining."

Remembering her own labor, Franny went over to where Olivia lay on the bed, exposed and humiliated but in too much pain to care. The girl looked up at her with wide, frightened eyes. "Make it stop," she begged. "I can't stand it any longer."

Franny took her stepdaughter's hand. "It will all be over soon," she promised. But even to her, the assurance sounded weak. Olivia let out another scream.

Ten long hours of labor. Screaming. Blood. More screaming.

As the evening wore on, the noise began to subside. By midnight, Olivia lay exhausted on the bed, her body covered in a layer of sweat, her damp hair stuck to her gray face. She could only groan weakly as the contractions ripped through her. There was no sign that the baby was any closer to coming out.

Franny went outside to take a break. But she found that she couldn't make herself go back in. Unable to stand the sounds, Max had retreated to his study a long time ago.

Even the usually calm Hilda looked frightened. "It shouldn't be taking this long." The grim-faced housekeeper had come to stand by Franny's side. "The baby's in distress. I've never seen anything this bad." She paused and then voiced what Franny had been thinking: "If we don't do something soon, I'm worried we'll lose them both."

Franny made a decision. "I'll talk to Max."

*   *   *

Max called his friend Dr. Robertson. The doctor had been at a dinner party and turned up wearing black tie. Franny and Max gave him a brief explanation of what had happened. He looked at them both with undisguised disgust and then got down to business. He could save the reprimands for later.

"Where is the girl?"

Max spoke. "In her room. I'll take you there."

He stood outside while Franny took the doctor in. Olivia did little more than whimper now as each new contraction came. It was obvious she was fading fast.

The doctor did a quick examination and then gave his assessment. "The baby's breech. That means its legs are coming out first." He was already rolling up his sleeves. "It's too late for a cesarean, but I'll see what I can do."

Franny and Hilda were standing by. "How can we help?" Franny asked.

The doctor looked between the two women. He nodded at Hilda. "You can stay." Then to Franny, "*You* just stand outside, please."

Franny and Max held hands together in the hallway. The door was slightly ajar, so they could hear the sounds from inside. There was one last low grunt from Olivia, then a long pause followed by the sound of flesh being slapped. Dr. Robertson murmured beneath his breath— whether it was words of encouragement or a prayer, Franny wasn't sure—but whatever it was must have worked, because suddenly they heard the first cry of the baby.

The door opened, and Dr. Robertson stepped out. Franny got a brief glimpse of Hilda holding out the baby to Olivia, who was lying back, exhausted. She felt relief run through her—they were both all right. She looked up at Max and saw that he, too, had seen that everything was fine. They exchanged brief smiles. The doctor came out then and told them that Olivia had had a little girl. Max offered him his hand.

"Thank you for everything. I-I can't believe they're both all right."

Dr Robertson pointedly ignored the outstretched hand. He looked exhausted. His shirt sleeves were rolled up, and his white dress shirt was smeared with blood.

"Let me get cleaned up, and we can talk" was all he would say.

Franny wanted to ask more but didn't dare.

Twenty minutes later, in the privacy of Max's study, Dr. Robertson broke the news to them. "Olivia's baby was deprived of oxygen for too long." He made no effort to hide his contempt. It was obvious where he felt the blame for the whole situation lay. Even friendship had its limits. There were some things that couldn't be excused. "I would say that she suffered massive brain damage."

"Oh God, no!" The words were out before Franny could stop them. She clamped a hand over her mouth to stop herself saying anything else.

The doctor carried on as though she hadn't spoken. "It's hard at this stage to say exactly how bad it is. But I imagine that she's going to need constant care her entire life."

There was silence. He'd made no effort to soften the blow, deciding they didn't deserve it. Franny glanced over at Max. He didn't look her way.

"And Olivia?" Max asked. He looked haggard, as though he was in shock, still waiting for his friend's words to register. There was no trace of the urbane businessman about him. Usually he was so composed, but after what he'd watched his daughter go through that night, he felt weak and ineffectual. "Is she going to be all right?"

"Physically, yes, eventually she will recover. But psychologically . . ." The doctor shook his head. "Someone her age should never have had to endure this trauma. I think we'll only know with time how badly she's been affected."

57

Cara drove back to Stanhope Castle as fast as she could. Seeing Sophie, finding out about her condition, had changed everything. It was time to act, she decided, clutching the steering wheel tightly as she sped along the twisting coastal roads. It was time to bring this all out into the open.

It was time to confront Max.

She was tired of his games. He was the one who'd invited her to come out here, who had said that he had something to tell her. And then, since she'd arrived, he'd gone out of his way to avoid her. She was going to demand that he gave her some answers.

Parking roughly in the driveway, Cara stormed into the house, calling Max's name as she went. She had never been so angry. Her mother and that husband of hers were no better than each other. Neither of them had thought anything of abandoning Sophie. They'd both been too concerned about themselves to care.

She marched straight to Max's study. Although she could hear voices coming from inside, she walked in without bothering to knock. Max and Hilda looked up as she came through the door.

"Excuse me!" Hilda was on her feet.

Cara ignored the housekeeper, focusing all her attention on Max. "We need to talk."

She'd caught a brief glimpse of Max two days earlier, when she'd been in the garden speaking to Gabriel. But this was the first time she'd met him properly. Up close, she could see just how ill he looked. There was little trace of the virile man he'd once been. The cancer had shrunk him, and she could see the liver spots on his hands as he wheeled out from behind his desk to face her.

"I'm sure you got my message," he said, his voice low and raspy. "I'll talk to you when I'm ready." He stopped, as though he was struggling to speak. "Whatever's bothering you can wait."

"No, it can't." She paused for a beat, and then said, "I *know*."

"Know what?"

"About Sophie."

That got Max's attention. His eyes flicked over to Hilda. "I think it's best if I talk to Cara alone."

The housekeeper didn't bother to argue. She hurried out, leaving Max and Cara alone.

"So how did you find her?" Max wanted to know.

"That's hardly the important point here, is it?" Cara snapped.

"Then what is?"

"That you've been lying all these years! Firstly, claiming that your child died. Not to mention it was never *your* child in the first place."

Max went very still. "What do you mean by that?"

"Oh, please. I know the child was Olivia's. I saw the doctor's records."

He couldn't keep the shock from his face. "How dare you dig into my family's lives like this!"

"Again, that's not important," Cara said dismissively, refusing to get distracted from the main point. "What *is* important is that you sent away that poor baby. What kind of people were you, to off-load a child like that, your own flesh and blood, simply because she wasn't perfect? Would it have been that much of an inconvenience to have her here? You could have hired the best nurses to look after her. You could have given her a home. But instead you abandoned her with people who could have been cruel and abusive."

"It was a good place!" Max retorted. "The nuns have given her nothing but the best care."

"Perhaps. But did you know that? Or did you just hope for the best?"

Cara was aware that somewhere along the way she'd stopped talking about Sophie and started referring to herself, as though this were a conversation she was having with her mother. All the resentment that she felt over the years was flooding out.

She shook her head in disgust. "You saw that Sophie wasn't the perfect little baby you wanted, and so you hid her away."

Max closed his eyes for a brief moment. "It wasn't like that. It wasn't because of Sophie's condition."

"Then what was it?" Cara pressed. "Why did you leave her there? What made you abandon your own grandchild to an institution?"

"Because of Olivia!" he burst out, finally cracking under the pressure of her questions. "Because my daughter blamed herself for the way Sophie was born. She was already fragile enough before everything that happened. Having the child here would have been a constant reminder of what she'd done!"

58

"It's my fault, isn't it?" Olivia stared up at her stepmother with dead eyes. "It's because I'd been drinking. That's why Sophie's the way she is."

The doctor had gone now. He'd given Olivia a tranquilizer before he left—something to calm her down and help her sleep. Hilda was looking after the baby and Max had holed himself up in his office, so Franny had offered to sit with her stepdaughter. Unfortunately, Olivia still seemed to want to torture herself over what had happened that day.

"You shouldn't blame yourself," Franny told her stepdaughter yet again. "It was a breech birth. That had nothing to do with you. If anything, your father and I are to blame. If we'd got the doctor sooner, then things would have turned out differently."

"I don't believe you." Olivia started to weep again. "You're just trying to make me feel better."

"No, I'm not."

But Olivia refused to listen. "It doesn't matter what you say, I *know* it was my fault. I'm a horrible, disgusting person." She turned away from her stepmother then, burrowing her head into the pillows as she cried.

Over the next few days, Franny, Max, and Dr. Robertson all tried to tell Olivia that she wasn't to blame, but it didn't make any difference—she wouldn't listen to them.

Franny still wanted to keep the baby, but Max wouldn't hear of it. "Olivia's hardly functioning as it is. How is she going to feel, seeing her child every day? A permanent reminder of everything that's happened?"

He was right, of course. Since the birth, Olivia had sunk into a deep depression. She didn't speak, eat, or sleep. She spent most of her time crying.

With the baby gone, left at the Sisters of Charity Orphanage one cold, foggy night by the troubled Max and the tearful Franny, it was hoped that Olivia might improve. But if anything, she seemed to get worse.

Max finally insisted on taking her to see a specialist, at Cranfield House, a discreet institution recommended by Dr. Robertson. Clayton Lorimer, the head psychiatrist at what was essentially an asylum, quickly delivered his assessment.

"Electroshock therapy is the only way forward."

Max couldn't conceal his horror. "Is that really necessary? There must be some other way."

The doctor sighed. The parents were always so squeamish, so ready to question his advice. "Olivia is very depressed," he told the businessman. "In my opinion, EST is the only way to jolt her out of that state. Otherwise she could be like this forever."

Max looked at his beloved daughter, staring glassy-eyed at nothing in particular, and reluctantly agreed.

Max insisted on being present while she had the treatment. Franny didn't think it was a good idea but agreed to go along with him for support. She hated Cranfield House: with its clinical white floors and walls, the terrified screams, and the lights that flickered from electrical surges. This was no place for Olivia to be, in her opinion. But Max felt it was for the best.

There was a glass wall that let him see inside the treatment room. He made himself watch everything. First two nurses led Olivia into the room. She looked calm, docile even, dressed in a simple white nightdress. Her feet were bare. The room was stark, apart from the array of contraptions that looked like medieval torture instruments. When she saw the gurney and realized what was about to happen, she began to protest. As the orderlies strapped her down, pulling the restraints tight around her wrists and ankles and across her chest, she began to beg for Max's help.

"Please, Daddy. Don't let them do this to me." She wriggled and twisted in vain. "Daddy, stop them, please."

"Try not to listen," the doctor said with an air of professional detachment.

Max wanted to say, "How can I not listen when my baby is pleading with me for help?" As the leather bit was fitted between her teeth to stop her swallowing her tongue, she was no longer able to speak. But Max could still see her eyes, beseeching him to intervene, reproaching him for having ever considered doing something like this to her. He wanted to tell them to stop, but then he remembered the way Olivia had been these past few weeks and how the doctor had assured him that this was the only way to help her.

The orderlies moved to a safe distance. The doctor pulled a lever down. Max could hear the electricity pulsing through the air. As the charge hit Olivia, her body began to convulse and spasm, her back arching off the table. Her eyes bulged; there was a smell of singed hair. Then mercifully, after thirty seconds, the machine was switched off. Olivia's body flopped limply down onto the gurney.

The doctor said, "We'll give her a minute's break, and then we'll go again."

Olivia must have understood what was being said, because through the mouthpiece she gave a groan of protest. She sounded weak. When the current struck again, her body still jerked, but there seemed to be less of a fight this time. When she came to rest, she emitted little more than a whimper.

Max turned to Franny, and there were tears streaming down his face as he said, "What have I done? What on earth have I done to my daughter?"

59

Cara faltered, her temples throbbing. She forced herself to focus. She could understand now why Max hadn't wanted to keep the child, why they had constructed an elaborate plan to conceal Sophie's birth. But it left Franny's death unexplained.

"So if Franny didn't kill herself over the baby, then what *did* happen to her?" She waited a beat and then said, "Did *you* have something to do with her death?"

"Why do you ask that?" Max looked coolly at her, his expression giving nothing away.

Cara's heart was beating hard: part of her was scared of the answer, scared of what he might do to her to prevent people finding out. But she had to know.

"Because right now it seems like the only answer is that you were somehow involved. Up until Franny met you, she was a famous actress with a good career. Then, within two years of marrying you, she was dead. Now, I don't know exactly what happened. But from what I heard, you had a lot to do with what went wrong."

"In what way?"

Max's tone was soft, but Cara could hear the latent anger simmering beneath the surface. She chose to ignore it. Instead, she began to list all the things she'd heard.

"You were controlling," she told him. "You hid her away up here and interfered with her career." As Cara spoke, she began to warm to her theme. "By the time she'd been living with you for two years, she'd changed from a confident, outgoing woman to a drunk who looked as though she'd gone a few rounds in a boxing ring."

Max's eyes hardened. "So, like everyone else you've chosen to believe idle gossip instead of trying to find out the truth for yourself."

"Well, give me a reason not to."

"Fine!" Max snapped. "You really want to know the truth?" He didn't wait for a reply. "I can tell you for a fact that your mother wasn't a drunk. Nor was I beating her. And I certainly, at no point, ever sabotaged her career."

Cara stared at him, trying to decide whether she believed him. He looked as though he was telling the truth, but it was hard to be certain. "Then what *was* wrong with her?"

"She was sick," he answered without hesitation. "Your mother was very sick. And she didn't want anyone to know."

60

As the months went by, Stanhope Castle settled back into some semblance of normality. Olivia was still in Cranfield House. Franny and Max went to visit her once a week. The doctors had declared the EST to be a success, but Franny was less convinced. Although Olivia had stopped crying hysterically since the treatment, now she simply stared into space all day.

Gabriel knew nothing of what had been going on with his sister. He was busy at Stanford now, and hadn't been home to visit in a while. Max still hadn't figured out what he was going to tell his son about what had happened to Olivia. It was something he was going to have to confront at some point, but first there was a more pressing problem concerning his wife to deal with.

It was Max who finally insisted that Franny go to see a doctor. It was after the mix-up over Hunter's birthday party, when she had completely forgotten about their plans to meet up at the venue. Franny hadn't seemed right for some months. She was tired all the time, staying in bed until late into the day, and when she was up, she seemed distracted, as though she couldn't focus. Not to mention the ongoing clumsiness. She was covered in bruises, and he knew that more than one person suspected that he was the cause of them. He'd been worried about her for a while now. This lethargic, defeated creature wasn't the woman he had married.

"This has gone on long enough," he said one day. "You don't seem well, my love. You haven't for a long time."

She turned listless eyes up at him. "I'm fine," she said flatly.

"No, damn it. I'm insisting on this." He took her in his arms. "You're too precious to me. I can't have something bad happening to someone else I love. I couldn't stand it."

Dr. Robertson had seen Franny several times in the past few months. Her depression had been obvious to him, but he'd assumed it was to do with the Olivia situation, which hadn't been easy on anyone. But it was Max's insistence that something more was wrong, that it wasn't all in her head, that made him look for another explanation.

It would have been easy enough to misdiagnose the real cause of her problems. The symptoms were so general: the anxiety and depression, the lack of coordination and memory loss. But watching her walk into the room, he saw that she no longer glided but her gait was ever so slightly off, her hand movements a little jerky. These developments, almost undetectable to the eye, rang an alarm bell in his head. To be certain of his suspicions, he referred her to an old friend of his, a Dr. Gillon, one of the leading neurologists in the United States.

He made Franny talk him through her symptoms in painstaking detail and then carried out some physical tests to measure her eye movement, hearing, reflexes, and coordination. Then he asked her to tell him about her family history. He seemed especially interested in her father's death, something she hadn't been there for, so she had to rehash what her mother had told her: that after years of sobriety, they suspected he had been drinking, and then one morning he'd driven the tractor into a ditch and died from his injuries.

Dr. Gillon nodded along as Franny spoke. She was getting increasingly worried throughout the appointment.

"Well?" she demanded finally, when she could stand it no longer. "Do you know what's wrong with me?"

His heavy sigh told her it wasn't good news. "I'm sorry to have to tell you this, but I think you have Huntington's disease."

Huntington's disease was notoriously hard to diagnose, Dr. Gillon told Franny. Before the nineteenth century, sufferers had often been persecuted as witches or thought to have been possessed. Even now, it was often misdiagnosed as alcoholism or insanity.

"You're lucky, really," the doctor said. "At least you know."

Sitting there in shock, listening to him run through the implications, Franny didn't feel very lucky—to learn that she had a degenerative disease that was going to erode her body and mind for the next ten or twenty years before she succumbed to pneumonia or heart disease. Because there was no cure, Dr. Gillon told her; no treatment, even, to ease the symptoms.

Max clutched her hand tighter. He had come with her to the appointment, waiting patiently outside, but once she'd heard the bad news she had asked him to come in and sit with her, knowing that she was still in too much shock to fully take in what the doctor was saying.

"But if this is a hereditary disease, why haven't any of her other family members had it?" Max asked. He looked over at his beautiful wife, fighting to understand how this could be happening to her.

"From what Franny's told me about her father, it may have been passed down on his side. As I've said before, the disease can be hard to diagnose, and it can often be mistaken for other ailments. He may well have died before becoming symptomatic."

Dr. Gillon suggested that Franny visit Mayfield Care Home, that it might help her to come to terms with the illness. "You can see how patients who are in a more advanced stage than you are coping with their illness. It might be therapeutic."

Franny knew that it was the doctor's way of getting her to face up to the realities of the disease. But even she hadn't been prepared for how bad it would be. On the day that he'd first diagnosed her, Dr. Gillon had run through the prognosis. But hearing him describe the breakdown of a patient's body in excruciating detail still wasn't the same as actually seeing it in the flesh: the bodies in spasm; the minds gone; the smell of incontinence. Standing in the ward, all she could think was: *That's going to be me.* It didn't matter what she did, she couldn't avoid the inevitable process: she was going to get sick, and after a long, drawn-out illness, she would die a painful death.

Max, who had insisted on coming with her, took her by the arm and said, "Let's go."

That whole evening, Franny could think of nothing but what she'd seen that day. She couldn't stand to end up that way.

So once Max had gone to bed that night, she crept downstairs, drank a bottle of brandy, and went out to her Pontiac.

61

Sitting in Max's study, Cara felt a chill pass over her as he reached the end of the story. She'd spent so long assuming that he was the bad guy, that he'd somehow harmed her mother, that it was a shock to find out that something else had caused her to go downhill.

"So you're saying that she found out she was sick and then—what? She killed herself? Have I got that right?"

Max hesitated. "Not exactly."

"Then what *did* happen to her?"

"It's hard to explain," Max said.

"Well, try."

He looked at her for a long moment. "I would, but it's not my secret to tell."

"Oh, for God's sake!" she exploded.

He held up his hands, to quiet her. "But maybe I can persuade the person in question to speak to you."

"Where is this mysterious person?" Cara couldn't keep the skepticism out of her voice.

"In one of the guesthouses."

The guesthouse—where Hilda lived.

"So? What are we waiting for?"

Cara followed Max outside and along the path to the guesthouse which she had seen him visit the night before. She was aware that she might have put herself into a dangerous situation: being alone with someone she suspected of killing her mother. But she needed to find out the truth.

The building was one of four guesthouses on the estate. This was the smallest of them all, a chocolate-box-style bungalow. Unlike the rest of the grounds, the garden was beautifully tended, and there were white sheets pinned onto a washing line, blowing in the afternoon breeze. A ramp led up to the front door. At the bottom, Max paused. "Please wait outside."

"No way." She hadn't come this far to be fobbed off again.

"Please." He looked weary. "Just trust me."

Something in his tone made her relent. "All right. I'll give you five minutes."

She watched him disappear into the house and settled down to wait.

Cara paced up and down the gravel driveway. Five minutes passed. And then ten. He'd been in the house for fifteen minutes when she finally gave up. Whether he was ready for her or not, she was going in.

Hilda opened the door to her. So it wasn't her that Max was talking to. "Mr. Stanhope asked that you wait outside."

"Well, I'm tired of waiting." Cara strode past the woman, refusing to be intimidated by the officious tone.

The house was all on one level, making it easy to search. Cara pushed open the doors to every room, looking for Max: a sitting room, a bright, airy kitchen, a small, neat bedroom that was clearly Hilda's, a family-sized bathroom. As she went, the housekeeper followed behind her. "Miss! Please, if you could just wait!"

Finally Cara reached a closed door at the back of the house.

"Please! Wait!"

Hilda grabbed at her arm, but Cara shrugged her off. She didn't bother knocking but threw open the door. She wasn't sure what she'd been expecting, but the scene drew her up short. It was a beautiful, spacious room, clearly the master bedroom, with French windows that led out onto the garden. The room was bright and cheerful, and feminine too: the wallpaper was white with large yellow and blue flowers. Another door opened into what was no doubt an attached bathroom. But Cara's eyes were drawn to the bed: a huge king-sized bed covered in floral sheets that matched the wallpaper. A woman was sitting up in the bed, clearly a very sick woman, her body twisted and jerking; Max had drawn his wheelchair up beside her and was feeding her.

As Cara watched him carefully, lovingly spooning food into the patient's mouth, she realized this man hadn't killed anyone after all.

Because the woman in the bed was her mother.

62

When Franny woke up in the hospital and found that she was still alive, she started to cry. The nurses assumed it was from relief, but really it was disappointment. Now she would have to find some other way to kill herself quickly. Because, whatever happened, she was determined not to die a slow, painful death.

Max came to see her. She'd never seen him so angry. "How could you do something like that?" he demanded, pacing the room. "How could you be so selfish?"

"Selfish?" Franny couldn't let that go. "Is it selfish of me to want to die with dignity? Is it selfish of me to want to avoid years of pain?"

He rounded on her. "Me, me, me. That's all you think about, isn't it? Yourself." His eyes blazed. "Well, it's not all about you. This affects me, too."

Franny looked at him. She genuinely didn't understand. "How?"

"How?" he repeated in disbelief. "Can't you see that this is as devastating for me as it is for you? How do you think I feel, knowing that our time together is going to be cut short? Knowing that my wife, the woman that I love, is going to get sick and there's not a damn thing I can do about it? And however awful that realization has been, it doesn't compare to finding out that you tried to end your life. Because however hard"—tears spilled down his cheeks—"because however hard these next ten years might be, I want that time together. So you have to promise me now that you won't ever do anything like this again, because I'm telling you, Franny, I can't stand to lose you!"

He fell to his knees then, burying his head in her lap as he sobbed.

Franny stared at him for a long moment, stunned by his reaction, his show of love for her. When she'd got into her car that night, Franny hadn't given a thought to anyone's feelings but her own. It hadn't occurred to her that there were people who would mourn her death. She'd assumed Max would meet someone else in time. And Cara—well, she'd failed her daughter for so many years now that she'd genuinely felt that Cara would be better off without her. But now, seeing Max like this, realizing how much he cared for her, changed everything.

She reached out her hand and began to stroke his hair. "Please don't cry," she soothed. "I won't do it again. I promise."

Max had always loved Franny, from the first moment he'd met her in Lloyd's office. True, she could be difficult and frustrating, and she'd hurt him terribly sometimes with her flirtations and ability to attract scandal, but still, he could forgive her anything.

She'd blamed him for what had happened to her career, but in fact it had been Lloyd's decision to end her contract. It was the same fate that a lot of former stars had faced in the late 1950s, under shrinking revenues from movies. Max hadn't intervened on her behalf, because he had stood by his word not to get involved in the creative side of operations. He'd learned his lesson in his early dealings with Lloyd. There had been that time he'd mentioned something to the studio head about it being awkward for Franny and Duke to work together. He hadn't meant anything by it, but the studio head had taken it upon himself to give the male lead in *Elizabeth* to another actor. When the businessman had figured out what Lloyd had done, he'd made it clear that in future any decisions were to be made on a strictly meritocratic basis— he didn't want special favors for Franny.

And that business with Leonard, the gardener. Max hadn't had anything to do with him leaving; from what he understood, the man had moved to Detroit, thinking he'd have more luck getting a recording contract there. And from what Max had heard, before Leonard left, *he'd* been the one to leak the story about him and Franny, wanting to make some easy money to tide him over while he tried to make it as a singer. Franny had blamed all of that on her husband only because the disease had made her paranoid and unable to think straight. But in truth, Max would do anything to make Franny happy—and that's what she was counting on now.

It was her idea, of course. Ever the romantic, she was the one who dreamed up the plan to fake her own glamorous, tragic death.

She brought it up the night she got back from the hospital, after the crash. She'd gone up to her room to rest, but when Max went to check on her, he found that she was awake and sitting up in bed with a copy of *Variety* magazine laid out in front of her. She was on the cover, a glamorous head shot, pouting over her bare shoulder at the camera, all big green eyes and sensual lips. The picture had been taken at the height of her career, just before they'd met.

"I want them to remember me like this." She looked up at her husband, her beautiful eyes bright with tears. "Those poor, poor patients in that home . . ." She shuddered. "I can't let anyone see me that way, to even think of me like that."

Max's heart melted. "Oh, Franny, love." He didn't know what else to say. Instead he walked over to the bed and sat down beside his wife. He tried to take her in his arms, but she squirmed away.

"No, don't try to comfort me," she insisted. "Listen to me instead."

He had so much that he wanted to say, but he could see that she was on the brink of cracking. "All right," he said. "I'm listening."

That seemed to calm her. She breathed in deeply, fighting to get her emotions under control, and then she started to speak.

"On the way back from the care home, all I could think about was James Dean. Dead at twenty-four, killed in a tragic car accident. Who knows what might have happened if he'd lived? He might have made a bad film, fallen out of favor, ended up as a bum. Instead, he's been forever immortalized as a promising young star who still had so much more to offer."

She took Max's hand then and looked him straight in the eye so he could see how serious she was. "I want that. I want to die young and pretty. I want my fans to mourn me, not pity me." She reached out and touched his cheek, and in that moment she looked almost serene as she said, "So I've come up with a plan. And if you love me, if you really love me, then you'll help me carry it out."

He listened as she told him that she wanted to fake her own death. He longed to argue back, to tell her that she was being ridiculous. But in some ways her words made sense. Looking at her then, beautiful and vibrant, perfect in every way, he wanted her to stay like that forever, too: to never grow old, to never lose her looks—let alone to suffer the humiliation of a long, drawn-out illness that was going to destroy her body and her mind. Her request might tear Max apart, but, as ever, he couldn't deny his wife what she wanted. And at least this way he could keep her with him for as long as possible. If he didn't agree, he was terrified that he would come home one day to find that she had taken matters into her own hands.

"All right," he relented. "I'll do it."

63

"So you faked her death?" Cara repeated, still struggling to process the details.

She and Max had gone into the kitchen to talk. Franny hadn't seemed to recognize her at first, and she'd become agitated, so Max had insisted they go outside, allowing Hilda to calm her down while he explained everything to Cara.

It made sense, she supposed. The beautiful actress not wanting the world to see what she had become. And Max obviously loved her enough to give up everything in order to make her happy. There was only one thing that was still bothering Cara: the body that had burned up in her mother's Pontiac.

"I thought the papers reported that there was a woman in the car."

"That's right. There was." Max bowed his head.

Cara swallowed. She wasn't sure she wanted to know the answer to her next question, but she had to ask it anyway. "Well, if my mother didn't die in the crash, then who did?"

64

Gabriel wasn't sure what was going on with his family. He was in his second year at Stanford now, and he'd gotten home for the Christmas holidays to find everyone at Stanhope Castle somber and subdued. Franny and his father were always closeted away together, being secretive. And Olivia—well, she still didn't seem *right*. He knew she'd been having some emotional problems, but what could be so awful that it had gone on for this long? She could only look at him with blank eyes, seeming to hardly register anything that was going on.

In the end Gabriel went to his father. "What's up with everyone?" he asked. "Dad, what aren't you telling me? I can't get a word out of Olivia. Is she sick or what?"

At first Max said nothing. He simply walked to the drinks cabinet and poured two large tumblers of whiskey. He brought them back to the table and set one down in front of his son. By then Gabriel was beginning to grow frightened. He'd never seen his father like this before. Whatever was going on, it had to be bad for Max to encourage him to drink.

"What I'm about to tell you must stay between us." His father's face was grave. "Last year, something happened to your sister."

As Gabriel listened to what his father had to say, the blood began to drain from his face.

Gabriel blamed himself. He could have done something to stop all this. He'd known Olivia was sneaking out to see someone when they were down in L.A., and he'd chosen to look the other way. If it hadn't been for him, none of this would have happened.

He listened to everything that his father had to say. It was the first time he'd felt a closeness between them, bonded in their concern for Olivia. They drank most of the bottle of whiskey together before Max said he had to go to Franny. Gabriel sensed that something was going on there, too, but he had enough to worry about without getting involved with that. His father counseled Gabriel to be careful about what he said when he spoke to Olivia. After all, she was still so fragile. Perhaps if the young man hadn't drunk so much he would have listened. But instead he found himself heading up to his sister's room.

Olivia was sitting on her bed reading. She looked up as he entered the room. Seeing his face, something in her expression changed. "You know," she said.

It was a simple statement of fact. Gabriel didn't bother to reply. Instead he walked over to where she sat, and took her in his arms. "I'm so sorry I wasn't here for you," he murmured into her hair as she rested her head against his shoulder.

After what seemed like an age, he gently pulled away. His eyes searched her face. "Olivia—tell me. Who was it? Who did this to you?"

Max had told him that Olivia refused to reveal the father's identity, and he was expecting her to say the same thing to him. But after a moment's hesitation she said, "It was Duke. Duke Carter."

Olivia didn't know why she'd told Gabriel who the father was. For months she'd refused to reveal Duke's identity to anyone, because she'd known how much trouble it would cause. She still couldn't believe she'd been quite so stupid. It was because of the night of her sixteenth birthday. At the end of the evening, the actor had given her his telephone number and told her to call if ever she was in town. During the next term at school, she'd allowed her crush to grow, daydreaming about what it would be like when they saw each other again.

During the Thanksgiving break, Gabriel had been going to meet friends in L.A., and Olivia had asked to tag along. It had been easy enough to call Duke and meet him then. She hadn't been sure he remembered her at first, but once she'd gotten a cab over to his place, he'd seemed pleased to see her. She'd spent the night with him and sneaked back to Holmby Hills early the next morning, before anyone had realized she was missing. She'd seen him a handful of times after that, since, whenever Gabriel had been going down to L.A., she'd go with him: at Christmas, on the odd weekend, and last, during the Easter break.

When she'd realized she was pregnant, she'd called Duke several times, feeling increasingly desperate as she left each message—wanting to tell him in person what had happened. But he'd never phoned her back. Eventually, his assistant had told her to stop calling, or he'd get the police involved.

Olivia hadn't known what to do after that. Then her stepmother and father had gotten involved, and she'd decided it was best to keep Duke's name out of it.

Then Gabriel had come home, and whatever their father had told him, he'd started asking those same old questions tonight, about who had fathered her child. Needing to confide in someone and thinking her brother would understand, Olivia had let him in on her secret. After all, he'd seemed so sympathetic about everything. It was only after she'd told him that his demeanor had changed. She could see his fury as he cursed Duke; she could smell the alcohol on his breath, fueling his anger. Now she watched as he headed to the door.

"Where are you going?" she asked, feeling frightened.

"To confront him." He spoke through gritted teeth.

"Gabriel! No!"

"I have to!"

Olivia saw the resolve in his eyes and made her decision. "Then I'm coming with you."

They hurried downstairs together. The garage had returned Franny's Pontiac earlier that day, repaired after her crash a few weeks earlier. It was parked in front of Gabriel's Mustang, blocking him in. Luckily, the mechanics had left the keys in the Pontiac's ignition. Perfect. He would take that instead.

Max was with Franny, in their bedroom, when he heard the squeal of the car. He hurried to the window and saw her Pontiac speeding out of the driveway with Gabriel at the wheel and Olivia in the passenger seat. He knew instinctively that it had something to do with what he'd told Gabriel earlier and cursed himself for thinking that his son would be able to handle the news.

"What is it?" his wife asked, alarmed, as he rushed for the door.

He didn't stop to answer. Instead, he ran down the stairs and out to his own car. The Pontiac already had a head start on him, but Max had seen Gabriel turn left out of the driveway and guessed that his children were on their way down to L.A. He sped off in pursuit, hoping to overtake them before Gabriel did anything crazy.

The roads were dark and empty, as always on this stretch of Highway 1. Occasionally Max would round a corner and catch sight of taillights ahead of him, and know that he was on the right track. Certain that he would catch up with them soon, he was just beginning to relax a little when he heard a screech of tires ahead and the crunch of metal on concrete. He put his foot to the floor.

As he rounded the next corner, he saw what had happened. It was the same hairpin bend where Franny had had her accident. The Pontiac had obviously plowed off the road and looked as though it had flipped over several times before coming to rest on the cliff's edge. Max brought the Lincoln to a halt and leaped out to help his children.

The Pontiac rested precariously on the edge, and as Max drew closer he saw that the front left wheel was dangling over, the car dipping forward and back, as though it was about to plummet downward. Gabriel had been thrown clear of the car during the crash, but Olivia was still inside. Max assessed the scene quickly. As his son was sitting up on the verge, apparently unharmed if a little dazed still, Max rushed to check on his daughter. Even from a distance he could see that she was slumped in the passenger seat, her eyes closed. The angle of her head suggested that her neck was broken, but Max wasn't about to give up. He ran toward his daughter, calling her name, already trying to figure out how he could get her to safety.

But just as he was about to reach her, there was one last creak of metal. Max stood frozen as he watched the Pontiac tip over the side and fall down the cliff edge, the car smashing on the rocks below, exploding on impact. Olivia was lost forever.

Max never knew whether he'd made the right decision that night. But having lost one child already, he had no intention of losing both. Having smelled the alcohol on his son's breath, he knew that he couldn't let him near the police. No one was around for miles, so he drove Gabriel, who was frozen in shock, back to Stanhope Castle, took him to his room, and warned him not to speak to anyone. Then he went to Franny to tell her what had happened—and what he planned to do.

"I can't let people know that Gabriel was driving." Max was focusing on the problem of his son at the moment, trying not to think of what had happened to Olivia. "The stigma of having been responsible for his sister's death will follow him around forever. It'll ruin his life."

"So what do you propose?" Franny could hardly take in what was happening herself, that her lovely, sweet stepdaughter, who had been through so much these past eighteen months, was dead.

"I'm going to go to the police and say that I was driving," Max told her.

"No!" Franny's voice was filled with panic. "You could go to jail."

"I know."

"But you can't leave me!"

Max knew it wasn't fair to her, especially now that she was ill. But he also knew he couldn't let Gabriel down either. He'd failed his children enough already. "What else can I do?"

Franny thought about it for a long moment. When she looked up at Max, she seemed very calm as she said, "Let them think I died in the crash."

Up until that point, Franny's plan to fake her death had been in its early stages; no details had been decided on. She and Max had assumed that they wouldn't put anything into effect until she got noticeably sicker. What had happened tonight stepped up her timetable, but it seemed like the best solution in the face of a horrible situation. Nothing could be done about poor, tragic Olivia, but at least this way Gabriel wouldn't be implicated in his sister's death. Franny would be sacrificing a few more months of the life she knew—there would be no going back after this. But that didn't seem like such a hardship if she could help her stepson, too.

Max and Franny agreed that there needed to be as few people involved as possible, to ensure that no detail was leaked. Their only accomplice was Hilda, trusted Hilda, who would do anything for the man she'd worked for most of her life. Hilda helped smuggle Franny out to one of the guesthouses that night and agreed to care for her when she got sicker.

As for Max's children, it was made known that Olivia had become something of a recluse at Stanhope Castle. No one thought to question the story, as it was common knowledge that she'd suffered from psychiatric problems. Gabriel was packed off to Europe until everything died down, his college place deferred for the following year. He'd reluctantly gone along with the plan, in too much shock to object. He blamed himself for what had happened that night and wanted to be as far away from any reminders of Olivia as possible.

No one thought to question that it was Franny who'd died that night. After all, she'd crashed her car once already, and it was widely known that she hadn't been herself lately.

On the day of the funeral, Max's grief was obvious to all—just that no one realized it was because he was burying his child rather than his wife.

That night Max went to see Franny. There was no turning back now, no shying away from what was to come. But Franny herself seemed almost serene, sitting up in bed in her bright, cheerful room. That was something she had insisted on—to be able to see outside, to have color around her—not to be shut away in some gray prison like Mayfield Hospital.

"There's one last thing you have to do for me," she told Max that night. "One last favor I need to ask of you."

It was something she had been thinking of ever since she'd found out about her condition. She had written to her mother, Theresa, telling her about the illness and how she wanted Cara to come to California to live with her. That had been several weeks ago, but she still hadn't heard back from her mother and she was growing worried—which meant she needed Max to help her out. She'd waited as long as she could, knowing the state he was in over Olivia. But she couldn't put it off any longer.

"Promise you'll do this for me," she said now. "However much you might not agree with what I ask."

"Anything. I'll do anything you ask."

Then she said, "I want you to bring me my daughter."

Epilogue

"Franny *told* you about me?" Cara couldn't keep the disbelief out of her voice.

His story had answered all her questions: about whose body was in the car; why Olivia had never been seen again; and why Gabriel hadn't spoken to his father for ten years—nothing to do with hating Max, as everyone assumed, but because of his guilt over the role he'd played in his sister's death. Max went on to tell her that when he'd found out from Gabriel that Duke had fathered Olivia's child, he'd made sure that he was blacklisted by every studio in town, destroying the actor's career as revenge for ruining his daughter's life.

But there was one revelation that had stood out most for Cara: that Franny had told Max about her existence years earlier.

"She should have told me about you from the beginning," Max said now. "But she thought I'd reject her. She didn't understand then that I loved her enough to accept anything."

"But why didn't she try to contact me sooner?" Cara asked.

"She wrote to your grandmother when she first found out about her illness, but Theresa was sick herself by then, so she never picked up the letter. With the time it took for the letters to go back and forth, your mother didn't realize at first that there was a problem. Once she told me about you and we'd sent someone to find you . . ."

"Theresa was already dead, and I'd gone to Saint Mary's," Cara filled in.

"That's right. My investigator managed to pick up your trail again when you were back in London with the Connollys. You seemed happy, so your mother decided to leave you. She felt that she'd done enough damage and didn't want to disturb your peace."

"Why didn't you tell me all this straight away when I arrived? After all, you were the one who invited me out here in the first place."

"Franny didn't want me to." He shrugged helplessly. "She wasn't ready to see you after all this time. She didn't know how you'd feel toward her."

Cara rubbed her hand across her face. It was impossible to take everything in.

Then Max asked the really difficult question: "Are you up to seeing her?"

It wasn't even a choice. After all this time, it was the only way to lay the ghosts to rest.

Cara's memories of her mother were distant, but she could remember a beautiful, special woman, someone she dreamed of being like one day. As an adult, she'd watched all of Franny's movies again and again, wishing she had just one fraction of her charisma. But this woman before her was someone different: twitching and messy, her vibrant red hair cut short out of necessity.

Tentatively, Cara approached the bed. Franny's eyes were on her now, and there seemed to be recognition there. Cara knelt down beside her mother so their faces were almost at the same level.

"Hello, Mum," she said. It seemed inadequate, but she didn't know what else to say.

Cara could see that her mother was struggling to say something. Her mouth was moving, forming words. Cara leaned closer, so she could just about make out what she was saying.

"I'm sorry," Franny stuttered. "I'm sorry."

Cara stared at her mother, broken and contrite. Franny had made so many mistakes. Cara thought of all the misery that she could have been spared if her mother had made different choices—but then she also thought of the journey she had come on and how she would never have met Jake, either. And apart from that, how would bearing a grudge help anyone?

So she reached out and took her mother's hand. "It's all right," she said. "It doesn't matter now. Everything is all right."

And she found that she meant it.

*   *   *

Later Cara stood by the door, watching Max and her mother together. It was Franny's dinnertime, and he was cutting the food into small portions, patiently feeding her and tenderly wiping any spills from her mouth. The way he was with her reminded Cara of how she had looked after her grandmother all those years ago. This was the kind of love that meant something: to be there for someone until the end.

Max had allowed people to assume that he had killed his wife. He'd been prepared to destroy his reputation rather than reveal his wife's secret. What her mother and this man had was a true love story.

Cara stayed in California to be with her mother. Franny died a few days later from a weakened heart, a common complication in Huntington's patients. Cara liked to think that she'd hung on until they'd had a chance to reconcile. Max went less than a week later, after his remaining lung collapsed. The couple were interred together in the family plot at Stanhope Castle. The headstone was left blank.

Gabriel went back to Morocco right after his father's funeral service. He had inherited Stanhope Castle, but from what Cara understood, he was putting it up for sale: it wasn't as though he had any good memories of the place.

Cara stayed one last night at Stanhope Castle. The following morning she sat alone on the cliffs, looking out over the dark sea. She felt more optimistic than she had for a long time. Knowing that her mother hadn't abandoned her had set her free. Now she wanted to go back home to England—and to see Jake.

Because now she realized that he was who she wanted to be with. She was finally ready to give it a shot with him. She knew she'd hung back these past years, and perhaps she'd waited too long, but at last she was ready to open herself up to the possibility of falling in love again.

Of course, she knew that she could end up like her mother; the knowledge was there, lurking at the back of her mind. And she would have to deal with that at some point. If Jake wanted to get out, this was the time. Because she wasn't prepared to settle for anything less than what her mother had had with Max.

The wind began to pick up, sending Cara's hair whipping around her face. Shivering, she pulled her jacket tighter. But instead of leaving right away, she closed her eyes and breathed in deep, filling her lungs with the cold sea air, certain that she'd never felt more alive. She stayed like that for a long moment. Only then did she get to her feet and, with one last look at Stanhope Castle and its dramatic coastline, walk across the mossy cliff top and back to her car.

As she drove away, she didn't look back. Her business here was done. Her eyes were on the road and her mind on the future. She had everything to look forward to. Finally she could start living the life she wanted—with the whole of her heart.

Acknowledgments

I would like to thank the following:

All my readers, especially those who took the time to get in touch to say how much they enjoyed *Daughters of Fortune*.

My wonderful editors, Suzanne Baboneau and Libby Yevtushenko in the United Kingdom and Sarah Durand in the United States, who read a very rough first draft of this manuscript—and an even worse second draft!—but still saw something worth pursuing and whose ongoing encouragement, extraordinary patience, and insightful suggestions shaped this into a much better book.

My amazing agent, Darley Anderson, whom I will always be grateful to for giving me this opportunity in the first place, as well as for everything else he has done for me over these past three years. Also at the agency, the foreign rights team, Maddie Buston and Kaisa Thompson, as well as Caroline Kirkpatrick, Rosanna Bellingham, and Sophie Gordon.

The hardworking, talented team at my publishers, who I'm still getting to know, but at the risk of leaving someone out, I'd like to mention a few names. At Simon & Schuster UK: Kerr McRae, Dawn Burnett, Emma Harrow, Amanda Shipp, Emma Lowth, Sara Jade-Virtue, and Rumana Haider. Also, webmistress and fellow *Buffy* fan Ally Glynn and the amazingly gifted Rafaela Romaya, who has designed the most wonderful book jackets I think I've ever seen. And at Atria in the United States: Judith Curr, Sarah Cantin, and Diana Franco.

Fellow author Milly Johnson, for her witty, warmhearted writing and for being such a genuine friend—I think I owe you several coffees now! And Lesley Pearse, whose books have entertained and inspired me for the best part of twenty years and who was so graciously welcoming and encouraging to a newbie like me.

The many family and friends who have supported and encouraged me. My dad, the most prolific reader I know, who always took me to the library as a child; and my mum, a wonderful storyteller in her own right. My oldest friend, Amanda O'Connor, for taking a beautiful set of wedding photos and for being so genuinely pleased for me when I finally got published. In Ireland, my uncles, Father Ray and Father Donald, as well as my uncle and aunt Damian and Alysha Hannon. In England, my aunt Maureen Golden and cousin Catherine Roper. The Tiffin girls: Liga Millers, Laura Martin, Lucy Taylor, Gemma Crane, Katie Fox, Sarah Burows, Lucille Pearson, Nicola Grant, and Jo Kapourta. The Bentalls bunch: John Pitts, John Foley, Matt Boyle, Richard Jones, and Adele Stevens. From Cambridge: Pia McGee, Andrew Besford, Reema Faridi, Jason Moss, Kristy Cooper, Sanjay Ojah, and Anjla Patel. At Newton: Raj and Meena Shant and Fred Moore. The Marks and Spencer Retirement Group in Kingston upon Thames for inviting me to speak and giving me such a warm welcome on the day. As well as Diana Pigg, Jenny Worsfold, Sandra Hendry, and Shirley Hunt.

And, as always, my most heartfelt thanks go to my intelligent, witty, and devilishly handsome husband, Tom Beevers, for reading far too many drafts of this manuscript and being prepared to endlessly discuss plot points over Saturday brunch. I hope you know how much you mean to me.

A Note on Huntington's Disease for Readers

Though obviously this is a fictional story, for one in ten thousand people Huntington's disease is a very real degenerative brain disorder. Onset typically occurs between the ages of thirty and fifty, and the average life span after symptoms appear is ten to twenty years. Particularly prior to the development of genetic testing in 1993, sufferers in the early stages of the disease were often misdiagnosed and thought to be simply depressed or alcoholics. There is currently no known cure for HD.

For more information or help on the subject, the Huntington's Disease Association has a very informative website, www.hda.org.uk, as does the Huntington's Disease Society of America at www.hdsa.org.